The Game

*Her Heart
was not a
Plaything*

The Game – a novel

First published by Arkhouse Press in 2009

This edition published by Free inDeed Media, 2023
12 Osmington Circle
Narre Warren Sth, VIC 3805
Australia
www.freeindeedmedia.com

© Amanda Deed, 2023

Cover Design & Typesetting by Book Whispers

ISBN 978-0-6458404-0-7 (paperback)
ISBN 978-0-6458404-1-4 (ebook)

AMANDA DEED

The Game

FREE inDEED MEDIA

Prologue

London 1835

'You ... you would banish me?' Jack Fordham's stomach clenched with horror and disbelief. What could have so suddenly and vehemently turned his father against him? The Viscount had just returned from Paris and without so much as a 'how do you do,' summoned Jack to his study, where he had let forth with a tirade like Jack had never known.

'Your uncle told me about Mademoiselle Antoinette de Louise,' his father gritted.

Jack froze at that, a new wave of shock assaulting him. 'He ... he did?' Why now, after two whole years?

His father paced up and down behind his desk in an agitated fashion, clearly at a loss for words. Eventually he sighed and turned pained eyes to Jack. 'How could you even think of carrying a girl off, let alone one who is already betrothed? You have scandalised her family and your own.'

'What? No.' Jack reeled in confusion.

'Indeed, you were fortunate your uncle intervened when he did,' his father continued. 'It is only through him the sorry ordeal remained secret, but even then, the damage was done. The girl was betrothed to the Marquis de Rouget, didn't you know. A brilliant match by all accounts. But when he learnt of your disgraceful behaviour, he would have none of her.'

Jack gulped, aghast. 'They have laid all this at my feet?'

His father's face reddened. '*She* laid it at your feet. After you returned

1

to London, Mademoiselle Antoinette told her father the whole sordid story.'

Jack's world span out of control. She wouldn't. She'd promised. They'd promised each other.

'How you wooed and cajoled her. How you promised her everything. How you convinced her to defy her father and run away with you.'

'That is not what happened.' Disbelief gave way to anger.

'I will have none of your insolence!'

'But what of the truth?' Jack pleaded with his father. 'Will you not hear me?'

Viscount Fordham's gaze held deep regret. 'Your silence for the past two years tells me all I need to know.'

'But they begged me …'

'Enough. I am done with you.'

Jack stared at the man who had raised him and when he spoke bitterness laced his words. 'So, you would send me to Australia as though I were a common criminal.'

The Viscount turned his back and gazed out the window. 'I've seen the way you allow the ladies to dangle after you; the way you charm them. I've seen the games you play. I will not have you destroy our good name with your reckless behaviour. You have grown too idle. The change will do you good.'

'But sir, it is a land of cut-throats and savages.'

His father turned back to him, his face softening somewhat. 'It is not as bad as all that. You have your sister to go to. And your brother-in-law has informed me there is good, fertile land there. I have procured some cuttings from France. You will establish a vineyard for me.'

Jack sighed, knowing his life in England was over. 'You will not reconsider then?'

The Viscount stepped closer to Jack. His eyes were glazed with emotion. 'You are my son and heir. One day, when you have purged yourself of this restlessness, you may return.'

Chapter One

Sydney, Australia, 1844

Jack Fordham ambled up the front steps of his large townhouse, on the coast east of Sydney. In the darkness, the butler held the front door open, lantern in hand, ready to receive him. 'Good evening, sir,' the man bowed a greeting.

'Evening, Miller,' Jack greeted as he entered the spacious dwelling. He shrugged off his coat and handed it to the servant.

'Did you find success at the docks today, sir?'

'I did. I have secured a passage for our upcoming shipment. In fact, I must compose a letter to my father the Viscount.'

Jack reclined in the leather chair at his desk and loosened his cravat. A warm fire blazed in the hearth and a decanter of wine rested on the desk. Jack smiled at the thoughtfulness of his servant. The wine remained untouched nevertheless, as Jack leaned back in the chair and gazed at the ceiling.

It was nine years since his father had sent him to establish an interest in the newly colonised country. Despite his unfair dismissal, in part Jack knew his father was right. Life in London had grown intolerably dull, save a few friends, and in the end, he quit the overcrowded city readily enough. The voyage to Australia had been long and at times sickening. Rough seas had churned his stomach for countless days, but eventually he recovered and looked forward to his new life as an adventure.

These years in Australia had been enjoyable for the most part, except the first two years. He had acquired good land within two days ride of Sydney in the Hunter Valley and established the vineyard as his father had commissioned. But it had been through hardship and toil. The land had to first be cleared of towering eucalypts, and then he built a homestead and huts for the workers. At first, they all lived in canvas tents without furniture or comfort. He had been assigned convict labourers to farm the land, and they were a troublesome lot to say the least. Everything; building materials, farming tools, food and other necessities had to be carried in by horse and dray, a costly and often perilous task.

Finally, though, the buildings were fully established, and the first batch of wine was cellared. He hired a man to manage the plantation while he moved to Sydney to be closer to his sister, Gwendolyn, and to conduct the trade wine from Port Jackson. Now, he was only months away from his first shipment.

He sighed as he turned to the letter and focused his thoughts on that task. He wrote to inform Father to expect the delivery of wine soon, knowing he would be pleased with Jack's success. At least Father might finally be proud of him.

It wasn't long before his thoughts began to trail off again. Of late, life in Sydney had grown tedious, just as London had. Though many friends and acquaintances surrounded him, something he could not name left him dissatisfied.

Only his relatives brought him real joy. It was grand to be near Gwen and her family. His brother-in-law, Philip, was a good friend and the children were a delight. He had not seen them in well nigh six months. It had been too long.

Glancing at the clock that ticked rhythmically from the mantle over the fire, Jack frowned at the time. He must have daydreamed for a long while. He finished his missive and returned the quill to the ink well. He pushed himself to his feet, turned down the lamps in the quiet study and headed upstairs to his room.

The staircase was wide and wound around as it ascended from the expansive entry way to the top floor of the house. Apart from his study, the ground floor held a spacious dining room, parlour, and a comfortable drawing room which had a wonderful prospect facing east over the ocean. At the back of the house were a good-sized kitchen and washroom and a few small bedrooms to house the staff.

The second story consisted of several large bedrooms which were mostly unoccupied unless he had friends visiting. He, of course, dwelt in the master bedroom which he had lavishly decorated to his taste.

Jack stared at the massive canopy bed with reams of lace spilling over it as he undressed and again knew discontent. He never had the lack of a woman who interested him, but he had failed to be happy with anyone. Not since Antoinette.

Lillian, the beauty who currently claimed him as her beau obviously used him for her own pleasure. He reflected on the dinner they had recently spent together. With a cynical smile he recalled the way she looked up from her plate and smiled seductively. 'Jack, darling,' she had purred. 'I saw the most dazzling silk today imported from France. I am told it will be the next rage of fashion. It is outrageously expensive, but I simply must have a gown made in it.'

The if-you-loved-me-you-would-buy-it-for-me look in her eyes angered him, although he did not show it. Instead, he smiled broadly at her and played along with her charade. 'We cannot have you looking out of fashion, my dear,' he drawled. 'Shall we go and see a dressmaker tomorrow?'

Lillian had clapped her hands, believing herself victorious. 'You shall not be sorry,' she told him with a delighted smile.

Jack shook his head as he thought over the incident. What was he going to do? It was obvious she hoped for an offer of marriage, but he knew her affection held no depth. She had no idea of the distaste she had stirred in his breast. He did not even wish to see her. He would send Miller with some flowers and a card, crying off their rendezvous at the dressmaker's. Instead, he would go into the country for a few days and visit with his sister.

His mind too occupied to sleep, Jack wrapped himself in a satin gown and moved to the far end of the room. Here, behind thick, velvet drapes, a set of glass doors opened onto a balcony overlooking the coastline to the south. Directly ahead, the earth seemed to stop short as sheer cliffs connected with the ocean below. Jack stepped out into the cold night air and leaned up against the balustrade, allowing his gaze to drift out to sea. In the moonlight, the white-tipped waves appeared luminescent as they rolled into the shore.

Restlessness. That's what his father had called it. But Jack believed the right woman would steady him. It was the only thing missing from his plentiful life. Alas, she eluded him. Why could he not find a woman who looked beyond his fortune or future title? Why could he not find a woman who was untarnished? The sea breeze whipped his brown hair about his face as he lingered. Unexpectedly a foreign thought dropped into his mind — *do you deserve a woman like that? Are you ... pure?* He sighed. It seemed probable he would remain a bachelor for the rest of his life. He shook these unsettling thoughts from his mind and turned inside. *Jack Fordham, you have run mad.*

Chapter Two

Meg, or Margaret Joy Wingrove as she was formally known, supervised the Sainsbury boys while they played in the yard of the sprawling homestead. Sainsbury Stud Farm was situated roughly five miles west of the Parramatta township, a good half day's drive from Sydney. The homestead buildings were spread in the centre of one hundred acres of land. The family used the property partially as a farm to meet their daily needs, but mostly for breeding horses. Philip Sainsbury made his income exporting horses to the Indian army for remounts; however, he also had a large trade locally, supplying animals to the new colonists.

The land had only cost Philip five shillings an acre; although with that came an obligation to sponsor labourers from England in order that they may travel to Australia. Thus, he had engaged Meg, a nursemaid come governess for his children, a house maid and two farm hands to assist him in his new enterprise. Of course, with the slow rate of travel, she and the other employees did not arrive for almost two years, in which time he had erected a temporary hut, built the house proper, and delivered his wife of their third child.

For ten years she had been employed in this household, first as a nursemaid when the children were all small, but now they were babies no longer, she functioned more as a governess. Only the boys had access to formal education, so the Sainsburys commissioned Meg to train the girls, teaching them sewing and housekeeping as well as basic reading and writing. The boys attended the King's School in Parramatta during most of the day; however, when they were at home they were in her charge as was the case this Saturday in July.

As the children played, each engrossed in their own activity, Meg's mind began to wander. The children grew rapidly and soon, her usefulness would expire. She needed to think about her future. She could gain employment as a nursemaid with another family or even as a teacher in one of the schools. She sighed. It would be much nicer if she could have a family of her own, but prospective husbands were hard to come by when one didn't get out much. And even then, the choices were not very appealing. Half the population were either convicts or ex-convicts and the moral state of the colony was characterised by profanity, drunkenness and Sabbath-breaking.

'Uncle Jack's here!'

Philip Sainsbury junior and William's united cry roused her from her reverie. Meg straightened to see the silhouette of a man on horseback in the distance. How her charges recognised him from this far, she had no idea. But in an instant, their game was forgotten, and they raced into the house almost falling over one another in their haste.

Jack Fordham was the last person she wanted to see. Unfortunately, she worked for his sister, so had no choice in the matter. All she could do was brace herself for unpleasantness. And as the children's governess, she needed to follow them inside, and apologise for their boisterous behaviour.

Gwendolyn Sainsbury, however, rose from where she played a board game with her two daughters, Mary, and Kitty, grinning at the news heralded by the boys. The two girls clapped their hands and their eyes lit up.

'Well then,' Gwen's eyes danced, 'that is wonderful. You boys had better go and wash up. You don't want your uncle to see you like that, with smudges of dirt all over your faces.'

Obediently, the young men hurried away to do as they were bid, while the girls rushed off to let their father in on the excitement.

Gwen turned back to Meg with a twinkle in her eyes. 'What have those boys been up to that caused them to be so grubby?'

'Only the most fearsome sword fight ever.' Meg rolled her eyes and laughed.

Gwen chuckled. 'And who won?'

'Well, neither actually. They were about to have a serious quarrel when they spied their uncle riding down the drive.'

Gwen sighed. 'I'm so glad he's come at last.' She rose from her chair. 'I dare say Jack will keep the children occupied for a while, you may as well have some time to yourself.'

Time to herself was always welcome when in charge of four energetic children. It meant time to stroll on the land in solitude.

⤜∘⤛

By the time Jack stabled his horse and made his way to the house, most of the family had gathered to greet him. As soon as he entered the room, Gwen jumped to her feet enveloping him in a warm embrace. 'Jack,' she cried. 'It is so good to see you.'

Laughing and holding her at arm's length, he looked into her eyes. Her hair was jet black and her eyes hazel, but her smile was identical to his, a smile that lit up her whole face. 'It has been too long,' he confessed.

'Too long indeed,' she frowned. 'Why, half the year has gone by.'

'You look well, my dear,' Jack told her, still clasping her hands. At thirty-six, she was still vivacious and exuberant. All who knew her loved her and she became instant friends with everyone she met.

'Even better, now you are here.'

Jack released his sister and turned to his brother-in-law. 'Philip.' They shook hands. Mr Sainsbury was the opposite of his wife, rather serious by nature. Responsibility and duty ruled his world making him a wonderfully devoted husband and father, but he often missed much of the enjoyment of life.

'How are you, Jack?'

'Well enough. How are the horses?'

Philip tried to answer but the clamour of two boys bounding into the room drowned out his voice.

'Uncle Jack,' they cried as one and threw themselves at him, grabbing hold of his arms.

'Whoa there, boys,' Jack laughed, extricating his arms, and ruffling the youngsters' hair.

'PJ! William! Where are your manners?' Their father rebuked.

The boys hung their heads in shame, but Gwen intervened. 'Let them be, Father. It has been an age since they have seen Jack.'

'As you wish, my dear,' Philip pressed his lips together and returned to his seat.

The two boys bounced around Jack again, firing questions over the top of one another, making him laugh again. When the noise died down enough, Mary and Kitty saw their opportunity to be noticed and approached slowly, Mary grasping her shy sister's hand. The older girl gently nudged her sister forward; and Jack crouched down to look her in the eye. 'How are you my little angel?' He held both of her hands in his.

'I missed you, Uncle Jack.' Her eyes were wide and earnest.

'I missed you too, Kitty.' His heart melted and he drew her into his arms.

She held him tight for a long while, but when she finally let go, he straightened himself to greet Mary. Taking one of her hands in his, he bowed low and kissed her fingertips.

'What a beautiful young lady you have become, Miss Mary Sainsbury. I am very sorry I did not attend your coming out party. Unfortunately, business at the vineyard detained me. I daresay every young fellow fell over himself to claim a dance with you.'

The seventeen-year-old girl blushed and giggled softly, while Jack searched his pockets for something. Finding the item, he withdrew it from its hiding place. 'As I could not be there, I wanted to give you something special instead.' He produced a red velvet case and opened it towards her. There, resting neatly in the container was a string of pearls. Mary gasped with delight. 'Oh, Uncle Jack,' she breathed, 'They are beautiful.'

'Then you and this necklace are a perfect match.' He removed the necklace from the case and expertly fastened it around his niece's graceful throat. Mary's hand fluttered to the expensive gift 'Thank you so much, Uncle Jack.' She threw her arms around his neck. Turning to her father, she asked, 'May I go and see in the mirror?' Philip smiled and nodded, upon which Mary fled the room, her hand still touching her pearls.

'Did you bring me a present, Uncle Jack?' Willy tugged at his sleeve.

'And me?' added PJ.

'Me too,' chimed in Kitty.

Jack threw back his head and laughed. 'But of course I did, you young scamps.' All three began to jump up and down. 'Now, who is first?' he teased, knowing full well they would all cry 'Me!' in unison.

Jack thoroughly enjoyed their animation and searched dramatically and laboriously through his pockets again, while the children watched his every move with rapt attention. Finally, after what would have seemed like an eternity to them, he produced something wrapped in a handkerchief. Carefully unfolding the cloth, Jack handed the object to PJ.

The young master withdrew an intricately carved figurine of a horse in a rearing position, its rider hanging on for dear life. PJ, who showed just as much love for horse flesh as his father, even at fourteen years of age, gasped over the wooden statue and marvelled at its detail. 'This is wonderful Uncle Jack. You can even see the flanks of the horse, and the creases in the man's shirt.'

Jack smiled. 'I knew you would like it.'

'Thank you, Uncle Jack.' PJ gave his uncle a fond handshake and ran off to place his figurine in a prominent place in his room.

'What did you bring me?' Willy jumped up and down impatiently. The twelve-year-old had inherited his mother's vibrant personality and was full of playful energy.

'Ah,' Jack held up a finger as if just remembering. He rummaged through his pockets again and this time withdrew a small, black leather case. 'Here you are my young adventurer.'

Willy opened the case and exclaimed in delight. 'Uncle Jack. My very own compass.'

Jack ruffled his nephew's hair again. 'I daresay you will not get lost now,' he teased. Everyone laughed, remembering how a year earlier Willy had taken it into his head to be an explorer like Charles Sturt and had wandered off into the bush. A search was sent after him when he hadn't returned by mid-afternoon. Thankfully they found him not too far away sitting by the edge of a brook. He had been crying, although not from fear. He was very disappointed he hadn't discovered anything magnificent.

A tentative tug on his sleeve, pulled Jack out of his reverie. He looked down to see Kitty's shy brown eyes staring up at him. 'Is it my turn, Uncle Jack?'

'I believe it is, sweetheart.' He leaned close to whisper in her ear. 'We must go outside to retrieve your gift.'

Kitty sucked her breath in, her eyes full of wonder. She followed him out and the other children who had returned from their rooms tagged along out of curiosity. Just outside by the door, a puppy was tethered and as soon as Jack and Kitty emerged, it began to wag its tail furiously and pounce all over them. 'She kept me warm all the way here,' Jack told Kitty as he untied the cord that held the puppy and handed it to her. Kitty knelt and put her arms around the dog, which licked her face all over. 'She's so beautiful, Uncle Jack. I shall call her Lady.' The next moment she sprang to her feet again and wrapped her arms tightly around his waist. 'Thank you, Uncle.'

Jack barely had time to respond before the two boys wielding make-believe swords, charged at him, yelling, 'On guard!'

Jack glanced around for another stick to use, while keeping an eye on the oncoming attack. 'You want to challenge me to a duel, what?' He lunged to pick up a suitable twig and swiftly turned to meet them, 'sword' aloft.

Glancing sideways at Kitty and Mary, he put on a dramatic flair, one arm stretched towards them, 'Stand back, my ladies, I shall defend thee.' The two girls giggled and ran to a nearby tree, pretending to seek refuge.

PJ and Willy renewed their charge with a yell.

'So, it's to be two against one, is it?' Jack pretended alarm as their sticks all clashed, and then recovered his courage. 'Well, I am renowned as Sydney's finest swordsman, don't you know.'

The three lunged and parried and laughed for a few minutes, while the girls giggled and Lady bounded around their feet, yapping, and trying to join in the fun. The battle ended when Jack stumbled over Lady and fell to the ground, both boys leaping upon him, holding their 'swords' at his throat. Between laughs and fighting off one very affectionate puppy, Jack panted out his dying words to Mary and Kitty. 'Forgive me, fair ladies, I have failed. I pray thee, run for your lives lest these blackguards lay hold of your jewels.'

Minutes later, the tribe, having brushed themselves off and straightened their clothes, re-entered the homestead still laughing. 'Have you ever fought a real duel, Uncle?' Kitty asked, clinging to one of Jack's hands.

'Yes,' he answered, 'A long time ago, in London. But I never killed anyone.' Jack's eyes met his sister's. Refreshments had been laid on the table, and it was obvious the elder Sainsburys wanted to spend time with him. He cleared his throat. 'I think it is time for tea, is it not, sister dear?'

'Yes,' she replied, a grateful look on her face. She rang the bell which would summon the governess and within minutes Meg appeared in the room.

'Meg,' Gwen turned to her, 'will you take the children to the playroom for a while?'

'Yes, ma'am,' she curtsied to her mistress and turned to the deflated children. 'Come along then.' She herded them to the door.

'Meg,' Jack nodded to her as she passed.

'Mister Fordham,' she replied with a curt nod and continued to the playroom.

Jack leisurely strolled over to a sofa and sat down; receiving the cup of tea his sister offered him. 'I see she still holds me in contempt.' He picked at some imaginary lint on his sleeve.

Gwen tossed her dark waves. 'You did treat that friend of hers rather poorly.'

'And she's not spoken above five words together to me since,' Jack feigned a yawn.

'She is very loyal.'

'Mountain from a molehill, that's what I say.' It shouldn't bother him. Except that he had found the governess a person of keen mind and enjoyed conversing with her. Jack shrugged and turned to Mary. 'So, tell me all about your debut.'

Chapter Three

Meg led the Sainsbury children to the playroom which had once been the nursery and encouraged them to practise their drawing. Still in an excitable state after meeting their uncle, it took several minutes for them to settle, squabbling about who'd received the best gift.

Meg smiled to herself. At one time, she thought Jack Fordham could have been a possible match for her. Seven years earlier, when he had first come to Sydney, she had developed a strong infatuation for him. He was the most handsome and dashing man she had ever seen, and the way he allowed the children to climb all over him melted her heart. Back then, the children were in her care much of the time, so she had enjoyed several conversations with Mr Fordham and found him a very good companion. Alas, he had not seen her as anything more than a household servant.

Some months later her brother, Brian, had come to visit her and she had gushed to him all about the wonderful Mr Jack Fordham. A frown had spread on his face when he saw her rapture. 'Meg, my dear,' he was firm but gentle. 'You must not become attached to Mister Fordham. He has a bad reputation. They say he is indifferent and uncaring; some say heartless. He would likely ruin you.'

Meg had gasped in disbelief. 'It cannot be so,' she argued and told him exactly how Mr Fordham behaved in the Sainsbury house.

'Well, I know naught about that,' Brian replied, 'But you may ask anyone in Sydney about Jack Fordham, and they will say he is a rake. He pours his attentions out on ladies until they believe he will make them an offer and then cuts them off.'

Meg could not endorse this remark. 'I do not believe you.'

Brian had sighed in frustration, taking a different tack to prove his point. 'Mister Fordham is a man of the world, and you know as well as I do it would do no good to attach yourself to a heathen.'

Brian's words hit home. Both of their parents had died when she was but sixteen-years-old, and he had cared for her ever since. Brian was her wisdom and counsel, even though only five years her senior. With his curly red hair, blue eyes, and freckled, fair skin, he always had a boyish appearance, belying a maturity that went beyond his years.

Meg admitted defeat but decided to pray that Mr Fordham would find faith.

Brian had chuckled and shook his head, his eyes showing how much he cared. 'You can do better than Jack Fordham, Meg. You want somebody who is as pure as you are.'

For all the truth in Brian's words, Meg found it difficult to conquer her infatuation for Mr Fordham. The cure finally came, but not without pain. An acquaintance of Meg's formed a tendré for Mr Fordham. That friend dallied after him and after a time he had returned her attentions. They were seen together many a time at balls and assemblies, card games and theatre presentations. The young woman believed herself to be completely in love with Mr Fordham and thought he would surely marry her. The awful day came however, when Mr Fordham ceased his romantic behaviour, leaving the young woman inconsolable. Meg secretly thought the girl had been more interested in Jack's inheritance than anything, but nevertheless, she became convinced of Mr Fordham's cruel reputation, just as Brian had told her.

Since then, she had tried to avoid meeting or conversing with him in any way. It was a simple matter to melt into the background as the governess. The children could be as devoted to him as they wished, but she had no obligation to feel anything towards him.

Supper was usually informal in the Sainsbury homestead. Most of the time, the family welcomed Meg to dine with them. However, when visitors were in the house, even if it was only Mr Fordham, all the staff ate in the kitchen, leaving the family and their guests some privacy.

So it was this Saturday evening, Meg took her meal in the kitchen, and enjoyed the company of the other staff. Nellie, the cook, fussed over the stove and thus was not in the mood for conversation. The two farm hands, Mick, and Joseph were amiable though, and she chatted with them. 'How goes the work, Mick?' she asked, filling her mouth with succulent lamb.

He nodded, a semi-toothless grin spreading across his face as he swallowed his own food. 'Not too busy, but not idle neither, eh Joe?' He nudged his fellow worker.

'Nah,' Joe agreed, 'But Mister Sainsbury's got some colts wot need breaking in soon, and then we'll 'ave plenty to keep us busy.'

'And outa trouble,' Mick chuckled and shoved a large spoonful of potato into his mouth.

She had eaten quickly while they talked to her so she could assist Nellie with her cooking. Nellie always became especially flustered when Mr Fordham was in the house, feeling under pressure to produce perfect food for such an important personage. After all, he was the son of a Viscount.

'Could you use some help, Nellie?' Meg dabbed her mouth with a napkin.

Nellie looked up from the stove; her face flushed with both heat and anxiety and blew a strand of fly away hair out of her face. 'Would y' mind taking a few of these platters in, so I can keep me eye on this pudding?' She asked in a lilting Irish brogue. 'I don't want to burn it, y' know.'

'Not at all.' Meg lifted a heavy silver platter piled high with steaming, thick slices of roast lamb and roasted vegetables. She was glad she had already eaten as it smelled delicious. She stepped out of the cook house and quickly covered the small distance to the main house, entering directly into the dining room via the veranda. A fire blazed brightly in the hearth, and the atmosphere was as warm as the air that greeted her on opening the door. She moved to the large table and placed the platter in the middle at which point Kitty noticed her.

'Winnie, Winnie,' she cried, using the childrens' pet name for their governess. Willy had not been able to pronounce Miss Wingrove when he was very young, and Winnie was all he could manage. It wasn't long before they all used the affectionate name for her. She gave the young girl her attention.

'Uncle Jack just told us about when he fought a duel.'

Obviously, the subject had not been forgotten since the afternoon. Meg gave a brilliant smile to match the child's enthusiasm. 'Oh, that sounds exciting.'

'It was only for a wager,' Willy informed her, sounding a trifle flat, 'And not even to the death.'

Everyone laughed at the lad's lust for blood and Meg gathered their soup dishes and headed back to the kitchen but heard the next part of the conversation on her way.

'You should fight a real duel, Uncle Jack,' Kitty said very firmly, 'because nobody could beat you and you could kill all the bad people.'

The table erupted in laughter as Meg shut the door behind her. She hurried to the cook house and returned with a jug of thick, brown gravy. Placing it on the table, she turned to her mistress. 'Will you need anything else, Missus Sainsbury?'

'No, thank you. Just dessert when we are done with this.'

Meg curtsied and went back to the kitchen again. 'You can relax, Nellie. They are happy with what they have for now. Why don't you have something to eat while I watch the pudding for you?'

Nellie wiped her apron across her brow and sighed. 'I confess I'm rather hungry. Thanks again, Meg.' She washed her hands and helped herself to a plate of food.

Meg busied herself at the stove, putting a large pot of water on to warm for the dishes to be washed later. She kept a close eye on the temperamental dessert in the oven and tidied up the kitchen so Nellie wouldn't have to work too late. All the while she hummed her favourite hymn, worshipping her creator as she worked.

Soon enough the evening meal was over, and the adults retreated to the parlour for tea and port. The Sainsburys summoned Meg to take the children and prepare them for bed. Once the youngest Sainsburys were settled into bed, Meg went to the parlour. Knocking gently on the door, she entered the cosy room and curtsied to the lady of the house. 'The children are abed Missus Sainsbury.'

'Good. I shall go and kiss them goodnight,' the loving mother rose from her seat and followed Meg out, leaving Mr Fordham and Mr Sainsbury alone to talk.

❧❧❧

Jack and Philip could spend hours discussing horses. Jack considered himself an excellent judge of horseflesh, and Philip often asked for his opinion on the quality of the horses in his yards. He had just recently completed breaking in and training several young colts and was keen to receive Jack's appraisal before he handed them over to the buyer. Jack, always eager to serve in this manner, agreed to test them in the morning.

'May I speak openly with you, Fordham?' Philip's face grew serious.

Jack wondered what troubled him. Was one of his brood mares carrying disease? Or was this about something else?

'What is it, dear brother?' Jack shrugged lightly, not comfortable with this level of solemnity.

Philip breathed deeply, poured two glasses of port, handed one to Jack and then plunged in. 'I have become rather concerned with all the talk I hear of you in town.'

'What talk is that?' Jack asked with an impish grin, fully aware of the gossip that trailed him.

'Talk of you and ... er ... women,' Philip showed obvious discomfort.

Jack chuckled softly, hiding his annoyance. 'Oh, that,' he waved his arm in dismissal. 'I shouldn't take too much notice if I were you.'

Philip frowned, clearly frustrated by Jack's blasé attitude. 'You must cease this dissolute behaviour at once, before...'

'Dissolute?' Jack almost choked on his drink. 'That is coming it a bit strong don't you think, Sainsbury.' His brother's harsh censure shocked him out of his flippant pretence. 'I am aware people call me a philanderer, but I do have morals. It is not as though I seduce every woman I meet. You would do well not to listen to rumours.'

Philip withdrew into silence, walking to the hearth and staring into the flames. Eventually he spoke again. 'Considering your past, I would have thought you'd be careful not to create a scandal,' he mumbled, still gazing at the fire.

'What scandal?' Gwen asked, wide-eyed as she returned to the parlour.

Philip turned his sombre countenance towards her, but Jack spoke first. 'Why, the latest rakish behaviour of that Jack Fordham fellow, of course.'

'Oh,' Gwen rolled her eyes, 'what has he done now?'

Jack looked evenly at Philip. 'Ruined some poor innocent girl's reputation, no doubt.'

Gwen gasped. 'Is it true?'

'I do not know. Ask your husband. He seems to know better than I.'

Gwen eyed him, then looked at Philip, and then back at Jack again. 'All right,' she said firmly, 'What is this about?'

Philip cleared his throat. 'I, uh, have heard some distasteful news about him. I questioned his behaviour. I should have asked him to tell me his version of the truth. I am truly sorry, Jack.'

Jack grunted. 'It is well.'

Gwen went to sit next to Jack, placing a hand on his knee. 'You mustn't scold him, Phil. He is a grown man after all.'

Philip seemed agitated. 'I am merely concerned for his future.'

'Come, come, Sainsbury,' Jack said, 'What is it you have heard?'

Mr Sainsbury sat down opposite his brother-in-law. 'It was about that Ambrose woman. They say you ruined her.'

Gwen screwed up her face. 'I never liked that one. She was the most self-absorbed creature I have ever met.'

'I quite agree,' Jack grinned at his sister's apt description. 'I confess I did keep her as a mistress for a time, but I certainly did not ruin her. I was not the first man to grace her bed, nor the last, I imagine. Since I have not seen her in months, I do not know what she is about.'

'I hear your current conquest is a lady named Lillian Charles,' Philip continued his interrogation.

'Yes,' Jack answered lightly. He turned to his sister. 'I am convinced you would not approve of her either. Indeed, I find I do not approve of her myself.'

'Jack,' Gwen chastised, her eyes wide. 'What a thing to say.'

'Well,' he explained, 'She is quite the fortune hunter for one thing, and I find she is a very quickly passing fancy.'

Gwen sighed and shook her head. 'Is there no hope for you?'

'I very much doubt it.' Although he answered with a nonchalant flick at his sleeve, Jack meant every word.

Gwen gazed at him with a motherly look in her eyes. 'Do be careful, Jack. Papa would likely cut you off completely if you brought us into disgrace.'

Jack took both of her hands in his and looked earnestly into her face. 'Never fear, my dear sister. I am always discreet, and I never behave dishonourably. I am very proper with most ladies, you know.'

'But you admit Miss Ambrose was your mistress.' Philip was still not appeased.

'Oh, come down from your high horse. She is one of a mere handful in my life if you must know.' Jack's voice had a slight edge to it. His annoyance was slipping out. 'And do not try to tell me *you* never tested the waters before you dived into matrimony, Sainsbury.'

Philip looked uncomfortably from Jack to his wife and back again but did not reply. He merely cleared his throat, went back to the fireplace, and leaned on the mantle.

Jack looked apologetically at his sister. 'Forgive me, dear. I should not have spoken so.'

Gwen squeezed his hand and shook her head.

Philip looked up from the blaze. 'As Gwen said, please be careful Jack.' He drained the last of his port.

Chapter Four

Mr Fordham and Mr Sainsbury were already out surveying the young horses when Meg made her way to the kitchen for breakfast. She had been awake for hours but had taken her time rising and dressing herself for church, the only day she wore anything but a plain blue dress with a white apron and bonnet. She donned a stiff, deep mauve dress with a tight waist and a modest bustle. She pulled her fair hair into a chignon, high on her head and placed a similar mauve hat at just the right angle over it.

It was the Sabbath, and she was not required to attend the children for any reason. Even so, she always went in and greeted them good morning. She gave each of them a kiss and then headed to the warm cook house.

Nellie had been up and working for a few hours, although on Sundays she started later than the other days. The fire glowed with blazing heat and a pot of warm porridge simmered over the flames. Meg served herself a bowlful and sat down at the large worktable to eat. 'Off to church then, are ya?' Nellie asked.

'Yes,' Meg answered between mouthfuls.

'I might just come along one of these days,' the flushed woman told her.

Meg smiled broadly at her. 'That would be wonderful, Nellie.'

The cook returned her smile and went back to cooking.

Cheered by her conversation with the Nellie, Meg headed to church. Although it was winter and the wind was icy cold, the sky grey with rain clouds and the ground sodden in places, Meg sang all the way. The small stone chapel which Meg attended was in the main street of Parramatta. Several of the members greeted her with warm embraces when she arrived, as though they were her own family. It was wonderful to be able to fellowship with other brethren. Soon they were all gathered and singing hymns of praise to their maker.

Their minister, Reverend Kilpatrick spoke a stirring sermon on faith. He taught that simply believing was not enough, but you had to outwork it in your lives for it to be truly considered faith. Meg was challenged anew to make her life a witness for the Lord.

Meg arrived home from church to discover Mr Fordham had been called away to his vineyard, leaving four glum-faced children and a disappointed sister behind.

'It will be weeks before we see him again,' complained Mary, while Meg warmed herself by the fire.

This news secretly pleased Meg, but she played her part properly. 'I see you miss him already,' she said with understanding.

'Ever so much,' Willy nodded. 'I wanted to play explorers with him today. PJ wanted to have a fencing lesson, and the girls wanted him to tell them stories. Papa didn't even manage to show him all the new horses and Mama, well, she would have him live here if she could.'

Meg laughed at this. 'Your poor Uncle Jack. I shouldn't be surprised if he was grateful to be gone from you. You would have exhausted him.'

Willy looked confused. 'But Uncle loves being with us.'

The governess laughed again. 'Of course he does,' she ruffled his hair. 'I am not at all serious, you know. Now if you will excuse me, I must go and have my dinner.'

The few yards of open air between the homestead and the kitchen were filled with large raindrops and Meg found herself a little damp once inside. 'It is far too cold out there,' she mumbled as she dried herself by the fire again.

'Spring will come soon enough.' Nellie ladled some hot potato and onion soup into a bowl for her and cut some slices of bread from a freshly baked loaf. ''Ere, come and warm yer insides.'

Once again dry, Meg followed the cook's suggestion and enjoyed the warm winter food. Nellie asked her about the church service that morning, and Meg repeated the contents of the sermon to her. Nellie eagerly absorbed every word and asked questions about faith. Meg told her about Jesus' death on the cross for our sins and how she could be forgiven.

When she finished, Nellie looked at her for a long while, her thoughts obviously elsewhere. Meg waited patiently for her to speak, occupying herself with her food.

'I'd like to learn more,' Nellie eventually said.

'Well,' Meg said, 'I managed to get you a Bible today when I was at church. Do you read?'

'A little.' The cook looked doubtful.

'Well, perhaps we could read it together sometimes,' Meg suggested.

Nellie nodded eagerly and Meg flashed her a huge smile.

Later in the day, Meg was relaxing in her room when she heard a knock on her door. The governess opened the door. 'Nellie. I was just thinking about you.'

The cook smiled bashfully. 'Mister Rod'rick is asking for you Meg.'

'Oh,' Meg tried to hide her disappointment.

''E's waiting in the parlour.'

'Tell me,' Meg said, 'are any of the family in there also?'

'The children are in the playroom, I think, but Mister and Missus Sainsb'ry are in the parlour with Mister Rod'rick.'

'Good.' Meg sighed a little in relief. 'Thank you, Nellie.'

The cook left her, and Meg smoothed her skirt and hair. Mr Gilbert Roderick had contracted with Mr Sainsbury a few weeks earlier to provide him with several horses for his stables. They had been discussing the terms when Mr Roderick had seen Meg walk past. He had stopped and stared, most impolitely at her for an uncomfortable length of time.

Since then, he had visited a few times, always with the excuse of seeing about his horses, but always asking if Miss Wingrove was at home. Meg wondered if he had a serious interest in her. Oh, he was amiable enough, but something about him held her in check. His looks were distinctive and refined with olive-skin, dark hair, black eyes, and a cleft chin. He was attentive, yes, and courteous, but she noted a hardness in his eyes which remained even when he smiled. Although he seemed to be well educated, she found him to be slow of wit and generally uninteresting. And apart from all that, she did not know the condition of his soul.

Gilbert Roderick stood as Meg entered the room. 'Good afternoon, Miss Wingrove,' he took her hand and bowed over it in polite fashion.

'Good afternoon, Mister Roderick,' she replied and sat down on a chair nearby Mrs Sainsbury. 'Good afternoon, Mister Sainsbury, Missus Sainsbury.'

'Philip has just been telling Mister Roderick how his horses are doing, were you not my love?' Mrs Sainsbury filled her in.

'Yes,' Mr Sainsbury answered. 'Another few months and he will have a pair of new Thoroughbreds to draw his carriage.'

'You must be pleased,' Meg said, 'I am told Mister Sainsbury breeds the best horses around.'

'That is why I chose him,' Roderick began in his monotone voice. 'I only want the best horses to draw my carriage. I imported it from America, you know, through Mister Cob in Melbourne. It is very well suited to these roads. I do not care much for a rough journey you know; it makes me feel excessively queasy. I once spent two days in a carriage, and I must tell you it was almost as bad as the voyage from England to the colonies. I rather thought I would perish with all that swaying and bumping. It took me a full week to recover. But tell me, how do you do today, Miss Wingrove?'

'I am quite well, thank you.' Meg was grateful for the opportunity to change the topic of conversation. 'I attended church this morning, which always gives me great joy and comfort.'

'You did not get caught in the rainstorm, I trust?'

'No,' Meg replied, 'I made it back just in time.'

'That is well,' he nodded. 'I once found myself trapped in a severe storm. Out in the open, I was. I must tell you the rain was so cold it felt like ice, and I became soaked to the bone. When the storm finally blew itself out, I had to dig my buggy out of the mud. It took me well nigh three hours to get to my lodgings and by then I had come down with the fever. Nowadays I dare not venture out if it looks as though it might rain.'

Meg wondered why he was here in that case, as chances were it would rain again this afternoon. But she kept this thought to herself.

'Speaking of rain,' Mr Sainsbury took the opportunity to make good his escape, 'I promised the children I would take them for a drive before it rains again. Will you excuse me?'

He rose from his seat and with a brief goodbye, left the room. Mrs Sainsbury picked up her embroidery and began to occupy herself.

'Well, Mister Roderick,' Meg tried not to appear uncomfortable. 'Would you care for some tea?'

'Thank you, no,' he replied, 'I am not partial to tea, I'm afraid.'

'A glass of water then?'

'I appreciate your thoughtfulness,' he answered, 'but I think I shall be all right without. Now, Miss Wingrove, I must tell you how becoming you look today.'

'Thank you, sir.'

'I would ask you to take a turn with me in the gardens, however I do not wish to catch a chill; or rather I do not wish you to catch one.' He smiled briefly, though it was merely a faint turning up of the corners of his mouth.

'You are most considerate, Mister Roderick.' Meg tried not to giggle, suspecting it was himself he cared about most.

'It is very easy to catch a chill during winter, I find. I seem to suffer almost constantly from either a raw throat or a hacking cough, and once that cough catches a hold of me it takes ever so long to be rid of it. Do you not agree?'

'On the contrary,' Meg shook her head. 'I find myself constantly in good health.'

'Providence surely shines upon you then, Miss Wingrove,' Roderick sighed. 'I seem to find no end of trouble in my life.'

'Perhaps you need a new outlook then, Mister Roderick.'

'I beg pardon?' he asked, his face blank.

Meg sighed. 'Perhaps you need to view your life with a positive attitude.'

'Oh,' he mouthed absently, 'yes, perhaps.'

Meg groaned inwardly. 'There must be something good in your life to be thankful for.'

He suddenly caught the idea and looked deeply into her eyes. 'Yes, there is,' he said in a meaningful tone.

It was all Meg could do not to laugh at his obvious affectation. She fought to compose herself before speaking. 'Are you sure you would not like something to drink, Mister Roderick?'

'Quite sure,' he became dull again. 'In fact, I will presume upon you no longer. It looks as though it may rain shortly and as I have mentioned, I do not care to be out in the rain. If you will excuse me, I shall depart from you. Forgive the brevity of my visit, and please do not harbour any ill feelings towards me. Good day to you both, Missus Sainsbury, Miss Wingrove.' He bowed deeply to them and took his leave.

Meg sank back in her chair, relieved he had gone. The next instant brought guilt for her attitude towards Roderick and then repentance and then relief again. The mixture in her emotions caused her to burst into a fit of giggles.

'What is so funny, Meg?' the lady of the house asked.

'Nothing,' Meg put one hand over her mouth to try and stifle her laughter. 'It just seems so ridiculous, Missus Sainsbury.'

'I do not follow you,'

'It appears Mister Roderick may be interested in me.'

'Why should that be ridiculous, dear?'

'Do you not think him a trifle ... er ... tedious, melancholy, and perhaps even a little proud? Oh, I know these are horrible things to say about him, but I can't help but feel impatient and frustrated the whole time he is here.'

'Well,' Mrs Sainsbury said sympathetically, 'He is rather uninteresting, I must say. But he is courteous and not without good looks. His manners are impeccable, and his attentions are very flattering. I believe he would make a good husband for you.'

'Husband?' Meg hadn't thought of him that way at all.

'Yes,' Mrs Sainsbury brightened. 'Why he would be good and faithful. He would take good care of you, certainly. And you have said yourself the children will be grown soon, and you will have to find a posting somewhere else. Would it not be much nicer if you could settle into a good marriage instead?'

'I agree,' Meg said, 'But I would much prefer to marry a man who is more lively and able to laugh, not to mention a man I love, rather than settle for Mister Roderick.'

Mrs Sainsbury sighed. 'What if another man does not come along?'

When she said no more, the weight of this question settled on Meg's heart. Perhaps she should not cast Mr Roderick off so soon. Perhaps she would grow to like him more in time.

Chapter Five

It disappointed Jack to be torn away from his family when he had just arrived, however business called. He rode back to his house in Sydney immediately upon receiving word from Miller that the estate manager needed his assistance urgently. The courier had delivered a message that trouble had arisen with the local aborigines. Miller had sent a reply straight away that his master would arrive as soon as was possible. Jack hoped the situation did not become dangerous before he got there.

Jack spent the afternoon preparing for his journey. It would take two days to ride to the Hunter Valley, a wide, green valley surrounded by mountains in the distance on each side, and he needed provisions for the journey. He also readied his pistol, as there were frequently bush rangers hiding along the roads.

Once everything was in order, he went in search of Miss Charles. He wanted to end their courtship before he left. To his great chagrin, a search of her favourite clubs only served to enlighten him she had gone out of town for a few days. Irritated he would have to leave without resolving the issue, he made his way home again.

In his study, he penned a quick note to Lillian to inform her of his whereabouts, and summoned Miller. 'When Miss Charles returns from her visit in the country, kindly see she receives this,' he told his manservant.

'Yes, sir,' he replied with a slight bow.

'I am to bed now, Miller. I want to get an early start tomorrow.'

'Very good, sir,' Miller nodded and headed for the kitchen. The servant would ensure breakfast was served before the sun came up.

Two days later found Jack at the Fordham Estate, named after his father. He had arrived just before nightfall and sat to dine with Mr North while learning of the problem in more detail. Originally, Jack had been assigned convict labourers to work the land, the grape vines, and the winery. He frequently had trouble with them, most likely due to the fact they were criminals, and it was forced labour. One time a pair of them had absconded into the bushland that surrounded the vineyard. The police went in search of them and finally caught them some hundred miles up the coast hiding out. They had been sent back to gaol and had been replaced with new workers.

Another time, a few of them had stolen different pieces of equipment, built their own distillery just off the edge of the property and were making potato rum. Those convicts had also been sent back to the depot. Then there had been others who refused to work or worked poorly, or most commonly, they got too drunk in the evenings and were of no use to anyone the next day.

There had been a few good convict workers over the years, but overall, it had been hard to get good labourers unless you enlisted free men or subsidised immigrants from the homeland. Then, three years ago, the assigned convict labour and the subsidising of immigrants had been abolished. He now had to hire all his workers, some of whom were free immigrants and others who were ex-convicts. Roger North was one of the free men Jack had hired, along with a few more free immigrants. He found he had to pay these men more to keep them on the job, yet he saved money because of the productivity increase.

The natives were a different story. They were not a problem as such. They were unpredictable and not always reliable, but not troublemakers. Often the local aborigines would come around and work for a day in exchange for some of white man's food, clothes or tools and then be gone again. Sometimes they would work for days in a row and sometimes they would disappear for months on end without even a sighting. Jack was happy to let them do their own thing.

On this occasion, however, as North filled him in, an argument had arisen between the ex-convicts and the aborigines. One of the ex-convicts accused the natives of stealing his rum. North suspected it was one of their own that stole the grog, but there was no proof to be had. The aborigines, of course were offended at the accusation, claiming they had worked for their share. Two nights ago, a worker named Barney attacked one of the aborigines and broke his nose with his fist. The following night the natives had retaliated. They crept up on Barney while he slept and stabbed him in the arm. With anger intensifying, it seemed there would be an imminent show down.

'Did you notify the authorities?' Jack asked of North.

'I did,' the manager replied. 'Two officers arrived yesterday. They are standing guard by the workers' huts, trying to keep the peace.'

'Trying?'

'Well, the men have fashioned themselves crude weapons and are preparing for a war of sorts. They have all gathered behind Barney and are threatening to kill any aborigines that set foot on the property.'

'Are they drunk?'

'Quite.'

'Mmm. And what of the natives?'

'They are camped not far from the edge of the bush.'

Jack frowned. The situation was grave indeed. He finished his meal while he contemplated his actions.

'Mister North,' he said with authority, 'tell the cook to make plenty of strong coffee. First, I shall try and sober these men up and then I will try and reason with them.'

North looked doubtful. 'I don't mean to contradict you, sir, but talking hasn't helped so far.'

Jack shrugged. 'Well, you never know. Perhaps they will listen to me.'

৵৽

Mary ran into the playroom where Meg instructed Kitty in needlecraft. 'Oh, Winnie, you will never guess what news I have.'

Meg looked up, startled from her work to see two wide brown eyes

31

shining down at her. She smiled at the young girl's enthusiasm. 'No, I don't suppose I will. What is it?'

'We have been invited to a ball in honour of Governor Gipps in Sydney a week following Saturday.'

'I am very happy for you.'

'But that is not all, Winnie,' Mary almost jumped up and down in her elation.

'What else could there be?' The governess had no idea what had gotten Mary into such a fidget.

'You are to come with us.'

Meg's mouth dropped open in surprise. 'Me ... I — no ... Whatever for?'

'I would dearly love you to come as my guest. I have asked Mama and she has consented. She thinks it is a wonderful idea.' She approached Meg and took her by the hands. 'Just think, Winnie. You may find a dashing young man there.'

Meg giggled at the face Mary pulled. 'Do you think it is really such a good idea?'

Mary's face fell. 'Don't you want to go with me?'

'Of course. I would love to go with you,' Meg assured her. 'I have never been to a ball. My parents died before I had the chance for a debut. I have always dreamed of what it would be like. But I have no dress to wear.'

Kitty piped up at this moment. 'You could borrow one of Mama's dresses she doesn't fit anymore.'

Meg turned to look at the young girl who had gone straight back to her cross stitch, intently concentrating on her work.

'You are right, Kitty. Let us go and see now.' Mary dragged Meg from the room and took her in search of the debutante's mother.

Mrs Sainsbury agreed Meg would fit into one of her older gowns. They were roughly the same height, and at one time, she claimed, just as slender as her governess. The girls went through a trunk of old clothes and finally decided on a pink silk gown with trimmings in cream lace.

Mrs Sainsbury held it up against Meg. 'This will do wonderfully with your colouring, dear.' She laid the gown on her bed. 'Do try it on.'

Meg removed her ordinary work uniform and Mary and Mrs Sainsbury assisted her into the gorgeous ball gown. They stood back from her and appraised Meg's appearance.

'How does it feel, Winnie?' Mary asked.

Meg felt like a princess already. 'It feels quite comfortable, thank you.'

Mrs Sainsbury came close, twisted the skirt, and pinched at the sleeves, her face a mask of concentration. 'A few minor adjustments and it will be perfect,' she smiled at Meg.

Meg threw her arms around her employer. 'Thank you so much for giving me this opportunity. I confess I'm quite dizzy with excitement.'

Mrs Sainsbury laughed. 'You are very welcome, my dear.'

❧⚘❧

Tension hung in the air and Jack knew he had to exude an air of extreme authority. His father had the knack of this, and he hoped he could pull it off himself. He had instructed the officers to disarm the men and burn their weapons. Then he had ordered the workers to have a cold bath and made them drink strong coffee until they had sobered up somewhat. The men were none too happy with this treatment, as the water in winter was like ice. Yet, as Jack had confiscated their entire rum ration, they were hesitant to anger him further.

North told the men to gather in front of the huts where Mr Fordham wanted to speak with them. They mumbled as they did so and moved slowly, but eventually they were in place. Jack stood up on a tree stump to address them. He wore the most serious, formidable expression he could muster and stared them down for a long moment. 'Those of you who have no grievance against the natives and who want no part in this quarrel, come and stand behind me,' he said in a stern voice.

A small handful of men moved to stand away from the workers, and those who remained grumbled against them.

Jack focused on the remaining group. 'Now, I have a good mind to sack the lot of you and hire new men, and I may do so yet. If any of you lays so much as a finger on one of the aborigines, I will have the troopers drag you out of here. Is that understood?'

The man named Barney spat on the ground in disgust. 'Dogs.'

Jack glared at him. 'Dogs, are they? You men behave more like animals than they. You, who are prepared to murder men over a few bottles of rum. May I remind you of what happened at Myall Creek only six years ago? Out of the nine men who were involved in that massacre, seven of them were hanged for their crimes; just as you will be if you carry out your threats. Is that what you want?'

Silence greeted him. 'Is that what you want?' he bellowed.

The men shuffled their feet, and he heard a few murmured 'nos'.

'There will be no rum for the next three days. Go back to your huts.' Jack jumped down from the box and turned his back on the labourers, heading straight for the small homestead he had built there. North fell in behind him and the two officers stayed to watch the men.

'I shall stay here for a few days and make sure everything settles down,' Jack told North once they'd entered the house. 'Besides, it will be good to see how the vines are coming along.'

'Your first shipment of wine will be ready in a month or so, and the grapes thrive in this climate,' North told him.

'Yes, I am pleased with how everything is progressing so far,' Jack grinned proudly, 'Except for the labourers, of course.'

North put a teapot on the stove to boil. 'You handled them well. I was impressed. They would not have responded so with me.'

Jack shrugged. 'Perhaps they know I have the last word around here.'

'I dare say,' North replied.

Jack leaned against the kitchen wall. 'Mister North, do you keep a record of every incident that happens?'

'I do as a matter of fact.'

'Do you list the names of the troublemakers?'

'Yes, I do.'

'I should like to have a look tomorrow, then.'

'Of course, sir.'

'For now, I am looking forward to that cup of tea you are brewing.'

North grinned. 'Yes, sir.'

The week before the ball dragged by for Meg, so great was her anticipation. Mrs Sainsbury had her dressmaker work on the gown, adjusting and modernising it a little. Meg tried the gown on several times before Mrs Sainsbury was happy with the fit. Then there was the matter of finding shoes and other accessories which involved a shopping expedition to Parramatta. Meg couldn't remember having so much fun in an age, and remembered her life in England before her parents were taken from her.

A new hope emerged with all the preparation. This ball would give her the chance to meet new people. She might meet a new family who could use her expertise as a governess. Or, dare she even think it, she could possibly meet an eligible young man. Dressed in a pretty gown, perhaps she might catch someone's eye. Perhaps this ball would broaden her prospects.

Jack had been on the estate for a week and things had finally settled back to normal. The men hadn't attacked the natives, but Barney and two of his mates had continued to stir up trouble. Reading North's ledger had shown these men, two of which were ex-convicts, had frequently been a problem on the plantation.

Jack decided very quickly to dismiss these men and have them replaced. He had them sent off the property with the troopers, although no charges were laid, and warned them never to return. As soon as they were gone, he sent a courier to Newcastle with an advertisement for three hands. Within a few days men began riding onto the property to fill the positions.

So, by the end of the week Jack had three new labourers and all was peaceful again. 'I shall depart on the morrow,' he informed Roger that evening at supper.

'You are satisfied, then?'

'Yes,' Jack replied, 'I believe everything is in hand.'

'Quite right, sir.'

Jack looked up from his meal and eyed the man. 'You are doing a fine job, North, keep it up.'

'Thank you, sir.'

Chapter Six

The day of the ball finally arrived, and Meg was so high in anticipation she couldn't shake the fluttering in her stomach. They were to prepare themselves for the ball at an inn, but Meg had organised to spend the night at her brother's house.

Excited chatter about the evening ahead filled the carriage ride to Sydney. Mary was so happy to have Meg beside her she clasped her hand most of the way.

'So, this is your first ball, is it Meg?' Mr Sainsbury asked her.

'Yes, I confess it is.'

'Well, I do hope you enjoy it, then,' he said. 'After a while they become quite tiresome.'

'Hush, Philip,' Mrs Sainsbury giggled. 'That is only because you do not dance with the ladies, nor gamble with the men.'

Mr Sainsbury smiled grimly. 'Just as I said, tiresome.'

Meg looked out of the window so he could not see the laughter in her face. How she dearly would love to dance. She could hardly wait.

'Oh, look,' Mary cried out. 'Here we are.'

Once the family had settled into their lodgings, they ate a light lunch and then rested from their journey. No-one wanted to be drowsy at the ball that evening. Meg lay down for a short nap, then spent some time reading.

Soon enough, it was time for an early supper. Meg and Mary were so excited they could hardly force themselves to eat, their minds fully occupied with dressing up the evening ahead. Mrs Sainsbury teased the girls, and it wasn't long before Mr Sainsbury was also laughing at them.

'All right, go, be off with you.' He waved the girls off, after they had picked at their food in distraction for some time. Meg and Mary bolted from the table, all etiquette forgotten, and raced to their room to get ready. A few minutes later, a beaming Mrs Sainsbury joined them, and the three women assisted each other in their attire.

Once they were in their gowns, a laborious task with stays to tie and buttons to fasten, they fixed each other's hair. All the while they laughed and chattered like children. Indeed, Meg might have been seventeen again and experiencing her own coming out party.

At last, Meg took her seat at the dresser. The girls pulled her hair up into a chignon but left several golden tresses to cascade in ringlets down her neck and around her face. They added delicate pink flowers to her hair and threaded a string of tiny pearls through it.

Having completed their coiffure, they next began to adorn themselves with jewellery. Mrs Sainsbury draped a beautiful string of pearls around Meg's neck and noticed she had not removed her locket. Meg's hand fluttered to the pendant. 'Must I take it off? It is the only thing I have to remind me of my mother.'

'What is inside?' Mrs Sainsbury asked.

'A tiny miniature of my mother and father.' She opened it to show the tiny portraits.

'It is hard to believe someone could paint something so small,' Mrs Sainsbury admired the artwork. Straightening, she returned to business. 'Nevertheless, it does not match the rest of your ensemble.'

Reluctantly, Meg removed the precious necklet and allowed Mrs Sainsbury to fasten the pearls around her neck. Finally, they completed their attire with shoes, gloves, and shawls. Just before they were ready to leave, they each had a turn to admire themselves in the full-length mirror that stood in the corner of their room. Mrs Sainsbury and Mary were very pleased with the outcome of their efforts. When Meg stepped in front of the mirror, she could hardly recognise the reflection she saw. Gone was the ordinary governess, and in her place stood a golden beauty. Meg gasped in surprise. She had never known she could look so fetching.

'I do not think it was wise to bring her to this ball, Mary,' Mrs Sainsbury feigned disgust. 'She is far too pretty and will outshine both of us.'

'Nonsense,' Meg blushed, still staring at herself.

'I daresay she will be the belle of the ball,' Mary agreed with her mother, sighing.

'I am too old to be noticed like that,' Meg dismissed their comments.

'If you say so,' Mrs Sainsbury gave a knowing smile. 'Just don't complain to me if every gentleman at the ball asks you to dance tonight.'

'Do stop it, you two,' Meg pleaded, heat rising in her face.

'Very well,' Mrs Sainsbury moved toward the door. 'Shall we go?'

⥲⥤

Jack rode up to his house in Sydney late in the afternoon. Saddle weary, he longed to collapse into his bed. Miller greeted him at the door, informing him a hot meal awaited him in the dining room. Miller always kept a fire burning in each of the main rooms, on the chance his master would return at any moment. He also made sure there was always food cooked for him if he appeared without warning.

Jack was grateful to have a servant with such insight and initiative. He smiled warmly at his butler and headed for the dining room. 'Will you have a hot bath prepared for me, Miller, and a fresh change of clothes laid out? I am covered in dust from the road.' He called to the butler behind him.

Miller went to do as he was bid and ten minutes later returned to Jack in the dining room. 'Your bath will be ready shortly, sir.'

'Excellent,' Jack looked forward to a good soak. 'I do not wish to be disturbed for a few hours, Miller, but is there any important mail for me?'

'Nothing that cannot wait, sir,' Miller replied, 'except for a message from Miss Charles.'

39

'Oh?' Jack yawned. 'What is it?'

'She has notified us of her movements each day in case you returned.'

'I see.'

'Tonight, I believe, she will be at Governor Gipps' ball.'

Jack scanned his memory for the details but came up blank. 'Did I receive an invitation to this ball?'

'Yes, sir, it arrived a few days after you departed for the vineyard.'

'Well,' Jack yawned again, 'right now I am far too fatigued to go anywhere. I shall retire to my room for a while. See to it I am not disturbed.'

'Yes, sir,' Miller bowed as Jack rose from the table.

❧

Mr and Mrs Sainsbury entered the ball room arm in arm just ahead of Meg and Mary, who clasped each other's hands nervously. Meg stared wide eyed at the scene around her. Hundreds of candles, chandeliers and lamps lit the room, so it almost dazzled in its brightness. The crystal chandeliers hanging from the high ceiling sparkled, sprinkling light in every direction. The wooden floor had been polished until it was so glossy you could see your reflection in it. Every where she looked, Meg saw brilliant gowns and glittering diamonds. She heard laughter and beautiful music emanating from every corner of the room. Huge fires burned in hearths at each end of the hall, filling the room with comfortable warmth.

In one corner, the orchestra was seated, and they played lively music to which there were already a few couples dancing. Most people, however, greeted their friends and acquaintances as they arrived. Meg and Mary followed the Sainsbury's to some of their friends. It didn't take long for the men to drift away from the women, leaving them to gossip and chatter about trivial matters. One woman pointed out several the guests to Meg and Mary, including the governor himself.

'... And over there, my dear Gwendolyn,' she pointed to a dark-haired beauty, who fanned herself demurely on the other side of the room, 'is your brother's latest conquest, Miss Lillian Charles.'

'That is Miss Charles?' Gwen repeated.

'Yes, indeed,' answered the lady.

Meg had a good look at the woman, trying not to appear too obvious. It puzzled her that a woman would lower her standards so much she would be seen with a man like Jack Fordham. She could only feel pity for the lady, as her heart would surely be broken.

It wasn't long before Meg noticed that many of the guests appraised her appearance. Several men smiled and bowed in her direction as she walked by, and a few ladies ogled her and whispered to each other behind their fans. If Meg had not seen how pretty she looked in the mirror, she would have thought something to be wrong with her gown or her hair. As it was, it seemed Mrs Sainsbury had been right. She had caused quite a stir in the room.

❧

Jack awoke with a start at the sound of Juniper barking somewhere in the house. He peered at the clock on the mantelpiece. Eight o'clock. The warm bath had relaxed him, and he had slept soundly for over two hours. Refreshed, he climbed out of bed and pulled the bell that would summon Miller.

When the valet entered, he found Jack dressing in his best evening suit. 'I perceive sir, you are going to the ball.'

'Yes, Miller,' Jack grinned. 'Would you see a light supper is laid out for me immediately, and then have my carriage brought around front?'

'Very good, sir,' the servant bowed and left the room.

Jack took his time over dressing. He loved the sensation of the exquisite fabrics on his skin and made sure every seam sat straight and in the right place. He meticulously tied his cravat, adjusting it until every fold sat perfectly, and examined the points of his collar, checking they were even and did not sag in the least. He ran a brush through his hair and smoothed it back with oil, so that it sat neatly against his head. He examined the details of his ensemble in his full-length mirror and adjusted until he was satisfied with his appearance.

Casually, Jack descended the stairs and went to the dining room once again to eat before departing. As he had requested, his supper awaited him, and he unhurriedly consumed this repast. Then, with a contented sigh, he made his way to his carriage.

❧❧

More guests arrived at the ball, and it became rather noisy and crowded. None of these things perturbed Meg; she revelled in the whole experience. Not too long after she arrived, she saw her brother enter the hall. 'Brian,' she squealed. She excused herself from her present company and almost ran to him.

'Brian,' she called as she approached.

'Meg.' His eyes lit with delight when he saw who called him. 'Is that you?' He clasped her hands and kissed her on each cheek. 'My, you look beautiful all dressed up. It is good to see you, dearest.'

'And you, Brian. How I have missed you.'

'Dance with me?'

'There is no-one I would rather dance with,' she grinned at him, and he led her to the dance floor.

It had been years since she had danced at all, but she was thankful she had not forgotten the steps. They danced several movements together until she was quite out of breath, and he led her to the refreshments table. She was just about to ask her brother about his work when he seemed to notice someone he knew. 'Excuse me, sister dear,' he said without looking at her, 'there is someone I must go and speak to.' He turned to her. 'I will catch up with you later. Enjoy yourself now.'

She smiled at him and watched him walk towards a honey haired, slightly stout girl on the far side of the room. Meg polished off her punch and began to find her way back to Mary's side, when she noticed Gilbert Roderick coming her way. She stopped still, wishing she could disappear into the background and considered turning her back to him, but her genteel upbringing would not allow her to. He looked at her as he approached and

42

then glanced away again. For a split-second Meg thought, with guilty relief, he didn't recognise her. But then his eyes suddenly flew back to her and the familiarity in them was unmistakeable.

Dressed entirely in black, he walked straight to her and bowed low over her hand. 'Miss Wingrove,' he breathed, 'You look like a goddess this evening.'

It was all Meg could do not to roll her eyes at him. 'Good evening, Mister Roderick,' she forced a pleasant voice as she curtsied, hoping he would not detain her all evening. 'You deceive yourself. I am no such thing.'

'An angel then,' he shrugged, 'It is all the same.'

'You flatter me, sir,' Meg blushed, 'But I do think you exaggerate.'

'I never exaggerate,' he said severely, 'In fact, it has been said I am on the tedious side of precision and detail. I am proud to say I never embellish the truth and am given only to the exact particulars.'

Meg tried to hide her laughter, although she was sure her eyes would give it away. 'Well then,' she said, 'the truth, on this occasion as you perceive it, is incorrect.'

'I am never wrong.'

'But I am neither an angel nor a goddess,' she told him, suppressing a giggle. She thought Mr Roderick's point of view quite absurd.

'Even so, may I have the honour of dancing with you?' He brushed off her argument.

'I do love to dance,' she admitted, glad for the change of subject. She took his proffered arm and followed him onto the floor.

Roderick danced wholly without enthusiasm, merely going through the steps as though they were a mathematic equation. He was lost in concentration on where he his feet were supposed to go next, rarely making eye contact or conversation, and thus was not an enjoyable dance partner. Meg found herself relieved when the dance finally came to an end, and even more so when a few gentlemen approached to beg an introduction and request a dance. Roderick had no choice but relinquish her to their attentions and he went in search of other distractions.

Time flew by for Meg as she danced with one partner and then another, meeting so many gentlemen, she could barely remember any of their names. She did manage to keep one eye on Mary, who seemed to have gathered a circle of admirers already, all competing for her favour. Mary behaved very properly and demurely, and Meg found her heart swell with pride. She sighed to herself. This night was indeed everything she had dreamed it would be.

The hour neared ten o'clock and Meg sat along the wall, caught up in a conversation with a gentleman of new acquaintance. Even so, her senses became alert when she heard the doorman announce, 'The Honourable Jonathon Fordham.'

Chapter Seven

Meg heard excited murmurs from women all around her. She looked up and followed their gaze to where Mr Fordham had just entered the ballroom. Tall and proud, he was dressed in an ivory silk jacket with long coat tails. His muscular legs were covered in deep green trousers and his heeled shoes sported a large, silver buckle. He wore an ivory, silk brocade vest and his cravat was fastened with a large emerald pin.

Reputed as the most handsome man in Sydney, Mr Fordham's jaw line was strong but not harsh, his nose straight, and his eyes a warm brown. His hair was dark and smoothed back from his brow. With every move he made, light sparkled and reflected from emerald cufflinks, the emerald buttons on his coat, and of course the emerald in his cravat. Meg found it difficult not to draw a sharp breath herself. She had always known Mr Fordham was good looking, but she had never seen him in full ball dress before, and she had to shake herself free from the effect he had upon her.

Most of the single ladies around her slowly began to make their way closer to this nonpareil, hoping for an introduction, or just to be noticed. Meg however, surprised the man she had been conversing with by ignoring the commotion and continuing their discussion. Even so, she kept a surreptitious eye on Jack Fordham.

Jack noticed his sister and brother-in-law almost immediately as he entered and, ignoring all the adoring glances that came his way, he moved in their direction to greet them. Before he could reach them, Miss Charles stepped in front of him.

'Jack, darling, there you are,' she almost threw herself at him. 'I have missed you so.'

He held her back at arm's length and looked her over. 'Lillian, my dear, how is it you are even more beautiful than when I left.'

Miss Charles demurely fanned herself. 'Why, thank you Jack. Charming as ever, I see.'

'Mmm.' He smiled and leaned forward to whisper in her ear. 'I must speak with you this evening. Do not leave without me.'

Lillian smiled broadly at him, hope lighting her face. 'Of course, my dear, whatever you say.'

He held her hands between his and looked into her eyes. 'Now, there are some people I must greet. Save me a dance and I will see you anon. Forgive me.' He kissed her hand, giving her an imploring look and took his leave of her, continuing towards his sister.

'You are back in Sydney, Jack,' Gwen greeted him with delight, kissing him on the cheek. 'I am glad you did not have to stay away long.'

'Fordham.' Philip nodded, shaking his hand.

'Trouble with the labourers,' Jack informed them. 'It did not take much to straighten them out.'

'Well, you must come back and finish your visit with us,' Gwen commanded. 'The children were sore when you left so quickly.'

'Believe me, I wasn't impressed either,' Jack assured her. 'I will return as soon as I can.'

They fell into silence for a time as a new dance started up and they watched the couples pair up on the dance floor.

Jack peered at one of the young ladies. 'Is that Mary, I see over there?'

Gwen beamed. 'Yes, it is. Doesn't she look lovely?'

'Indeed,' Jack agreed. 'I must ask her for a dance. Although, from the looks of it she has the young men queued up waiting for the chance.'

Gwen laughed in delight. 'She is a great success, is she not? And Jack, do you want to know who else is here?'

Jack was about to ask who when several his friends strolled up.

'Fordham!' One gentleman slapped him on the back.

Jack turned to see who had thumped him. 'Bart,' he exclaimed, pleased to see his closest friend in Sydney. 'Excuse me, Gwen, Phil. I have not seen this fellow in an age.'

Jack drifted off with his friends. 'When did you return, Bart?' he asked as they strode away.

⁂

Meg had furtively watched Mr Fordham's interchange with Miss Charles, only half listening to her admirer. Mr Fordham played his part well. Miss Charles appeared to be completely beguiled by him. How could a man use a woman so? She had half a mind to go and warn the lady herself.

Instead, Meg excused herself from her companion and went in search of her brother, finding him quite close at hand. 'Meg,' he called her as she almost walked by him.

'Oh, Brian,' she turned to him. 'I was just looking for you.'

'Is there something you need?'

'No. I just wanted to spend some time with my brother.'

He gave her hand a squeeze. 'Are you enjoying yourself?'

'It is wonderful.' She gazed around the room. 'I am so glad I have come, and grateful to the Sainsburys for bringing me.'

She glanced across to see Mr Fordham had made his way to the Sainsburys and engaged himself in conversation with them. Shifting her gaze away from them, she caught sight of Mr Roderick coming towards them.

Meg made the necessary introductions between Mr Roderick to her brother and then they were both forced to listen to his dull chatter. He continued to bore them for some minutes when Brian finally excused himself to go and bring Meg a drink. Not wanting to be left alone with Mr Roderick, she quickly decided to join him. 'Excuse me Mister Roderick, I have not seen my brother for a long time. You understand, don't you?'

Roderick, who had been in the middle of a speech advising about the best way to invest one's funds, found his companions were gone before he was fully aware of the fact. He shrugged his shoulders and went in search of a card game.

Brian and Meg, glasses of punch in hand went to stand at the edge of the dance floor and admire the graceful movements. 'Who was that young girl you spoke with earlier?' Meg asked her brother.

'Her name is Miss Katherine Montgomery.' Slight colour rose in his cheeks.

'You are fond of her?'

'I like her very well, yes.'

'Come now, Brian,' Meg pressed. 'It is me you are talking to. I can see plain as day you have feelings for her.'

'Feelings, yes,' he replied honestly and sighed. 'I am just not sure of my intentions yet.'

'You don't know if she's the right one?'

'No,' he gave a brief smile.

'Then I shall pray for you,' she squeezed his hand.

Meg made a furtive glance towards Mr Fordham who now conversed with his friends and noticed with alarm that he looked directly at her.

৯৯৯

Jack gazed around the ballroom, mostly without interest, whilst chatting with his friends, when the vision of a woman across the hall arrested his attention. He let out a low whistle and put down his glass of punch. 'Who is that exquisite beauty over next to the dance floor?' he interrupted Mr Bartholomew mid-sentence.

Bart stopped and followed his friend's line of sight. 'She is rather pretty, isn't she?'

'I have never seen her equal.' Jack was unable to take his eyes off the golden-haired beauty.

Another of his friends, Mr Neville, laughed. 'Fordham, from what I see, she is beyond your touch.'

Jack's attention was at last diverted. 'Beyond my touch? What the devil do you mean?'

'He means she is too good for you,' teased a third friend, as he took a bite from an apple.

'Too good?' Jack was astounded. 'I have never heard such nonsense. You want me to prove you wrong? Very well, I shall ask her to dance.'

'She'll refuse you,' Mr Neville baited him with laughing eyes.

'What woman ever refuses me?' Jack boasted.

'Suppose this one does?' Mr Neville provoked.

Jack took the bait. 'I will wager you twenty pounds she will dance with me.'

'Done,' Mr Neville grinned, and Mr Bartholomew shrugged his shoulders.

❧

A red-haired gentleman took the beauty's empty glass and his own and walked away to dispose of them. In the moment she was alone, Jack took his opportunity to approach her. As he neared her, he summoned his best debonair smile and bowed deeply before her. 'Jack Fordham at your service, my lady.'

The lady neither put her hand out to receive his greeting, nor displayed any elation at his attention. She merely eyed him suspiciously for a moment, then something that looked like surprise crossed her features. 'Mister Fordham,' she greeted. 'I have heard much about you. I quite feel as though I know you.'

He frowned slightly. There was something about her. 'Oddly enough, ma'am, I feel the same,' he told her. 'There is something very familiar about you. Have we met before?'

'Perhaps we have,' she lifted her shoulders and moved away from the dance floor. He followed her.

'May I inquire as to your name, my lady?'

'If you know me, then you would know my name, would you not? Do you need time to think?' Mischief sparked in her eyes.

But he could not answer, though he wracked his brain.

'I am surprised a man of your reputation would use such an old cliché to lure a girl.'

'Cliché?' Jack was confused.

'Come now, Mister Fordham. Do not attempt to deny that you and your friends over there conspired together, daring you to try and win my favour.'

Jack gave an empty laugh. She was bold … and harsh … and right. 'My dear lady, I can assure you I am in earnest. Something about you is very familiar; your face, your voice, why, even your gown is impressed upon my memory somehow. I just cannot place it.'

'Well, Mister Fordham,' she sighed seeming disappointed. 'Perhaps I should be insulted. Here you are trying to flatter me, professing to know me, and yet not remembering me. I must, indeed, be intolerably dull.'

Jack stared at her for a moment and then laughed heartily. 'Very well, I am undone. I do not know how I could forget such a uniquely beautiful face, nor such a sharp-witted tongue in the same person. Please, do tell me your name.'

She pressed her lips together, although her eyes danced. She put out her hand in greeting. 'Miss Margaret Wingrove, sir. Glad to have made your acquaintance.'

Jack bowed again, his mind already scanning his memory for any recollection of that name — still coming up blank. By the time he gave up thinking about it, she had escaped him. He looked around the ballroom to see she now danced with a young gentleman. Slightly mystified, but infinitely more amused, he returned to his friends.

Mr Bartholomew, Mr Neville, and Mr Smithson all guffawed at the look on his face. 'You got her to dance with the wrong man, Fordham,' Mr Smithson laughed.

'Hand over the twenty pounds, my friend, you have lost this wager,' Mr Neville held his hand out.

Jack turned his back to them and fixed his gaze on the young beauty he had just been speaking with. 'Not yet, Nev. I am not done.'

'So, who is she?' Mr Bartholomew asked him.

'A Miss Margaret Wingrove,' Jack informed him. 'Only I am sure I have met her before.'

'Where?' Mr Bartholomew inquired.

'That is the thing,' Jack replied. 'For the life of me, I cannot remember.'

They watched her dance for a while. 'She is the most intriguing character, Bart,' he said quietly so only his close friend could hear. 'She gave me a tidy set down, I can tell you.'

Just then the dance ended, and Jack moved to try and intercept Miss Wingrove again. He was not swift enough however, as the red-haired young man claimed her for the next set before he could get near her.

⤞⤝

Meg was glad to be in her brother's hands again. It was very comfortable to dance with one's brother, especially when they had practised all their dance steps together growing up. 'Brian, do you wish to stay much longer?' she asked him, conscious Mr Fordham kept a close eye on her now.

'Why? Do you wish to leave?'

'I am a little tired, I confess.'

'Then after this dance, I shall take you home. All right?'

'Thank you, Brian.'

A few minutes later the music wound down and Brian went to collect their coats, bidding her to remain where she was. She nodded, stifling a yawn, and waited for him to return.

Jack saw Meg standing alone and made his move. He quickly approached and stood before her, sporting his most dazzling smile. 'Miss Wingrove,' he said, 'May I have the honour of leading you out onto the dance floor?'

'I beg pardon, sir,' she replied, 'but I find I am rather weary and ...'

'May I escort you to the refreshments table, then?' he interrupted.

'No, thank you, I just need to rest.'

'A chair perhaps?' He waved his arm toward the seating along the wall.

'Mister Fordham,' she sounded annoyed. 'I am waiting here for my brother, who is about to take me home.'

'My presence offends you, I see.' Jack frowned. 'I beg pardon, ma'am. I only wished to spend a few moments with the prettiest girl in the room.'

Miss Wingrove's lips pressed together, and her eyes flashed. 'And yet, the lovely Miss Charles waits just over there for your company,' she looked past him to where that lady sat.

Jack glanced over his shoulder at Lillian who watched their interchange with a possessive eye, and he wished her grasping attitude to Hades. He turned back to Miss Wingrove, shrugging off the discomfiture she roused. 'Your loveliness far outshines that of Miss Charles,' he said smoothly. 'So much so, I had quite forgotten she was even here.'

Miss Wingrove gasped but locked onto his gaze with a challenge in her eyes. She spoke quietly and directly. 'And how long will it be before you speak sweetly to another lady, while I am the one left along the wall? Two, perhaps three weeks? If that is all I must look forward to, then I beg you will find someone else who can appreciate such a brief liaison.'

Once again, her set down left Jack dumbfounded. He struggled to find a smile. 'Very well, Miss Wingrove, you have made your point. I shan't detain you any longer.'

The golden beauty said nothing. Her red-headed brother emerged from the cloakroom and waved to her from the entrance.

Jack looked at her intently, still trying to place her. 'Tell me one thing, Miss Wingrove. Have we, indeed, met?'

Her smile was thin at best. 'Many times, Mister Fordham.'

'May I ask where?' he pressed.

'You really do not know, do you?' she sighed. 'Perhaps you should ask my young charge over yonder.' She pointed towards the far wall.

Jack turned to where she indicated, but only saw Mary. 'But that is my ...' He turned back at that moment to see she had escaped him once again. He shook his head in bewilderment and watched as her brother wrapped her in her shawl. Then he noticed Mary approach her from the other side of the ballroom. They kissed one another on the cheek like old friends, and then the mysterious girl was gone.

All at once everything fell into place in Jack's mind and a wave of shock hit him with force. 'Meg?!' he exclaimed in disbelief, causing many heads to turn his way.

Chapter Eight

Brian and Meg descended the stairs at the front of the building to meet their carriage as it drew up. They were not far outside the doors when Mr Roderick appeared from the shadows at the corner of the building and approached them.

'Miss Wingrove,' he called after her. 'May I have a word?'

The hairs on the back of Meg's neck stood on end. She shook off the eerie feeling and told Brian to go on ahead. 'I shall join you presently.'

She turned to the strange man. 'What is it, Mister Roderick?'

'I saw you with Mister Fordham tonight. Take care he doesn't deceive you with his charms. He is a scoundrel of the worst kind.' There was an inexplicable glint in his eyes.

'I can assure you I am no fool,' Meg wondered at his motives.

'Do you know then, he entered into a wager on your account tonight?' When Meg remained silent, he added, 'I just wanted you to know the kind of evil he will stoop to.'

Meg could not fathom how he could know this information, but instinctively knew it to be true. 'Do not concern yourself with my welfare, Mister Roderick.' She tried to sound confident, shaking off the alarm he roused. 'I am aware of Mister Fordham's devices. Now, if you will excuse me, my brother awaits.'

Roderick bowed and let the matter drop. 'Good night, Miss Wingrove.'

Meg hurried down the stairs and the footman handed her into the carriage with Brian.

'What did you say that fellow's name was again, Meg?' Brian asked her as she made herself comfortable.

'Mister Roderick,' she replied. 'Mister Gilbert Roderick.'

'Hmm,' Brian rubbed his chin. 'That name sounds familiar. I wonder where I have heard it before.' He became silent for a while, clearly trying to remember. In the end he shrugged. 'Well, no matter. What did he want?'

Meg grinned mischievously at her brother. 'He wanted to warn me away from the dastardly Mister Fordham.'

Brian laughed. 'I saw you speaking with Fordham tonight. You do not still fancy yourself in love with him, I hope.'

Meg put a tender hand on his knee. 'You know I changed my mind about him long ago. In fact, until this evening, I am sure I have not spoken above ten words to him in the last few years.'

'So, what was different about this evening?'

'Would you believe, he did not know me?'

'Did not know you? How so?'

'He seemed to think I was rather captivating.' She pretended to examine the lace at her wrists.

Brian laughed again. 'And what did you do?'

Meg smiled wickedly at him and then bit her lip.

'What did you do?' he insisted.

Meg shrugged. 'You know how I am. I couldn't resist.' She sighed. 'I teased him a little, and then I gave him a delicious set down.'

Brian stared at her open mouthed for a moment and then clapped his hands. 'Bravo to you, sister. I would that I had been there to witness it. I dare say it has been a long time coming for him. Tell me how it went.'

Meg giggled. 'Well,' she began and launched into a word-for-word description of her encounter with Mr Fordham, leaving her brother both gasping in shock and roaring with laughter. Soon enough they arrived at his home, where they enjoyed a nightcap of hot chocolate together and continued their conversation late into the night.

For Jack, the rest of the evening went by in somewhat of a daze. In a state of disbelief, he had returned once again to his friends who forced him to pay out the twenty pounds he had staked. They had laughed and slapped him on the back, but Jack's mind still reeled from the knowledge that all along he had been speaking with Meg, the governess of his nieces and nephews. He told himself it couldn't be true. Meg, the governess and Miss Margaret Wingrove, the enchantress, could not possibly be one and the same person.

When he had finally caught up with Mary, she asked him if he had seen their dear Winnie that evening. 'Yes,' he had affirmed, though his voice sounded full of doubt.

'Didn't she look magnificent?'

'Yes,' he had replied weakly, receiving the unwanted confirmation of the truth.

So distracted was he, that he almost forgot his meeting with Miss Charles. When she stepped into his pathway, he suddenly wished he didn't have to perform this bothersome task, longing only to be alone with his thoughts. Nevertheless, he had taken her aside to where they could speak without being overheard. He had showered her with compliments and then gently told her he no longer wanted to continue their liaison. She flew into a rage, slapped him on the cheek, told him in no uncertain terms what she thought of him, and then stalked off angrily. Jack had sighed, stood for a moment in silence, collecting his thoughts, and headed for the cloak room.

Now at home, Jack lay on his bed staring at the ceiling, his hands folded behind his head. He could not erase a pair of almond shaped clear blue eyes from his thoughts. She was a perfect angel to look at — slender in form, but shapely. She moved with ease and grace. Never in his entire memory had Jack been so captivated by a woman at first glance. And yet, it wasn't first glance. How had he not noticed her before?

How she had spoken to him. Remembering the gleam in her eye he realised she had mocked him throughout their conversation. Why, she enjoyed putting him in his place. Jack smiled despite himself and then chuckled softly. She had been at an unfair advantage. 'The next time you will not be so lucky, Miss Wingrove,' he murmured aloud. The game had begun.

❧❦

Meg cherished every moment she could spend with her brother, the only real family she had left in the world. He was the one person she could speak completely openly and honestly to, and he felt the same way about her. So, at these times together, they usually shared the things that were deepest in their hearts.

Over breakfast, Brian talked at length about his feelings for Miss Montgomery, and Meg told him of her concerns for her future. They then spent time in devotion together and prayed for each other before heading to church.

Brian's church was much bigger than Meg's and had a large stone chapel in Sydney. The children went to Sabbath School while the adults benefited from the main service. The church had a very informal and friendly atmosphere, and Meg rather enjoyed herself. She noticed Miss Montgomery enter a little late while they were singing a hymn and watched her secretively throughout the service.

After the service, Meg saw Brian approach Miss Montgomery, and made her way to join them as quickly as possible. As she arrived at her brother's side, he introduced her.

'Pleased to meet you, Miss Wingrove,' the shy young girl said.

'And I you, Miss Montgomery.' Meg offered a warm smile. They chatted together about the service for a few minutes and then Meg asked, 'Do you have any family here, Miss Montgomery?'

'Just my mother over there,' she pointed.

'Why, you should both join my brother and me at his home for lunch today,' Meg suggested as if the idea had just come to her. She received a gentle pinch on her arm, Brian warning her not to be too forward. 'I am yearning

57

to make new friends in Sydney,' she added. Brian would likely scold her later, but she wanted them to have the chance to get to know one another better.

'I am sure Mother would be delighted,' she replied, her eyes wide. 'We are just new to Sydney and looking for new acquaintances ourselves. I shall go and ask her, that is, if it is all right with you, Mister Wingrove.'

'It would be my pleasure,' Brian bowed slightly, and Miss Montgomery turned to speak with her mother.

'You should not be interfering, Meg,' Brian whispered, his lips barely moving while nodding at a church member who passed by.

'Nonsense, Brian,' Meg pretended to examine the floor, 'What ever happened to your Christian charity?' She looked up with a twinkle in her eye, to see Miss Montgomery returning.

The young woman blushed as she spoke. 'My mother and I would be pleased to accept your invitation.'

As it was, Meg had barely finished eating her dinner when the Sainsburys arrived to take her back to Parramatta. She excused herself from Miss Montgomery and her mother, apologising for cutting short her time with them. She was secretly glad Brian would be able to spend more time with them though, without having to involve her in the conversation.

Brian had her portmanteau collected and brought to the carriage and he escorted her out to bid her farewell. 'It has been wonderful to see you again, Brian,' Meg told him, clasping his hands.

'And you, my darling sister.'

'Farwell my dear,' she kissed his cheek affectionately.

'Goodbye, Meg,' he returned her kiss. 'By the way, thank you for inviting Miss Montgomery. I truly am grateful to you. It is the opportunity I have hoped for.'

Meg grinned at him as he handed her into the carriage.

∽∾

A week had almost passed before the journey to Parramatta was possible for

Jack. The weather turned sour right after the ball and it had rained for days on end, making the roads too boggy to pass. Jack wasn't at all put out. It afforded him time to inspect his own interests in Sydney.

By the time the roads had dried enough for travel, the week's end was almost upon him. Once the way was clear, he wasted no time in gathering some belongings, climbing on his horse, and making a beeline for his sister's estate.

Jack arrived at the homestead soon after lunch on Saturday to the delight of the whole family, although Meg made no hurried appearance. As per his usual custom, Jack greeted each family member and produced gifts for the children. The Sainsburys were very good at keeping him busy with talk and play and it would be difficult to escape them with any reasonable excuse.

The time came when Gwen summoned Meg to take the children out of the parlour so the adults could converse in peace. He focussed his attention on Philip, ignoring her presence in the room. He did not want his sister guessing his thoughts. He caught Meg wearing a smug expression in the one glance he sent her way, just as she was leaving. She believed he'd forgotten already. This would be diverting, indeed.

Chapter Nine

The sun had escaped the cloudy sky for the present, and Meg took advantage of it, leading the children into the yard to play. She was sure her encounter at the ball with Jack Fordham was the first and last of that nature. Why would an unmatched paragon of society pursue a simple governess? In her mind there was simply no reason why he would. She was relieved he'd paid her no attention since he arrived, and she could put that incident to rest.

Meg challenged the children to a game of croquet which kept them occupied and out of mischief. Eventually, she went to sit on a nearby bench and watch as they enjoyed themselves. She hadn't been resting long when Mr Fordham emerged from the house and joined in the fun with them. Always the good sport, he allowed Kitty to beat him every time. After they had played together for a while, Meg saw Mr Fordham lean down to Kitty and whisper something in her ear while pointing in Meg's direction.

The next thing Meg knew, Mr Fordham turned towards her and for a moment her nerves fluttered. With great displeasure she realised he would not forget Governor Gipps' ball as quickly as she'd hoped.

'Miss Wingrove, I presume,' he placed a bold finger under her chin, turning her face up to his. He looked into her eyes, searching. 'Ah, yes, there she is,' he drawled in satisfaction.

'Good afternoon, Mister Fordham,' she stiffened.

He sat down beside her, stretching his long legs out before him. 'How it is I did not know you the other night, I cannot fathom.'

'Why it is simple, sir,' Meg explained, 'You have never seen me in a ball gown.'

'And yet, as I recall,' he rubbed his chin, 'I recognised the dress.'

Meg chuckled. 'Of course you did. It belonged to your sister.'

Mr Fordham seemed thoughtful. 'I see,' he smiled at her. 'Though I dare say it never looked as well on her as it did on you.'

Meg gasped. 'How could you say such a thing about your sister? Mrs Sainsbury is a very beautiful woman. Perhaps I should pass on your insult.'

'You wouldn't dare,' he eyed her with a challenge.

Meg laughed.

'Besides I said it to compliment you, not to insult her you silly goose.'

Meg widened her eyes. 'So, I should be flattered then?'

Mr Fordham's eyes flashed at her. 'Do not poke fun at me. I am serious.'

Despite his words, he appeared to be stifling laughter. The man was absurd.

'If you wish me to be serious, then do not compliment me at all.'

'Why ever not? I find you surpassingly lovely. Does that surprise you?'

'In fact, it does. How long have you known me?'

Mr Fordham looked sheepish. 'As Winnie, the governess — many years. Although, our conversations have been rather infrequent of late,' he hinted at the contempt she'd shown him of late.

'Your behaviour with Susanna was deplorable.'

Mr Fordham sighed. 'Do you really think her heart was broken?'

Meg remained silent, reluctant to admit her doubts.

'No, neither do I,' he answered for her. 'So may I be forgiven?'

Meg did not answer him, pretending her attention was taken up with the children. Unfortunately, Mr Fordham ignored her reluctance to continue their conversation.

'I was never aware that underneath that servant's garb was a diamond of the first water. The lady I met at the ball was a breath-taking vision.'

'Please, sir,' Meg's hackles rose. 'I seem to recall your name is connected with Miss Lillian Charles. Is it prudent for you to admire me while she is elsewhere?'

'I see,' He frowned. He leaned forward and rested his elbows on his knees, staring at the ground. 'You charge me with unfaithfulness.' He pulled a blade of grass from the earth and slowly twisted it around his fingers. 'Well, you may put your mind at ease. She will no longer be seen on my arm—not since after the ball last week.'

'And you already pursue another?' Meg challenged. 'Rather heartless don't you think?'

Mr Fordham was silent briefly and then leaned close to her. 'Am I pursuing you?'

A thrill shot through Meg at his nearness, but she also knew a moment of doubt. Was it possible she had made the wrong assumption? It would be frightfully embarrassing. She opened her mouth to stutter an awkward reply when her intuition reminded her that this man was an accomplished flirt. She decided to call his bluff. Fortifying herself, she looked him directly in the eyes. 'Do you mean to tell me, Sir, that you are not?'

Mr Fordham grinned at her. 'You are very sure of yourself.' He returned his attention to the blade of grass. 'To own truth,' he said after a time, 'I decided to dissolve my relationship with Miss Charles almost a month ago but was unable to. So, you see, in my mind it has been over for some time. Do you understand?'

Meg pressed her lips together. 'I do. But I am not so sure society will. Please excuse me, Mister Fordham, but I must take the children inside, it is almost time for supper.' She rose and called them to her, leaving Mr Fordham sitting on the bench to ponder her words.

Meg found it disturbing that Mr Fordham had renewed his attentions to her. She would have much preferred he left her alone. She was thankful she would not have to eat with them. That is, until Mary asked her mother if Winnie could join the family for dinner. She had asked at Jack's suggestion, Meg suspected, though he probably made it so subtly Mary thought it was her own idea.

'Winnie, you must join us tonight,' Mary commanded her with a smile, 'Mother has consented.'

Meg groaned inwardly. 'No, you need to spend time as a family without me.'

'But Winnie, you are practically family,' the young girl insisted. 'We miss you when you aren't there.'

Meg rolled her eyes and smiled. 'Very well, then. I would not wish you to miss me too much.'

Although Meg looked forward to the meal with trepidation, it turned out to be a wasted worry. Mr Fordham dined at one end of the table with Mr and Mrs Sainsbury, while she sat with the children at the other end. Meg tried to ignore him the whole way through dinner, and she made sure she involved herself in the children's conversation. Mr Fordham neither spoke to her nor looked her way.

The children chattered on about everything from the games they had been playing that day to what they were going to do at school next week. Willy asked questions about how the sun and the stars got into the sky and Kitty wanted to talk about her favourite doll. Although never tired by their conversation, she was relieved when dinner was finally over, and she could remove herself from Mr Fordham's presence.

❧

'How is it with Miss Charles?' Gwen asked Jack when they were alone in the parlour playing cards after dinner.

'It appears you haven't heard the latest gossip, my dear,' Jack replied lightly, putting a small pile of buttons, their pretend money, in the centre of the table. He leaned forward confidingly to whisper. 'It is said the cruel Mister Fordham has dashed her hopes of becoming a Viscountess.'

Gwen sighed and shook her head as she equalled his bet. 'And I suppose you have your eye on a new beauty already.'

Jack eyed his cards carefully and pushed a few more buttons forward. 'That, my dear sister,' he drawled, 'Is for me to know and for you to hear on the grapevine.'

Gwen groaned. 'Will you not be serious?' She laid her cards facedown and folded her hands over them. 'How can you speak so flippantly?'

Jack shrugged. 'It is naught but a game of chance, Gwen, just like these cards, what?'

'How so?'

'The woman plays her hand, I play mine.' Jack said simply. 'She stakes her bet, and I wager against it. The one of us with the strongest suite wins. Now are you going to finish this round? Make your bid.'

Gwen held his gaze for a moment and then returned to her cards. 'That is a sad tale. How many women have laid their heart on the table, only to lose?' She pushed all her remaining buttons to the centre pile.

'Alas,' Jack said with feigned regret, 'it is known I possess no heart to bid against it. Am I to blame for that?'

He laid his cards on the table and Gwen groaned, losing the hand and all her betting tokens to Jack.

'Let that be a lesson to you,' he grinned.

'What, little brother?' she teased.

'Never risk more than you are prepared to lose. And *never* assume you have a better hand than Jack Fordham.'

Meg happened to enter the room as Jack made his point and no doubt, she saw his smug expression.

'Pardon my interruption, sir,' she gave a polite curtsy.

'Never mind,' he grinned. 'My sister has just discovered how devilish lucky I am at cards.'

Mrs Sainsbury laughed. 'Yes, don't try and beat him,' she rolled her eyes. 'He always wins.'

Meg shrugged. 'It is unlikely, as I don't play cards.'

Jack gave her a shrewd look. 'No, I daresay hide and go seek would be more to your liking.'

'Jack, don't tease the poor girl.' Gwen scolded.

'Or perhaps a good game of chase is your preference,' he continued, holding Meg's gaze.

The governess blinked then ignored his insinuation, turning to Gwen. 'The children await their goodnight kiss, ma'am.'

'Yes, of course,' Gwen responded. 'Excuse me, Jack.' She gave him a warning glare, rose from the table, and swept out of the room.

Meg turned back to him, then, with a frosty glare. 'I think you are better suited to childish games than I. Good night, Mister Fordham.' She turned to make a hasty retreat.

'Join me, Miss Wingrove,' he moved to the sideboard, not ready to let her go.

'I do not think that would be appropriate.' Meg cleared her throat.

Jack rolled his eyes at her. 'My sister will return directly, you need not fear.'

'I have no wish to …'

'Do you take sugar?' He ignored her and poured her a cup of tea.

Meg stood there unmoving. Perhaps she could not find a reasonable excuse to leave. Perhaps she enjoyed their tete-a-tete more than she let on.

'One lump, please,' she mumbled and sighed as she sat in a chair by the fire, folding her arms across her chest.

He passed her the cup and relaxed into a chair opposite her.

She stared into the flames, sipping her tea, while he watched her. When minutes passed by, she became irritated, much to his delight.

'Has no one ever told you it is impolite to stare?'

Jack leaned forward and smiled archly. 'Was I staring? I do beg your pardon. But if you would stop being so devilish beautiful, I'm sure I would not be so ill-mannered.'

A gurgle of laughter erupted from Meg, and she seemed to relax a little. 'As though I designed my own features just to trip you up. What a harebrained notion.'

Jack smiled indulgently at her and sipped at his tea.

'What is it you want from me?' Meg raised her eyes to his.

'I find you very diverting, though I think you know that already. Will you accompany me on an outing tomorrow?'

'No, Mister Fordham, I do not think so.'

'Why ever not?' he raised his eyebrows.

Meg sighed. 'I do not wish to continue this …,' she waved a hand back and forth between them, 'whatever it is.'

'I explained to you about Miss Charles …' he began, and Meg rolled her eyes. Jack leaned towards her and spoke in confidential tones. 'Are you concerned about my reputation? Perhaps you wonder how I could wish an alliance with a humble governess. Is that what you think?'

Meg almost choked on her tea, placing the cup down with a loud clatter. 'What is so shocking?' Jack frowned.

Meg stood up and moved to the hearth. 'That is so very condescending of you, sir,' she said with sarcasm. 'It is so kind of you to grace me with your attentions.'

'Your station does not bother me,' he explained.

'No, of course it doesn't,' Meg's eyes flashed. 'There is less scandal when the woman is of no consequence.' She paused, but he remained silent. 'I am not entirely without connections, Mister Fordham.'

Jack leaned back in his chair rubbing his chin, amusement lifting the corners of his mouth. 'I see,' he said, 'So, I am now charged with the worst of arrogances. What an awkward faux pas on my part.'

Meg turned away from him and gazed into the flames, but he caught the smile she tried to hide.

Jack scanned for her family name in his memories of England. 'I take it you are of the Herefordshire Wingroves, then?'

Meg turned back to him. 'Yes.'

'Your father was Percy Wingrove?'

'Again, yes.'

'I remember him.' Jack nodded. 'He was quite fond of the gaming houses as I recall.'

Meg pressed her lips together. 'A fact neither my brother nor I knew about. He died leaving enormous debts and we were left without a feather to fly.'

'And so, you came to Australia and employed yourself as a nursemaid,' he finished the story.

'I cannot remember precisely how it came about, but my brother and I discovered there was work available here. Landowners here sponsored labourers to emigrate and work for them. Also, our local church offered to contribute towards our passage overseas to help lighten the burden. Brian and I had a long talk together one night, and we eventually decided to take the plunge and try to improve our prospects here.'

Mr Fordham examined the tea leaves in the bottom of his cup. Her story held familiar pain. Neither of them was where they were entitled to be. 'I am very sorry for your misfortune. I would that I had known. I would have come to your rescue.'

⁂

Meg eyed Mr Fordham. His words were gallant, his tone sounded artificial and yet, when he looked up, there was something genuine in his eyes. Meg did not know what to make of it and giggled nervously. She changed the focus of their conversation. 'In all these years, I've not heard how you came to be in Australia, Mister Fordham.'

Mr Fordham seemed surprised but covered it with an inane response. 'Why, I do believe I came on a ship.'

Meg could not hold back the laugh his dry wit forced from her. 'How absurd you are. You know what I meant. What made you decide to come across the sea?'

'I'm afraid I made no such choice,' Mr Fordham let out a dramatic sigh. 'The decision was not of my making.'

Meg's curiosity awakened. 'Do you mean to say …?'

'That is exactly what I mean to say.' Mr Fordham declared as though he were sharing a tasty morsel of gossip. 'I am in exile.' His manner was so careless Meg could not be sure if what he said was true. Once again, she giggled nervously.

'What an outlandish thing to say about oneself. You are either funning me or you are indeed a bad apple.'

'Who is a bad apple?' Gwen returned just then.

'As if you don't know, sister dear.' Mr Fordham drawled as he rose from his chair and stifled a yawn. 'This bad apple needs his beauty sleep. Goodnight, ladies.'

The women chuckled at his inanity and wished him good evening. Once he had gone, Meg turned to Mrs Sainsbury. 'Is it true he was banished?'

Mrs Sainsbury sighed. 'Unfortunately, so. I will not distress you with the details. But when he came to Australia, he was not the same young man I remember growing up.'

Chapter Ten

The morning sun was out, and it was a cheerful day although Meg was tired. She had tossed and turned, uneasy about what she had learned of Mr Fordham. Most of the time his brazen attitude irritated her, but then she would catch a glimpse of something that made her curious about the man behind the arrogance. Part of her fervently wished he would just stay away from her, but part of her wanted to find out more about him. If only he would cease his ridiculous flirtation.

'Top o' the morning to y' Meg,' Nellie greeted as Meg entered the cook house.

'And you Nellie.' Meg glanced around the room and noticed all was tidy and a pot sat on the stove.

Nellie must have noticed Meg's observations. 'I started early this morning. Breakfast is in that pot. I'd like to come to church with y' if that's alri'?'

Meg's heart lifted. 'It is more than all right, Nellie.'

'I've been thinking about what y' said, and I read a little bit o' the Bible. I wanna hear more.'

'I know you will find the answers you're looking for,' Meg squeezed her hand. She glanced around the kitchen again. 'Where are Mick and Joe?'

'Still sleeping it off, I'd reckon. They was drinking rum half the night.' Nellie sighed. 'Well, I'd better go and put a decent dress on, I s'pose.'

'All right, Nell. I will meet you at the stables in half an hour.'

Very soon, Nellie and Meg climbed in a buggy and drove down the long driveway. Meg saw, away off to her right that Mr Fordham was up and putting one of Mr Sainsbury's Thoroughbreds through its paces. She kept her eyes on the road and refused to acknowledge him there. However, Nellie also spotted him. 'Oh, there is Mister Fordham. He is so 'andsome, don't y' think?'

Meg gritted her teeth but didn't want to sound rude. 'Yes, quite dashing.'

Nellie grasped Meg's arm. 'He's seen us, Meg. He's coming this way.'

Meg groaned inwardly.

'Oh, and he's a master in the saddle. Look Meg.'

Meg reluctantly followed her gaze to see Mr Fordham ride the horse through the yard gate at a graceful trot. It was true; Mr Fordham looked splendid upon a horse. He wore a riding coat, and the tails flew out behind him as he rode, and he seemed to move as one with the animal. As he neared them, he reined in.

'Good morning, ladies,' he nodded to the two women. Nellie withdrew in silence, bashfulness tying her tongue.

'Good morning, Mister Fordham,' Meg answered. She did not stop the buggy, forcing Mr Fordham to ride alongside of them.

'You look very becoming today.'

She ignored his flattery. 'That is a magnificent horse you are riding.'

'I quite agree,' Mr Fordham nodded. 'I told Sainsbury I would test him to see if he was ready for the Indian Army, but I think I may keep him for myself.'

'Even though Mister Sainsbury has already sold him? I do not like your chances.'

'Don't you know? I always get what I want.' Mr Fordham looked her in the eyes, and she read deeper implications there.

Meg could not keep the amusement from her face. 'Is that so? Then I fear you will be disappointed.'

'We shall see,' he promised and pulled the stallion's head around to turn back. He nodded to Meg in farewell and rode away.

When they were out of earshot, Nellie found her voice again. 'He's so nice an' friendly like.'

'Mmm,' was all Meg replied, fearing the girl's opinion was somewhat too high.

'You spoke very bold to him.'

'He was very bold towards me,' Meg shrugged, unmoved.

❧

Meg soaked every moment of the church service into her soul. It was like satisfying food to her. She saw that Nellie also took in every word eagerly. After the closing prayer, Nellie began to ask questions. Meg sat with her a while and answered as best she could. Eventually Reverend Kilpatrick joined them.

'Reverend,' Meg said as he sat. 'I would like you to meet a friend of mine, Miss Nellie Finnegan.'

'Miss Finnegan, Miss Wingrove,' he nodded to each in turn.

'Miss Finnegan would like to know peace with God, Reverend,' Meg told him, joy making her heart dance.

'Oh. Wonderful!'

Reverend Kilpatrick prayed with Nellie while Meg's heart swelled with happiness. When the prayer was over, a tearful Nellie wrapped Meg in a tight embrace. 'Thanks so much for showing me the way o' salvation.'

'I am so glad you are part of our family now.'

'That's right,' the pastor agreed. 'Welcome to the brethren, Miss Finnegan.'

Meg went through the drive home, her midday meal and part of the afternoon as if in a dream. The joy she experienced sharing her faith with Nellie was intoxicating.

Around mid-afternoon, Mrs Sainsbury sought her out to inform her Mr Roderick had called. 'He is in the parlour, my dear.'

Meg's stomach sank and she rubbed the back of her neck. She wanted to retain this glorious elation. Mr Roderick would, no doubt put a damper on her mood. In the next instant she repented. She knew she should accept this man as he was.

Roderick stood by the sideboard, admiring several statuettes Mrs Sainsbury had on display there.

'Good afternoon, Mister Roderick,' Meg forced a warm greeting. He came to her and bowed. She looked over his shoulder at the sideboard. 'It is a lovely collection is it not?'

He followed her gaze. 'Yes, most fascinating. 'How do you do, Miss Wingrove?'

'I am well thank you, sir.'

'And I am glad to hear it. It is rather fine out at present. I thought perhaps we could take a turn about the garden.'

Meg agreed, collected a warm wrap, and joined her sombre companion in the garden. 'You look as charming as ever, Miss Wingrove,' he complimented her as they strolled along leisurely.

'Thank you, sir.'

Silence reigned for a time and Meg noticed he kept moving his hands. In his pockets, then clasped behind his back, then tugging at his cravat.

'Is everything all right, Mister Roderick?'

The gentleman cleared his throat. 'I noticed Mister Fordham is here.'

'Yes …'

Mr Roderick opened and closed his mouth and then sighed. 'You must heed my warning about him. If he has come all the way out here to win your favour, then …'

'No, no, Mister Roderick,' Meg interrupted, halting to face him. 'You do know he is Missus Sainsbury's brother, do you not?'

Mr Roderick took in this information in surprise. 'No, I did not realise. I … that is … I am just concerned for you.'

'You need not be,' Meg assured him.

'Even so, I would not trust him. He is very smooth of tongue and has beguiled even the most intelligent of women. It would be best if you stayed away from him.'

Meg clenched her teeth. 'Mr Roderick, I think it is improper of you to tell me what is best.' She turned and began to walk again, although a little more briskly.

Roderick pulled a handkerchief from his waist coat and mopped his brow before he jogged to catch up to her. 'I … I am very sorry … Miss Wingrove …

That was ... unbefitting ... of me.'

Meg continued to walk but nodded an apology to him. Inadvertently, in his agitated state, Mr Roderick caught his foot on a stone and stumbled to his knees. Meg immediately stopped to see that he was all right and put her hand out to help him up.

'How clumsy of me,' he mumbled, clearly embarrassed. 'I beg your pardon.'

Jack rounded the corner of the homestead at that moment. His eyes widened in shock, and he cleared his throat. 'Uh, forgive me,' he said, 'I did not realise you were here.' As quickly as he had come, he vanished, and Meg burst into a fit of laughter. The corners of Roderick's mouth lifted and fell again, his eyes clouding.

'Forgive me, Mister Roderick,' she sighed. 'I was not laughing at you. It was the look on Mister Fordham's face. I believe he thought ... never mind.' She doubted he would appreciate the humour in what she had just seen.

Finding his feet again, and apparently his confidence along with them, he looked at Meg.

'Miss Wingrove I, uh, came here today to tell you I would like to get to know you more.'

'You would?' Meg was unsure if she should be pleased or not.

'Yes, you hale from Herefordshire, do you not?' he asked, continuing their stroll around the gardens.

'Yes, I do,' she replied, surprised he should know such information.

'I also, am from Herefordshire.'

'Oh?'

'Yes. I believe I knew your father. I did some business with him at one time.'

'What kind of business were you in?'

'Uh,' he stuttered, 'investments.'

'Oh.'

'Yes,' he continued. 'Your father made a few investments with me.'

Meg's laugh was hollow. 'Well, I can tell you he gambled them all away.'

Yes, I am aware of that,' he admitted. 'Did your mother have any investments?'

'My mother? What a strange question. Why would she? My father looked after all our assets.'

'She may have had a fortune of her own,' Roderick suggested with a shrug.

Meg frowned. 'If she did, I dare say my father lost that in a wager also.'

'Are you saying there was nothing left?'

'Nothing. Not even our home.' Meg sighed. 'Mister Roderick, at the risk of sounding impolite, I do not think these things concern you.'

He stiffened and coughed uneasily. 'Forgive me. I did not mean to pry. As I said, it was my line of business in England. Inheritance and fortune have always interested me.'

Chapter Eleven

Later that afternoon, Meg sat in the study, availing herself of Mr Sainsbury's writing desk to pen a note to her brother. She had just finished when she became aware of a movement just inside the doorway.

'So, Miss Wingrove,' Mr Fordham's voice was both cheerful and insinuating. 'Now I know why you have refused me all this time.'

Meg jumped and wondered how long he had stood there.

'May I offer you my felicitations,' he bowed.

She grinned at him, sorely tempted to let him remain ignorant. Yet, her moral convictions would not allow her to deceive him any further. 'Alas,' she feigned a sigh. 'There is no need. You have mistaken a clumsy accident for an offer of marriage, Mister Fordham.'

He measured her for a moment. 'You are not betrothed, then?'

'No.'

'But he is courting you?'

She lifted her chin. 'I don't think it is any of your concern.'

'Who is he, anyway?' He ignored her rebuke. 'Should I be jealous?'

'His name is Mister Gilbert Roderick.' Meg rose from her chair. 'And as to jealousy, well, I would not wish anyone to be jealous over me.'

Mr Fordham looked her without flinching. 'How could anyone not be jealous over someone of your exquisite beauty?'

Meg's heart fluttered in her chest unexpectedly and knew she should make her escape. 'I must go and prepare for supper.'

'Running away?'

How could he see through her, so? Meg turned her back on him. She would not allow him to defeat her with gallantry.

Misreading her stance as an admission of weakness, Mr Fordham pressed on. 'Has no-one ever told you that you are the image of perfection? Your eyes are …'

'I have a mirror, Mister Fordham. I know what I look like,' Meg gritted, turning around again.

Mr Fordham appeared to be annoyed momentarily, but then broke into a hearty laugh. 'You are a shocking mischief.'

Relaxing a little, Meg pretended despondency. 'It is incurable I'm afraid.'

Mr Fordham chuckled. 'But do tell me, Miss Wingrove. Does your heart belong to another … to Mister Roderick, for instance?'

If only it did. But she could not lie to him. She opened her mouth to tell him her heart was still free when another idea occurred to her. 'It is very ill-mannered of you to pry into my personal affairs.'

'I must know,' Mr Fordham disregarded her objection. 'Are you attached? Do you have an understanding with him?'

'It is none of your concern,' she held her ground.

Mr Fordham stared at her. 'I shall take it then, that you are still unspoken for, and therefore fair game.'

Keeping her face straight, Meg shrugged. 'You may believe whatever you wish.' She made to brush past him, but Mr Fordham quickly stepped in her path and Meg looked up to find herself uncomfortably close to the gorgeous man. Heat rushed to her cheeks, and she gasped in dismay.

'You know, you are disturbingly pretty when you are flustered,' he murmured with a warm glint in his eyes.

Once again Meg's heart lurched, but aggravation flickered at the same time. 'Excuse me, Mister Fordham. I have no desire to continue this … this …'

'Delightful moment?' Mr Fordham finished for her, one eyebrow raised optimistically. He stepped aside with a slight bow.

Meg snorted. 'Travesty is the word I was searching for.' She glared at him as she sauntered past.

Meg made a beeline for the kitchen, hoping fervently she would not bump into anyone on the way. Mr Fordham's advances were hard to ignore, especially when they made her heart race. Why should it be so when Mr Roderick's compliments did not move her at all?

On the one hand there was Mr Fordham; charming and yet insincere, handsome, and yet incredibly arrogant. On the other hand, there was Mr Roderick; courteous and yet intolerably dull, attentive, and yet uncomfortable. Mr Fordham was too dangerous. Mr Roderick was not dangerous enough. And neither was a Believer like her. She would have to disappoint them both. But how would she make Mr Fordham lose interest?

She must avoid him at all costs.

She let out a long breath when she closed the cook-house door behind her. Three pairs of eyes shifted to her in question.

'It … it's very cold out there,' she made an excuse.

'And it'll get colder yet,' Mick assured her. The two men returned to their plates.

'Here's yer supper, Meg,' Nellie handed her a plate.

Meg nodded and took the meal to the table. 'How has your afternoon been Nell?'

'Oh, wonderful.' Her face lit up.

Joe peered at her over his fork. 'You met a bloke, Nell?'

Meg and the cook exchanged knowing glances and giggled. Meg changed the subject. 'Do you have a busy week ahead?'

'Yep,' Joe replied. 'We gotta start breaking in the colts tomorrow.'

''Though with Mister Fordham 'round, it won't be too busy.' Mick added.

'Why is that?'

''E likes to help. 'E's very good with horses ya know,' Mick told her.

'Does anyone know how long he's staying?' Nellie asked.

'Dunno,' Joe said, and Mick shrugged.

When Meg rose the next morning, she learnt that Mr Fordham rode off the property at first light. Mick and Joe would be disappointed. It meant more work for them. A little later, she discovered a note had been left on the hall table for her. Immediately curious, she bent to pick it up and broke open the seal.

Miss Wingrove,

Forgive my sudden departure. I have business to attend to in Sydney, but I shall return in a few days. Until then I beg you will accept a gift as a token of my sincerity.

Yours etc, Jack Fordham.

What gift? Meg looked around her, but nothing caught her eye. Perhaps he forgot to leave it. But it did seem unlike him to be so absent-minded. Meg traced her fingers over the words, admiring Mr Fordham's expressive hand. Realising once again his expert devices were having the desired affect, she growled at herself and hastily threw the note into the fire, putting it out of her mind at the same time.

Hours later when Meg entered the playroom to give the girls their lessons, she noticed a bolt of fabric leaning against the wall. Mary and Kitty saw her frown and followed her gaze. Mary gasped and ran over to take a closer look, Kitty on her heels.

'It is silk, I am sure of it,' Mary exclaimed as Meg approached.

'Mama, come see,' Kitty called.

Meg touched the soft lilac fabric and then saw another note inserted in the end of the roll. She retrieved it and read.

Miss Wingrove,

I am told this will be the next rage of fashion and I know you will look charming adorned in it. I look forward to the day!

'Who is it from?' Mary's eyes were wide.

Meg sucked in her breath and shook her head. 'Odious man,' she mumbled. Aloud, she uttered a half laugh, loath to admit the truth. 'Your Uncle Jack.'

Mrs Sainsbury entered the room to a chorus of squeals from her daughters, each clamouring to tell her the news. She confirmed the material was indeed a costly silk and admired it with wonder. She also shot Meg a questioning look. 'And you say it is a gift from Jack?'

'Yes,' Meg confirmed through gritted teeth. 'Although I will tell him I cannot accept it. Perhaps you should have it.'

Mrs Sainsbury still looked puzzled. 'Why would you not accept it?'

'I have no use for it.' Meg shrugged and then twinkled at her mistress. 'It really is too exquisite for household duties.'

'But, why …?'

'Who knows what goes on in the mind of Jack Fordham?' Meg tried to be flippant, misdirect her mistress.

'Well,' Gwen sighed. 'You have a point there.'

Later, in the kitchen, Meg had all but forgotten the incident with the silk and cheerfully chatted with the other employees. She was grateful to have a few days reprieve and was satisfied within herself she could hold Mr Fordham at bay effectively and he would soon give up in his pursuit.

Nellie had been reading her Bible and had a few questions for Meg, which she answered thoroughly and clearly.

'You're a good teacher. I can see why the Sainsbury's have kept y' all these years.'

Warm patches of self-consciousness developed on Meg's cheeks. 'Thank you, Nell, that means a lot to me.' She placed a mouthful of salt pork into her mouth and let her mind wander. She loved those children. Ever since the first moment she met them, they had stolen her affections. Meg understood the burden of responsibility when tutoring the Sainsbury children. What they learnt now would stay with them forever. It was so important to instil godly principles into them. Meg realised with wonder it was the same with infant Christians and she looked at Nellie in a new light.

She gave the young woman a spontaneous hug. 'I'm here whenever you have more questions, Nellie.'

Nellie smiled gratefully. 'Thank y', Meg.'

∂∞∞

Although life on the farm kept her busy, as time wore on Meg found her thoughts wandering to that disarming smile. Much to her chagrin she caught herself reliving his romantic advances and realised with more than a little surprise she had enjoyed their confrontations. Guilt assailed her as she realised her infatuation was not as dead as she believed. This must stop. She must face him and make it clear she was not available.

So, with her face set in grim determination, she waited for Mr Fordham's return. Indeed, when the children came to her excitedly, calling out 'Uncle Jack's back,' far from hiding from him, she went outside with them to receive him. She stood resolutely, telling herself she was in control of her emotions and Mr Fordham had no power over her.

The exquisite gentleman dismounted near the house and handed the reins to Joe who took his horse to the stables to be cared for. As he approached, gorgeous in his riding coat, his eyes locked on her, and his smile told her he was more determined than ever.

'So, you came to greet me,' was all he said, but Meg caught his insinuation. Her resolve crumbled and all she could do was search her mind for a way to escape.

Chapter Twelve

In the safety of her room, Meg leaned with her back against the closed door. What was wrong with her? Why did her heart beat so hard? Why had she been so weak? 'Lord, give me the strength to stand up to his charms,' she whispered to the ceiling. She must not let him see how he affected her. He must not know.

She spent time praying and composing herself and then went in search of the children. After all, they were supposed to be in her charge. She found them playing croquet with their uncle and decided to join in. She paid scant attention to Mr Fordham, focusing on Kitty, assisting her with her game and trying to help her win. Thankfully, Mr Fordham did not trouble her, involving himself in the game as well.

This exercise helped her to regain her good sense and her tension melted away. Mr Fordham was no-one to be feared, he was just like any other man. Yes, like any other ordinary man. He could only manipulate her if she allowed him to. When Mary invited her to eat with them for supper, she refused without any qualms. The more distance she kept between herself and Mr Fordham, the happier she would be.

Once supper was over, she busied herself tucking the children into bed, lingering over their bedtime stories, and chatting with them until well past their bedtime. She hoped Mrs Sainsbury would come and say goodnight to them without having to be summoned, but alas, their mother did not appear. Reluctantly, Meg went in search of her, hoping she would not encounter Mr Fordham in the process.

As it turned out, the siblings were strolling in the garden and Mr Sainsbury was the only one in the house. She informed him the children were in bed and he went to tuck them in himself. Meg almost made it to her room when the inevitable happened. She had her hand on the doorknob when she heard Mr Fordham's insinuating voice from the end of the hall. 'A word with you, Miss Wingrove.'

She paused, somewhat deflated. 'Must you say my name in that horrid way? I confess it puts me out of all patience with you.'

'And how is it you have managed to elude me all afternoon?' He ignored her protests.

'Did I? How fortuitous.' She raised her eyebrows at him.

'Well,' he narrowed his eyes, 'I will not allow you to escape me forever.'

'Oh,' Meg feigned disappointment, 'Dear me.'

'You are incorrigible.'

Meg grinned at him. 'I am contrite. Forgive me.'

He glared at her, though she suspected him to be in jest. He then shook his head as though clearing his mind. 'Would you do the honour of joining me for a picnic tomorrow?'

'No, Mister Fordham.' She did not hesitate.

'No?'

'I have told you before I do not want to be seen with you.'

'Why ever not? My reputation is not that bad.'

Meg crossed her arms over her chest and laughed. 'Perhaps not to some, but it does not change my answer. I do not wish for my name to be connected with yours.'

'You insult me.' This time his frown seemed genuine.

Slightly taken aback, Meg pressed on. 'I do not intend to insult you. I have merely seen the way you trifle with women. You sweet-talk them, you use your charms until they fall into your arms and then…then you say goodbye. I have no wish to be your next conquest. I am not a toy for your amusement, Mister Fordham.'

'Your accusations are harsh.' His face was grave.

'Do you deny them?' Meg challenged.

When he remained silent, Meg opened the door of her room.

'They are not entirely true,' he said at last. 'Would it make a difference if I told you I have no intentions of doing the same with you?'

Meg looked at him evenly. 'That is just the problem, Mister Fordham … you have no intentions.'

❧

Jack watched the door close in his face, more than a little ruffled. Never in his entire life had a woman resisted him with such determination. He had thought she would be like butter in his hands by now. Instead, she had turned the tables on him every time. And, devil take it, he enjoyed every moment of it. The more she rejected him, the more he wanted her. If it wasn't for his damned reputation …

He thrust his hands into his pockets and headed for the parlour. She was not indifferent towards him, he was sure of that. He could feel the pull between them. Somehow, he had to get through her defences. Even as he stood there, he vowed to redouble his efforts on the morrow. There must be a way through to her heart.

❧

On Friday morning Meg occupied herself with chores while the girls spent time with their mother. She had been quite firm with Mr Fordham the previous evening and hoped it was enough to make him quit his pursuit of her. Part of her regretted she had been so blunt with him, hoping she had not hurt his feelings. Nevertheless, she felt confident she had done the right thing.

She was engrossed in polishing some furniture, when she realised Mr Fordham stood lounging in the doorway. She straightened and offered him a genuine smile. After all, she didn't want him to think she was completely disagreeable. 'Good morning, Mister Fordham.'

'Good morning to you, m'lady,' he replied, clear appreciation in his eyes.

Meg put down her polishing cloth for a moment and looked at him. 'I hope your pride has not suffered too greatly since last evening,' she teased. 'I was very bold, I know.'

Mr Fordham narrowed his eyes at her mockery. 'Looking divinely beautiful as usual, I see.'

Meg saw a dangerous gleam in his eyes and knew he had not given up his flirtation. Gathering her courage, she gave him a cynical roll of her eyes. 'Perhaps you should see a doctor. I think your eyesight is failing.'

'My eyes are working quite well, thank you. However, I am glad you have found one way to care for me, even if it is only for my health.'

Meg laughed out loud. 'You are preposterous. Now, is there any particular reason you are here, or is it merely to entertain me with your absurd humour?'

'If I have brought you joy then I am honoured to be of service.' Mr Fordham kept a straight face, though his lips twitched.

Meg shook her head at him and returned to polishing.

'Actually, I have come to ask you to accompany me for a turn about the garden.'

'No, Mister Fordham.' She replied without looking up. 'As you can see, I am quite busy.'

'Then I shall remain here and watch you work until you are free.' His voice held a challenge.

Meg stopped polishing and paused before she raised her eyes. 'I see you are determined to have your way.'

'Yes,' he gloated.

She sighed in resignation, wishing to be away from him. If only Mrs Sainsbury would summon her at this moment. 'Very well, then,' she pulled off her gloves roughly and untied her apron, leaving them on the table.

Mr Fordham offered her his arm and they slipped out into the garden.

Being so close to Mr Fordham made Meg's resolve waver. A sidelong glance at his face made her heart skip a beat; it was no wonder the term nonpareil was attached to him everywhere he went. At that moment she couldn't blame any of the women who had succumbed to his charms in the past. Who, in their right mind, would reject such an example of superb manhood? And now here he was, determined to win her over while she fought him tooth and nail.

He led her to a quiet part of the garden and begged her to sit with him on a whitewashed, wrought iron bench.

'Mister Fordham,' Meg muttered. 'This is quite improper.'

Ignoring her objections, he flashed her an impertinent smile and patted the seat next to him. 'You are not in any danger you know,' he drawled. 'Now come down from your high horse and sit.'

Meg could very easily argue that point. Being near Mr Fordham was too dangerous for her liking. But, with a grumble of resignation she sat stiffly beside him and folded her arms across her chest.

'There now, that's better,' he said with a smug grin.

Meg, irritated with him, could not keep her exasperation quiet. 'You know you waste your time, do you not?'

'Is that so?' He gazed into her eyes as if he were reading her thoughts. 'I wish you would reconsider,' he murmured. 'I can give you whatever you desire, you know. I would treat you like a queen. We could share something wonderful together.' He reached forward and caressed her cheek with the back of his hand.

Against her will, Meg knew colour rose in her face. 'Mister Fordham ...'

'Fate has brought us together,' he continued. 'Do you not feel it?'

Meg reined in her faltering emotions. 'To be quite candid, no,' she lied, pushing his hand away from her face.

'Do you not care what you do to me?' he became impassioned. 'I am so distracted I cannot sleep. My every waking moment is consumed by thoughts of you. I cannot concentrate on anything else. Please grant this fevered mind a reprieve — allow me to court you.'

Meg wavered again. No-one had ever spoken to her like that before. Could he be serious? No, no, no. This was more of his guile, that's all. She took a deep breath. 'It is just like poetry.' She sounded more confident than she felt.

'Poetry?'

'You speak many beautiful words. They sound like poetry, but I'm not sure they mean anything.'

'Have you not been listening?' He pleaded. 'You have been naught but cruel and unfeeling towards me these last weeks, while I have done nothing but shower you with affection. Deny me again and I will be a broken man. Do you not realise, my heart is in your hands?'

Meg studied his expression and saw a flicker of challenge in his eyes. A smile played at the corners of her mouth. 'I doubt your heart is in the least affected. In fact, I do not believe your heart is involved at all. It is all a game to you, a game you shall not win.'

Mr Fordham met her gaze as though they both held swords aloft. 'A game, is it? Then you already know; I always win. And what a prize you are.'

Meg began to wonder how long she could hold her ground. She was sure he must be able to hear her heart pounding in her chest. She swallowed. 'I am no prize ...'

Mr Fordham reached inside his jacket and pulled out a small leather case. 'I have a gift for you,' he said and opened it to face her.

Inside the case a silver chain with a diamond and sapphire pendant rested. Meg gasped at the beautiful piece of jewellery. 'I cannot accept this.'

'Yes, you can, and you must.'

Her hand flew nervously to her throat where she touched the familiar locket her mother had given her. Her presence of mind returned as she clasped it. 'No, Mister Fordham. I am wearing the only jewellery I have, and I will not take it off. I will return the silk to you too.' She swallowed again, regaining her self-control. 'Those gifts are designed to manipulate me. I am not a fool.'

Mr Fordham snapped the case shut and placed it back inside his coat. His eyes reflected a mixture of frustration and admiration. 'You are a merciless woman.' His voice trembled with both annoyance and suppressed laughter. 'I know you have feelings for me, Miss Wingrove. I do not understand why you resist me, but I will not give up until you are mine.'

Chapter Thirteen

Upon leaving Meg, Jack returned to the house, frustration churning within. How could one woman be so alluring and yet so exasperating at the same time? He made his way to the guest room, his strides long and heavy. In the hallway he almost collided with Gwen.

'Why Jack, my dear,' she smiled, 'I was just coming to look for you.'

Jack ran a hand through his hair. He just wanted to be alone with his thoughts. 'Yes, what is it?'

'A message from Miller.' She handed the note to him.

Jack broke the seal and scanned its contents briefly. 'A deuced nuisance.'

'Is something wrong, Jack?'

He shook his head, suppressing his annoyance. 'It seems there is a pressing matter I need to attend to. Regrettably, I must leave you again.'

Gwen scanned his face, clearly trying to read him. 'Are you all right, Jack?'

Jack flashed her an impressive grin. 'Of course,' he laughed. 'Why do you ask?'

'Well,' she grasped his elbow and led him into the parlour, 'you have been coming and going a lot recently. And you have been rather distracted of late.'

Jack waved an arm in dismissal. 'It is nothing. You know I frequently have business to attend to in town. I have a lot on my mind with the vineyard and so on. I could stay at home, but it is refreshing to be around my family. Is there anything wrong with that?'

'No Jack,' she sighed. 'But when you came in just now you were rather worked up.'

Jack opened his mouth to speak but she continued. 'Do not try to deny it. I am your sister and I know when you are upset.'

'Perhaps I was a little frustrated,' Jack admitted. 'Just a passing irritation, nothing more.' He examined his fingernails, pretending boredom. Hopefully it would throw her off. 'You see, I have already recovered.'

Gwen chuckled. 'This doesn't have anything to do with a certain pretty girl with strawberry-blonde hair, does it?'

Jack looked at her with mock disgust. 'Do not be absurd,' Jack arched one eyebrow. 'Since when have I ever been ruffled by a woman? Now, if you will excuse me, I must go and gather my belongings.'

He strode out of the room, his irritation back in full force. Now his sister was going to plague him as well.

❧❧

Meg sighed heavily. Mr Fordham had made it abundantly clear he would not relent in his ambition to have his way. Resisting him wasn't enough. He had left her shaken on the bench with his intense, insistent gaze. Masking indifference had been completely ineffective. Mr Fordham had obviously seen through her pretence. It would take a great deal of effort and a lot of courage to be rid of him.

There was only one thing to do, and Meg's nerves fluttered just thinking about it. She knew not why, but although sharing her faith with Nellie had been natural and gratifying, Mr Fordham was another matter. For some reason she'd never had enough nerve to speak to him about it. Perhaps because of his contempt for religion. Perhaps she feared his disapproval. Either way, it was time to face her fears, and confront him with the truth. Meg sat on the iron bench for a long while, trying to decide how she would approach the incomparable Mr Fordham.

Word spread quickly on the farm that Jack was leaving again and when Meg heard this, she was disappointed. She had planned to put an end to their farce that night. Now she would have to wait until whenever he chose to return. Or would she? An idea came to Meg that made her smile and she hurried to her room to gather her hat and some leather gloves.

❦

Jack had said his goodbyes, not promising when he would return. The children had bid him an affectionate farewell, Kitty in particular. She wrapped her little arms around his neck tightly. 'I love you, Uncle Jack,' she whispered in his ear.

'I love you too, my sweet,' he whispered back.

Gwen also embraced him tenderly. 'Take care, Jack.'

Jack swung up into the saddle, tipped his hat to them all and nudged the horse onward. The family went into the house, and he was finally alone with his thoughts. Clearly, Meg would not give up without a fight. Perhaps he should stay away for a week and give her a chance to pine for him. They did say absence makes the heart …

Wait. There she was, walking beside the driveway, cutting sprigs of flowers from the wattle trees. He pulled the horse to a stop and flashed her a roguish grin. 'Can that be the lovely Cinderella I met at the ball a fortnight ago?'

Meg appeared startled. 'Why Mister Fordham,' she straightened. 'Are you following me?'

'Do you want me to?' he parried and received one of those mischievous grins he adored.

'Alas, I am leaving. I have been summoned back to Sydney on urgent business.'

'Whatever will we do without you?' she threw him an arch look.

Jack was mesmerised by those dazzling blue pools and had to force his gaze away to break the spell. 'If only you meant that,' he said wistfully, adjusting the bridle unnecessarily. When he looked back at her, he was defiant. 'When I return, I will take you on a picnic whether you agree to it or not.'

'You would resort to abduction?'

Memories of London and Paris flooded him, and anger rose. He could not keep the bitter edge from his voice. 'Have you been listening to gossip, Miss Wingrove?'

Meg frowned. 'Gossip? What do you mean?'

Jack watched her, trying to read her. She seemed genuine. Perhaps she'd never heard about that time. He shrugged nonchalantly. 'Never mind,' he glanced away again. 'I believe you thought I would like to carry you off against your will. I am sorely tempted. I am a desperate man after all.'

Meg gurgled with laughter. 'You were born for the stage, Mister Fordham.'

'The stage?' he repeated. 'Now I am acting a drama? What will you accuse me of next?' He gazed at her in mild frustration. 'You make it devilish awkward for a man to bare his heart.'

'Then, I pray you, do not try.'

Jack frowned at her. 'You have not got the better of me yet, my dear. I promise you I will make you fall in love with me.'

'That sounds more like a threat than a promise.'

'Enough, you young rogue.' Jack tried to glare at her, but his lips trembled with mirth. 'I am going before your sharp tongue does me an injury.' He flicked the reins on the horse's neck. 'Good-day, Miss Wingrove.'

❦

Meg watched him ride away and her stomach fluttered with anxiety. If she didn't speak now, it could be weeks until she would have another chance. 'Mister Fordham.'

He stopped immediately and looked over his shoulder. Meg walked up to him and smiled, suddenly shy.

'I must confess, I deliberately came to wait for you.' Her cheeks heated with the admission.

Mr Fordham's eyebrows went up at that. 'Did you now?'

Meg chuckled self-consciously. 'Yes. I wanted to talk to you about something in particular.'

Looking more optimistic than Meg thought it warranted, Fordham dismounted so they could speak face to face. 'I find myself daring to hope.'

Once again Meg laughed nervously. 'No,' she said, 'I wanted to ask you about — that is — I wanted to know … how is it … with your soul?'

Mr Fordham stared at her blankly and then repeated. 'My soul?'

'Yes.'

'Good God! Have you not heard; I do not possess a soul.' He rolled his eyes. 'Indeed, I daresay I never had one, and if I did, I am sure I signed it over to the devil a long time ago.'

Meg looked at him with a bewildered gaze. 'Must you trivialise everything? It saddens me to hear you say that.'

'Oh, no. Don't pity me,' he said cheerfully. 'I have it on good authority I am beyond saving.'

Meg gasped. 'Whose authority?'

Mr Fordham rolled his eyes again. 'Well, I would not take it from a regular Joe Smith on the street. No, no. It was an esteemed clergyman, no less.'

Meg could only stare at him, horrified.

'Don't look at me like that. You need not concern yourself. I am happily bound for the Other Place.'

Meg almost choked. 'You don't know what you're saying. How can I not be concerned?' She looked earnestly into his eyes. 'It is not true you know. No-one is beyond saving.'

For a moment Meg thought she saw a desperate and vulnerable look flicker in his eyes, but then it faded again, and he resumed his careless tone, picking at lint on his sleeve that she doubted existed. 'Why bother discussing something as uninteresting as my soul, Miss Wingrove?'

Meg drew a deep breath. 'Because, Mister Fordham, my soul is bound for heaven, and if I am to court a man, he must share my faith in Christ.'

'Faith in Christ?' Mr Fordham looked bewildered.

Meg sighed. 'I have devoted my life to God.'

Mr Fordham stared at her for a moment and then laughed. 'You?' He thrust his hands in the pockets of his coat. 'I don't believe you.'

Meg felt at first affronted and then ashamed. She hung her head and kicked a stone at her feet. 'You are right. I am not a very good Christian.'

'No, no,' he shook his head. 'I meant that all the church-goers I have ever encountered are intolerant, narrow-minded, judgmental and hypocritical— not to mention self-righteous.'

'Well,' Meg said, embarrassed, 'I try not to be those things. I try to be gracious and forgiving. However, I am very narrow-minded. I believe Jesus Christ is the only way and we are all sinners in need of salvation.'

Mr Fordham looked at her as though she were a stranger. 'You believe that?'

'Yes, Mister Fordham. And that is why I cannot accept you as a suitor; you do not hold to the same belief.'

'Are you serious?' he seemed incredulous.

'Quite.'

❧

Jack scanned her face for that familiar twinkle of mischief, but it was not there. She must be funning him. He wagged his finger at her. 'Aah. You almost fooled me,' he grinned at her. 'When I return —'

'Will you not stop playing this absurd game?' Meg rolled her eyes heavenward.

At last Jack understood her sincerity, and at once became impatient. Of all the hypocritical … 'Correct me if I am wrong, but you are just as guilty of playing games. And you enjoyed yourself too if I am not mistaken.'

Meg's gaze fell to the ground, and she kicked at the root of a tree. 'You are right,' she said softly with a defeated shrug. 'I did enjoy our banter. It was excessively diverting and a wicked indulgence on my part. I am an incurable mischief, you know. Will you excuse my imprudence?' She lifted her gaze to his.

Jack chuckled at her confession, seeing the glint once again flash in her eyes. 'Only if you will consent to my courting you.'

'I cannot,' she insisted.

Jack looked at her, bewildered.

'Mister Fordham,' she explained. 'I like you very much. I enjoy your company. You are charming and entertaining, and yes, rather handsome. I am very flattered you want to pay your attentions to me. But my feelings are not a part of this decision. I need someone who shares my faith in God, and on that basis I cannot, will not, *ever* become involved with you.'

Jack still had trouble comprehending the finality of her words.

She continued. 'We once used to have enjoyable conversations together. Can we not return to that? Friendship is all I can offer, and it is something I would value from you.'

Jack held his silence for a long while, staring at the ground and pondering her words. At length, he looked up at her and shook his head. 'I do not pretend to understand your reasoning,' he told her. 'But I see you have made up your mind. Very well, from now on I shall be your most loyal friend — but there are two conditions.'

'And what are they, Mister Fordham?' Meg asked, a smile creeping back into her face.

'One: you will not presume to preach your religion to me, and two: since we are going to be such good friends, you must call me Jack.'

'As long as you stop calling me Miss Wingrove in that ridiculous fashion.'

'Very well Meg, we have a bargain.' He put out a gloved hand to shake.

Chapter Fourteen

With Jack gone and knowing he finally understood her position, Meg relaxed. She enjoyed days of undisturbed peace and thanked God for giving her the strength to be honest with him without backing down. It troubled her the way Jack had denounced himself so carelessly, though. If it weren't for the flash of pain she had caught in his eyes, she could easily believe he was as heartless as he claimed. But she had seen it and it compelled her to pray for him earnestly.

Meg spent most of Sunday afternoon curled up with a good book until Mrs Sainsbury knocked on her door. 'Mister Roderick is here to see you, Meg.'

Meg smiled wanly. 'I will be out shortly,' she replied, folding the blanket that covered her knees and putting her book aside. Mr Roderick's visits had become quite regular. She straightened her skirt and checked her hair in the mirror to make sure it didn't appear dishevelled and made her way to the parlour.

'Good afternoon, Mister Roderick,' she greeted him as warmly as she could, thankful to see Mary and Kitty playing a board game in another corner.

'And you, Miss Wingrove.' He bowed low over her hand.

'I trust you are well.'

'Yes,' he replied, 'that is, apart from a slight sore throat. It is this blasted cold weather, you know. I have tried drinking lemon and honey and gargling salt water, but I fear it grows worse. I am afraid I will lose my voice soon.'

'That would be an inconvenience, indeed,' Meg nodded sympathetically, although she held back amusement at his melodramatic belief.

'Do you never fall ill, Miss Wingrove?'

'Rarely, I must say. I suppose I owe it to being raised in the country with fresh air and much to keep me occupied.'

Roderick's smile was flat. 'Ah, yes, Herefordshire. Tell me more about the home where you grew up.'

Meg sat down into a comfortable chair and allowed herself to reminisce. 'Wingrove Hall was rather a large house, our ancestral home. It was made of grey stone, with ivy climbing all over it and stood proudly amongst very old oak trees. It was a beautiful home. I grieved a long time over the loss of the estate. There were so many memories and so much of our heritage there. I loved every room in that house, and every inch of the grounds. My brother and I were used to go exploring together when we were quite young. We had our own horses and our own dogs. I had a special place I liked to visit, down by the brook that ran through the property. There was a weeping willow I used to sit under and watch the water trickle by.' She giggled, suddenly self-conscious. 'But you do not want to hear all of this sentimental nonsense.'

'On the contrary,' Mr Roderick inclined his head, 'I want to hear every detail.'

Meg smiled at him. 'Well, when we were very small, my father would chase us around the house. Mother would always scold him for teaching us to be so unruly, but he would go on and do it anyway. He would finally catch us and then it became our turn to chase him. I can remember running through the hallways after him and then he would just disappear.'

Roderick raised his eyebrows. 'Did you have secret passages?'

At that, Kitty burst into the conversation. 'Oh, did you Winnie?'

Meg shook her head, laughing. 'I don't think so. But there were definitely secret hiding places. It took us years to figure it out.'

'Oh,' Kitty breathed, her imagination obviously captivated.

'Secret hiding places,' Mr Roderick repeated. 'You don't say. Some of those English ancestral homes are fascinating.'

After he had gone, Meg sat thoughtfully pondering his visit. It had been nice to have someone show interest in her life for a change, and she hadn't expected such concern from Gilbert Roderick. She recalled Jack had never asked about her past other than who her parents were. He had only shown interest in her beauty and having her for a prize. She shook her head, realising how selfish it seemed. Even so, although Roderick may be more attentive to her, she wasn't sure about the state of his soul either.

Mr Roderick's visit left Meg feeling nostalgic and she retired early to think back on her life in England. She had been devastated when her parents departed this life so suddenly. They had both been lost to a raging disease whilst Meg had been visiting with a good friend in London and Brian took a tour of Europe. She had grieved for a few years before she could look to the future with any joy again. It had been a difficult process. Forgiving her father for his gambling had been the hardest part. Now though, the pain had subsided, and she could look back with fondness at her childhood.

Absentmindedly her fingers felt for the locket around her neck. She ran her fingertips over the engraving in the silver pendant and thought about her mother. She had only been eight years old when Mama had given her the necklace. Tears had glistened in the older woman's eyes and on her cheeks as she had knelt before her daughter. Meg could remember the late afternoon sunlight streaming in the bedroom window, giving a golden glow to her mother's flaxen hair.

'What's wrong Mama?'

'Nothing, my love,' she had sniffed. 'I am just so happy to have such a beautiful daughter.'

Her mother had then clasped the pendant around Meg's neck. 'I want you to always wear this to remember us by.'

Meg's eyes had moved from the necklace to her mother's face and back again.

'No matter what happens in the future, remember you are always loved and always provided for. This locket will help,' her mother had said.

Meg fumbled with the clasp and opened the pendant to see the miniatures inside. 'These are beautiful, Mama.'

'Yes, they are more than just pictures, darling,' her mother had told her.

Now, Meg opened the locket to look again, as she had thousands of times since then, at the small paintings of her parents. She gazed affectionately at their dear faces for a time and then closed the clasp again with a sigh. She kissed the pendant tenderly and turned down her lamp, ready at last for sleep.

∾∿

In Sydney, Jack spent his time catching up on business matters. He needed to finalise arrangements for his first shipment of wine to be transported back to England. He also had other business matters to attend which required his full attention. But, when he was not otherwise occupied, he mused over his last conversation with Meg. He could not fathom how a woman could reject a man based on her religious beliefs. After all, religion was only for women and children, wasn't it? It gave them something to do and it was a good social activity, but it was different for men.

Men didn't need a crutch, a higher power. They were like gods themselves, self-sufficient and in control of their own fate. Why would Meg demand that her suitors also be involved in religion? No matter how much Jack pondered the question, he could find no answer.

In the evenings, most often Jack would go to one of the gaming houses and meet with his peers. Most of them had forgotten about the ball and the episode with Meg. Only his closest friend, Bart, remembered.

'So, Fordham,' Mr Bartholomew inquired when they were seated together alone one night. 'Have you seen any more of that exquisite you met at Governor Gipps' ball?'

Jack smiled at him. 'You mean, Miss Margaret Wingrove, governess to my sister's children?'

Mr Bartholomew gaped at him. 'She is Sainsbury's governess? But how …?'

'I know, Bart,' Jack pre-empted his friend's question. 'It was an infernal piece of mischief, but I did not recognise the girl.'

Bart threw back his head and laughed. He slapped Jack on the back. 'What a fool you must have felt.'

Jack smiled and sipped at his glass of port. 'I tell you what though, my friend, she is the most captivating creature.'

'Are you courting her, then?' Mr Bartholomew leaned forward with interest.

'I have tried,' Jack drained the drink. 'But she'll have none of me.'

Mr Bartholomew slapped the table and laughed. 'It cannot be possible.'

'Alas, it is true.' Jack sighed.

The pair were silent for a time and then Mr Bartholomew said, 'So, I suppose we shall have to find you another charming young wench to hang on your arm.'

Jack shook his head slowly. 'Ah, Bart, old chap. Did I say I had given up on Miss Wingrove?'

His friend frowned. 'But I thought you said …'

'Merely that she is somewhat of a challenge,' Jack finished with a sly grin.

'You old fox.' Mr Bartholomew slapped his shoulder again. 'What tomfoolery are you up to?'

Jack chuckled but chose not to elaborate. He sighed. 'You should see her, Bart,' he tried not to sound wistful. 'She is beautiful and charming, as you know. But, added to that she is wonderful with the children, has a sharp wit and is quite intelligent. She also has a rather mischievous sense of humour.'

'What a strange mixture of characteristics,' he said, his head cocked to one side.

'Intrigued, Bart?'

'Very much.'

'As am I, my friend.'

'Jack,' Bart hesitated. 'I do not mean to sound presumptuous, but it sounds like she has the stuff one would wish for in a wife.'

Jack looked at him in contemplation for a while. 'You are right. Perhaps I should marry her.'

'But if she'll have none of you …?'

'Oh, she'll have me,' Jack interrupted confidently. 'You see if she doesn't.'

Chapter Fifteen

Parramatta, September, 1844

The first day of spring broke with the scent of flowers in the air and the sound of birds chirping at the promise of warmer weather. Meg rose early to go for a solitary ride in the open countryside where she could be alone with her thoughts and spend time communing with her Father in heaven. A month had gone by, and Jack had kept to his word. His visits to the stud were still regular, spending days at a time with his family. Thus, he and Meg had spent many hours together while she supervised the children and they had become fast friends.

Meg found Jack to be a constant source of amusement. He was always carefree and playful with the children, and they would often band together and tease her. At other times the children would side with her and play tricks on him. Jack had ceased every form of flattery and merely behaved as a companion. He had even attended church with her and Nellie on occasion, despite his warning to her. When she had queried him, he had simply replied. 'If it is so important to you, then the least I can do is come and see what it is all about.' Not that he took the services seriously. He constantly distracted her, often whispering in her ear some ridiculous remark, causing Meg to almost erupt into a fit of giggles. She had received many strange looks from other worshippers and was forced to tell Jack to sit somewhere else. He complied, but she doubted he paid any more attention to the sermons than before.

Not to be outdone, Mr Roderick also joined in on the Sunday morning party. Previously he had insisted he attended his own church in Richmond, but now made sure he was present in Parramatta every Sunday. It appeared he saw Jack as competition where Meg was concerned and tried to keep up to the same standard the handsome bachelor had set. Meg could only shake her head at this foolishness, but if they were in church, there was always the chance the Truth would enter their hearts.

Mr Roderick continued to visit with her every week, returning to the farm after church and joining the family for dinner. He persisted in asking her every detail about herself, particularly her past in England, until she became weary of talking about it. What had begun as a pleasing experience was now just as insipid as the rest of his conversation. Yet, he still had not made his intentions clear to her. She did not know if he was happy to be acquainted with her or if he had plans to deepen their relationship. She couldn't very well beg him to leave her alone if he only wanted to be friends.

As Meg rode along with the crisp morning breeze blowing through her hair, thanked God for his blessings in her life. Two months ago, there had not been much variety in her life, but now there were new opportunities at every corner and Meg looked forward with eagerness to the future.

That Friday afternoon, Jack rode in for one of his frequent visits. The boys and Kitty had seen him coming and immediately engulfed him in a rough but affectionate welcome. Meg watched with enjoyment as Jack tussled with the young men and then swung Kitty up and around until she was quite dizzy.

'Poor children,' Meg defended the young assailants with a grin after they had scampered off to notify their parents of their uncle's arrival.

'Poor children?' Jack breathed harder than normal. 'Poor Jack would be more fitting.'

Meg laughed.

'Those young rascals are trying to slay me with affection, I am sure of it.'

'And you delight in every moment of it, Jack,' Meg gave him a knowing look. 'Do not deny it.'

'More's the pity,' Jack grimaced.

'Scoundrel,' Meg scolded him light-heartedly, chuckling.

Jack picked up his satchel from where it had been dropped when the children accosted him and walked to the house. Meg joined in step with him.

'Have you been well, Meg?'

'Very well, thank you.' She appreciated his thoughtfulness. 'And you?'

'I declare I feel quite full of life,' Jack announced. 'I have a yearning to go on a frolicking adventure.'

'It must be the spring air,' Meg crossed her arms.

'I dare say. I have decided to take the children on a fishing expedition tomorrow. Will you join us?'

'A fishing expedition...it sounds like fun. I would love to join you.'

⇄◦↶

So it was that after breaking fast the next morning they set off for the Parramatta River. Mary declined to go, believing herself too grown up for a fishing expedition. Thus Meg, Nellie and Kitty were the only females in the party. Meg organised a large picnic hamper which Nellie had stowed, along with blankets, cushions, and her favourite book, away in the buggy.

An hour later they stopped by the river and tied the horses in the shade of a large tree. PJ and Willy were eager to begin fishing and whisked their uncle away to the water's edge. The girls wandered down towards the bank and sat down in the grass. Kitty began to pick daisies and the older women showed her how to make a daisy chain. Frequently, Meg glanced across to see Jack showing his nephews how to cast their line into the water, or how to put the worm on the hook. She admired the way he put so much time into the boys and never got impatient with them.

Meg gazed at the view around her from underneath the rim of her wide hat. The scene reminded her of a beautiful oil painting. The river was unhurried in its journey as it flowed by, framed on one side by an orange grove. The bank where she sat was covered with luxurious green grass dotted with flowers. She could hear kookaburras laughing in the distance and galahs squawking nearby. Beauty surrounded her and Meg thought she could easily dose off to sleep in such a peaceful place.

'I got one!'

Willy's excited exclamation interrupted Meg's reverie.

Scrambling to her feet, she took Kitty's hand and ran over to see the catch. It was a very small fish, but Willy held it up with pride. 'May I eat him, Uncle Jack?'

'No, Will,' Jack answered, 'We need to throw him back so he can grow bigger.'

'Oh.' Willy looked disappointed but accepted this decision.

'May I learn to fish, too?' Kitty looked plaintively at her uncle, tugging at his sleeve.

'If you really want to,' Jack told her, and Kitty nodded her eagerness.

'Well,' Meg clapped. 'I shall go and help Nellie prepare our lunch while you all enjoy your fishing.'

The two women spread blankets out under the shade of a group of tall gum trees a fair distance from the water's edge and scattered the cushions on it. Meg laid out the food Nellie had packed: bread and butter, cold ham, boiled eggs, fruit, and a flask of water. There was also some delicious looking tea cake and cookies for those who were extra hungry.

Once it was all set out Nellie draped a shawl over the food to keep the flies away and they sat back to watch the activity down at the river. It appeared PJ had now also caught a fish, one that seemed a good size, but out of fairness Jack had also thrown it back into the water. Jack crouched with one arm around Kitty's waist, helping her to hold the rod as she cast the line. It seemed he was explaining to her how to know when a fish had taken the bait and she nodded frequently, ringlets bobbing up and down.

Eventually they all put their rods down and headed towards her. 'I hope there is a lot to eat, Nell,' PJ said as he approached, 'because I am starving.'

'Me too.' Kitty plopped down beside Meg.

Nellie laughed softly. 'There's plenty for all of y'.' She lifted the shawl from the spread of food.

True to their word, the children ate hungrily, along with Jack, until everything was gone, including the cake and cookies. With their bellies full, a new lease of energy hit the boys and Kitty, and they ran off to play hide and seek, begging Jack to join them. Endlessly indulgent, he did so for a time, pretending he had no idea where the young scamps where hiding.

Meg and Nellie cleared up all the empty plates and put them in the picnic basket, and then Nellie excused herself to go for a walk. 'It is so lovely 'ere,' she sighed. 'I kept some crumbs so I could go an' feed the ducks. Do y' want to join me?'

'No, you go ahead,' Meg smiled. 'I am going to read for a while.'

Nellie nodded and headed off while Meg settled down against some cushions with her book. She enjoyed this time of solitude and peace and was thankful for the opportunity. So engrossed in her reading did she become she didn't hear Jack approach.

'Judging by that smile on your face, it must be a good book,' his voice startled her.

'Oh, Jack,' she said, recovering her composure, 'How long have you been standing there?'

'Only for about half an hour,' he exaggerated.

Meg grinned. 'Is that so?'

'Never mind,' Jack feigned a woeful look, 'I have grown quite accustomed to being ignored.'

'Nobody ever ignores you, Mister Nonpareil,' Meg growled good-humouredly, slapping him with her book.

Jack chuckled.

Meg looked at him with a mischievous twinkle. 'Although, it would be a good thing if you *were* ignored.'

'How so?'

'Perhaps you would not be so superior.'

Jack narrowed his eyes at her. 'Abominable girl.'

Meg laughed. 'What are the children up to now?'

'Well, I happened to mention to Willy that Charles Sturt has set out from Adelaide on an expedition to explore the inland. He is looking for an inland sea, I believe. Anyway, Willy has now gone exploring and PJ and Kitty are his travelling companions.'

Meg smiled. It was just like Willy to set off on an adventure. 'I wonder if he will still dream of exploration when he is older.'

'Perhaps he will.'

'I could not do that,' Meg shuddered.

'What?'

'Travel into the unknown. Make my bed in the bush. Risk life and health to discover what is "out there".'

'Mmm,' Jack agreed. 'I imagine it would be devilish uncomfortable.'

Meg looked over at the children playing in the distance.

'What would you do?' Jack asked.

Meg's gaze swerved back to Jack. 'What do you mean?'

Jack eyed her intently. 'If unfortunate circumstances had not befallen you, what path would your life have taken?'

Meg thought for a moment. 'Well, I always imagined I'd marry and have a quiverfull of children. That is why, when those unfortunate circumstances occurred, I chose to be a nursemaid. Children are so precious to life and if it weren't your sister's lambs in my charge, then it would be someone else's I care for. Perhaps even orphans, the poor little souls. I myself, if not for the hand of Providence, would have been a homeless waif. So, my heart goes out to them. Oh, but I am running on, aren't I?'

Meg looked up to see a glimmer of admiration in his eyes before he turned his face away from her.

'What about you, Jack?' Meg returned the question. 'What did you imagine your life would be before you were exiled as you put it?'

Jack glanced at her briefly, and then looked away with a half laugh. 'I never had much of an imagination,' he said airily. 'Except to tie an excellent cravat.'

'Jack!'

'What?'

Meg groaned. 'Sometimes I wonder who the real Jack Fordham is.'

He frowned at her. 'You're looking at him, dash it all.'

Meg shook her head. 'No, Jack. I am looking at an enigma.'

'An enigma?'

Meg scanned her mind for the right words. 'What is real; the unguarded and carefree uncle or the fastidious and debonair bachelor, the affectionate brother or the heartless nonpareil? Every time you are confronted with a serious question, you hide behind a trivial answer. Are you afraid of sharing your mind? I want to know what you really think. What does Jack Fordham deeply care about?'

Jack stared at her in silence, his eyes wide with disbelief. He opened and closed his mouth a few times, but no words came. At that moment they heard a shriek and a splash from the water's edge.

Jack immediately sprang to his feet, tearing his jacket off and flinging his hat aside as he ran. Meg followed close on his heels calling the children each by name.

'Kitty's fallen in,' PJ's frantic voice reached them from the bank where she had gone over. 'There, there!' he pointed.

Within seconds Jack was upon the water's edge and without hesitation, dove straight in. Meg could see Kitty's struggling form a small distance downstream and heard her cries for help. *Lord God, keep her safe, please.*

In a few powerful strokes Jack had the little girl in his arms and hauled her to safety. Despite her panic, Meg was awed by the ease at which Jack moved through the water. He handed Kitty up to her and she pulled the quivering child into her arms and held her tight. Kitty wailed from both fright and cold but was otherwise unharmed. Jack pulled himself out of the water, wordlessly lifted the little girl into his arms and headed towards the buggy.

Meg grabbed hold of the boys' hands and followed their uncle. The two young men were trembling with shock. 'It is all right now,' Meg assured them, though her own voice wavered. Nellie ran to join them, alarm written on her face. 'What happened?'

'Kitty fell in,' Meg answered in dismay. 'But Jack got her in time. She is safe.'

Instructing Nellie to take the boys to the buggy, Meg stopped with Jack at the picnic site. Jack put his niece down so Meg could wrap a blanket tightly around her. Hugging her and whispering comforting words in her ears, Meg looked up to see if Jack was ready to leave. He was dripping wet, his shirt clinging to his body, revealing powerful muscles in his chest and arms and Meg looked away in discomfort. 'There is another blanket over there,' she suggested, indicating with her eyes.

'I will be fine.' His words were curt as he pulled his jacket over his wet clothes. He packed the remaining blanket and picnic items in the buggy and returned for Kitty.

❧❦

After what seemed an eternity, they were finally heading home. Jack drove with Meg sitting beside him and Kitty in between. The boys rode silently in the back with Nellie. Kitty had fallen asleep from her ordeal even though she was soaked through. Jack looked across at Meg and saw she still looked pale.

'Are you all right?' he asked her.

'Yes,' she replied, her voice shaking. 'That is, I will be. We could have lost her, Jack.' She swallowed hard. 'I was so scared.'

Jack pressed his lips together but said nothing. How could he express the panic that had taken hold of him when he saw his niece in the water? The dread he wouldn't get to her in time?

'Are you all right, Jack?'

Jack let out an unconvincing laugh. 'No. Botheration,' he said with a frown. 'My shoes are likely ruined.' As he spoke, Jack remembered what Meg had said just before Kitty fell in the river and drove on in troubled silence.

Back at the farm, Gwen and Meg swept Kitty off to be dried and cosseted. Gwen was clearly upset by the accident, scolding all in the party for allowing Kitty to be so close to the water's edge. Jack was not fazed by her — it was the natural, alarmed reaction of a parent. Meg however had crumbled into tears, obviously feeling responsible for the mishap. Once Gwen's fright had worn off, she calmed down somewhat and apologised for her outburst, embracing Meg, and assuring her she was not to blame.

Once the fuss had died down and all had returned to normal, Jack took himself off to groom the horses. Those hard-working animals received the reward of an extra vigorous rubdown, while Jack communicated with them at intervals.

'Insufferable girl,' he gritted as he brushed one of the horses. 'I do not hide behind triviality.' He revisited his discussion with Meg by the riverbank. 'And I am not afraid to speak my mind.' And yet, when she had asked him about his feelings, he'd feigned concern about his shoes. Damnation. His shoes were the last thing he worried about. He'd very nearly watched his precious niece drown, and it scared him half to death.

He worked in silence for a time, regaining his equilibrium through exertion. Once the horses were brushed, he draped blankets over them for warmth. He picked up a handful of sugar cubes and went to the horse's head to give it a treat. While the horse nuzzled his palm, Jack stroked its neck.

'If she wants to know what I care about,' he told the animal, 'Perhaps I should show her.' The horse nickered as if in agreement. Jack smiled. 'Ah yes,' he argued. 'But can she be trusted?'

The horse pawed the ground and shook out its mane. Jack gathered another handful of sugar for the other horse. Jack chuckled. 'I daresay you're right, old chap. If I am to exchange vows with her, I will have to take some chances.'

He was thoughtful again for a moment, while the other horse ate its treat. He stroked her nose and stared into the animal's eyes. 'Well, my dear,' he sighed. 'It seems it is time for some very subtle romancing.'

Chapter Sixteen

Sleep eluded Meg for a long while that night. Jack remained a mystery. He was clearly shaken by Kitty's accident, she had seen it in his eyes, and yet he had remained aloof. It stunned her that he could maintain a mask of indifference, even in the face of a crisis. She wondered what took place underneath that carefree exterior, and what caused him to hide his emotions away.

She was further perplexed the following day at church. She noted he mixed easily and comfortably with the church folk without carrying any airs of superiority. He behaved with genteel propriety, and he mixed easily amongst farmers and officials alike. He did not behave as though he were an unmatched paragon of nobility. Perhaps arrogance was part of the charade he played at times. She also noticed he did not search out the single young damsels in the congregation, which surprised her knowing his reputation. Meg was thankful he showed at least a little respect in a house of worship.

❧

Jack was, at first, rather surprised at the lack of attention he received within the congregation. But, as time went on, he found it quite a pleasant change not to be sought out by all and sundry. They all knew who he was, of course, but they did not seem to place importance on wealth and title like the rest of the world as he knew it. There were a few shy, admiring glances directed his way by young girls, but there were none who made the bold advances he was accustomed to.

Jack was impressed, but wished they weren't all religious fanatics.

As the party rode home in the warm, spring sunshine, Meg, and Nellie riding together in a buggy, Jack and Mr Roderick riding horseback beside them, the conversation was full of laughter. Jack's wit was in fine form, making both girls erupt in laughter time and time again with his ridiculous statements. Meg's dry sense of humour complemented Jack's wit and poor Nellie had tears of hilarity streaming down her face. Mr Roderick made a few attempts at humour himself, only succeeding to draw uncomfortable silence each time. Eventually he gave up trying while the other three continued with their merriment.

❧❧

When they finally arrived back at Sainsbury Stud, Jack took the horses and buggy to the stable and Nellie went off to the cook house to prepare the midday meal. It fell to Mr Roderick to escort Meg indoors. Meg sighed, contented. 'I have not laughed so much for a long time.'

'If only I could make you laugh like that, I would be a happy man.' Mr Roderick sounded sullen.

'I am sure you can,' Meg assured him, while scanning her mind for an instance where he had. She came up blank. 'Perhaps the wit was just with Mister Fordham today.'

'He is a hard man to compete with.'

Meg stopped walking. 'Why would you want to compete with him?'

'You don't know?' Mr Roderick's face fell.

'Mister Fordham may be rich and ...' Handsome, intelligent, witty, commanding, charming, '... and all those things, but he is just a man.'

Mr Roderick didn't look convinced.

'Will you join us for dinner?'

Mr Roderick looked at the ground. 'No, I don't think so,' he answered. 'Forgive me, I do not feel I would be very good company today. Perhaps I am coming down with something.'

Meg tried to find sympathy, although she suspected all he suffered was self-pity. 'I hope you feel better tomorrow, Mister Roderick.'

He gave her a half smile, bowed over her hand, and bid her good day, then walked away to retrieve his horse.

Later that afternoon, Meg, Mrs Sainsbury and her two daughters were spending some time together in the playroom. The four were sitting in a row on the floor; Kitty in front, Mary behind her, then Meg and last of all, Mrs Sainsbury. They all practised dressing each other's hair and a myriad of pins, ribbons, flowers, brushes, and combs surrounded them on the floor. Whilst they braided and pinned and decorated, they talked of fashion, ball gowns, shoes, dashing young men and dolls.

Jack unexpectedly entered the room, and he watched with amusement from the doorway for a moment before speaking. 'I must have misplaced my invitation to whatever soirée you are dressing for. Will you remind me?' he drawled.

Gwen chuckled. 'Jack, we are having some feminine fun. Be off with you.'

'No! No!' Kitty squealed. 'Uncle Jack, come here. I want to braid your hair.'

Meg gasped.

Gwen almost choked. 'Kitty, men do not have their hair braided.'

Jack raised his hand in protest. 'Forgive me, but I am in such sad want of feminine attention I will accept anything.' He settled his tall frame on the floor in front of Kitty. 'Braid away, fair one.'

Gwen and Meg laughed out loud and shook their heads in disbelief.

Mary blushed. 'Uncle Jack, you are very silly.'

Meg was amazed at the lengths Jack would go to when enjoying his family. He sat very still while Kitty pulled and twisted his hair into two very short and uneven plaits which she tied with two very pink ribbons. He joined in on their dainty conversation, commenting that it would be very agreeable to dance with Mr Benedict, another esteemed bachelor, as he is so very elegantly dressed, which sent the girls into fits of laughter.

When eventually they all finished and turned around to face each other, the girls could not help but burst into giggles at the comical appearance of Jack with plaited hair.

'You look very beautiful, Jack,' Meg said with dramatic flair.

'Thank you very much, ma'am,' he nodded and then smiled. 'Now we are all dressed up it seems a shame we have nowhere to go.'

'I don't know,' Meg looked at Mrs Sainsbury and then back at Jack. 'I am sure there is a party somewhere we could all go to. I am certain you would outshine every other woman there.'

Jack grinned at her. 'Minx.'

'Kitty would you please put these pins and ribbons away,' Gwen handed the little girl a box, her lips still twitching. Kitty took the box, shining with pride at her work, and skipped out of the room.

'Do you know,' Jack looked at his sister, 'the Philharmonic Society are giving a recital next week?'

Gwen's face lit up. 'Are they really?'

'Yes,' Jack replied. 'I would like to take my favourite ladies along.'

Mary clasped Meg's arm. 'Did you hear that, Winnie? We are going to a musical concert.' She turned to her uncle. 'Can Winnie come?'

'Mary.' Gwen scolded.

'I was referring to you and your mother,' Jack told Mary with an affectionate smile, 'but Winnie is welcome to join us if she wishes.'

'I would enjoy that very much.' She could not deny it. 'If it is all right with you, Missus Sainsbury.'

Gwen opened her mouth to speak when Jack interrupted.

'No, wait, I have a better idea. You can all come and stay in my home next weekend. PJ and Willy, too. I am sure Meg would be more comfortable supervising those young scamps while we go to the recital. And she can also keep you ladies company while I take the boys out adventuring on Sunday.'

'Jack!' Gwen gasped at him.

'It is all right, Gwen,' he laughed. 'Meg knows I am merely teasing her, don't you Meg?'

'Worse than any rumours you have heard so far, Missus Sainsbury, your brother is a complete cad.' Meg narrowed her eyes at him.

Jack pulled a face as though he was insulted. 'I implore you, sister dear, to ignore this woman. She does naught but slander my good name all day.'

'Oh, stop this absurdity, both of you.' Gwen fell into a fit of giggles.

'All right,' Jack conceded, a wide grin on his face. 'I was serious about you all coming for a visit though. I am sure we will have quite an adventure.'

Chapter Seventeen

The following Friday afternoon, the four children, Gwen and Meg piled into the family's coach and headed for Jack's town house. The two boys were all agog with excitement for their upcoming adventure. Mary, Gwen, and Meg looked forward with anticipation to the concert recital, especially the two younger women. Neither had ever experienced a musical performance before. Kitty was rapt in the knowledge she would spend the night in Uncle Jack's house.

Consequently, due to all the excitement in the carriage, the trip seemed to pass by quickly, even though it was dark when they arrived. Meg was curious to learn more of Jack Fordham's nature and as she stepped out of the coach she looked around, taking in every detail that met her eyes. She slowly climbed the wide steps that led to the front door where lanterns burned on either side to light their path. The Sainsbury children raced up to the entrance in their anticipation and hammered on the door.

Moments later it was opened by a short, greying man with a friendly face. He bowed low before them, welcoming them in his master's name and waved them inside. Meg gazed around in awe at the well-lit entry way. Ahead of them, a wide staircase wound around towards the upper floor. Four doors opened from the entrance hall, plus another that was almost hidden by the staircase at the rear.

The serving man led them to the second door on the right-hand side. They entered what appeared to Meg to be the drawing room. It was a large and luxuriously furnished room. There were velvet drapes hanging in front of the windows and intricately woven Persian rugs on the floor. A grand piano sat in one corner, to which Mary immediately ran to play. There were several small tables, various chairs and lounges sprawled about. There were sideboards gracing delicate china ornaments and beautiful paintings hung on the walls. The fireplace was surrounded by a marble hearth and mantel. Candelabras burned with light all around the room and a large chandelier sparkled with numerous candles from the centre of the ceiling.

'Mister Fordham will be with you shortly,' the servant told them.

Here, Jack's wealth was made abundantly clear. It was on show for all to see. She glanced at Mrs Sainsbury and noticed the other woman watched her attentively.

'It is beautiful, is it not?'

'I have never been in a house like this,' Meg breathed. 'It is ... overwhelming.'

'Interesting choice of words, Meg.'

She spun around to see Jack had entered the room. Dressed in his town finery, he blended in perfectly with his gorgeous surroundings. His face beamed with pride and as much excitement as the boys had shown on their journey. For a moment, Meg felt infinitely inferior. Jack, in all his elegance, amongst such luxury, cast her completely into the shade. She stammered to find words. 'I ... uh — what I meant is ... this house is ... uh ... beyond compare.'

Jack laughed, his face softening. 'I am glad you approve of it.'

Meg felt compelled to curtsy and Jack laughed again.

'Welcome to my home,' he bowed deeply and kissed each of the girls' hands in turn. Then he shook hands firmly with the two boys.

'I am sure you are all ravenous,' he rolled the r in an exaggerated way. 'I have some supper laid out for you in the dining room. Will you join me?' He offered his arm to his sister, and they led the rest of the party across the hall into the large dining room.

Meg was dazzled by the opulence which surrounded her with renewed force. A very long table graced the centre of the room and a uniformed attendant stood beside each place. Once again sideboards lined the walls with expensive looking knick-knacks on display, and lights blazed from every corner of the room. The table itself was spread with all kinds of delicacies, much more than they could possibly eat. Meg was overwhelmed, and Mrs Sainsbury was obviously not far behind.

'Jack, you did not have to go this far,' she exclaimed. 'We are not royalty.'

Her brother was clearly tickled by her objection. 'I know,' he gave her shoulders a squeeze, 'but it has been an age since I have entertained at all, and I must say I feel rather extravagant at present.'

'Extravagance puts it quite succinctly, my dear,' she responded. 'What do you think, Meg?'

Meg thought of all the hungry people that could be nourished with this food. However, she did not want to seem ungrateful or impolite. 'It is an unexpected indulgence, I must say.'

Jack eyed her for a moment as if reading her mind and then pulled out a chair for her next to the head of the table. 'Please, have a seat,' he urged. Meg sat down compliantly, Mrs Sainsbury opposite her and Jack to her right at the head. The boys hungrily fell into their meal, their attendants filling their glasses with water, milk, or juice, whatever their wish was, and serving them tender portions of meat and garden greens, tarts, and jellied fruit.

The girls ate well also, but Meg ate sparingly, unwilling to gorge herself, no matter how sumptuous the meal appeared to be. She didn't want to appear gluttonous and waste precious food on greed.

࿐

Jack could see plainly Meg thought the meal excessive and wasteful. He tried to converse with her but found she had become shy and reclusive for the present, so he turned his attention to Gwen and the children. The latter bubbled with gaiety and were in obvious high spirits. He managed to halt their racing tongues for long enough to tell them his plans for the next two days. 'Tomorrow morning, I have a little business to attend to, but I have requested a friend of mine come here to entertain you. He can do magic tricks.'

115

The boys gasped, looking at each other with wide eyes, and Kitty clapped her hands.

'In the evening, of course,' Jack continued, 'I will escort the ladies to see the Philharmonic Society. On Sunday morning I shall take PJ, Willy, and Kitty on an adventure.'

'Where to? Where to?' Kitty bounced up and down in her seat.

'That, my sweet, is a surprise,' Jack grinned at her.

'Uncle Jack,' a serious Willy said. 'I do not think I can wait until tomorrow. I think my head shall pop before then.'

Everyone laughed and when a measure of quiet returned, Gwen spoke. 'I have a solution for you, my darling,' she said to Willy. 'Off to bed with you and tomorrow will come very quickly.'

'May we go down to the beach, Uncle Jack?' PJ asked.

'Of course, you may,' Jack answered. 'There will be plenty of time tomorrow for that.'

❧

Once their appetites were satisfied, Jack handed them all over to Miller who showed them to their rooms. The servants had already delivered their portmanteaux to the second floor. Mary and Kitty were given a room to share. They squealed with pleasure over the comfort of their bed and the warmth of their room. PJ and Willy were also given a room to share, and they immediately took to thumping each other with pillows, much to their mother's chagrin.

Gwen and Meg were each directed to a room for themselves. Meg entered hers somewhat hesitantly. She felt at odds sleeping in this man's beautiful house. The room was painted white, and the bed was of whitewashed wrought iron. A white stone hearth surrounded the fireplace and a white dresser sat against one wall. The bed cover was white also, of course, but was embroidered with small, lilac flowers. The same embroidery decorated the pillow covers. The wash basin and jug were white porcelain and had the same purple flowers painted on them. The dresser had sticks of dried lavender tied together with lilac ribbon lying across a lace doyley on it, filling the room with a soft scent. The mantel piece carried two vases of fresh white and purple blooms.

Overall, the room had a very feminine feel. Meg sat on the bed to drink in the luxury and then lay down to test the comfort. She discovered a sachet of dried lavender under the pillow and smiled at yet another indulgence. Everything, every little detail in this house spoke of sumptuous luxury. She wondered what it would be like to live in such a home.

As she lay there, she noticed a card sitting on the dresser with her name on it. She quickly jumped off the bed and retrieved it. *Meg*, it read, *I hope you will be comfortable here. Jack.* Meg put the card down thoughtfully. Every little detail. She wondered if the others received cards like that.

The children had retired, and the two older women returned to the lower floor to join Jack in the drawing room. They found him reclining indifferently in a lounge chair, a glass of port on a table at his elbow. He stood politely when they entered. 'A glass of wine for either of you?'

'Perhaps I shall have a nightcap,' Gwen agreed, 'and then I am to bed. I am rather fatigued from the drive, you know.'

'Indeed,' Jack poured her a small glass. 'Meg?'

'No thank you, Jack.'

The master of the house returned to his lounge and the women sat in comfortable chairs nearby.

'Are you both cosy in your rooms?'

'Of course we are, Jack,' Gwen scoffed. 'How could we not be?'

She rolled her eyes and Meg giggled.

'Jack, my darling brother, what is this dreadful business that will take you from us tomorrow morning?' Gwen pouted.

He laughed at her. 'I must see Mister Brown. You may come with me if you like.'

'I should like that,' Gwen replied.

'And you, Meg? Would you care to join us?'

Gwen jerked upright, her eyes wide with question, but she said nothing.

And Jack gave her a wordless stare. Meg watched this exchange with curiosity. What was going on?

'Who is Mister Brown?' she asked. 'That is, I have heard you mention his name before, but…'

'Mister Brown is a very dear friend of mine,' Jack answered her with an enigmatic smile.

'I suppose I should be happy to meet him.'

'It is settled then,' Jack gazed into the glass of port he held.

Mrs Sainsbury coughed and set down the glass of wine which she had barely sipped at. 'I will bid you both goodnight,' she said. 'Sleep well.'

'You too, dear,' Jack replied, rising to kiss her on the cheek.

'Goodnight Missus Sainsbury,' Meg added as the older woman swept out of the room, leaving Meg and Jack in uncomfortable silence.

'So, you like my home?' Jack eventually spoke.

'Like it?' Meg struggled to find words. 'That is not the word I would use. This house is wonderful. It is …enchanting.'

He seemed pleased to hear her praise his home. He opened and closed his mouth a few times, as if choosing his next words carefully. 'And yet, you have been uneasy since you arrived.'

He had noticed that? His insightful observation surprised her. 'It is just…I am not used to such—such…'

'Opulence?' Jack finished for her. 'You think it is overdone?'

'No,' Meg said slowly. 'I just did not realise that you — I mean, I knew you were … wealthy, but I feel — dwarfed by all this … luxury.'

'You need not be, Meg, I am still the same old Jack.'

Meg finally smiled.

'You did not approve of the supper I provided. You can be honest with me. You believe I am overly extravagant and wasteful, do you not?'

Meg's gaze fell to her lap. How did he read her so well? 'Yes, that is what I thought,' she admitted and then boldly returned her eyes to his in challenge.

'You could not be more mistaken.' Jack's face was unreadable.

'But, all that food …' Meg pleaded.

Jack stared at her intently, and a hard glint crept into his gaze. 'Do not judge me, Meg.' His voice was harsh. 'Pious criticism is the last thing I want to hear from your lips.'

Chapter Eighteen

Meg rode silently in the carriage with Jack and Mrs Sainsbury. His comment the previous night had been sharp and unexpected. Jack had never spoken to her in such a way before. Where could such a reaction stem from? Jack had not yet explained himself, but even so, she could not ignore the note of disappointment she'd heard in his voice.

The carriage drew up in front of a large, sprawling, two-storied house, a small distance from the city. The house was situated on one hundred acres, centred in a large clearing amongst untouched bushland, which gave the place a very private atmosphere. There were various sheds and outbuildings dotted around the clearing, with smoke rising from some. There were also many fenced yards with a variety of animals penned in them. Meg could hear chickens, sheep, cows, pigs and dogs as Jack handed her down from the coach.

Jack turned to his sister while Meg looked at her surroundings, drinking in the fresh air and scent of eucalyptus. He escorted Gwen towards the house and Meg followed closely behind. 'What a beautiful property.'

Jack smiled, seeming pleased at her approval. 'It is, is it not?' He banged on the door, and they could hear the sound resonating through the large building. Presently a robust woman opened the door and peered out. 'Ahhh, Mister Fordham,' she greeted, obviously pleased. 'Good morning to you.'

She opened the door wide, and Jack stood aside to let the ladies enter first. 'Missus Sainsb'ry,' the lady nodded to Gwen.

'Hello May,' Gwen returned the greeting.

'Ma'am,' May curtsied to Meg as she passed.

'Good-day,' Meg answered.

'This is Miss Wingrove, May,' Jack told her as he entered. May nodded another greeting to Meg.

'Where shall I find them this morning?' Jack asked the woman once the formalities were over.

May pulled a fob from her apron pocket and examined the time. 'They'd be at their studies at this hour, sir,' she answered in a thick cockney accent.

'Very well,' Jack nodded and headed for the staircase at the end of the hall.

Meg was puzzled. Jack had a friend who studied? Was he a scientist? She shrugged to herself. No doubt it would all become clear shortly. In contrast to Jack's townhouse, this place appeared understated. It was comfortably furnished and seemed a pleasant home to live in, yet it was not embellished at all. She followed Jack and Mrs Sainsbury up the stairs to the second floor. For such a large house, it seemed all too quiet. Meg imagined she would jump at the slightest noise.

Jack led them to a door at the far end of the building, motioned for them to be very quiet and edged open the door. He stood back to allow Gwen and Meg to peek in. Meg became increasingly curious about this strange behaviour. When Mrs Sainsbury stepped back, she moved to the gap in the door. What she saw puzzled her further. It appeared to be a schoolroom. There were at least twenty young men seated at desks, all with their heads bent low over their work. A teacher paced the floor at the front of the room frowning and not a sound could be heard from anyone.

Meg backed out of the doorway and looked at Jack who grinned at her but said nothing. He gently closed the door and led them to another door opposite. Once again, he silently opened the door for the ladies to look inside. This time the room was full of younger boys and there was a little more noise. Meg could see feet swinging under chairs, boys whispering together and a teacher who carefully assisted one student. A few heads turned her way and smiled before they went back to their work, one young boy became quite animated when he turned around.

Their spying expedition complete, Jack led them away from the schoolrooms. 'I think I shall go and speak with May and the kitchen staff,' Mrs Sainsbury said abruptly.

'If you wish.' Jack shrugged and Gwen strolled away down the stairs.

Meg looked suspiciously at Jack. 'What is all this about?'

Jack offered her his arm and led her back to the stairs. 'It is an orphanage, Meg.'

'An orphanage?' Meg repeated, even more bewildered.

'Yes,' Jack replied. 'After what you told me the other day, I thought you might like to see it.'

Meg could find no words to respond.

'Shall I show you around some more?'

'Yes,' Meg found her voice. 'Please do.'

As they walked Meg wondered what this had to do with Jack's friend Mr Brown. Was he one of the staff that worked here or was he one of the orphans? Meg's curiosity grew by the minute, but she told herself to be patient. Jack walked her around the outbuildings and explained to her how the boys could learn a trade in ironwork, carpentry, farming, or domestic serving. Meg was impressed. She imagined the dramatic impact such a place would have on these children's lives.

Once the tour was over, they returned to the house. 'So, what do you think?'

'What can I say? I am inspired,' she replied earnestly. 'It does my heart good to know such a fine establishment exists. Thank you for bringing me here, Jack.'

Smiling, Jack pulled the fob from his pocket. 'Shall we go and see the children?'

'Yes please,' Meg allowed him to lead her back up the stairs.

They stood outside the schoolroom doors waiting for the class to be over. Jack told her they were learning to read and write.

'I did not know you had so much interest in the welfare of orphans.' Meg noticed Jack kept his eyes diverted from her and he was clenching and unclenching his fists. He also licked his lips several times and Meg was astonished to realise he was nervous about something. He swallowed carefully and at last spoke.

'Yes,' he said quietly. 'I too, have a fondness for children.'

She had known this, of course, but she had never heard him admit it. Neither had she known his interests went beyond his family.

Jack finally turned and met her gaze, smiling briefly and self-consciously. 'I would like to tell you more. However, what you are about to learn is a very well-guarded secret. You must promise me you will never speak of it to anyone.'

'Jack,' Meg frowned, mystified, 'What do you mean?'

'Promise me, Meg,' Jack insisted.

Meg scanned his face for answers he only offered a grave countenance. He was serious.

'Very well, I give you my word.'

Jack's anxiety returned. This was the moment. It was time to tell her. Once again, he moistened his lips. 'You told me recently you wanted to know what I … deeply cared about.' He cleared his throat. 'Well, I — er … this orphanage …' he struggled to find the right words to use. 'I … I …'

Just then the doors burst open, and boys flooded out of the rooms. 'Brace yourself, Meg,' Jack warned. 'In fact, you should stand over there.' He pointed to the wall, well away from him. Alarmed, Meg did as he said and turned to see the boys flocking to Jack. One little boy ran straight to him and threw himself on Jack, full force. 'Papa!'

'Come here, you young ruffian,' Jack tussled his hair and lifted the five-year-old into his arms. 'How do you do, Cedric?'

Jack managed to extricate himself from the swarming children around him for long enough to glance at Meg, only to see a look of mixed shock and grief on her face. She had paled, as though she might even swoon. He put Cedric down, her reaction heightening his anxiety, and moved away from the crowd. 'Meg, what is it? What is wrong?'

'You … you have a — a son? Is that the secret you were been about to tell me? Is it Cedric Brown? Why would you want me to know this?'

Now Jack was confused. He glanced back over his shoulder and then back to Meg. All at once he realised her train of thought and his anger rose. 'Good God! No. Must you think the worst of me?'

The mystified look on Meg's face increased and the children slowly filtered away. 'That child called you Papa,' she hissed. 'I only have your reputation to go on, and the fact that this is such a secret. What else am I to believe?'

Jack stared at her for a moment and then coughed lightly, trying to throw off his irritation. '"Papa John" is their pet name for me. What I wanted to tell you before is this orphanage — well — it is mine.'

'Yours?' Meg looked incredulous, disbelieving.

'I built it.'

&⤙

Slowly, as Jack's words sank in, Meg relaxed into relief and understanding, then to admiration and finally to embarrassment.

'What is it now?' Jack asked.

Meg sighed and lowered her gaze to the floor. 'You are right, Jack,' she admitted. 'I am far too quick to judge.'

'Never mind, Meg,' Jack dismissed her error and slowly led her down the stairs again. 'That was an honest mistake to make. And as for last night, the attendants were all boys from here whom I offered some work for experience, and all the leftover food was theirs to feast upon and to bring back here for the others.'

'Oh,' Meg let the truth settle in her mind. 'I shall reserve my judgement where you are concerned in the future, until I know all the details. Jack, I had no idea you had a heart of gold. I cannot tell you how much I admire what you have done here. Those boys obviously adore you.'

'Yes,' Jack grinned sheepishly, 'particularly Cedric. It appears he truly sees me as his father. He was only a few months old when he came here.'

'Well, I must say I have been pleasantly surprised. If you don't mind my asking, what moved you to build an orphanage here?'

Jack drew in a deep breath and let it out slowly. 'Well, back in London, before I was — er — cast off,' he began, 'I was witness to a horrible accident. I saw a young lad run over by a carriage. The details are not fit for a lady's ears, but the sum of it was the poor child had no father or mother to nurse his injuries. I could not, in good conscience, leave him, so I took him back to my lodgings and called for a doctor. I kept him with me until he was well again, but it concerned me that he had no home to go to.

'I began to investigate the plight of young fellows such as he. I was appalled to see how many fatherless urchins roamed the streets without a soul to care for them. No-one that is, except perhaps some corrupt character who could use them for his own means and send them out to thieve. The orphanages in London were overflowing and I had thought to build one there, but before I could, I found myself on a ship bound for Australia.

'When I settled in Sydney, I was horrified to find the same thing happening in the colony. I saw several homeless children sleeping in the street and made up my mind to do something about it at once. It was a simple matter to engage the services of a respectable clergyman to head up a committee, appointing myself as the sole patron. The Reverend heeds my wish for anonymity and he communicates any needs or decisions from me to the committee or vice versa.'

Jack stopped talking and watched her. He wanted to know her reaction, she could tell. Her mind spun at this new knowledge, like she'd been run down by a speeding carriage herself. Who was this man — the same and yet so, so different? She smiled uncertainly at him, unsure how to respond.

'The welfare of these children is what I care about,' Jack told her then swallowed. 'No hiding behind trivial remarks.'

'Yes, Jack. So I see. Thank you.' It was clear he'd made a significant disclosure to her, one he was not comfortable with.

Not long afterward, when they were back in the carriage and on the way home, Meg frowned once again, still processing all she'd seen and learnt. 'Jack,' she said. 'After all that, I still have not discovered who Mister Brown is.'

Jack and Gwen looked at each other and laughed.

Puzzled by their reaction, Meg said 'What is so funny?'

Mrs Sainsbury smiled at her. 'Mister Brown is the surname of the boy Jack rescued in London. Jack and I, and now you, use his name as a code for the orphanage when we want to discuss it.'

Meg stared at them both. 'Are you saying we three are the only people who know about this aside from the Reverend?' Jack had told her it was a secret, but she had no idea how close.

'And my man, Miller, of course,' Jack added. 'And May. The other staff probably think I am a patron of some sorts, I suppose, but they do not know the whole truth.'

'Do the boys know?' Meg asked.

'They do not know my full involvement, no.' he replied. 'I am sure one day knowledge of my patronage shall leak out somehow, but for now I am trying to keep as many people unaware as possible.'

The enormity of this weighed on Meg. 'So, why tell me, Jack?'

'Yes, Jack. Why tell Meg?' Gwen echoed, eyes wide in question.

Jack shrugged nonchalantly. 'You are a governess and one day you may be looking for a new post. Besides, my sister here has entrusted her children to you all these years, I believe I can depend on your discretion.'

Meg looked at him in amazement. 'Are you serious?'

'Yes,' Jack chuckled and leaned back in his seat, closing his eyes. He practically offered her a secure future beyond the Sainsbury children. She could work in his orphanage. She had no words.

❧❦

Jack strolled along the beach later that afternoon while the children ran and played with Juniper ahead of him. A slight breeze ruffled his hair and whisked the waves into white peaks before they tumbled into the shore. Seagulls flew just above the surface, trying to catch any fish that ventured too close. Mary and Kitty had their heads together searching for pretty shells on the shoreline, and the boys had found a stick which they repeatedly threw into the mild surf for Juniper to fetch.

Jack's thoughts roamed, as they frequently did, to Meg. Had he been able to win her affection today? She had shown no sign. She had openly admired the boys' home and said she was inspired, but beyond that he had no indication his device had worked. It surprised him to find that making himself vulnerable to her like that had impacted his own feelings. Suddenly it became even more important to him that she approved of his character. How could the opinion of one governess become so significant to him?

❧

Meg sat at her dresser, fixing her hair in readiness for that evening's entertainment. She had trouble concentrating on her task, however. Now that she'd had time to digest the information she had learned that morning, she couldn't keep her mind from it. When Jack first told her he owned the orphanage, she had been too shocked to comprehend the full meaning. Now, the more she thought about it, the more her heart swelled.

Tears sprang to her eyes at the generosity of this man. Jack had depth of character after all. She began to wonder what other virtues he had hidden beneath his indifferent exterior. Up until now, he had only allowed her to see his affectations, but today, he had let her peek beneath the surface, and what she had seen moved her deeply.

One thing puzzled her. He had made it clear the boys' home was highly confidential, and she was now part of the inner circle. If it was that important to him, why had he told her at all? He could have shown her without telling her he owned the home. He could even employ her there without her knowing. Did he have another motive? Was it just because they were alike in their love for children, and he wanted to share it with someone else? Whatever his reasons, it was an honour he had entrusted this valuable part of his life to her, and she was more drawn to him than ever.

Chapter Nineteen

The Australian Philharmonic Society performed at the Royal Victoria Theatre. Jack and his escort of ladies pulled up at the special entrance to the dress circle where Jack had a box with some of the best seats in the house. He gallantly took his niece by the arm and accompanied her inside, while Gwen and Meg followed behind. Mary shone with pride at such attention.

Jack, of course, had dressed in the height of style and fashion, with not an item or hair out of place. Gwen, Mary, and Meg were all dressed up in beautiful silk gowns with full bustles and lace trimmings. Meg wore another of Gwen's old dresses of pale blue silk with white embroidery on the bodice. The colour made the governess' eyes seem an even deeper blue than usual and the cut of the gown accentuated her slender form.

Jack was once again entranced by her beauty. He had not seen her so dressed up since Governor Gipps' Ball and had all but forgotten just how alluring she could be. He had difficulty keeping his eyes from her and hoped he could hide his attraction. He wondered if she felt just as drawn to him.

❧

Meg had trouble keeping her focus diverted from Jack. Flawlessly dressed as he was, and now knowing the goodness in his heart, she became more fascinated by him every moment. She took a deep breath to still her swirling emotions. Jack must not know how her heart tumbled for him. If he did, he may try to renew his advances again and she did not want to go down that road.

Meg sat quietly throughout the performance, drinking in the harmonies that filled the theatre, soaring with a high melody on the flute at one moment and wallowing with the hum of a deep cello the next, but always trying to ignore the fact that Jack was nearby. Unexpectedly, she heard his voice in low undertones speaking into her ear and she jumped, a thrill running through her body. 'Are you enjoying yourself, Meg?'

She gasped, a hand flying to her heart. 'I am sorry,' she said, 'you startled me.'

'I beg your pardon,' he smiled. 'I did not mean to.'

'I was engrossed in the music.'

'So, you are enjoying it then?'

'Well,' she told him in a loud whisper, 'I was until you interrupted me.'

His eyes flashed with amusement. 'Rogue.'

'Seriously, Jack,' Meg continued, 'I have never experienced anything quite like it. I feel as though I am floating.'

Jack grinned. 'Mary said the same thing.'

'She did?'

Jack nodded. 'I confess I am partial to a good melody myself.' His smile made Meg's heart flutter.

'Thank you for bringing me, Jack.' There was no harm in showing her genuine gratitude, was there?

A strange look came over his face and his Adam's apple bobbed. He took in a sharp breath and glanced away. Roughly, and with an air of indifference, he drew her hand to his lips. 'Any time, my dear friend.' He then excused himself to go and meet with some other folk, leaving Meg to wonder at his odd behaviour, although her knuckles burned where his lips had brushed them.

ॐॐ

Back at the townhouse, Meg was only too happy to pardon herself quickly and go to bed. She truthfully explained how tired she had become, even though her weariness was due more to her emotions than the activities of the day. She had experienced enough of Jack's disturbing new face for one day and yearned for the privacy of her room where she no longer had to hide her spinning emotions.

She paused at the door and looked back. 'Jack,' she asked, 'would you mind very much if I called on my brother tomorrow?'

Jack's face fell a little. Was he disappointed? If he was, he didn't let on.

'No, of course not,' he replied amiably from the chaise where he stretched out leisurely by the fire. 'You are welcome to my horses and a carriage to take you there. Treat my stables as if they were your own.'

Meg made him a curtsy. 'Thank you again, Jack. Good night.'

Jack and Gwen watched Meg's retreating figure until she had disappeared and then Gwen sighed. 'She is a wonderful girl.'

Oh, how he agreed, but he would not admit so to his sister.

'Mmm,' was all he replied, and then changed the subject. 'Did you not enjoy the Society's interpretation of Mozart this evening, my dear? I thought it quite superb.'

'They performed very well,' Gwen replied. 'I was deeply moved.'

Jack stared into the flames.

'I noticed the charming Miss Charles there tonight.' Gwen seemed intent to dig.

Jack frowned. 'You must remind me,' he drawled. 'Who is Miss Charles? I regret my memory is fading in my dotage.'

Gwen rolled her eyes. 'Dotage. You are little more than thirty. Anyway, Miss Charles has not forgotten you. She appeared to be keeping a close and jealous eye on you.'

Jack waved his arm in dismissal. 'Let her eyes do what they like, as long as the rest of her stays away.'

'Was there no young enchantress there to entice you?'

'In case you have forgotten, m'dear,' Jack replied dryly, 'Mary was the girl on my arm this evening. I was far too busy to search the crowd for a prospective bride.'

'Yes, Mary is quite stunning, is she not?' Gwen grinned in pride.

'Rather.' Jack agreed. 'I saw a number of young gentlemen looking her way.'

'And I'll wager double the number gazed upon Meg,' Gwen chuckled.

A knot twisted in Jack's stomach at the mention of her name. 'I did not notice,' he lied with a shrug. In fact, Gwen was right; Meg's pure and lovely face had drawn many adoring stares from around the theatre, a fact that had inexplicably disturbed him.

'Speaking of Meg ...'

Here we go. Why would his sister not let it drop?

'... why did you tell her about Brown today?"

'Struth my dear, I told you this morning.' Jack watched the flames dance in the hearth with a feigned yawn.

'Jack,' Gwen's voice was stern. 'I am your sister; you can be plain with me. In all these years you have not once shared your secret with anyone. Why now? Why Meg? And don't try that excuse you used this morning.'

Jack wanted to get away from the topic of Meg, but he could see his sister's determined face. He shrugged. A half-truth it would be. 'It was no excuse. I am thinking of making her a business partner of sorts.'

'What?'

'In a few years the children will not need her anymore and she will need a new posting. She has expressed an interest in homeless children, and I believe she would make an excellent den mother in a girls' home.'

Gwen stared at him open mouthed.

'She knows nothing of this yet,' he warned, 'so you must not tell her. I will do nothing until your children are old enough.'

'Of course,' Gwen readily complied. 'Jack, you are too good. This is exactly what she needs. I have been concerned about her future, but now you have provided one for her. Thank you for caring.'

'It is nothing.' He examined his fingernails.

'You have no idea, Jack,' she shook her head. 'Philip and I are so fond of Meg, we just want to see her happy.'

'I know.' And Meg's happiness could be his happiness, too. His heart leapt at the thought.

'Well,' Gwen said, rising, 'You have taken a great deal of worry from me, my dear brother. And now, I shall bid you good night.'

Jack stood and kissed his sister tenderly on the cheek. 'Good night, Gwen.'

At the door, she turned back to him. 'Are you sure it will only be a business partnership, Jack? Nothing more?'

'Good God, Gwen. What are you implying?' She was getting too close.

'I'm only saying you could do much worse than marrying Meg.'

And there it was.

'Struth Madam, you well know that matrimony and I don't suit. I am a confirmed bachelor. End of story.'

Gwen sighed and rolled her eyes. 'If you say so, Jack.' She turned and left.

Jack fell back into his chair and stared at the ceiling. He sighed inwardly, hoping he had successfully diverted his sister's curiosity. He did not want her to know his plans went further. The time was not right. He needed to be sure he had won Meg's heart before he made any declarations. Indeed, she had seemed distant and withdrawn since this morning. Had he been wrong about her? Only time would tell.

Chapter Twenty

Meg awoke to the distant sound of waves rolling onto the shore and sunlight streaming into the pretty lavender and white room. Looking at her surroundings she immediately thought of Jack and her pulse quickened. This would not do. For a moment she considered not going down to breakfast, but very quickly disposed of that idea. It would serve no purpose to hide.

The only thing to do was to keep on a brave face and look Jack in the eye. She climbed out of bed and paced the room. She quaked at the thought of seeing him and then shook her blonde locks. This was ridiculous. She needed to stop allowing her emotions to run wild and start to think rationally. Jack was just Jack. He was no-one out of the ordinary. Just because he was extremely handsome and owned an orphanage, it didn't change anything. Jack remained the well-known breaker of hearts and set firmly on the path that leads to destruction.

This thought sobered her. She stopped pacing and prayed earnestly for his soul. Focusing on Jack's spiritual status helped to calm Meg's emotions and she was finally able to head down to the morning meal at peace.

Much to her surprise, Meg was next to last to arrive in the dining room. Everyone had risen early, excited for the day's plans. Only Mary still slumbered.

They greeted Meg warmly and her personal attendant drew her chair for her. 'I feel so spoiled with all this treatment,' she commented as she sat.

'You deserve it, Meg,' Mrs Sainsbury said. 'After all, it is usually you that does all the serving.'

'Thank you, Missus Sainsbury.'

'I heartily agree,' Jack toasted her with his cup of tea, also in a good humour.

'Then I shall make the most of it.' Meg was served a large slice of salt pork and a pair of poached eggs.

'Gwen, how shall you entertain yourself this morning?' Jack asked his sister.

'I am sure I shall find something to do,' she answered. 'I shall probably go and visit some friends. I must catch up on all the latest news.'

'So long as you do not spread any scandalous rumours about me,' Jack drawled.

Gwen laughed and then touched him tenderly on the cheek. 'I could never say a bad word about you, my dear, sweet brother.'

Jack turned to Meg with a doubtful look. 'Perhaps you should stay and nurse my sister, Meg,' he said dryly. 'She seems to be ailing in her upper works, this morning.'

Gwen giggled. 'Is a woman not permitted to have an affectionate moment with her brother?'

'Lord!' Jack rolled his eyes and turned to Meg again. 'Next, she will try to embrace me in the market square and crease my coat. How mortifying.'

Meg could do naught but shake with silent laughter at this sibling banter.

'Uncle Jack.' Willy interrupted their inane conversation. 'Where are we going today? Are we leaving soon?'

Jack, now laughing himself, gave his attention to the youngster. 'We shall leave shortly after breakfast.' His voice still quivered with amusement. 'As to where we are going … well … I have hired a yacht. We are going sailing.'

Both boys' mouths dropped open, and Kitty squealed and clapped her hands. 'Winnie, are you coming?' The little girl asked eagerly.

'Unfortunately,' Jack answered before the governess could speak. 'Winnie is deserting us this morning. Apparently, her brother is more important than an adventure out to sea.' He put on a disgruntled face and then shook his head in mock disappointment. 'Well, if we all drown, we shall know who to blame when you are not there to rescue us.'

Meg imagined heroically diving into the ocean to save a pathetically drowning Jack and fell into a fit of giggles. It was a totally nonsensical scenario, and yet it held some truth. At present Jack *was* drowning in a life without God. Could she save him – or lead him to salvation at any rate?

Meg exited the rear of the house to locate Miller who had been sent to organise her carriage. As she rounded a corner, she saw Jack in conversation with one of the young attendants from the orphanage. She stopped, staying close to the wall, and watched.

'Are you enjoying yourself, Henry?' Jack asked the lad.

'Well enough,' the boy answered.

Jack reached into a pocket inside his coat and pulled out a silver coin. Handing it to Henry, he said, 'a little something extra for you.'

'Thank you, sir,' the young man said gratefully.

Jack pulled his fob from his pocket and checked the time. 'Forgive me, Henry, I must be on my way.'

Henry craned his neck to look at the watch. 'May I see it, sir?'

Jack removed the time piece and handed it to the boy, who gazed at it in admiration.

'Do you tell time?' Jack asked.

'I am learning.' Henry ran his fingers over the engraved golden surface.

'You like it … the watch I mean?'

'It is rather splendid.'

'It is yours then lad.'

Henry looked up at him sharply. 'Sir, I didn't mean …'

'I know,' Jack cut him off.

'But, sir, I …'

'Hush now,' Jack gently scolded. 'We will speak of it no more. Besides, I have another I can use. Now, be off with you.'

'Thank you, sir,' Henry began to move away. 'I shall never forget this.'

Jack smiled warmly as the boy ran off.

Meg backed quickly around the corner before either could see her, her heart beating loudly in her ears. Seeing Jack part so selflessly with such a costly and necessary item, undermined her resolve to dismiss her feelings. Jack was not just an ordinary man. There was something very special about him, she could no longer ignore it.

She ran to the stables to find Miller. She must depart immediately before she saw Jack again, lest he see the truth in her eyes.

In the end Miller himself drove her to town. She gave him the address of the little church her brother attended, knowing it would be there she would find him. She entered the building unobtrusively and sat in a back corner. The service had just begun. Meg tried to sing with her whole heart and be attentive to the sermon, but her mind kept wandering to one six-foot tall, gorgeous man with a smile that warmed her and a generous spirit that moved her heart. Frequently Meg shook her luxurious locks and tried to focus, but every attempt was in vain. What was she going to do with herself?

She doubled her efforts to concentrate but found herself looking around for her brother. She finally spotted him in the front row of pews where he sat beside Katherine and her mother. Meg smiled to herself. Progress had clearly been made between them. She was happy for her brother. If only her own life could be so simple.

Meg was relieved when the service ended and then knew a pang of guilt for feeling that way. At least she would find something to take her thoughts away from Jack. She edged her way through the crowded room until she neared Brian. It was only a moment before he noticed her, and his face lit up.

'Meg.' he exclaimed. 'What a surprise. What are you doing here?'

'Hello Brian,' she went forward and kissed him on the cheek. 'I have been staying in town with the Sainsburys.'

Brian opened his mouth to speak again, but hesitated and looked her carefully in the face. He turned to Miss Montgomery. 'Excuse me Miss Montgomery,' he said, 'I wish to speak to my sister privately.'

'Of course,' the shy girl replied, and Brian drew Meg aside.

'So, you are sitting together in church now?' Meg teased.

'Yes,' Brian replied, but his face showed a mixture of joy and worry. 'Oh, Meg, I have so much to tell you...but right now I am concerned about you.

You seem troubled. What is it?'

Meg lowered her eyes. 'I am — it is nothing,' she tried to cover herself.

'Meg, I am your brother. I know when something ails you.'

'Really Brian,' Meg said earnestly, 'It is nothing important. This is not the time to talk about it. I will be all right.'

Brian watched her for a moment, measuring her words. 'Very well, then,' he relented, 'if you are certain.'

'I am, Brian,' Meg insisted.

Brian scanned her face again and then appeared to let the matter drop. 'I am so glad you are here,' he told Meg. 'I have wanted to speak with you.'

'You have?' Meg asked, curious.

'Yes,' her brother answered. 'How long are you staying?'

'Not long, I am afraid. I am due to return with the Sainsburys early this afternoon.'

'That is a shame,' Brian looked disappointed. 'I have an engagement to dine with the Montgomerys today.'

So, Meg thought sadly, she would not be able to spend time with her brother. Aloud, she said, 'Perhaps another time, then.'

Brian looked unresolved, but they turned back to Katherine and her mother. The younger woman smiled shyly at Meg. 'How nice to see you again, Miss Wingrove.' She stretched out a gloved hand.

Meg received her hand warmly. 'Please call me Meg. I am happy to meet you again, too.'

Katherine glanced at her mother who almost imperceptibly nodded and looked back to Meg. 'My mother and I would like to invite you to join us for dinner along with your brother — that is, if you are free.'

Meg looked at her gratefully. 'I should like to join you very much.' She glanced happily at Brian, thankful she would be able to spend some time with him after all.

The Montgomerys lived in a small, but cosy cottage. Mrs Montgomery had been widowed a few years earlier and the two women had survived by building a small business as seamstresses. They were both experts with the needle and thread as well as gifted in design, and their enterprise had become quite successful.

Meg was admiring some of their recent work when dinner was announced. 'I must acquire your services when next I need a special dress, Katherine,' she told the modest girl once they were seated. 'You have a great talent.'

Katherine blushed. 'Do you really think so?'

'Yes, I do.' Meg told her sincerely.

As the party ate and conversed it became very clear to Meg that Brian and Katherine were deeply in love. Katherine's face glowed when Brian looked at her, and Brian's eyes were full of tenderness as he gazed upon her. They exchanged many meaningful smiles, and it seemed an effort to acknowledge the others in the room.

Unexpectedly, Meg found herself beginning to feel a little envious of their affection for one another. Why couldn't she have such a beautiful relationship? Why did her life have to be so complicated? At present she had fallen for a man who was all wrong for her, while at the same time a more decent man showed interest in her whom she did not care for in the least.

Meg found herself longing for her mother, wishing she could be there to comfort her and guide her. She always missed her most when illness or malaise took hold. She yearned for the grey stone walls of Wingrove Hall. She wished she were a child once again, carefree, and ignorant of pain.

As the meal progressed, Meg became more withdrawn, retreating within herself and her tumbled emotions. Eventually the happiness around the table became too much for her and she quietly begged to be excused, hurrying out into the rose garden to breathe some fresh air.

Within minutes, Brian approached her from behind and put a hand on her shoulder, causing her to turn around.

'Meg,' his eyes were filled with concern. 'I have never seen you like this. What is troubling you?'

'Nothing, Brian,' Meg shook her head in frustration. 'It is just silliness. I am sorry I am ruining your dinner party. I should not have come. I am not good company today.'

'Nonsense. What is making you feel this way?'

Meg looked up at him, her lips trembling. 'Will you call me a carriage? I should be getting back.'

Brian frowned. 'Not until you tell me what ails you.'

Meg sighed. 'I cannot tell you in one sentence. I wish Mama were here.'

Brian wrapped her tightly in his arms. 'Oh, Meg,' he whispered into her hair, 'I miss her too.'

They held each other for a while and when Brian pulled away, he cupped his sister's chin in his hand and looked into her eyes. 'You need to take leave of the Sainsburys and come and stay with me for a few days. You need to rest.'

'Brian, I ...' Meg protested.

'Tell me you will do it,' he insisted. 'You need to spend some time with your big brother. Besides,' he smiled sheepishly, 'I have been suffering toothache recently, but I have been putting off having my tooth pulled. I shall take a leave of absence from work to do so, and then we can nurse each other. What do you say?'

Meg relented with a half smile. 'Very well, Brian. I shall stay.'

Chapter Twenty-one

The little guest room in Brian's small townhouse was snug and comforting. As instructed by her brother she had sent a message to Gwen and requested a few days' leave. In return she had received her travelling bags and a note permitting her to take a leave of absence.

Not able to shake her loneliness or nostalgia, Brian had called her a carriage and sent her to his home. She had gone almost straight to the guest room where she had lain down and thought about her mother a great deal, removing the silver locket from around her neck, and gazing at her portrait.

This was a time in her life where she keenly felt her mother's absence. She greatly needed her wisdom and counsel. What was she to do about Jack? How would she face him in the future? Every time she thought about him her heart somersaulted. And she thought about him a lot. In fact, it became increasingly difficult to think of anything else. She wondered what he did, who he was with and if he thought about her at all.

But although she was rapidly losing her heart to this man, she was no less aware of his staunch dislike of all things religious and his rakish reputation. She fervently wished he were otherwise, and they could have a future together. The battle in her emotions confused and exhausted her and she eventually fell asleep, still dressed and without even a blanket to warm her.

She awoke hours later, surrounded by darkness and shivering with cold. She fumbled around the unfamiliar room to light a candle. The house was quiet and still. Meg sighed. There was nothing for it but to get into her nightgown and go back to sleep.

❧❧

When Meg descended the stairs to join Brian for breakfast, her stomach growled with hunger. Refreshed and in brighter spirits, she greeted her brother with a warm embrace.

'How are you, this morning, Meg?'

'I feel a great deal better than yesterday,' she admitted, 'but still not quite myself.'

Brian nodded but didn't press her any further. 'I have sent a message to the Colonial Secretary's Office this morning. I shall see the doctor about my tooth directly after breakfast.' Brian had been well educated and skilled in business and administration, and since they'd been in Australia he had climbed ambitiously through several different positions until now he worked as a clerk in the Colonial Secretary's Office.

Meg smiled at him. 'Soon you will be as miserable as I.'

'I dare say,' he agreed. 'However, while you are here, you are not to lift a finger to work. You may lounge around in your nightgown all day if you wish. You have no obligations and no responsibilities … except to ease my suffering, of course.'

Meg chuckled softly. 'So, you are going to pamper and cosset me, are you?'

'You are worth a little pampering from time to time, you know.'

Meg smiled and wondered if Jack would do the same for her.

They lingered over breakfast and then drifted into the parlour where Brian had stoked a cosy fire in the hearth. Once he saw that Meg was comfortable, he made his way to the doctor as promised.

When he returned just over an hour later, he was a little pale and obviously in pain. Her compassion stirred, Meg fetched him some laudanum from the top shelf in the pantry.

'I will be fine.' Brian tried to refuse the medicine.

'Just take a little, Brian, until the worst of the pain is gone,' Meg insisted.

Brian soon capitulated, the throbbing in his jaw getting the better of him.

Having seen to her brother, Meg curled up on a comfortable sofa and Brian stretched out on a nearby lounge chair. Meg sat, staring into the flames, her mind wandering to Jack again. She wasn't surprised when after a few minutes of silence, Brian questioned her.

'Are you going to tell me why my normally vibrant sister is so distant and quiet? What occupies your thoughts so completely?'

'Pardon?' She dragged her attention to him. 'Oh, my thoughts are very uninteresting,' she waved her hand in dismissal. 'You must tell me all about Katherine.'

A light came into Brian's eyes at the mention of Miss Montgomery's name. 'Ah, yes.'

'I can see you are very much in love with her.'

'Is it that obvious?' Brian coloured.

Meg laughed.

'Do you think she feels the same?'

Meg rolled her eyes. 'Do you even need to ask?'

Brian smiled briefly. 'I suppose not. I want to ask her for her hand.'

'You do?' Meg clapped her hands. 'Brian, that is wonderful.'

'Do you approve, then? Do I have your blessing?'

His question both surprised and touched Meg. She placed her hand on her heart. 'Brian, I am very honoured you would even seek my blessing. You have it with all my heart.'

Her brother let out a short laugh of relief as though he had been apprehensive of her answer, and then winced as pain shot through his jaw. 'Thank you, Meg.'

'Now, Meg sat forward on her chair. 'Tell me all about how it happened.'

☙❧

'… I could talk about her all day, and I probably will,' Brian laughed. He had been gushing over his sweetheart for over an hour. 'But Meg, I would really like

142

you to tell me what is bothering you.'

Meg stared at her brother then shook her head. 'I do not think you would understand.'

'Try me, Meg,' he pleaded. 'I do not like to see you so withdrawn.'

Meg stood up and paced in front of the fireplace. 'Brian, I know what you will say, so there is no point in telling you.'

Brian rose and went to her, clasping her shoulders. He looked into her eyes. 'Please, Meg. Let me help you.'

Meg sighed, although it sounded more like a groan. 'It is just …' she had trouble finding the words. 'What has been on my mind … that is … what has me in confusion … well … Brian … I think I am falling in love …'

Brian's face brightened in excitement.

'… with Mister Fordham.'

Her brother's face fell as the words sank in. 'Fordham?'

She nodded.

'Meg, I thought you had gotten over that infatuation.' He put a hand to his tender mouth. 'You wrote me recently that he tried to carry on a flirtation with you. In your letter you assured me you were not fooled by him. You know what kind of man he is. What has happened since?'

Meg shrugged. 'It is hard to explain,' she said. 'I convinced him his advances were not welcome and we agreed to be friends.'

'Friends?'

'He is very good company. He is excessively diverting. We have spent quite a lot of time together in the past month or so, always with the children or the Sainsburys. But the more I know him, the more I like him.'

'So, he has won you over, has he?' Brian gritted, clearly suspicious.

'Brian, it is not like that,' Meg explained. 'Jack has not tried to flirt with me or flatter me in the least for weeks. He pays me no special attention. We have just been friends, and that is all. I have fallen in love with who he is, not his romantic behaviour.'

'Do you know who he is?'

'I know more than some,' she replied. 'Jack is everything I could ever want in a man.'

Brian looked exasperated. 'You want a rake? You want a devout pagan?'

Meg sighed. 'No,' she acknowledged. 'I do not want those things.' She raised her voice again. 'But I think you may judge him too harshly.'

Brian stared at her, eyes wide in incredulity. 'I cannot believe what I am hearing. You have seen his conduct with women firsthand.'

Meg lowered her eyes. 'I know he is a dreadful flirt, but I do not believe he is completely dissolute. *And* he has been attending church with me.'

'Meg, you know that does not mean anything,' Brian's voice held a note of pleading. 'Fordham would do anything to turn a girl's head.'

Meg wrung her hands and paced again. 'I know he is not there for God, Brian. But he *is* hearing the Word and that gives me hope.'

'You cannot base a relationship on that. You have no guarantees. Please Meg, do not tell me you are serious about this man.'

'You know,' Meg gave vent to her pain. 'I watched you and Katherine together yesterday, so obviously happy together. You make it look so easy and uncomplicated. Why can't I have that? Why can I not just fall in love and get married? Is that too much to ask? Jack and I would be so perfect together.'

Meg looked at her brother whose face had filled with anguish, and she pressed her lips together. 'I am sorry, Brian. I speak as though I am about to throw myself at Jack, and you are afraid for my future. Well, I have no intentions of ever putting action to my words. I just need to unburden myself. The problem is … how can I overcome these emotions? How can I put it behind me when every moment I want to be with him? If Jack were a Believer, I would marry him in a heartbeat. Brian, what am I going to do?'

Brian remained quiet for a long while, deep in thought. Meg returned to her sofa, leaned her head back and closed her eyes. Eventually her brother spoke again. 'I perceive you really do love him,' he said, 'though I am at a loss to know what you see in him.'

Meg was grateful he made an effort to understand. She wished she could tell him about the orphanage and Jack's generosity with homeless children.

Alas, all Brian knew of Jack was he cared little for anything but his clothes and the pretty ladies around him.

'The Jack Fordham you know and the Jack Fordham I know are two different people,' Meg told him.

Brian raised one eyebrow. 'That does not improve my opinion of him.'

'I understand that,' Meg conceded. 'But I believe his pretence is born of fear, not of wicked design.'

Brian's brow furrowed. 'What possibly could a man like Jack Fordham be afraid of? He has everything one could ever want — looks, charm, money, skills — he has no enemies. He has more security than anyone I know?'

'You speak of physical things, Brian. Perhaps his fear is emotional or spiritual.'

'Humph. I have never seen Jack Fordham anything but calm and controlled. They say he is heartless.'

'Heartless is one thing he most certainly is not. Brian, you know I have struggled with my feelings for Jack since the beginning. I know what he is. But, despite his faults, I feel drawn to him. He has virtues I cannot begin to tell you about. You would never understand unless you knew him like I do.

'But, enough about that. What I must do now, is figure out how to put those feelings aside and focus on a future without Jack Fordham in it. Brian, how am I to forget him when I am forced to see him so frequently?'

Brian looked at her, his eyes soft with compassion. 'Right now, I cannot answer you. But I *can* see now why you have been so distracted and confused. Give me some time to think and rest this sorry mouth of mine. Then, we can try to answer your questions.'

Meg agreed to a break from such a serious conversation, and she returned to the kitchen for a small luncheon. Brian declined any food but contented himself with a cup of lukewarm tea.

Later that afternoon, they spent time talking about her situation again.

'I have tried to put myself in your shoes,' Brian told her. 'If Katherine were not a believer or had a ruined reputation, I confess I would find it hard to give her up. I can well understand the weight of your struggle.'

'Thank you, Brian,' she replied. 'Your understanding gives me some comfort at least.'

'I still cannot comprehend how you have fallen for Fordham ...'

'As I mentioned ...'

'Yes, yes. You know him better. But we must find a solution.'

Brian encouraged her over and over and reminded her that a relationship with Jack would most likely end in pain. They were headed on separate spiritual paths. He read to her from the Bible reminding her why God wanted her to choose a better life.

'Meg,' he explained, 'In the Old Testament, God forbade the Israelites from intermarrying with foreigners.' He thumbed through the pages of his Bible. 'Here it is. Deuteronomy chapter seven, verse three. *Neither shalt thou make marriages with them; thy daughter thou shalt not give unto his son, nor his daughter shalt though take unto thy son. For they will turn away thy son from following me, that they may serve other gods.* God knows in an intimate relationship like marriage, one is influenced by the other. Jack would only lead you away from everything you believe in.'

'I know, Brian,' Meg nodded. 'Keep talking though, I need to hear it again.'

'You can see instances where the Israelites did not obey, and it did not turn out well for them. Think of Solomon. He married, how many women?' he paused to turn the pages of his Bible again. 'Ah, yes, seven hundred wives and three hundred concubines. It says here they were all foreigners and they *turned away his heart after other gods: and his heart was not perfect with the LORD his God, as was the heart of David his father.* Further on it says: *And the LORD was angry with Solomon.* As a result, Israel split into two kingdoms, and nothing was ever the same again.

'Remember, this is the Old Testament,' he added. 'Today we have the grace of Jesus through the cross. We can be forgiven for our mistakes, but it still grieves God when we drift away from him. And it would happen, even if only gradually.

'The kingdom of God and the kingdom of this world do not mix. You would be pulled in opposite directions which would only cause dissent. In Romans 8:5, it says: *For they that are after the flesh do mind the things of the flesh; but they that are after the Spirit the things of the Spirit.* It would either drive you apart, or one of you would give in, and the Bible is very clear about which it is likely to be.

'Meg, I cannot imagine having to turn away from my love for Miss Montgomery. It would be the hardest thing in the world to do. But it is something you must do. There is someone for you; someone who is, by far, better than Jack Fordham.'

Meg let his words sink in. Her brother was right, of course. She already knew everything he said, but his words strengthened her. 'Pray with me, Brian,' she said, determined to make the right decisions and put her desire for Jack to rest.

Chapter Twenty-two

Brian and Meg spent time praying for each other that afternoon, and then Meg spent the rest of the day reading chapter after chapter in her Bible. Every now and then she would stop and pray some more and then continue with her reading.

The next morning, she awoke with her spirits uplifted and strong enough to conquer any difficulty. The bounce returned to her step and her smile was never far from her lips. She greeted her brother cheerfully at breakfast and he seemed relieved see her back to her normal self.

'Brian,' she said in between mouthfuls of oats, 'Thank you for making me stay here with you. It has done me the world of good. My mind is clear, and I am able to focus again. I must have just needed to have my big brother's encouragement and some time alone with the Lord.'

Brian gave her a warm smile. 'You are very welcome, my dear,' he said. 'And if you begin to struggle in this way again, come to me at once.'

'Thank you, Brian, but I think I will be all right, now I have my priorities back in order. How is your tooth this morning?'

'There is a great deal less pain today, of which I am thankful. I find myself rather hungry this morning.' He grinned.

Having eaten, Meg curled up in the parlour and returned to reading more of the Scriptures. Brian left her to her quiet time and busied himself making a few repairs to his house. He had a maid who helped with the domestic work, but fixing broken chairs and the like were his responsibility. Thus occupied, the two remained until they heard a knock at the front door.

The maid opened the door and presently ushered Mr Roderick into the parlour where Meg reclined. She was surprised to see him there but greeted him amiably. 'Mister Roderick, I did not expect to see you?'

Roderick bowed deeply. 'Yes, I called on you yesterday at Sainsbury Stud, but Missus Sainsbury informed me of your convalescence here in town. I do hope I find you well.'

'Yes, yes,' Meg smiled at him. 'I am quite all right.'

'You are very lucky,' Mr Roderick said gravely. 'Some people take weeks to recover from their illnesses. I, for one, find once a bout of sickness takes hold of me, it simply refuses to let me go.'

Meg chuckled at his melodramatic nature. 'But you are mistaken, Mister Roderick. I was not ill. I merely suffered from a bout of nostalgia.'

Brian entered the room at that moment. 'Ah, Roderick, it is you,' he greeted. 'Good to see you.' He went forward and shook the sullen man by the hand.

'I have come to call on your sister. I heard she was unwell, but now I see she is quite the opposite.' He turned to Meg. 'In fact, I would say you are aglow with health.'

'Do sit down, Roderick,' Brian instructed, 'and I shall have some tea brought in.'

Mr Roderick moved to a seat near Meg. 'Do not trouble yourself. I shall not stay above a few minutes.'

Brian joined them in another chair. Meg was thankful for his protective presence, even though Mr Roderick was not someone she feared.

Roderick eyed Meg's Bible sitting beside her. 'You have been reading your Bible, I see.'

'Yes,' she replied. 'I derive great comfort from the Scriptures.'

Mr Roderick nodded. 'As do I. I have been reading lately from the Psalms. They are a great source of encouragement.'

'Yes, indeed they are.' Meg's interest was stirred. She had never really heard Mr Roderick speak of spiritual matters before.

'I must confess,' he went on to say, 'I had been neglecting my religious obligations until I met you. My attendance in church was somewhat lacking. I have tried to put things right of late.'

Meg could not help but be impressed. 'I am so glad to hear you say that. Indeed, I was not sure, and I say this without contempt, whether you were a Believer at all.'

'I can assure you I am.'

'Good for you, sir,' Brian cheered.

'Thank you, Mister Wingrove,' Mr Roderick nodded to him.

When he left, Brian stayed in the parlour to talk with Meg.

'What are you thinking about, Meg?'

She turned her attention to him. 'I have just been pleasantly surprised by Mister Roderick.'

'How so?'

'I truly doubted whether he shared our faith. But this morning, he has proven me wrong.'

'What are his intentions where you are concerned?'

'I am not sure,' she answered honestly. 'Sometimes he pays me the most over-exaggerated compliments and I wonder if he is enamoured with me. He can be rather melodramatic, you know. And other times he behaves more like a friendly companion. He has not made any declaration, but he has said he wants to know me better.'

'Mmm,' Brian mumbled. 'It is unclear. But I am sure he will come around to it sooner or later.'

'I suppose so. Although, I do not find him very interesting, and no matter how courteous and attentive he is, I do not think I could accept his suit.'

'Mmm,' Brian murmured again, his thoughts drifting. 'You know. There is something familiar about him. I just cannot place it. I wonder if we have met before.'

Meg smiled. 'It is possible, I suppose.'

'Yes,' he mused and then slapped his thighs. 'Never mind, I am sure it will come to me directly.'

The day continued to pass in peace and harmony until another visitor arrived. Brian answered the knock at the door this time, to find the honourable Jonathon Fordham standing on the threshold, unshaven, with a tricorne hat tucked under his arm, and a cutlass sheathed in its scabbard hanging at his side. He wore sea-faring clothes and held an eye patch in one hand.

~∽∾

When Meg had not returned to his townhouse to go with Gwen and the children, Jack had inquired after her. Gwen informed him that Meg remained at her brother's as she was out of sorts. Knowing Meg was unhappy did queer things to Jack's heart. He wondered what could have upset her so. Did it have anything to do with him? He spent the next day racking his brain for a reason to call on her; a reason that did not appear to be romantically inspired.

His answer came early on Tuesday morning when he received a message from the vineyard. The wine was ready to be shipped and Mr North required his presence at the estate. Jack quickly formulated a plan. He would ask Meg to pass on a message to his family that he would be out of town for at least a week. He went on to devise a madcap idea that would cheer up the young governess and make her laugh.

That idea saw him arrive at Brian Wingrove's house dressed as he was. Jack glanced at the red-headed young man and seeing a suspicious frown form on Mr Wingrove's face, he spoke quickly and quietly. 'Mister Wingrove,' he bowed. 'I know we have not yet been formally introduced, but would you honour me by playing along with a little charade for a moment? I promise you, you shall not be harmed.'

Mr Wingrove seemed to scan him from head to foot, as if analysing him, but continued to frown at him. 'Fordham,' he acknowledged with contempt. 'What is the meaning of this?'

'All will become clear to you presently,' Jack assured him, still speaking in a loud whisper. 'Will you direct me to your sister?'

Mr Wingrove pressed his lips together, clearly of a mind give him a dressing down and send him on his way. The young man probably thought him impertinent on top of his rakish reputation. Thankfully, Mr Wingrove's curiosity won out, as he reluctantly he stepped aside to allow Jack to enter. Jack carefully donned the eye patch and the hat and withdrew the dangerously shining sword.

'I need you for my hostage,' Jack swiftly moved behind Mr Wingrove and grasped him around the shoulders. He held the cutlass in a threatening manner near the alarmed man's neck.

'This is a great piece of impertinence. How dare you …'

'I have no intention of injuring you, Mister Wingrove,' Jack whispered. 'It is all part of a theatrical display. Remain still and all will go well.'

'This is preposterous.'

'Quite,' Jack agreed. 'Where is she?'

'In there,' Mr Wingrove pointed to the parlour.

∾∾

Meg still had her focus on the Scriptures when the door knocker sounded. Believing this visitor would be for her brother, she did not move from her position where she reclined on a sofa. The next thing she knew, the door burst open and the vision that met her eyes alarmed her momentarily. A dangerous looking pirate held her brother at knife point. She jumped up and backed towards the fireplace.

'Right there lassie,' came a drawling, rough brogue. 'Hand over all yer gold and jewellery and pieces o' eight, or I'll slit yer brother's throat.'

Meg gasped and looked from the pirate's menacing face to her brother's, which instead of showing fear, only held distaste and contempt. Her eyes swerved back to the pirate, whose appearance at once became all too familiar.

Her sense of mischief was awakened, and she held back a chortle. She reached slowly behind her and took hold of the fire poker. With a graceful movement she drew the poker from its stand and brandished it in front of her like a sword. 'Unhand my brother, now, you blackguard.'

Jack's eyes flashed with amusement and regard. 'So, it's a fight ye be wanting?' he growled. 'Very well,' he roughly pushed Brian aside. He stepped towards Meg and swung the cutlass lightly.

Steel met iron and a gentle sparing match began. A few strokes in, however, and Brian called a halt. 'Not in my house, you don't,' he said sternly, probably worried about his furniture as much as her safety. After all, Jack held a real sword.

Jack and Meg fell apart, laughing. Brian looked from one to the other, his face a mask of incredulity. He shook his head. 'Why you two are naught but little children.' This set them off into more gales of laughter. 'And behaving quite badly too,' Brian added for good measure.

When Meg composed herself enough to speak, she looked at Jack. 'What harebrained scheme made you come here dressed as a pirate?'

Jack removed the hat and patch, sheathed the cutlass, and put it aside. 'Your young charges are convinced I should take up piracy after our adventure on Sunday, so I thought I would give it a try. Do you think I make a fearsome buccaneer?'

Meg erupted in giggles once again and then remembered her brother who still watched them in a daze. 'Poor Brian,' she said and looked back at Jack. 'What an introduction you have made yourself.'

'I beg pardon, sir,' Jack bowed. 'However, as you can see, it worked.'

Brian and Meg spoke at the same time, asking 'What worked?'

Jack paused, glancing from one to the other, and seemed to realise he had not given a reason for his appearance. 'Oh. Gwen informed me you were out of sorts. I thought you could use some cheering up.'

Meg's heart fluttered but she ignored it. 'How thoughtful of you. However, I am quite well.'

'And I am glad to hear it.'

Meg smiled. 'So, the Sainsburys think you should become an adventurer, do they?'

'Yes,' Jack replied. 'Shall I tell you about our sailing expedition?'

Meg settled down in her cosy chair. 'I am anxious to hear the tale. I am sure it is full of mishaps.'

'Shall I have some tea brought in?' Brian interjected, reminding Meg of his presence in the room.

'Yes, thank you Brian,' Meg acknowledged him and returned her attention to Jack who began to regale her with an exaggerated version of events as they took place that Sunday. It appeared PJ had almost gone overboard trying to catch a fish; Willy had attempted a mutiny and tried to take over the helm while Kitty had been content to watch the porpoises play around the hull of the yacht.

By the time the tea arrived, Meg had erupted in gales of laughter again and Jack also trembled with mirth as he tried to finish his story. Brian sat quietly, watching and listening, clearly unsure what to make of Jack.

❧

Neither Wingrove nor Meg was aware of how difficult it was for Jack to keep his guard down in front of a stranger. He had to remind himself that this was Meg's brother, and if he were to wed her, he would also have to win his approval. Nervous energy kept him moving and talking. He must seem a right dolt.

The three drank tea together, Wingrove eventually joining in the conversation which covered a broad range of topics. The afternoon passed quickly and when Jack looked at his timepiece the hour surprised him. 'I do apologise. I am sure I have overstayed my welcome. But I must speak of the main reason I came to see you.'

Meg lowered her gaze to her lap. Was that disappointment he'd seen?

'I am leaving for the vineyard tomorrow,' he told her. 'I shall be gone for at least a week. Would you inform Gwen and Philip I shall not be visiting this week and I shall see them when I return?'

'Certainly, I will,' Meg nodded.

'Give my love to the children as well.'

'Of course.'

'Well then,' he rose reluctantly. 'I shall bid you good-day.'

'Good-day, Fordham,' Wingrove shook his hand.

Jack took Meg's offered hand and bowed deeply. 'Until I return.'

⋙ ⋘

'I shall see you out,' Meg said impulsively, not wanting to be parted from him just yet.

'If you wish,' Jack replied and held out his arm.

Meg walked with him down the steps to his carriage.

'Your brother looks at me with distrust.'

Meg smiled. 'What do you expect, Jack? You know society thinks you are a philanderer. Well, the church thinks you are completely immoral.'

'Do *you* think I am any of those things?' Jack sounded serious.

'I have seen how you trifle with women, but I reserve my judgement.' There was more to his story, she was sure of that now.

'I see.'

'Forgive my brother. He is afraid you will try and break my heart.'

Jack turned to her as they reached his carriage. 'Alas,' he said with a smile that didn't quite reach his eyes. 'Your heart has a lock for which I could never find the key.'

Meg looked at him, carefully measuring her words. 'The key will be easily found by the right person.'

Their eyes locked momentarily and then Jack looked away. 'Just so you know,' he said, placing his pirate disguise in the vehicle, 'I have never set out to break any girl's heart.'

'Why is it you have never married, then?'

Jack drew in a deep breath and let it out again. 'I ... I guess — I ... don't ...'

Meg searched his eyes and saw a hidden pain in them. 'Oh, Jack. She must have hurt you very deeply,' she said in a compassionate murmur.

Jack's gaze shifted away from her. He coughed, straightened his shoulders, and when he turned back to her, she could see his walls were back up.

155

'I have no idea what you are talking about,' he said with his familiar drawl. 'I shall see you in a week or two. Good-day, Meg.' With that he swung into the carriage and drove away, leaving Meg standing thoughtfully by the side of the road until the retreating vehicle turned out of sight.

Chapter Twenty-three

'Are you all right?' Brian asked her as soon as she came back inside.

'Yes,' Meg replied though her thoughts were still with Jack and what he'd almost admitted.

'Fordham is certainly not what I expected.'

'He is a very good friend.'

Brian walked over to the mantel and leaned against it. 'As you said, he does not appear to be dangling after you. He does not behave like an enamoured suitor at all.'

'Which is a good thing, do you not agree?'

'I begin to see the struggle which you face.'

Meg shrugged. 'It is of no consequence now,' she sighed. 'My path is laid out before me, and it is one that does not contain Mister Jack Fordham.'

⇠⇢

Jack so occupied himself with preparing for his trip into the country, he had no time to reflect on his conversation with Meg until he sat astride his horse early the following morning on his way to the vineyard. With nothing to do but breathe the fresh air and admire the landscape, his thoughts quickly turned to the lovely blonde.

Meg had given him a very clear message yesterday which answered the question that had been occupying his mind of late; had his scheme of showing her the orphanage worked? While standing by his carriage she had told him the right person would be able to unlock her heart without any difficulty. This evidently meant he was neither the 'right person' nor had he won her heart.

Despite that, he felt closer to her than ever. Their friendship had deepened, or so he believed. He had been close to revealing his heart to her when she reminded him of Antoinette. Even after all these years, the memories of that season in France stung him and he forcefully pushed them from his mind.

There was no point in dwelling on the past, and he tried to focus on Meg. Since she had admitted her heart remained closed to him, he now had to decide whether he should admit defeat and give up on her or keep on trying. Was she worth this much risk — making himself vulnerable again and opening himself to betrayal? He was on dangerous ground as far as his heart was concerned. After a great deal of thought, he decided the stakes were too high. If he bared his soul, there was no guarantee she would accept his hand. Besides, it had been hopelessly uncomfortable revealing even a few of his deeper thoughts. He would leave things as they were and remain her loyal friend.

❧❧

The sun shone as it did almost every spring day and the air was fresh and crisp as Brian drove Meg home. She was happy and ready to return to the Sainsbury farm. Her strength had returned, and she was at peace once again. Brian said he was very proud of her for the stand she had taken. He knew she had struggled with her decision and yet she bore it with a smile.

Mary and Kitty ran to greet her when they drove into the yard. They met her with hugs and kisses as she descended from Brian's buggy. 'I have missed you so,' breathed Kitty.

Meg hugged her. 'I have missed you, too.'

The boys were still in school, so Meg had time to take her bags to her room and unpack. Brian stayed with them for dinner, but bid her farewell shortly afterward, having to be back in Sydney that night. Once she had waved him off, she went in search of Mrs Sainsbury whom she found in the parlour stitching embroidery.

'I have a message for you from Jack,' she told the older woman.

Mrs Sainsbury looked at her with surprise. 'You saw him?'

'Yes,' Meg glanced at the sideboard she stood by and swiped at an imaginary speck of dust. 'He called on me specifically to tell you he has been summoned to the vineyard. He left this morning and will not be back for a week at the least.'

Mrs Sainsbury looked at her for a moment and then went back to her embroidery. 'Thank you, Meg.'

'You are quite welcome.'

'I assume you are feeling better.'

Meg sat down in a nearby chair. 'Much better, Missus Sainsbury.'

'May I ask what troubled you?'

Meg waved a dismissing hand. 'Oh, I still grieve for my mother on occasion. I felt rather homesick.' It was half the truth, but Meg couldn't tell her about Jack. She changed the subject. 'Jack tells me the children's seafaring adventure was a complete success.'

Mrs Sainsbury grinned. 'I suppose he told you they have got a romantic notion in their heads their Uncle should take up piracy?'

Meg laughed. 'I dare say.' She remembered the costume Jack had worn.

'They are still talking about it. Mary regrets she did not go along, and the boys are constantly playing pirate games.'

'Speaking of the boys,' Meg interjected, 'I will go and fetch them from school.' She rose and went to the door. 'Thank you for allowing me to spend some time with Brian. It means so much to me.'

'You are welcome, Meg. You know you are just like family to us.'

Later that evening, after the children were in bed, the two women were seated in the parlour, enjoying a peaceful evening.

'What are you reading?' Gwen asked Meg, who was curled up by the fire with a book.

Meg looked up. 'It is a book Jack loaned me from his library.'

'Oh.' Gwen seemed surprised. 'Did he show you his collection?'

'He knows I love to read.'

'He has a fine library, has he not?'

'Yes, and quite comprehensive too,' Meg agreed. 'He has many volumes I would like to read.'

'Did you enjoy your stay at his house?'

Meg rolled her eyes. 'It was rather daunting to be surrounded by such affluence, I must say.'

'But you were comfortable?'

'Strangely, yes,' Meg answered thoughtfully. 'Jack is a very attentive host.'

Gwen smiled. 'Yes, he is one of the best men I know…aside from Mister Sainsbury, of course…and I do not say that just because he is my brother.'

'He is certainly full of surprises.'

'You speak of our visit to Mister Brown, of course,' Gwen interpreted. 'It is only a surprise to those who do not care enough to really get to know him.'

Meg did not reply, musing over Mrs Sainsbury's words.

'You and he have been quite sociable of late. Do you…like him?'

Oh dear. Gwen was fishing for something. How to lead her off? Meg stretched her smile wide. 'He is a very good friend, and wonderfully entertaining.'

Mrs Sainsbury's eyes sparkled. 'He will make someone an excellent husband one day.'

'I daresay he will,' Meg replied with equal mischief, 'but I pity the poor woman if he is to take up the buccaneering life, dragging her off to live among blackguards and savages.'

Both women erupted in giggles and Gwen did not pursue her point any longer. Much relieved, Meg returned to her book.

❧

Sunday came around very quickly, and Meg headed to church with Nellie. Mr Roderick attended as usual and Meg noticed he sang along to the hymns, although reading the words from the psalm book. Reverend Kilpatrick's sermon captured her full attention, and it seemed like she had only been in the church for a few minutes when he gave the closing prayer, and it was time to go. Mr Roderick rode along side their buggy back to the Sainsbury's farm where he joined the family for their Sunday dinner. Mr and Mrs Sainsbury indulged him with polite chit-chat about the weather and the progression of Mr Roderick's new horses. The children were on their best behaviour, although Meg noticed they frequently suppressed their giggles over the way Mr Roderick dramatised every little detail in his conversation.

When all were satisfied with their meal, Mr Roderick suggested he and Meg take a walk in the surrounds of the house to enjoy the afternoon air filled with fragrant pollens. Meg agreed, and soon they strolled amongst blooming roses and other flowers imported from Mother England.

'Reverend Kilpatrick spoke well today, did he not?' Meg stopped to examine a pink blossom.

'Yes,' Roderick replied. 'It was very … inspiring.'

'I always find his sermons inspiring.'

'He is quite skilled in giving speeches,' Mr Roderick analysed. 'His message is very clear.'

Meg only smiled and continued to roam through the gardens.

Mr Roderick followed and resumed his conversation. 'Do you think you will ever return to England?' he changed the subject unexpectedly.

Meg thought about his question for a while before she answered. 'Part of me wishes to,' she replied after a time. 'There are so many cherished memories I have of home. But they were a long time ago now. I think it is best to look to the future. There are many opportunities here in Australia and I have made this my home. I do not think I will return.'

'It is well you do not wish to go back,' Mr Roderick nodded. 'How can one compare these wide spaces and this clean air with the cramped streets and fetid air of London?'

'You are quite right,' Meg laughed. 'They are completely different places.' Just like Mr Roderick and Jack were completely different people.

'I like to hear you laugh.'

Meg tensed, fearing he was about to become romantic.

'I like to laugh,' was all she could find to reply.

He rounded on her suddenly and clasped her hands in his. He looked earnestly into her eyes, putting her into a mild state of alarm. She was not prepared for this.

'I have received an invitation to a ball that is to be held in the assembly rooms of the Banks Inn. Would you do me the very great honour of accompanying me?'

Meg tried to hide her relief and smiled broadly. The thought of attending another ball excited her and Mr Roderick would be a very courteous companion, if not her first choice as an escort. He had become less distasteful too since she could now discuss her faith with him. 'I would be pleased to go with you.'

'You would?' Mr Roderick seemed both surprised and delighted, a smile lighting his normally serious face.

Meg chuckled softly again. 'Yes, Mister Roderick,' she assured him, 'I would.'

Chapter Twenty-four

Although Jack's journey to the vineyards gave him time to ponder over his situation with Meg, once he finally arrived at the estate, all thoughts of her were swept away as the demands of the business filled every moment. A slightly perturbed Roger North welcomed him on arrival. Indeed, he sighed with relief when Jack rode up on his mount. 'I am ever so glad to see you, Mister Fordham.'

'What is the trouble, North?'

North's mouth was set in a grim line. 'We're a little behind in getting the shipment ready. The natives 'ave decided to go walkabout. Sorry business or something, they said. So, we're shorthanded by 'alf a dozen men, just when we needed 'em most.'

'Hmm,' Jack frowned and rubbed his chin. Sorry business meant someone in their family had probably died and they had gone away to complete their rituals and mourn. The aboriginals would most likely be gone for a few weeks. 'Have the other men been working well?'

'Well enough. If they stay off the rum in the evenings, they're all right. They're sleeping it off today, tho'. They were drinking up plenty last night.'

Jack thought for a moment then dismounted and removed his riding gloves. 'Well, there is no time like the present. You have another pair of hands now; let us get this shipment ready.'

North stared at him. 'I don't mean to question yer judgement sir, but it be getting dark soon.'

Jack walked towards the workers' huts and his manager followed. 'Gather as many lanterns as you can find. We shall work by lamp light. If we are to get this load to the ship on time, we must work as many hours in the day as possible.'

'But the men … It's Sunday.' North began to protest.

'I shall take care of the men,' Jack replied confidently. 'There will be no trouble. Now, go and do as I have bid.'

Indeed, with large doses of strong, black coffee and a promised reward of doubled rations of rum once the shipment had left, Jack did get the men working without much opposition. It wasn't long before they were hard at work, where Jack kept them busy for a few hours before releasing them for the night. The men were sent back to their quarters with the instructions they were to be back in the cellars by dawn the following morning.

·∾·ᗒ·∾·

Meg awoke on Monday morning with an excitement she hadn't known for many weeks. She would attend another ball, and this time she would accompany a gentleman. A man who became a little more agreeable to her each time they were together. Still, it would have been delightful to attend a ball on the arm of a certain nonpareil, but, no, she could not allow her mind to stray that way.

She bounced out of bed and entered her daily chores with a song on her lips. Once she had driven the boys to school she went in search of Mrs Sainsbury, whom she found still lingering over her breakfast in the dining room.

'Good morning, Meg,' the lady of the house greeted with a smile.

'Good morning,' she dipped a curtsy. 'Before I begin the girls' lessons this morning, I wanted to ask you something.'

'Yes, my dear, what is it?' Mrs Sainsbury replied, taking a sip of tea.

'Mister Roderick has invited me to a ball on Saturday next, and I wondered if I could prevail upon you to lend me another of your dresses.'

Gwen set her teacup down and eyed Meg with a small frown. 'Mister Roderick, you say? So, things are progressing between you?'

'Perhaps,' Meg replied with a shrug.

Well, of course you may borrow one of my dresses,' Mrs Sainsbury twinkled at her, 'but I have a better idea.'

Meg looked at her quizzically.

'Remember that beautiful lilac silk?'

'Yes,' Meg hesitated.

'Well, Mrs Sainsbury sighed. 'Jack gave it to me.'

'Oh.'

'I think we should have a dress made for you.'

Meg gasped in surprise. 'That material is exquisite. You should have a dress made for yourself.'

Mrs Sainsbury shook her dark hair. 'I have plenty of gowns. Wouldn't you like one of your very own? You deserve it you know.'

Meg laughed uncertainly. 'I don't know what to say … but I do know a good dressmaker.'

Mrs Sainsbury clapped her hands. 'Good then, it is done.'

Before the end of the day the roll of silk was wrapped up and sent with an urgent message to Miss Katherine Montgomery. She drafted a note begging the seamstress to design and make her a gown for Saturday next and included her measurements to make this possible. She promised to call on her early on that morning to fit the dress and have any minor adjustments seen to.

As it turned out, Mary had been invited to the same ball by one of her young admirers. So, together the girls planned to travel into Sydney with Mr Sainsbury on Friday night, so they would be able to do some last-minute shopping for the event. They sent letters to their respective partners that they should be collected from the Hero of Waterloo Hotel on Saturday evening. With those arrangements made, all that remained was for them to wait for the week to be over.

❧❦

Jack, Roger North, and the labourers had worked solidly since Sunday night, only stopping for food and sleep. When Tuesday rolled around, the shipment was all but ready to depart. Huge wagons had been loaded with large numbers of kegs and bound with many yards of rope to make sure they were secure. The wagons were very high, and each barrel had to be lifted very carefully by ropes onto the bed of the dray, and then cautiously moved into position. They had to be sure none of the kegs would fall off on the rough road, lest it burst open, and the wine be lost.

Four strong draught horses were hitched up to each dray and finally the wagons were ready to leave. A cheer went up from the men. Jack was pleased with their hard work and issued them with their promised double ration of rum. From his seat, up in the saddle of his horse, he called out to the workers. 'Go and take a week's leave, all of you. Go and visit your families and friends. Come back fresh, next week to begin work again. Thank you for your efforts. I bid you good day.'

Jack pushed his leather hat onto his head and wheeled the horse around amidst another cheer from the men. He rode up to North. 'That week of leave includes you, my friend,' Jack grinned at him.

'Thank you, sir,' North smiled back.

'I shall be back to see how things are in a few months unless you send for me,' he told the foreman. 'Until then, North, I bid you good health.'

'God speed, sir,' North tipped his hat to Jack.

Jack nodded and gave a loud whistle, signalling the drivers of the three wagons to head out.

Travelling with the heavy-laden drays slowed down the journey considerably and it wasn't until late on Wednesday night the convoy arrived in Sydney Cove. Jack had ridden in front of the wagons, watching for bush rangers and deep ruts in the road. Fortunately, there were no bush rangers hiding out at present, and Jack carefully guided the drivers through the roughest parts of the track. Thus, they avoided any mishaps and successfully transported the wine without losing a single barrel.

Jack accompanied the shipment all the way to the harbour where he and the drivers bunked down for the night, one on each wagon, while one kept watch. They took turns sleeping and watching so no-one could try to thieve any of the kegs during the night.

The following morning, although exhausted from lack of sleep preceded by the long hours in the saddle, Jack went in search of the ship's owner he had engaged to transport his wine. It took him several hours to locate the seafarer, only to discover some other cargo was being loaded and he would have to wait longer.

Having this unexpected time on his hands, Jack found his thoughts once again drifting to a beautiful face with sparkling blue eyes. His heart leapt at the vision he saw in his mind's eye and at that moment a great longing to see her swept over him. It would be so refreshing after being around foul mouthed, labouring men this past week. He decided as soon as his duty was finished there, he would go and visit her. Eventually, just after luncheon, the captain of the ship gave Jack the go ahead and the men began loading his precious cargo onto the ship.

Jack kept a couple of barrels aside to sell to the local drinking establishments, hoping to create a strong local market for his produce. The rest would travel aboard the *Madeline,* which would depart for Melbourne in a few days. Once there, the wine would be transferred to another transport bound for England, where Jack's father would sell it.

Hoisting the kegs onto the deck of the ship and then lowering them into the hold was a slow and arduous task, and it wasn't until another night of limited sleep and another day of heavy labour that they completed the job. As the last barrel was safely and securely stored in the ship's hold, Jack looked up into the cloudless sky to see the sun beginning its slow descent towards the horizon.

Completely drained of strength and energy, Jack paid his hired men and dismissed them, thinking only of a long soak in a hot tub and the still and silent relaxation of a deep sleep. Miller was ready and waiting for him when he arrived at his town house. He had received word from Jack earlier in the day that he would be home.

Jack dragged his feet up the short flight of stairs and wearily took off his riding coat. Miller took the jacket. 'Good to see you home safely, sir.'

Jack managed a genuine, although sleepy smile. 'It is good to be home,' he replied. He sighed deeply as he took in the familiar and luxurious surroundings. Camping out in the bush, and sleeping by the harbour were not altogether bad, but they were nothing compared with the comforts of his home.

'Your supper is ready, your bath has been drawn and your bedchamber is prepared,' Miller informed him.

'Just so,' Jack slapped him on the back. 'What would I do without you?'

Miller grinned at such high praise.

'I am for the tub,' Jack said starting for the staircase. 'Have my supper served in my bedchamber. I do not wish to be disturbed until morning.'

'Yes, sir.'

Jack paused halfway up the staircase and turned. 'Oh, and Miller,' he added, one finger raised in the air as a thought came to him. 'I wish to breakfast early tomorrow. I am heading to Parramatta first thing.'

'As you wish, sir,' the servant bowed lightly.

'Have a horse ready, not Sally, she needs to rest. And put out my best riding clothes for me.'

'Yes, sir,' Miller nodded, 'Very good, sir.'

Jack turned again and continued up to his room, happily anticipating a visit with Meg.

☙◦❧

Meg and Mary settled into their room at the Hero of Waterloo Hotel, in Sydney. Once they had unpacked their small portmanteaux, they skipped downstairs to join Mr Sainsbury in the private dining room for supper.

As they sat together in the cosy room, Mr Sainsbury reminded the girls of the arrangements for the ball on the morrow. He would accompany Mary and her young gentleman as their chaperone, while Meg was left to travel alone with Mr Roderick. 'I think you are old enough to look after yourself, Meg,' Mr Sainsbury winked at her, although he looked rather serious. At twenty-seven, she was almost considered a spinster and therefore, not in need of a chaperone.

'I wonder if Uncle Jack will be there,' Mary remarked with a mischievous smile. 'He could keep an eye on you, Winnie.'

'Do you think I am that depraved I need to be watched?' Meg affected a scandalised face.

'He will most likely be there, though,' Mary continued. 'Don't you think so, Papa?'

'If he is back from the vineyard, I dare say he will,' Mr Sainsbury answered wryly, 'seeing he is the most sought-after bachelor in town.'

Meg chose not to comment. Part of her hoped Jack would be there. She had missed him dreadfully this past week and a half. Not a day had gone by without her having a thought she wished she could share with him or a humorous anecdote she knew he would enjoy. They were moments that could not be shared with Mr Roderick, as he rarely saw the funny side of anything.

On the other hand, seeing Jack might just stir up those unwanted sentiments again. Perhaps it would be better if he did not appear at the ball. It would be easier to tame her interest in him if this distance remained between them.

Meg shook thoughts of Jack Fordham from her mind and focused on her meal with Mr Sainsbury and Mary. 'We must not stay up too late tonight, Mary. We have an early appointment to keep tomorrow.'

'We have so much to do.' Mary's eyes shone.

'Well, I shall leave you ladies to your feminine preparations,' Mr Sainsbury said with a sigh. 'I am going to meet with my bank man.'

'How dull that sounds,' Mary told him.

Mr Sainsbury looked at her, and as he did on rare occasions, chuckled softly.

Chapter Twenty-five

True to his word, Jack was in the saddle and on his way to Sainsbury Stud soon after eight o'clock in the morning. He had slept like the dead, and awoke much refreshed, although his body ached from days on horseback and hard labour. As he rode, he gazed towards the horizon. The day had begun with clear, sunny skies, but there were now dark clouds forming in the distance and the wind began to pick up.

Jack nudged the horse into an easy canter, not wanting to get caught in a downpour. Despite the threatening weather, Jack's mood was light and cheerful. Every time he thought of Meg, his heart swelled with expectation. It suddenly occurred to him he had missed her. He realised with some surprise that instead of longing to see his nieces and nephews, the pretty governess was foremost in his mind. Had he become so attached to her? It was an alarming thought. It would not do. He refused to allow himself to become emotionally entangled with a woman. She was but a friend, he tried to remind himself, but another thought intruded on him. She was a friend who would make a very comfortable wife.

His heart thumped at the idea, and his throat became dry. However, he could not fathom why these sensations should take hold. Frustrated, he told himself that the sooner he saw Meg, the better. Her presence would banish this foolishness. His mind had been too free to roam while riding on the open road.

'I believe rain is on the way today,' Mr Sainsbury remarked over breakfast, once again in the cosy private dining room.

Mary pouted in an affected way. 'How dare the weather be so beastly, when I am in such high spirits.'

Meg laughed. 'Isn't it funny how one wishes it to rain only when one is sad?'

'Precisely.'

Mr Sainsbury merely shook his head. 'Feminine reasoning,' he commented, 'I shall never comprehend it.'

'Papa! Don't you ever get cross when the weather turns sour, and just when you expect to have a grand day?'

'Not at all, my love,' he answered with a shrug, picked up his napkin and dabbed at the corners of his mouth. 'The rain is very good for the gardens; it helps them to stay green.'

Mary looked sheepish. 'Yes, there is that I suppose. But could it not rain on another day than today?'

'Who are we to argue with Providence?' Mr Sainsbury rolled his eyes. 'I just wanted to make sure you young ladies are prepared in case it does rain. Take your coats along. Now, I shall leave you to your Grand Day, and I shall see you this afternoon.'

He had no sooner left the room when Mary, a little frustrated, said, 'Sometimes, I cannot talk sensibly with Papa.'

Meg tried not to laugh. 'Never mind Mary,' she said consolingly, 'Men think differently than we do. One day you will understand.'

'I do hope so.' Mary sighed.

'Now,' Meg said, rising from the table, 'Shall we call for a cab?'

⁎⁎⁎

An eternity had passed by the time Jack rode into the yard at Sainsbury Stud, or so it seemed. He had but one thought on his mind. Where would he find Meg at this time of the morning? Before he could contemplate the answer, three excited children burst from the house and ran towards him.

'Uncle Jack! Uncle Jack!'

Jack slid off his horse and hugged each one in turn.

'Do you have a present for me?' Kitty asked when he turned to her.

Jack crouched down to look her in the eyes. 'I have not had time to buy you anything, my sweet. I promise you next time I will bring you something special.'

Kitty broke into a huge smile. 'All right.' She hugged him again.

'Where is Mary?' Jack looked around, realising one of his young relatives was missing.

'She has gone into Sydney with Papa and ...' PJ answered him.

'They are going to a ball,' Kitty finished.

Jack looked at her with interest. 'Are they now?'

'Yes, she nodded. 'When I grow up, I shall go too.'

Trying to keep his focus on his niece, Jack said, 'And I am sure you will look just like a princess. You must promise to give your old Uncle Jack the first dance.'

Kitty's face lit up. 'I promise.'

Jack stroked her cheek and smiled affectionately at her, and then he straightened. 'Excuse me, children, I must go and see your Mama.'

ॐ

'It is good to see you again, Katherine,' Meg said warmly as the young lady welcomed them into her house. 'I would like you to meet one of my young charges, Miss Mary Sainsbury.'

'Good morning, Miss Sainsbury,' Katherine gave Mary a slight curtsey, 'I am honoured to make your acquaintance.'

'Pleased to meet you, Miss Montgomery.'

Katherine turned to Meg. 'I am sure you are eager to see your dress. That silk is so beautiful. I cannot wait to see what you think.'

Meg was intrigued. 'You make it sound wonderful. You must show me at once.'

Katherine giggled. 'Come this way, then.'

She led them into her sewing room where her mother fussed over her work. Meg scanned the room until her eyes fell on a wooden torso which had a magnificent gown adorning it. Meg gasped and heard Mary's sharp intake of air at the same time.

'Mother and I have worked ever so hard on this one. It is our best piece of work so far.'

'Why, it is…it is simply magnificent.' Meg circled around the dress, admiring every detail.

The gown was made primarily of the lilac silk. The bodice was embroidered with intricate patterns in a darker purple, interlaced with sparkling glass beads. Lace, dyed the same lilac colour, flowed from the cuffs, and adorned the throat. The skirt was full and dotted here and there with glass beads surrounded by a small, embroidered flower. The hem was trimmed with lace and satin ribbon that was a few shades darker. The rear of the dress was drawn up into a bustle and decorated with a large bow of wide satin ribbon in the same darker shade.

'We have also made a wrap for the coolness of the evening.' Katherine handed Meg a soft satin shawl. It was the same darker shade of purple as all the trimming on the dress and had glass beads in the shape of tear drops, dangling from the corners.

Meg still stared in amazement at the gown when Mary nudged her. 'Why don't you try it on?'

Meg came back to earth and nodded. 'Of course.'

Mary helped her out of her town dress, and then Katherine and her mother helped Meg put the ball gown on. They twisted the dress here and there, adjusted, and threaded a few pins into the material. At length they stood back and appraised their glowing customer. 'It shall do nicely,' Mrs Montgomery nodded.

'It shall do …?' Meg expostulated, 'Why it is incomparable. I don't know how to thank you.' She made a move to embrace the women, but they held her back.

'We need to make a few alterations,' the elder Montgomery said sternly, 'then you can do as you wish in this dress.'

Meg turned to Mary. 'So, what do you think?'

Mary narrowed her eyes at her governess. 'I think I am quite jealous, that is what I think.'

Meg laughed.

'I wish I had a dress like that.'

'And so you shall,' Meg told her still laughing, 'once you ask your father to have the Montgomerys make you one.'

Mary's face brightened. 'Of course.'

⤬

Jack found his sister in the parlour. 'Greetings dear sister,' he said cheerfully as he entered the room, pulling off his riding gloves.

'Jack.' Her face lit up with delight. She put her cross stitch aside and rose to embrace him. 'You look tired.'

'I have good reason to be.'

'The wine is ready, then?'

'Yes. We leave on the morrow.' Jack informed her. 'I have managed to bottle you some. I want you to have the first taste and see if you approve.'

Gwen clapped. 'We shall serve it with our dinner.'

She returned to her seat and Jack sat opposite her. 'I believe our young debutante is going to a ball tonight?'

'Yes,' Gwen replied. 'She and Meg both received invitations.'

Jack had not expected this and knew immediate frustration and disappointment. 'You say Meg is going as well?'

'She is accompanying Mister Roderick.' Gwen eyed him, no doubt trying to read him. 'Why do you ask?'

Jack forced a nonchalant shrug. 'I had wished to discuss something with her, that is all.'

'It must have been important for you to have come all this way when you are already exhausted and must be back in Port Jackson by tomorrow morning?'

She raised her eyebrows at him, insinuating.

Jack looked at her, keeping his face a mask. 'I have not seen my family in over a week,' he tried to convince her, 'And I will probably not see you again for at least another two weeks. Do you blame me for wishing to spend these precious few hours with you? My discussion with Meg was not of great significance, but I had thought to include it in this visit.'

Gwen grinned at him, a mischievous twinkle in her eyes. 'I do not believe you. I think you missed our governess so much you had to rush out here and see her before you board your ship tomorrow.

Jack screwed up his face at her. 'That is absurd. Why should I do such a foolish thing?'

'Because ... you are in love with her.' Gwen declared. 'Admit it.'

Jack scowled at her. 'I will do no such thing. You women are always full of fanciful, romantic notions.'

Gwen merely grinned at him. 'She has won your heart.'

Jack rolled his eyes in contempt. 'Come now Gwendolyn. You and I both know I do not possess a heart.'

Her eyes narrowed. 'You had better not be toying with her, Jack. If you ruin her, I will never forgive you.'

Jack's irritation grew, but he shrugged indifferently. 'That is rather ungracious of you, sister dear. Why would I wish to ruin Meg?'

Gwen threw her hands in the air and snapped at him. 'You have a history of it, in case you have forgotten.'

'Will I never outlive that accursed event?' Jack was exasperated.

Gwen looked at him with shock and even disgust. 'You abducted a girl! Have you no shame?'

'I never abducted her!' Jack thundered, no longer able to restrain his anger. 'You have all of you damned me without once asking for my version.'

Gwen gasped and fell silent, shocked.

'What — what are you saying?' she seemed confused.

Jack paced across the room and back again before he answered resentfully. 'The only thing I am guilty of is being too green to recognise the warning signs.'

Gwen searched his eyes. 'Jack, what are you talking about? What warning signs?'

He raised his eyes to the ceiling in frustration. 'There is no use dragging it up now. It was too long ago.'

'But Jack,' Gwen insisted, 'if there is something I should know …'

'Will it make any difference now? My reputation has been shattered beyond repair.'

'Your reputation has never bothered you before …'

'It *always* bothered me!'

Gwen stared at him, her mouth open to speak, but she shook her head. 'This is getting us nowhere. Let us go back to the beginning. What happened in France?'

Jack groaned. He knew Gwen would not let him go without hearing the whole, now he had let the truth slip out. He ran his hand through his hair and sank into the nearest chair.

'I was too young,' he began, 'and naively fell in love with Antoinette. We had a whirl-wind love affair, and my foolish passion ruled my head. Antoinette had me believe her father was a tyrant and was forcing her into marriage with a man she despised. She insisted we keep our rendezvous a secret. I should have known then something was amiss. But, like an imbecile, I let her lead me around like a foolish puppy. At the height of our madness, Antoinette gulled me into that harebrained scheme of eloping. I had no desire to run away in secret; I wanted to marry her properly, but she swayed me with her tears.'

Jack paused to pour himself a glass of water, while Gwen merely looked at him in dismay.

'The rest,' he continued, 'you already know. My uncle and her father overtook us on the road and "rescued" her. I was quickly and quietly sent back to England.'

'Papa said it was two years before he found out,' Gwen spoke softly. 'Why did you not say anything to him? You know he would have taken your word.'

Jack looked at the ground in obvious pain and regret. 'I know he would have … then. But the Compte de Louise begged me to remain silent to protect his daughter. I now suspect she had duped other young mooncalfs before me. But at the time, I ... I loved her Gwen, beyond all reason,' he looked up and knew she could see the brokenness in his eyes. 'How could I dishonour the woman I worshipped?'

'But it was she who accused you was it not?'

'Little did I know she would turn on me.' His voice shook with years of buried pain. 'The lies she told ... but by the time Papa heard of it, any explanation I had fell on deaf ears, and he sent me away.'

Gwen sat back, aghast. 'Why did you never seek to set us right?' she questioned. 'Indeed, you have done naught but prove your waywardness since you came to Australia.'

'Your expectations were so high,' Jack replied with biting sarcasm. 'I could not bear to disappoint you.'

Gwen sat back, stung. He knew his words hurt her, but it was time she heard them.

'In faith,' Jack continued, 'I had thought to start afresh here, but by the time I came to Sydney, my reputation as a lecher was already set in stone.'

'How could it be so?'

Jack sighed impatiently. 'How many of your confidants did you unburden your cares upon; worries about your poor errant brother, banished to the colonies?'

She opened her mouth and closed it again, colour rising to her face. 'I didn't tell anyone the reason, I swear ...'

Jack eyed her seriously. 'No. But perhaps enough to set curious tongues wagging. A few inquisitive letters to Mother England would have sealed my fate.'

Gwen shook her head defiantly, although flushed with shame. 'You cannot lay the blame at my feet, surely? Your behaviour has not been above reproach. You persist in your flirtations to this day.'

When Jack spoke, his voice shook with suppressed hostility. 'Do you know how many fathers warned me away from their daughters? Can you imagine the injustice I felt? The only women who will tolerate my reputation are desperate fortune hunters whom I cannot abide, or those who are well seasoned in the art of seduction. I indulge in light flirtation because there *is* nothing else. Any chance of happiness I might have had was ruined by Antoinette.'

Suddenly, understanding dawned in Gwen's eyes and her lips trembled. 'You have treated every lady since as though she were Antoinette all over again.'

Jack swallowed and tried to maintain his composure. He stood up and went to the fireplace staring into the flames. 'Have I been mistaken? Has not every woman proved to be shallow, insincere, and selfish?'

Gwen rose and touched his arm. 'Until now, perhaps,' she agreed softly. 'But Meg is different. She is very special. Please do not play your games with her. If you hurt her, I will …'

Jack shrugged her off. 'I do not know why you keep bringing Meg into this,' he said, annoyed. 'I am too wise to become a lovesick sap-skull again. Not when I am still being punished for the first time.'

Tears appeared in Gwen's eyes at his vehemence. The truth had wounded her. 'Our family has done you a great wrong,' her voice broke. 'I am so sorry. I had assumed Papa's letter contained the whole truth, but if I'd known any different … I would never …'

Jack could not find any compassion for her in that moment, his anger was still too raw. 'Do not fret, my dear sister.' His voice sounded overly harsh. 'I blame myself for being fool enough to fall in love, and for being naïve enough to believe my family would rise to my defence.'

Gwen gasped in dismay. 'Jack …' she pleaded, tears spilling down her cheeks.

'I shall see you when I return from Melbourne.' He said stiffly and brushed past her to the door.

Chapter Twenty-six

Jack pushed his horse at a gallop for a long time, furious at himself for becoming emotional and speaking of things he'd promised himself he would take to the grave. Why could he not maintain control over his sentiments like he had for the past ten years? He had poured out resentment and accusation on his sister. Until that moment, he had been unaware of the depth of his bitterness. He had even left without saying goodbye to his nephews and niece. He never behaved with such ill manners. What had gotten into him?

Something within him had been unaccountably altered. In the past few weeks, he had begun to experience disturbing emotions, and for some infuriating reason, they would not be suppressed. His reputation troubled him more than usual. The judgement of others aggravated him. Meg's opinion of him had become too important. And now he had spoken of Antoinette, the betrayal refused to be buried again. He found it more and more difficult to remain aloof.

Gwen was convinced he was in love with Meg. He quaked at the thought. 'I am not in love with her,' he told himself defiantly. Love was for ignorant clods. Why should he take note of Gwen anyway, she had abandoned him to the injustice he suffered long ago. Jack made a contemptuous sound, much like a snort. And to suggest she wouldn't forgive him if Meg's feelings were hurt, well, it seemed blood was not thicker than water after all. 'Insufferable!' he urged the horse to gallop faster to help him ease his irritation.

Meg and Mary spent the morning pleasantly wandering the streets in Sydney, shopping for all the little accessories one needed for a ball. Among their purchases were hair pins and adornments, gloves, hose, and shoes.

By the time they returned to the hotel, the clock struck the lunch hour, so they sat in the hotel's dining room and ordered a meal. Meg's gown had arrived while they were shopping, and the owner of the establishment had seen that it was stored in her room. As soon as they had filled their stomachs, the girls hurried to their room to gaze at the stunning dress again.

'You are going to look *so* lovely tonight,' Mary, awestruck, fingered the delicate lace.

Meg tried to brush her compliment aside. 'So will you, my dear.'

Mary was quiet for a moment, her head to one side. Then she pouted, and a small frown creased her pretty brow. 'It is a pity such a gown should be wasted on Mister Roderick.' She finished this comment with a roll of her eyes.

'Mary! That is a wicked thing to say. Mr Roderick is a fine, upstanding gentleman.'

Mary looked sheepish, but not repentant. 'I just think you would look better on a more dashing man's arm. Just think what a stir you would cause.'

Meg busied herself unwrapping her purchases. 'I am not interested in causing a stir.'

Mary flopped down onto her bed. 'But just imagine,' she sounded dreamy. 'What would it be like to enter on the arm of ... say ... Uncle Jack, for instance?'

Meg froze for a moment, and then began unwrapping with somewhat more energy.

'Every head would turn and gasp. Why, you would be a sensation, the talk of the town.'

Meg straightened and eyed Mary severely. 'That is enough nonsense from you, Miss. I cannot fathom what would be so wonderful about having

180

the entire assembly gawking at me. I would much rather be unseen with the common folk. Now, I think you and I should have a short nap before we prepare for our evening's entertainment.'

Mary did as she was bid, removing her dress, and hopping into bed in her unmentionables. Meg did the same, although her emotions were in a little turmoil. Mary's fairy tale ideas had drawn pictures in her own mind; pictures she did not want to dwell upon. Even though she had denied it, she knew it would be wonderful to be escorted to a ball by Jack, to know she belonged to him and to see his pride at having her on his arm. Meg pushed these fanciful illusions aside, not without a little sadness. It was not meant to be, and the sooner she stopped pining after Jack Fordham, the better.

As she lay on her bed, she forced herself to think about the character traits she appreciated in Gilbert Roderick. She must not go to the ball still dwelling on Jack. It would not be right to be in the company of one man while yearning to be with another. 'Pull yourself together, Margaret Wingrove,' she whispered forcefully to herself and concentrated on going to sleep.

By the time Jack reined in at the front of his house, it was late in the afternoon. He was worn out and dripping wet, having been caught in the promised downpour. Still churning with volatile emotion, he took Juniper down to the beach for a run, careless of his saturated clothes.

The deep green waves seemed to churn as much as his thoughts did. Juniper rushed back and forth into the foam, in his element, barking at the white tips as though they were the enemy. The wind blew right through Jack's wet clothes, and it wasn't long before he was chilled to the bone. He realised he had not eaten since breakfast and if he didn't get dry, he would make himself ill. He called Juniper to him and headed back to the house.

'Miller,' he called as he entered. 'I need food. I need warm bath and dry clothes.'

'Yes, sir,' the valet answered as he appeared from the back of the house, holding a vase he had been polishing. He almost dropped the vase when he saw Jack's condition. 'Mister Fordham, are you well?'

Jack realised he had a scowl on his face and forced a smile. 'I am fine,' he said gruffly. 'Or will be, once I am warm and dry.'

'I will see to your bath at once, sir,' Miller said quickly and hurried off upstairs, leaving the vase on the hall table.

Jack rid himself of his riding coat and stalked into his study, where he knew Miller always kept a fire burning. He stood in front of it, allowing the heat to thaw his chilled bones and an incredible weariness swept over him. 'That is what is wrong with me,' Jack sighed. 'I am far too fatigued.' He turned and dragged himself up to his bed chamber where Miller had just poured the last kettle of water into the tub.

'That was swiftly done,' Jack was grateful.

'I commandeered the hot water from the cook. She can always boil more.'

'Good thinking, man.' Jack peeled off his damp clothes.

Jack's eyes began to droop minutes after getting in the tub. He lifted his heavy limbs out of the warm water, wrapped himself in a robe and lay down on his bed. He would eat soon, he just needed a little rest.

❦

Refreshed after their nap, the two young ladies began their lengthy toilet so they would be ready for the ball in time. Philip had returned from his appointments and after calling on the girls to see if their day was indeed 'Grand', had gone to rest and read a newspaper in his room. Meg and Mary spent hours fussing over each other's hair, curling, pinning, and adorning with fastidious care until they were both satisfied with the effects. Mary fixed a fashionable patch to her left temple, and Meg fixed on one high on her right cheek.

Amidst giggles and squeals they sprayed scent on each other and tightened each other's stays and at long last they were ready to put their gowns on. However, they had ordered a light supper to be served in their room, so they covered themselves with dressing gowns and sat down to eat. Flushed with excitement they both chatted incessantly while they picked at their food. Neither was particularly interested in eating. They just wanted to be dressed and on their way to the ball where they could spend a fairy tale evening.

When Mr Roderick and Mr Greenfeld, Mary's admirer, were announced as waiting below, the girls squealed and rushed to put on their gowns. Meg helped Mary into hers and fastened the buttons at her back. Mary spun around and examined her reflection in the mirror. 'You look perfectly adorable,' Meg announced. 'Now help me into mine.'

Once the ball dress was on and fastened, Meg also studied herself in the mirror and could not help but smile. This was indeed a magical gown.

Mary gasped. 'You look even more stunning than I imagined you would. I am sure every man at the ball tonight will be looking at you.'

'Nonsense,' Meg frowned, but then immediately smiled. 'Shall we go?'

Mary nodded, her eyes shining, and hooked her arm through her governess'.

Mr Roderick and Mr Greenfeld were seated in the parlour of the establishment, waiting expectantly for their respective partners to descend. Following closely behind Mary, Meg noticed Mr Greenfield's adoring gaze, and knew the poor youth had become infatuated beyond all sensibility. She smiled, her lips quivering with laughter. Then she noticed Mr Roderick, who appeared to be likewise entranced, for his eyes were frozen upon her. His mouth moved but no words came forth. Meg resisted the urge to roll her eyes, and instead forced a welcoming smile to her mouth. 'Good evening, Mister Roderick.'

'G … good evening, Miss … Miss Wingrove,' he stuttered, bowing deeply over her hand. 'May I have the honour?' he held out his arm for Meg to escort her to his carriage.

Meg looked over to see Mr Sainsbury joining the young couple as they headed for the front entrance. She slipped her hand into the crook of Mr Roderick's arm, and he led her outside.

ʆʢ

The Banks Inn had become a very popular place to hold assemblies since it opened two years earlier. The gardens were magnificent and were a favourite for romantic strolls and scenic picnics. On this evening, inside the grand ballroom, it seemed a thousand lights and chandeliers burned, and the enormous hall was bathed in brilliant light. Fires blazed in hearths at either end of the room, and there was a platform on one side of the hall. Seated on the platform was a small orchestra, who filled the air with resonant music. On either side of the stage, a wide staircase wound gently up towards a balcony which overlooked the hall.

Meg gazed around at the assembly and the ball room into which they entered with a renewed sense of wonderment. She had been mesmerised at Governor Gipps' ball but was even more so now. Mr Roderick must have noticed her admiration because he leaned in close and said, 'A magnificent piece of architecture, don't you think?'

'Yes, it is wonderful,' Meg replied earnestly.

'I believe it took some years to build and they came across many obstacles in the course of construction,' Mr Roderick told her in confidential tones.

'I am sure it was a difficult task,' Meg replied, not really interested in the details of building hotels.

'You see that platform?' he pointed.

'Yes.'

'I'll lay you odds it is made of pure marble.'

Meg merely nodded.

'And the balustrade,' he pointed again to the staircase, 'African Mahogany.'

'From Africa, you say,' Meg repeated, attempting to show appreciation for these details.

'Yes. And I dare say,' Mr Roderick continued pointing around the room, 'those figurines are artefacts from an island of savages.'

Meg shuddered, not wishing to speak of savages, although the figurines did look rather sinister if one looked hard enough. 'Mister Roderick,' she tried to distract him, 'Would you be so kind as to procure me a drink?'

'Of course, Miss Wingrove,' he said with a small bow. 'Forgive me. I am forgetting my duties.'

Mr Roderick took her coat and went off in search of the cloak room and the refreshments table, leaving Meg to enjoy a few moments relief from his dull conversation. All the way to the ball he had explained to her the importance of having a tightly sprung carriage, interspersed with various overly dramatic compliments on her ensemble.

With regret, Meg realised the only time she enjoyed their conversations was when they discussed matters of faith. But it was not realistic to talk about doctrine all the time, and it would be selfish to expect it. He was a very attentive and thoughtful man. She should be grateful for the blessings in her life.

Meg turned her attention to Mary, already surrounded by many admirers, each trying to claim a moment with her. Mr Greenfeld hovered closely by, guarding his prize, and trying to stake his territory. Meg noticed that Mr Sainsbury stood not too far away, keeping one eye on her while conversing with a gentleman friend.

Meg had not been noticed by anyone yet. She stood in the shadows of the entrance, waiting for Mr Roderick to return, and scanned the room for anyone else she knew. But apart from a few new acquaintances, she recognised no-one. She knew a small stab of disappointment but pushed it aside as Mr Roderick returned with a glass of punch for her. She flashed him a large smile and allowed him to lead her into the throng.

❧

When Jack awoke, darkness surrounded him. He still did not feel fully rejuvenated, but the sleep had taken the worst of his fatigue away. He sat up with a start. Meg was at that ball — with Roderick. The urge to see her again took hold of him and he rang his bell furiously. Had Meg formed an attachment to Roderick? A strange uncertainty crept into the pit of his stomach. 'What in God's name is wrong with me?'

When Miller appeared a few moments later, he found Jack already searching through his wardrobe.

'How may I serve you, sir?'

'Did I receive an invitation to a ball that is being held this evening?'

'I believe so, yes,' the servant replied. 'You have not seen it yet, I expect. It arrived while you were away.'

'I have decided to go,' Jack ran agitated hands through his hair.

Miller stared at his master, unmoving, questions all over his face.

'What are you gaping at, man?' Jack growled. 'Help me dress.'

'Yes, sir,' Miller set to work.

Jack refused to wear almost everything that his manservant suggested, nothing being good enough for that evening.

'May I speak candidly, sir?' the valet asked eventually.

'What is it, Miller?'

'You do not seem yourself, Mister Fordham,' he suggested. 'Are you ill? Do you have a fever?'

Jack stared at him momentarily and then threw his head back and laughed. 'As a matter of fact, I do, of sorts.'

Miller continued in his boldness. 'Do you think it is wise to venture out in such a state?'

Jack eyed him again, weighing up his words. 'You are right,' he said simply. 'This will not do. Choose me an ensemble and I will accept your judgement. I will return presently.'

Jack strode out of the wardrobe and out to the balcony. With his hands clenched around the railing and his face set towards the sea, he made a decision.

With a supreme effort of will he reined in his confused and turbulent emotions. The only way to regain control of himself again, was to put an end to this perilous attachment that threatened to derail him. He would finish it tonight.

Chapter Twenty-seven

As soon as Meg stepped from the shadows on Mr Roderick's arm, many faces turned to gaze at her. Several women, she noted, stared covetously at her dress, while several gentlemen looked at her with barefaced admiration. Within minutes, young bachelors began to drift towards her to request a dance or to make her acquaintance. A few young ladies also came to greet her, wishing to know who had created such an exquisite gown.

Roderick had danced the first couple of movements with her and had then gone off in search of his own entertainment, leaving her to socialise with the crowd. Dancing was not his forte and so it did not appeal to him. He much preferred to sit with his friends and throw dice or drink port and smoke a pipe. Meg, on the other hand loved to be amongst the throng, meeting new people, and whirling about on the dance floor.

Most of the guests were powerful landowners. They ran sheep over enormous tracts of land and made a fortune in selling wool. These settlers were the 'aristocracy' of this young colony, and their daughters and sons were the ones who tried to form connections at the jovial assembly.

Meg chatted with the women, making new friends, promised a few dances to some admirers and began to enjoy herself thoroughly. The quick tempo of the music made her spirits soar, and she imagined herself floating as she twirled about on the dance floor.

'Meg?' a familiar voice called from behind her in a moment when she had stopped to drink a refreshing glass of punch.

Meg spun around. 'Brian!' she kissed him warmly on the cheek.

Brian stood back and took in her lovely appearance. 'My,' he exclaimed. 'You look positively radiant tonight. And where did you get that gown?'

'As if you don't know,' said a soft voice approaching the pair. Katherine blushed with pride. 'Meg, you look better than I could have dreamed.'

'Katherine,' Meg greeted her new friend. 'I must confess it appears I have been transfigured. I cannot tell you how many mooncalves have told me I am either an angel, or a fairy queen, or even a princess.'

The three of them laughed. 'If they only knew …' Brian rolled his eyes.

'Oh Katherine,' Meg told the shy girl, 'You will be all the rage after this. I hope you have a lot of time on your hands.'

Katherine's face brightened and then fell a little, looking unsure. She glanced across at Brian who smiled warmly at her.

Brian turned to Meg. 'She may not have a lot of time to spare, actually.'

Meg glanced from one to another of them and understanding slowly dawned. 'Are you saying …?'

'Yes,' Brian laughed. 'We are betrothed. And she will need much of her time to make her own wedding gown.'

Meg squealed in delight. 'I am so happy for you both,' she kissed them both.

She took hold of her future sister-in-law's hands. 'Katherine, you must tell me everything. Was he romantic? If he wasn't I shall clobber him for you.'

Brian laughed as Meg drew Katherine away. They sat at the side of the hall for a time and talked. Katherine told Meg all about Brian's proposal. By the time Katherine had finished her tale, Meg had to dab at her moist eyes with a handkerchief. 'I am so happy for you,' she told the young woman for the second time. 'I know he will make you a wonderful husband.'

Just then, Mr Roderick strode up and interrupted her. 'I came to see if you are enjoying yourself comfortably.'

Katherine chose that moment to excuse herself, and though Meg was disappointed to have her time with her future kindred cut short, she accepted it without a fuss.

'I am having a splendid time.'

'May I be of any service to you? Do you require a drink?'

'No, thank you,' she was impressed by his thoughtfulness. 'I have just finished one.'

'Would you care to dance?'

'Forgive me, Mister Roderick,' she replied, 'But I am enjoying a little rest at present.'

'Well, then,' he sighed contentedly. 'It appears everything is as it should be. Perhaps, if you do not mind, I shall return to my game of whist.'

'Go ahead, Mister Roderick,' she nodded. 'I am happy to sit here by myself.'

⌒∽⌒

Dressed at long last, Jack descended the stairs, resplendent in a navy blue, satin dress-coat which had flowing tails and sapphire buttons. Beneath the coat Jack wore an ivory silk vest, inlaid with tiny glass beads. His silk cravat was arranged perfectly as always. Ivory satin leggings hugged his muscular thighs, and navy-blue shoes with large silver buckles, adorned his feet. 'Is my carriage ready?'

'Ah, Mister Fordham,' Miller said hesitantly. 'You have not yet eaten your supper. It has been kept warm for you.'

An impatient grunt escaped Jack. The last thing he wanted to do was waste more time eating. However, he had not eaten all day, and it would not help him to maintain his equilibrium if he had a growling, empty stomach. 'Very well, Miller,' he walked into the dining room. Normally, Jack took his time over a meal, savouring every morsel. On this occasion however, he shovelled large forkfuls of food into his mouth, chewed quickly and swallowed, washing it down with great gulps of water. Fifteen minutes later, he was ready to depart.

He strode swiftly out of the front door, and almost leapt into his carriage. He tapped loudly on the roof and the coach lurched forward. As they drove along, Jack peered into the darkness outside the window. In the moonlight, he could see his jaw flexing in his reflection, the only indication of his unrest. How one woman could have him in such a whirlwind was beyond his comprehension. All he knew was he had to put it to a stop before he lost his sanity, or worse …

≈∞≈

Meg had not been left sitting by herself for long. Within minutes, her admirers began to gather around her, hanging upon her every word. One young man had told her of his younger siblings, inspiring her to talk about her favourite subject. She began to tell him humorous stories about the Sainsbury children when they were just toddlers. Before long she had an audience of laughing subjects, all engrossed in her animated storytelling.

Amidst one guffaw, Meg noticed heads turn away from her and towards her left, and women whispered excitedly together. She turned to see what had caused such a commotion and her stomach fluttered uncomfortably. Jack. More handsome than she had ever seen him, her heart somersaulted in her chest. He was just a friend. She tried to suppress the emotions that threatened to surface.

Jack scanned the room, obviously looking for someone, when his eyes met hers. Something dangerous seemed to flash momentarily in those brown eyes and then he gave her his most charming smile, but he did not approach her. Instead, he continued scanning the hall until he located Mr Bartholomew and headed towards him.

'Do you know Mister Fordham?' one of her companions asked.

'Yes,' Meg tore her eyes away from that vision of magnificence. 'He is Uncle to my charges.'

'Oh,' many voices breathed with keen interest.

≈∞≈

Jack had not been prepared for Meg's appearance. He remembered her beauty had first caught his attention at a ball, not unlike this one. However, since then he had grown to know and appreciate the person behind the lovely face. As his eyes locked with hers, his heart thumped in his breast. She appeared more exquisite than ever before, and his emotions surged dangerously.

The vision of an angel, draped in soft lilac silk and sparkling from each glass bead, with ringlets cascading delicately around her perfect face, she had smiled demurely at him. Her face was delicately flushed with excitement, and her eyes danced. She was obviously in high spirits. He noted the crowd around her and decided it would not be a good time to approach her, not until he could look at her without turning to water.

'Fordham. Good to see you.' Mr Bartholomew greeted as Jack approached him on the balcony.

'And you, my friend,' Jack replied, lacking the zeal his friend had shown. He leaned on the balustrade with his forearm and glanced down at Meg, a slight frown creasing his brow.

Mr Bartholomew followed Jack's line of sight. 'She has the look of a woman in love,' he commented quietly. 'Either that or she is in her cups.'

'In her cups?' Jack repeated with a scornful laugh. 'That, I can assure you, she most definitely is not.'

'She certainly is radiant this evening, though.'

Jack tore his eyes away from the enchanting governess. 'Roderick must have succeeded where I did not,' he told his friend matter-of-factly.

'So, you are giving up, then?'

Jack's set his face like flint. 'She has occupied far too much of my time. I weary of her. Besides, she appears to be happy with Roderick. Why should I stand in his way?'

Mr Bartholomew shook his head. 'I cannot fathom what she admires in that insipid fellow.'

'Blast!' Jack slammed his fist on the railing. 'Nor can I.'

They fell silent again, absent-mindedly surveying the couples dancing.

'Hang it,' Jack cursed again. 'She deserves better than that dull clod.'

Mr Bartholomew seemed to study Jack. 'Oh my,' he said after a moment.

'You are in love with her.'

Jack turned to him intensely. 'I am not in love with her. The game is over. It finishes tonight.' He strode off to mingle with the other guests.

⨳

Meg managed to extricate herself from the group surrounding her long enough to find Mary and see how she progressed. The young lady's attention had been claimed by a good-looking youth, while Mr Greenfeld sat, somewhat sulkily, nearby. Meg approached him first. 'Would you mind if I stole your companion for a few minutes?'

'Of course,' Mr Greenfeld replied. He appeared to be relieved it was not another suitor come to draw her attention away.

'I shall return her to you presently,' Meg assured him, and he nodded.

Meg moved towards her charge and interrupted with a light cough. 'Excuse me Miss Sainsbury and, I am sorry, I have not had the pleasure?'

'MacCullum's the name, Miss,' he told her without hesitation.

'Pleased to meet you, Mister MacCullum. I am Miss Wingrove.' Meg told him. 'Forgive me, but I wish to take a turn about the room with Miss Sainsbury if you will permit me?'

'I should not like to stand in your way, ma'am.' He bowed briefly to Mary. 'Good evening, Miss Sainsbury.' He winked at them and strolled casually away.

'What is it you want, Meg?' Mary asked.

'Come and walk with me,' Meg said, taking her arm. 'Are you enjoying yourself?'

'Oh yes,' the young girl answered, 'I have ever so many admirers.' Mary had clearly let her success go to her head.

'You must not neglect Mister Greenfeld,' Meg scolded her gently.

Mary pouted a little. 'But I wish to become acquainted with more than *one* gentleman. They are all very nice and I wish to be able to have a few to choose from when it comes time for me to marry.'

'Which shows why you are not ready for that yet,' Meg mumbled.

'I beg pardon?'

'Never mind,' Meg patted her hand. 'You do not need to worry about marriage yet. You still have a few years to get to know many young men. The point is you may be hurting Mister Greenfeld's feelings.'

Mary eyed her governess suspiciously. 'I do not see you hanging off Mister Roderick's arm. In fact, I have barely noticed you together all evening.'

Meg smiled knowingly. 'That is different. Mister Roderick is hardly sitting by my side looking morose, while I chatter to everyone else but him.'

Mary looked guilty. 'Have I been that bad? Very well, I shall be more attentive to him for the rest of the evening.'

'Good girl,' Meg gave her a quick squeeze. They had returned to where Mr Greenfeld awaited her. 'Now, go and enjoy yourself.'

৵৽৵

Jack had spent a pleasant time conversing with some of his acquaintances. They were all in light spirits and laughed and joked together. As Jack entered into their humorous conversation, his tension melted away. Perhaps all of his angst was from spending too much time alone. He accepted a glass of port from them while they bantered words about, and his mental stability slowly returned.

He noticed Roderick through an open door, sitting around a card table with some other gentlemen, engrossed in his gaming. He briefly wondered why, if the man was so enamoured with Meg, he did not stay by her side. He shrugged the thought away. It was none of his business. He returned his concentration to the discussion that took place around him.

After a while he decided it was time to do what he had come to do and excused himself from the group. Descending the stairs, he encountered Philip Sainsbury who was on the way up.

'How are you this evening, brother-in-law?' the elder man asked.

'I have never felt better.'

'Good to hear, good to hear,' Philip slapped him on the back.

'Mary is here, is she not?' Jack asked politely.

'Yes,' Philip chuckled unexpectedly. 'She is quite the thing, I am told. She is feeling rather triumphant, it seems. She has all those young chaps in a spin, I can tell you.'

Jack smiled. 'I must see if she will stand up with me for a dance.'

'If you can find her amongst the throng worshipping at her feet.'

It was Jack's turn to laugh.

'Meg is causing no little sensation this evening, either,' Philip told him. 'Have you seen her? Gad, but that woman is a rare beauty when she is done up to the nines.'

'I dare say,' Jack lowered his eyes.

'I am surprised you have not made her the object of your charm, Jack.'

Jack shrugged, forcing a light smile to his lips. 'God save me, she is too good for me.'

Philip chuckled again. 'Yes,' he nodded. 'I dare say you are right.' He continued on his way, still chortling. 'Too good. Yes, yes, yes.'

Chapter Twenty-eight

Jack shook his head with a grin as he watched his brother-in-law walk away. He was obviously tickled by his daughter's success. He turned around and glanced down into the brilliantly lit room. Where was Mary? Ah, there she was, dancing with a youthful looking gentleman. He descended the remaining steps two at a time and moved swiftly to where he had seen the couple. He tapped the young man on the shoulder. 'May I cut in?'

When Mr Greenfeld saw who had asked, he merely nodded, probably intimidated by Jack's reputation. So, when Mary turned back from the dance steps she had been performing, she saw Jack in place of her handsome escort. 'Uncle Jack,' she clapped, and almost missed her next set of steps.

'I hear you have conquered every young scamp here,' Jack teased.

'It is amazing is it not?' Mary ignored his jibe.

'And they shall adore you even more now they have seen me dancing with you.' His lips twitched.

'Why is that?'

'Because anyone, of whom Jack Fordham approves, must be the catch of the town.'

'But you are my uncle, you are obliged to approve of me,' Mary informed him.

'Is that so?'

'Yes.'

A mischievous idea sparked in Jack's head. 'I wonder what would happen if

I suddenly scowled at you and left you standing here on the dance floor, alone.'

'Uncle Jack, you wouldn't dare.' Mary looked panic stricken.

Jack threw his head back and laughed. 'You see,' he boasted. 'You know I am right.'

Mary looked daggers at him.

When the dance brought them closer together, Jack looked at her solemnly. 'Do not let your success go to your head, my sweet. A conceited woman is not an attractive one.'

Jack rarely ever lectured his nieces or nephews, so Mary quietly accepted his rebuke with respect.

'I am sorry, Uncle Jack.' she said gravely. Jack smiled warmly at her and kissed her on the forehead as the dance wound to a close.

As he handed Mary back to Mr Greenfeld, Jack saw Meg being led off the floor by another gentleman. He watched her part from him and head towards the refreshment table. There was a bounce in her step and a large, contented smile on her face. Now was his chance. He moved swiftly to intercept her at the refreshments table and picked up the glass she reached for. 'May I?' he asked with a charming smile as she turned to see who this intruder could be.

She grinned with amusement and allowed him to fill her glass. 'How are you this evening, Jack?' she asked. 'You look positively hagged.'

'Damned hard work,' Jack drawled as he handed her the drink. 'Thank you kindly for noticing. But enough about me, let's talk about you.' He led her away from the table.

ॐ

Meg studied his face. Something about him was not quite right, but she could not place it.

'I see you are wearing the silk I once gave you. I knew it would become you,' Jack said suavely, his voice smooth. 'In fact, you take my breath away.'

Meg stared at him for a moment, wondering why he would put on a charade for her. 'Jack, this is me here. Meg. You are talking nonsense. No games, remember.'

Jack swallowed and turned away from her. 'This hotel is quite splendid, is it not?'

Meg frowned. What was going on in that addlepated mind of his? Then she shrugged and shook her head. There was nothing for it but to play along.

'Very much so,' she agreed. 'I was rather overwhelmed when we arrived.'

'We?'

'I came with Mister Roderick.'

Jack pulled a face. 'Lord, what dull company he must be.'

'I cannot say,' Meg told him, 'Since I have barely seen him all evening.'

'Fool.'

'Jack Fordham,' Meg gasped. 'Why would you say such a thing?'

Jack turned to look at her. The dangerous gleam returned to his eyes. 'If it were I who brought you, I would not let you out of my sight.'

Meg was astonished and uneasy both at once. 'Jack, why do you speak so?'

He glanced away and back again, and his eyes now had a mischievous twinkle. 'Who knows what roguery you might get up to while my back was turned?'

Meg laughed. 'Odious man.'

A loud voice called out the next dance, only Meg did not pay attention. Her mind still puzzled over Jack's strange behaviour. She sipped at her drink thoughtfully. One moment he seemed almost angry, and the next he played the cool, enigmatic nonpareil again. Perhaps she imagined things. Perhaps this was just his usual outrageous behaviour. She swallowed the remainder of her punch and took her glass back to the table.

When she returned, Jack looked at her, his eyes bright. 'Dance with me?'

Meg wavered. Should she? Realistically, she knew she aught to keep her distance from him. But she was having such a wonderful time, and she had always wondered what it would be like to dance with him. They were only friends, she reminded herself. One dance wouldn't hurt, surely.

She smiled up at him and took his proffered arm. Before she realised what had happened, the music began, and he swept her up in a waltz. *A waltz?* Hadn't all the mothers warned her and other girls about the waltz? For a moment, she panicked, knowing she should run away. But the dance had started, and she did not want to embarrass Jack and subject herself to hideous gossip, so she decided to make the best of it. She looked uncertainly at Jack who seemed to study her every expression. 'Is everything all right?'

'Yes. I just ... did not realise this was a waltz,' she admitted.

A distant look appeared in his eyes. 'Are you uncomfortable?'

'No...no, I am fine.'

As the dance progressed, however, the music seemed to fade into the background as well as the rest of the crowd and there was only Jack. He was so near she could smell his scent. She could feel the warmth of one hand penetrating into her back and his other hand clasped hers. When she looked up, his eyes were fixed on hers, and they were anything but cold. It unnerved her, and for the rest of the dance she focused on one of his sapphire buttons. Masterfully, he guided her around the dance floor with graceful steps and she felt as though she were in a dream.

Being in such proximity to this man whom she loved dearly brought all her longings to the surface. She found herself wishing the dance would go on forever. She wanted to be with him and no-one else, right, or wrong. She wanted to be in his arms. She wanted to tell him how much she loved him. She wanted ...

Slowly, she came to realise they had stopped moving. The music had finished, and couples were drifting away from the dance floor. In a haze, she lifted her eyes to Jack's and a surge of emotion swept over her. She had to get away from him. She pulled away and hurried for the nearest door.

つや⌒ら

All of Jack's emotions churned again as he danced with this delicate flower. How could she hold such a power over him, and yet manage to keep herself distant from him? Or did she? He noted how she focused intently on his button and, although she moved in step with the music, her body was almost rigid with tension. Perhaps she was not as indifferent as she had wanted him to think. Did he dare hope?

The music wound down, but Meg appeared slow to realise the fact. He opened his mouth to ask her if she was well, when her face lifted, and their eyes met. What Jack saw in her eyes undid him. In them was written everything he had wanted to know and everything he, himself felt. It had only been the briefest of moments, but the longing in those blue pools was undeniable. He awoke from this revelation to see her escape through the garden doors, and he immediately went after her.

As his eyes became accustomed to the dim light, he saw her shimmering dress disappear into the shadows down the path and away from the hotel. He dashed after her and found her just beyond the last reaches of light, seated on a bench. As soon as she saw him, she rose to hurry away from him, but he caught her by the arm, and he turned her around.

'Meg.'

❧

'Jack,' Meg protested weakly, but could get no more out before he swept her up in a passionate embrace. Not that she cared at that moment. She wanted to be kissed by him and returned it ardently.

After what seemed like a blissful eternity, Jack and Meg pulled away from each other. 'Meg, my darling,' Jack murmured, his eyes caressing her face. 'How I have longed for this moment.'

As he spoke, reality crashed in around Meg, and she realised she had just done the one thing she had promised herself not to do. She had given in to her emotions. 'We ... we are supposed to be friends,' she whispered in confusion, 'Why did you kiss me?'

She tried to escape from his arms, but he held her tight. He looked at her possessively. 'No you don't, Meg,' he said firmly. 'I will not let you deny me again. I know you care for me. I can see it in your eyes.'

She could not argue with him. What would she do? What could say to him? 'Jack, I ...'

'Marry me, Meg.' His voice was husky.

She gasped. She had not expected this. Not from Jack. Her moment of weakness would have devastating consequences. She swallowed hard.

'Marry you?'

'Yes,' he searched her eyes, 'Marry me.'

'Jack, please don't ask.' Her whole body shook. 'I can't.'

He abruptly let her go and stared at her in disbelief. 'Can't?' he repeated as though he did not know the meaning of the word. 'Did we not just share a very meaningful kiss?'

'Jack, I …'

'I believe you wanted that, just as much as I did.'

'It was a mistake,' Meg sank to the bench beside her, her legs weak.

'A mistake?' Jack's voice rose in astonishment. 'I can still feel the warmth of your lips upon mine, and you are saying it was a mistake?'

'Jack,' she pleaded.

'Perhaps you are just like the others,' a bitter edge came into his voice. He sat down close to her and cupped her chin in his hands firmly. 'Only interested in what you can take from the moment.' His hungry gaze roamed her face. 'I suppose you want to …'

'Jack, stop.' Meg whispered, dismayed by the resentment and accusation in his voice. 'I am not like that.'

Jack released her and stood up abruptly. 'Forgive me, I don't know what came over me.' He shoved his hands deep into his coat pockets, but the wild look on his face remained. 'Why do you refuse me when you have just proven to me you truly care.'

'It was wrong,' Meg insisted, though her voice was low.

Jack stared at her in disbelief. 'How can something so wonderful, that felt so right, be wrong? We belong together, Meg. Nothing else matters.'

'But it does matter,' Meg argued, her voice rising in confidence. 'It matters to God.'

'To God?' Jack's words were edged with scorn. 'What has this got to do with God?' He looked at her angrily. 'I am tired of the way you hide behind your religion and don't face your true feelings.'

Meg's anger rose and she stood up to face him. 'I do not hide behind my religion,' she glared at him. 'You want to hear what my feelings are? Fine. I will tell you. I am insanely in love with you. There. Are you satisfied? I love you. And yes, I wanted that kiss; I wanted it more than I can say.' Meg's voice began to shake. 'But I should not have allowed it. Regardless of my feelings, I do not belong to you, and you do not belong to me. I told you once I could not, would not, ever, be involved with you. I told you it is a decision not based on emotions, but based on the knowledge that a relationship between a believer and a non-believer will not work. This here, this argument,' she waved her hand between them, 'is exactly why I cannot marry you. It would be the first of many.'

Jack stood there shaking his head. Her explanation had obviously not satisfied him. In a bitter, half laugh, he said to her, 'You are far too idealistic for me, and far too good. I am sorry I do not measure up to your standards. I hope someday you find someone flawless enough for you.'

'Jack, please don't …'

He began to walk away, but turned back, resentment twisting his face. 'In case you feel the need to tell your friends you were the one to break Jack Fordham's heart, don't waste your breath. I merely proposed to you out of respect to what I supposed to be your innocence.'

With that he stalked away, and Meg collapsed to the bench and allowed heart-wrenching sobs to flow freely. What a mess. Despite his resentful comments, Meg knew she had hurt him deeply. Why had she even agreed to dance with him? She stayed there until she could cry no more, and then waited until she calmed enough to return to the ball room.

Chapter Twenty-nine

In a fury, Jack walked briskly away from Meg. He was enraged with himself for behaving such a fool. She had always resisted him, why should tonight have been any different? He should have stayed with his original plan, which was ... which was what? Only to try and shut off the emotions Meg constantly stirred in him. What had possessed him to offer for her? He must have looked as ridiculous as one of those love-sick puppies mooning about Mary's feet. Now he just wanted to leave.

Jack skirted the hotel and re-entered the ballroom through a different door. No doubt many observers had seen him follow Meg into the gardens, and he did not want to feed their already gossiping tongues. He quickly made his way to Mr Bartholomew to bid him good evening, flashing debonair smiles at any who caught his eye.

'Bart,' he said as he approached. His comrade looked up from where he sat at a card table. One look at Jack's face and he quickly rose from his chair and went aside with him.

'What is it, Fordham?'

'I am leaving,' Jack told him frankly. 'I just came to say good night.'

'What happened? You look a trifle pale.'

'I told you,' Jack said through gritted teeth. 'It is over.'

No doubt Bart would see through his charade, but right then he didn't care. He just needed to escape, so he strode away, leaving his friend to ponder.

Jack instructed his driver to take him to a well-known gaming house, situated nearby. There were people in the club whom Jack knew, but he wanted to be alone. He ordered a drink and went to sit by the fire, where he nursed his bruised ego for a time.

He could not understand why Meg refused him. Her piety infuriated him. If two people desired each other, then they should be together, to put it simply. Why God had to come into the equation he could not fathom.

❧

Meg tried to enter the ballroom unnoticed, and hurried to the powder room, keeping her eyes lowered. She checked her appearance in a mirror. If there had been any puffiness around her eyes, it had mostly subsided now. Apart from looking a little pale and dishevelled, no one would notice she had been crying. The memory of Jack's arms around her kept flashing in her mind, threatening to make her dissolve into tears again, but she desperately pushed those thoughts aside.

Meg dabbed at her face with a moist towel and pinched her cheeks to give them some colour. She tidied her hair and straightened her skirt. While she fixed herself up, two ladies entered the room to touch up their own appearances. They were in the middle of a conversation which Meg had no choice but to listen to.

'He said goodbye to me when he left,' the first lady informed her friend as they entered. She was obviously excited about the fact.

'Yes, but did he notice you?' the second woman asked.

'He smiled at me,' the first lady said, as if that would be enough.

'And what a heart-melting smile it is,' the other said dramatically. 'May I borrow your comb, dear?'

'They say he's a shocking flirt,' the first woman said, passing over the requested comb.

'Mister Fordham would say anything to a girl to win her heart. Why I believe he would even go to church for a lady if she wanted him to.' Both women giggled, and the second woman continued. 'And you know he cannot abide religion.'

Meg froze, her hands grasping one of the pins in her hair at the mention of Jack's name, but neither woman seemed to notice her.

'I heard he has had his eye on a particular girl for a few months now, but no-one seems to know who she is. Someone's house maid, I believe,' prattled lady number one.

'I am sure it is the longest he has carried on a flirtation with anyone.'

'The woman must be mad if she will not receive his addresses.'

'My, yes.' Number two agreed. 'He is such an attractive man. And his fortune. Well, what is there to say? Thank you, dear, here is your comb.' The item was passed back.

'I shouldn't care if he was the most wicked rake in the world,' the first woman said naively, 'If Mister Fordham came my way, I would snap him up like a good bargain at the markets.'

The second lady laughed, and they left the room. Meg sank into a nearby chair, suddenly ill again. The way those women had talked about Jack disgusted her, speaking as though he were a trophy. They said he would say anything... could it be possible Jack had manipulated her the whole time, even after he had promised not to? And if it were true, how could she not have seen it? She was suddenly overcome by a strong desire to go home. She quickly finished fixing herself up, noticing all the colour had drained out of her face once again, and went in search of Mr Roderick.

❧

Sitting alone dwelling on Meg's rejection did nothing to alleviate Jack's distress. He polished off his glass of wine and rose from his chair. He needed distraction. He approached a card table where he knew a few gentlemen. 'Good-evening Davidson,' he greeted one of them.

'Fordham,' the man exclaimed cheerfully. 'I did not see you there. Pull up a chair.'

Jack dragged a chair over from a nearby table.

'Hello Fordham,' another acquaintance greeted.

'Harris,' Jack nodded.

He looked around the table. The rest were strangers and one by one they were introduced to him.

'And this is Miss Coventry, visiting from Melbourne with my family.' Davidson leaned back so Jack could see the woman sitting next to him.

Miss Coventry was a sultry looking brunette with luscious lips and a silken voice. She smiled invitingly at Jack. 'The pleasure is all mine,' she held out a gloved hand. Jack raised her hand and kissed it boldly.

'My, you have a lovely acquaintance there, Davidson,' Jack turned on his charm.

Jack joined in their game for a while and before long he found himself sitting next to Miss Coventry. They chatted amiably while intermittently throwing their cards on the table, laughing gaily at each other's humour.

'So, Mister Fordham,' Miss Coventry leaned in close after a time, so they could have a private conversation. 'Are you married?'

'No,' Jack replied smoothly. 'I am a confirmed and dedicated bachelor.'

'Why so devout?'

Jack laughed scornfully. 'I do not believe in love.'

'You must be very lonely,' she said in mock sympathy.

Jack looked her in the eye. 'Are you offering to keep me company?' he said in a low voice, flashing her a disarming smile.

'It depends,' she gave him a flirtatious look. 'What will you offer in return?'

'I suspect you have something already in mind,' Jack smiled wryly. This woman wanted him, even if Meg didn't. His mind in a fever of bitterness, he ceased to think about his actions.

Miss Coventry leaned even closer and whispered in his ear. 'Diamonds.'

'I think I can arrange that,' Jack told her smoothly. 'Shall we?' He offered her his arm and rose from the table.

Gilbert Roderick could not be found. Meg searched the gaming rooms, the refreshments tables, the gardens — everywhere. When she finally made enquiries as to his whereabouts, an attendant informed her he had departed over half-an-hour earlier. It angered Meg that he would leave without her. She became increasingly distressed and did not know how much longer she could force a smile.

She remembered Mr Sainsbury and Mary were there and went to find them, only to discover they had left not five minutes earlier. Abandoned by everyone, panic rose. Then she noticed her brother and his fiancé were still on the dance floor. She sighed in relief and waited for their dance to finish. As soon as they moved off the dance floor, Meg intercepted them.

'Brian,' Meg could not hide the desperation in her voice, 'I need you.'

'Gracious Meg, you look as though you've seen a ghost.'

'Mister Roderick has left without me; Mister Sainsbury and Mary are already gone, and I have ruined the whole evening ...' Meg's words tumbled out over one another and she began to shake.

Brian wrapped his arms around her. 'It is all right, Meg,' he soothed, 'I shall take you home.'

He led her and Katherine towards the entrance. 'Stay here while I fetch your coats,' he told them.

Katherine grasped Meg's hand to comfort her as they waited.

Behind them and unaware of Meg's presence, she heard several men in a discussion.

'Is he still trying to turn the young lady's head, then?' one man asked.

'No,' Bart replied. 'He is done with his game, it seems. He told me he has finished it this evening.'

Meg's grip on Katherine's hand became tighter. 'Please, let us go outside,' she whispered, tears brimming in her eyes again. She pulled the worried girl towards the door.

Meg's stomach churned so much she thought she would be sick. Brian found them outside a few moments later. 'Brian,' Katherine sounded relieved.

Brian hurried to Meg's side and put his arm around her.

'How could this have happened?' Meg asked.

Thinking Meg referred to Mr Roderick's disappearance, Brian scowled. 'He is obviously not as well mannered as he pretends to be. I shall have words to say to him when next I see him.'

He led the women down the steps and handed them gently into the carriage. Meg trembled violently and tears began to fall.

'It is all right now, Meg,' Brian reassured her. 'We will take you to your hotel. Mister Roderick will be dealt with. There is no need for such high fidgets.'

'Mister Roderick?' Meg finally realised they had no idea what had happened. 'It's Jack!' Her voice broke with the agony she'd been holding back.

⥓⥔

Jack emerged from the gaming house with Miss Coventry on his arm. As they strolled towards his coach, another carriage went past, splashing muddy water from a puddle in the road. A few drops landed on Jack's satin pants, and he cursed after the vehicle. 'Just a moment,' on a second glance at the receding coach, he changed his attitude. 'That was Philip's coach.'

'Who is Philip?' Miss Coventry asked.

'My brother-in-law,' Jack answered simply. 'He breeds horses. I would know his get up anywhere.'

Miss Coventry smiled boldly at him. 'The only "get up" I am interested in, Mister Fordham, is yours.'

Jack gave her another of his charming grins. 'Has anyone ever told you how alluring you are?' He opened the door of his coach.

She looked over her shoulder as she stepped up, her eyes teasing. 'I am?' She sat down in the carriage.

Jack climbed in behind her, shut the door and tapped on the roof. Before the carriage had barely begun to move, Miss Coventry fell into his arms and their lips were pressed together.

But Jack could only think about the moment he had shared with Meg. That had been real and heartfelt, nothing like he'd ever felt before. This was shallow and meaningless. He did not even know this woman. How could he trap himself in another futile liaison? Was he insane?

Moments later he pulled away from Miss Coventry and moved to the opposite side of the carriage. He ran his hands through his hair in confusion. 'I am sorry, Miss Coventry, but I cannot ...' He told her in a somewhat shaky voice. 'I will return you to your friends. He tapped the roof again and the coach stopped. He ordered the driver to turn around.

The woman appeared to be rather annoyed at this change in Jack's manner. She stared at him for a while. 'There is someone else, isn't there?'

'Yes and no,' Jack sighed in frustration.

Miss Coventry unashamedly showed her disappointment. 'So much for being a confirmed bachelor.' The coach stopped. 'We could have shared some beautiful moments, Mister Fordham,' she said in a seductive voice, and stepped outside.

Jack sank back in his seat with a heavy sigh. He was more miserable now than when he departed from Meg. The worst part was, he was due to sail for Melbourne in the morning and he would have no chance to resolve anything. Then again, perhaps the sea air would help him clear his mind of all this confusion. Right now, he wished only for the pain free unconsciousness of sleep.

❦❧

'What about Jack?' Brian asked Meg between sobs.

Meg covered her face with her hands and rocked back and forwards on the seat. 'Oh Brian,' she cried. 'I have been such an imbecile.'

Brian seemed to give up drawing any information from her while she was in this state. Not that she could get the words out anyway. The coach seemed to take forever to get back to the hotel. Meg occasionally groaned and pounded her fist into the leather on the seat, until eventually the driver reined in at the Hero of Waterloo.

'Stay here,' Brian told his fiancé when she began to follow the Wingroves out of the carriage. 'I'll have the driver take you home and then return for me. Otherwise, your mother will begin to wonder about you.'

Katherine accepted his wisdom, although she seemed torn. She offered Meg a sad smile and squeezed her arm. 'I hope you feel better soon.' Brian kissed her hand tenderly and closed the door upon her. He left Meg for a few seconds to give the driver instructions and then returned to escort her inside.

As Mary was already asleep in her room, the only place where they could be alone was in the small private dining room. Thankfully due to the late hour, this room was deserted, so Brian pulled two chairs close to the dying fire in the hearth and sat Meg down.

'Now, Meg dearest, tell me everything, from the beginning,' he instructed her gently.

Meg swallowed, her eyes closed in pain. 'You ... you know how I — told you ... I was in love with Jack ...' she began.

'Yes,' Brian nodded.

'Well, I thought ... I thought I had my feelings under control.'

'But you did not?' her brother guessed.

'No.' She admitted. 'And then I stood up with him, and it was a waltz. But I didn't know it was a waltz at first and then it was too late.'

'Too late for what?'

'To say I didn't want to dance. But it was so wonderful. My heart soared, Brian, and I wanted ...'

Meg stopped in her sentence, remembering the longing that had swept over her. She could not express that to Brian.

'Go on,' he encouraged.

'I ran away ... out the nearest door, which led into the garden, only I did not know that until I was out there.'

'Yes?' Suspicion crept into his voice.

'He followed me ... and I was so — I kissed him, Brian. That is, he kissed me, but I did not stop him.' Tears spilled down her cheeks anew.

Immediately infuriated, Brian jumped up from his chair. 'That insolent rake. I shall call him out for this.'

'No, wait,' Meg tugged at his sleeve, pleading. 'He offered to marry me after that.'

'He did?' Brian sat down again in surprise.

'But I said no.' Meg dabbed at her eyes with Brian's handkerchief.

'You what?' Brian's astonishment increased.

'I told him I would not marry him.'

Brian shook his head. 'Why ever not? You have compromised yourself. Don't you see? You should have said yes. If gossip gets out about this, you will be scandalised.'

'Then that is something I shall just have to face,' Meg sobbed. 'He only offered for me to save my reputation anyway. I would not marry him now for all the money in the world.'

Brian frowned at her. 'A minute ago, you told me you were in love with him.'

'I was,' she nodded. 'But now I feel ill just thinking about him.'

'What did he do to you?'

'He tricked me.' Her voice was laced with bitterness. 'I have been so blind, so naïve. And you warned me so many times, but I didn't listen.'

Brian wrapped one arm tightly around her shoulders. 'Tell me how he tricked you.'

Meg tried to stop crying to tell him. 'I overheard some people talking about Jack tonight. He has been playing a game from the start.'

Meg collapsed into uncontrollable sobs again and Brian pulled her into his arms. 'Oh, my poor darling,' he rocked her gently.

When her sobs finally faded, Meg mumbled into her brother's coat. 'I don't know what is real anymore. I am confused, and oh, I feel so humiliated. How could he do this to me?'

Brian sighed. 'I have no answers for you right now, but I promise you this,' he told her earnestly. 'I will deal with Fordham for treating you so shamefully, and I will deal with Roderick for deserting you in your time of need.'

It was late when Meg slipped into her room, emotionally and physically exhausted. She had finally been able to convince her brother she would be all right alone now. He had almost insisted she return to his house with him where he could keep an eye on her. But now she had blurted out the whole story to Brian, and cried for a good long time, she felt a little better. Eventually she told him to go home with a grateful kiss.

Mary slept soundly, and Meg was so tired she could not be bothered trying to undo her dress. She flopped onto the bed and fell asleep amidst visions of whirling ball gowns and bright lights. Her last thoughts before she succumbed to sleep were of Jack and wishing she had never known him.

Chapter Thirty

Early in the morning, while a sleepy mist still hung over the harbour, Jack boarded the vessel that would take him and his shipment of wine to Melbourne. Still weary from lack of sleep, and heavy of heart, he crossed the gang plank and instructed Miller to have his travelling bags stowed in his cabin. Jack went in search of the captain to discover how soon they would be departing.

'Everything is ri' to go,' Captain Thomas Connelly informed him in a rolling Scottish brogue. 'Just as soon as this fog thins a wee bit, we'll be on our way.'

Captain Connelly had a thick black beard, and wavy black hair. He was a tall man with a broad chest and wide set shoulders with muscles bulging from every inch of his body. When he walked upon the deck, his feet fell heavily with a loud 'thud'. He was obviously a sea lover and kept himself busy checking and re-checking every piece of rigging on the sturdy ship. He looked towards the horizon and his dark eyes gleamed from beneath his bushy eyebrows. 'I reckon half an hour and we'll be sailing into the sunrise. I cannae think of a better way to start the day. Can ye?'

In a subdued mood, Jack could not enter into jovial conversation. He gave the sailor a brief smile and turned to lean on the rail, where he remained until well after they set sail.

The day opened into a perfect blue sky with a crisp breeze, ideal sailing weather. The ship gently rolled with the mild swell and spray occasionally splashed up from the bow as it forged through the green water. At times dolphins played alongside the vessel, leaping out of the waves in a majestic arc before disappearing below the surface again.

Apart from the sounds of the ship moving through the water and the intermittent snap of the sails as they filled with wind, quietness surrounded him, and Jack had naught to do but reflect. He stared into the fathomless depths and examined his heart and his conscience. It had been a very long time since he had been brutally honest with himself, and what he now saw repulsed him.

For the first time in years, he knew regret and perhaps, yes, also shame. He had gone from professing a wish to marry Meg one moment, to engaging a high-class whore less than two hours later. Unfaithfulness. Meg had seen through him from the start. *How long will it be before you are talking sweetly to another lady, and I am the one left behind?* Her words echoed in his mind.

She had been right, of course. All these years he had harboured resentment for Antoinette's betrayal, but he had become just like her. How many women had he hurt with his heartless attitude? He didn't dare think.

And now Meg was just another name he could add to his list. If only she had not denied him, he would never have even left the ball. None of this would have happened. Why did she have to refuse him? She had admitted she loved him. She *loved* him. Oh, how his heart had surged for her in that moment. Alas, only for a moment. She had gone on to deny him the one thing he yearned for above all. That denial taxed his already strained emotions to their limit. He could not comprehend how her religion could be so important to her that she would sacrifice her happiness for it.

The sun rode high in the sky and light glistened off the uneven surface of the ocean, when Jack realised the captain stood silently beside him at the rail.

Eventually the captain broke the silence 'There's nothing like being at sea.'

Jack stirred from his reverie. 'It is certainly different from the hubbub I am used to.'

Captain Connelly smiled. 'It'll be dinner time soon. Why don't ye join me in me cabin? I could use some fresh company.'

Jack shook his head as though trying to clear the cobwebs in his mind. 'Thank you, but no,' he replied. 'I would prefer to be alone.'

The captain nodded. 'Very well,' he said. 'But I'll leave the offer open if ye change yer mind.'

Jack gave him a half smile and turned back to the sea.

The seaman remained at his side for a little while longer, staring into the blue sky.

'Is she very beautiful?' he asked after a time, and immediately Jack stiffened and his grip on the railing tightened.

'How did you know?' Jack asked without turning.

'I just did,' the captain said simply. 'Ye've been standing here for hours looking miserable. If I can be of help, let me know.'

Jack turned to him, appreciative that the man took the time to ask. 'Thank you, I will.' Part of Jack desperately wanted to talk, but he wasn't ready. His thoughts still tumbled too much.

Most of the day passed before Jack found the courage to approach Captain Connelly and ask him if his offer of a shared meal remained open.

'Of course 'tis, lad,' he replied with a grin.

A couple of hours later they were seated in the captain's cabin at a small table, filling their mouths with tasty gruel and mashed potatoes, and talking of commonplace things. They washed their hearty meal down with ale and before long their stomachs were satisfied, and they could focus on more important things.

'That food certainly pleases one's appetite,' Jack complimented as he dabbed at the corners of his mouth.

'Aye,' Connelly agreed. 'I have an excellent cook on board.'

Jack leaned back in his chair with his mug of ale and took a swig. He lapsed into quiet thoughtfulness wanting to talk, but not knowing where to start.

Captain Connelly leaned his elbows on the table and looked at Jack. 'Ye got any family here?'

Warm affection filled Jack at the thought of them. 'Yes. My sister and her husband live out in Parramatta. They have four children — two girls and two boys.'

'Do ye see much of them?'

214

'I visit them regularly. I am very fond of them, especially the children.'

'Aye,' the captain drawled. 'Children are a precious gift.'

'I must admit I have always had a soft spot for them.'

'Well, that ain't a bad weakness to have,' Connelly sighed. 'If ye call it a weakness at all, that is. Ye want children of yer own one day?'

'That would be pure delight.' Jack admitted. He did not have the energy for pretence of any kind. 'But it seems I am doomed to remain a bachelor.' He laughed uncertainly and withdrew a little.

'Finding the right woman is the hard part.' The captain rolled his eyes.

'Finding her,' Jack argued quietly, 'was the easy part.' The one thing Jack was sure of — if he was ever to marry, Meg was the one he wanted.

'So, the difficulty would be …?'

Jack looked him in the eye. 'She will not have me,' he shrugged.

Captain Connelly's eyebrows rose. 'Did she give you a reason?'

Jack gave a half laugh. 'Many, actually. I do not pass her standards of what a man should be. Of course,' he added regretfully, 'she is quite right in her judgement of my moral character.'

'I see,' the captain responded and watched Jack intently as though reading him. Jack shivered a little under his penetrating gaze. Could this man see right through him?

'Something more troubles ye, does it not?'

Jack eyed him, wondering how much to share. Although it seemed this captain had some keen insight.

'It is the main reason she denies me. It is more important to her than all her other sentiments, and I cannot understand why.'

'What's her reason?'

'She is religious; very devout in her faith. She will not marry me because I am not a believer like her.'

Thomas leaned back in his chair, with a grim smile. 'I begin to see your confusion.'

'You do?' Jack knew he sounded desperate. 'Because no matter how many times I turn it over in my head, I still cannot understand her actions.'

'Well,' Thomas leaned in again. 'I understand it completely.'

Jack stared at him. Would this man with a bushy beard and simple life be able to answer his questions? Did he dare hope? 'Will you explain it to me then, Captain?'

Captain Connelly looked at the beams above his head for a moment. Then he looked Jack in the eyes. 'Mister Fordham …'

'Jack, please.'

'Very well. And I am Tom.'

'Yes … go on Tom.'

'Jack, ye were telling me a few minutes ago that children are a vital part of yer life.'

'Yes.'

'Ye want some of yer own?'

'Definitely.'

'Then let me ask ye something. If this woman had absolutely no interest in children, even if she were the most beautiful woman in the world, would ye still want to marry her?'

Jack frowned at him. 'Gracious, no. I'd have to be mad.'

The captain nodded. 'Just so. In the same way I could no' marry a lass unless she had a hankering for the sea like me. I'd be a fool to marry a land lubber. Perhaps, while we were newly in love it would work. But after a while, she would want to be in a cosy house somewhere and I'd be pining for the swaying of a ship beneath me. It would draw us away from each other and only end in unhappiness.'

Jack absorbed every word. He stared at the roof reflecting over the captain's explanation. 'So, what you are saying,' he said after a time, 'is Meg values her religion just as I value children or as you value the ocean. She believes that because I do not value religion at all, we cannot be happy together …'

Tom smiled broadly. 'Aye. Ye understand now?'

'I think so,' Jack was hesitant. 'Although, it doesn't make me feel any better.'

The captain looked at him with sympathy. 'Perhaps, in time, ye'll be able to accept it.'

Chapter Thirty-one

Mary had already gone down for breakfast when Meg awoke. She first noticed the sunlight stream in through a gap in the curtains. Then all at once the memories from the previous evening came flooding back in a tide of pain and she buried her face in her pillow and groaned. How would she be able to face anybody? How could she smile and be pleasant company when Jack's deception ripped at her heart with every breath?

Meg remained silent for most of the trip home. Not that the others noticed. Mary constantly chattered, first about one boy and then about another, leaving little room for either Meg or Philip to get a word in. Meg's initial shock and anguish over the events of the previous night eventually passed, and now she quietly seethed. Her anger centred mostly on herself for trusting Jack. She had known of Jack's rakish character from the beginning. But he had beguiled her with his charm, on the pretext of being her friend and she had fallen completely into his trap.

Why would he change his ways just for her? She realised now how ludicrous it sounded. After all, she was the only one to see the "deeper side" of Jack. He was probably basking in his glorious victory right now, laughing at how easily he had duped the naive Miss Wingrove. And to think at first, she believed she had hurt him. Meg almost groaned out loud, but clenched her fist instead, so tightly her nails began to dig into her palms.

As soon as they arrived back at the stud farm, Meg engrossed herself in catching up with the other children and helping in the kitchen; anything to get her thoughts away from Jack Fordham and anything to keep from facing his sister.

Late in the afternoon, Mrs Sainsbury came to inform Meg that Mr Roderick had arrived to see her. In the face of Jack's betrayal, Meg had forgotten about Roderick's disappearance from the ball until that moment.

'What is it, Meg? I confess you look rather pale.'

'I do not wish to see Mister Roderick.' Meg's words seethed with contempt. 'He abandoned me at the ball.'

Mrs Sainsbury gasped. 'Do you mean to say he left without you? How shocking. That is excessively ill-mannered of him. What did you do?'

'My brother brought me back to the hotel.'

Mrs Sainsbury shook her head. 'Of all the thoughtless — why it is shameful,' she scorned. 'I shall throw him out on his ear.'

Meg thought that would be a good idea and then reconsidered. 'No, please Missus Sainsbury,' she said crossly. 'I think I shall confront him myself.'

Mrs Sainsbury's lips pressed into a thin line. 'Are you sure?'

Meg nodded and stepped past her out of the room.

Roderick waited for her in the parlour. His back was turned, and he stared into the small fire that burned in the grate. Meg watched him, irritation churning within.

'I am surprised to see you here,' she eventually said, a sharp edge to her voice.

Mr Roderick turned around, his expression somewhat dark. 'I do not doubt it.'

Meg turned her back to him and walked to the sideboard where she fiddled with the nick-nacks. 'I do not pretend to understand why you left me stranded at the ball. Fortunately for you, my brother was there to assist me, although he has sworn to call you to account.' She turned to face him again. 'I can only hope you are here to apologise for your shabby behaviour.'

Roderick appeared to be stunned at her outburst. 'You wish for me to apologise?' he scoffed, his eyes glinting harshly. 'It is you who ought to be sorry, Miss Wingrove, for your offence far outweighs mine.'

Alarm shot through her. Had he seen something? Heard something? 'What...what are you talking about?' Meg dreaded the answer.

'I think you know.' His eyes did not swerve from hers. 'I saw you and Mister Fordham in the garden last night, locked in an embrace.'

'Oh,' Meg cried and sank into a chair, her hands over her face.

'I thought we had an understanding between us,' Roderick accused, and Meg looked up sharply.

'What understanding?'

'Come, come, Miss Wingrove,' he came to stand in front of her, his eyes burning. 'You must know how ardently I adore you. You were on my arm at the ball. How do you think I felt when I saw you and Fordham together? I could not stay another moment.'

Meg dropped her head into her hands again. The whole situation was more of a confusing mess than ever. She had no idea anyone had seen them in the garden. She could only hope Roderick was the only one. Somehow, she had to fix things. 'You are right,' she groaned. 'My indiscretion far outweighs yours, and I am truly ashamed. I am so very sorry for causing you pain. I only hope you can forgive me.'

Roderick stared at her for a long while, breathing deeply. 'So, you heart belongs to him, then?' he asked stiffly.

'The ... er ... incident with Mister Fordham should never have happened. You know what he is. You warned me yourself.' Meg's lips trembled and tears welled yet again.

Mr Roderick rubbed his chin, eyeing her carefully and then moved to a chair. After a time, he spoke again. 'If that is true,' he said solemnly, 'then I must bring him to book. Just tell me one thing. Do we have a foreseeable future together?'

Meg sniffed and dabbed at her eyes. This was a question she could not deal with at present. 'Mister Roderick,' she began. 'Thank you for being so gracious and patient with me, but I am too confused to focus on the future at the moment. I need time to clear my head.'

Mr Roderick sighed. He had obviously hoped for a different answer.

'Very well, Miss Wingrove,' he said. 'I am due to collect my new horses next Saturday. May I call on you then?'

Meg nodded. 'Yes, I am sure that would be better.'

'Well, since you are clearly distressed, I shall not trouble you further. I bid you good day.' Mr Roderick stood up.

Meg watched him walk out of the room, her tongue frozen in her mouth. She could think of nothing appropriate to say. She stayed in the parlour for a long while, guilt gripping her heart. She was a traitor too, and it mortified her that she had hurt Mr Roderick. God forgive her, she had been so wrong.

ೊ಄ೕ

The *Madeline* had been at sea for two days and yet melancholy clung to Jack. Although he now understood why Meg held so tenaciously to her decision, it didn't change the way he felt about her. His heart still leapt when he pictured her face or remembered her voice.

Added to that was the incredible weight of remorse and shame of how he had treated her and how he had treated women in general. Was there any way to remove this disgrace? He certainly could not undo what he had done.

Jack was so engrossed in his thoughts he did not notice the captain appear beside him.

''Tis not easy to let go of a woman once ye fall in love, eh?'

Jack was startled out of his reverie. 'Love?'

Tom grinned. 'Ye do love her don't ye?'

Jack clenched his jaw. 'Love is for fools,' he almost hissed. But regret once again overrode his reactions. 'Others — seem to think so … that I love … her,' he admitted.

'Others?'

Jack squared his shoulders and tried to look indifferent. 'My heart and I have been estranged these ten years. We are not well acquainted anymore.'

Tom grinned at him. 'Fair enough,' he said with a shake of his large head. 'But she is important to ye, is she not?'

'Too important,' Jack said vehemently and then lapsed into silence.

If the captain had something to say to that, he held it back. He just stood there, quiet. Waiting.

'You know what is so maddening,' Jack suddenly became impassioned. 'She confessed to me she loves me. Now, I can understand she thinks our ideals are too different, but, for the life of me, I cannot fathom how she finds religion so important. It is nothing but a narrow-minded view and a list of dos and don'ts. Why ... *why* would she sacrifice her happiness to a set of rules? It doesn't make sense.'

The captain's lips twitched, but understanding lit his eyes. 'Perhaps she's not sacrificing herself to a set of rules.'

Jack frowned at him. 'What do you mean?'

'Maybe your perception of religion is the problem here.' The captain said candidly. 'I'm saying maybe yer lady friend sees her faith as something far greater than a list of rules.'

Jack stared at him, taking in this explanation. 'I see,' he replied. 'I mean, I understand what you are saying, but I still don't ... never mind.' Jack turned back to the ocean, lost.

The captain turned and scanned the horizon. 'Ye still don't understand what could be so great that it transcends the fulfilment of loving and being loved in return.'

Jack turned back to him and nodded. 'Exactly.'

The captain still gazed out over the sea, a small smile turning up the corners of his mouth. 'Nothing.'

'I beg pardon?'

Captain Connelly sighed and turned around to lean against the railing. 'Nothing is better than loving and being loved,' he elaborated. 'Nothing in earthly terms, anyway.'

Jack looked at him, waiting for further explanation, but nothing came. 'What do you mean?'

Tom flashed him a broad grin and slapped him on the back. 'Join me again for supper tonight,' he said, 'and I'll tell ye the greatest love story ever told.' He began to walk away but paused and turned back. 'And Jack,' he added, 'come with an open mind.'

Chapter Thirty-two

Jack watched the large man trudge across the deck and laughed softly to himself. The captain certainly knew how to whet one's interest. Jack was more than intrigued and impatiently waited for the day to pass and supper time to arrive.

In fact, Jack's impatience took him to Tom's cabin before the man himself arrived. The captain had hardly sat down to eat when Jack reminded him to tell the story. Tom grinned at him and told him to wait until he finished his meal.

When the captain's plate was clean, and he had even mopped up his gravy with some crusty bread, he got up from the table and stretched himself out upon his bed to relax. Jack pulled his chair around to face the sea farer. With his hands behind his head and his eyes on the ceiling Tom began his tale.

'It all started when God created man …'

'Oh.' Jack scowled in disappointment. He had been tricked. 'You are not going to read me a sermon are you, Tom?'

The captain rolled onto his elbow and gave Jack a challenging look. 'It depends, Jack,' he said. 'Do ye want to understand why yer lady cherishes her faith so, or not? I told ye to come with an open mind.'

Jack rolled his eyes. 'All right, all right,' he grumbled. 'I'll listen.'

Tom rolled back to his former position and continued. 'God made the man, Adam, and the woman, Eve, in the garden of Eden. He had created something very good, and he loved them with a perfect love. And they were free. God only asked one thing of them; not to eat the fruit from a tree called the Tree of the Knowledge of Good and Evil, or they would die.

'However, God had an enemy. Lucifer was jealous of God and hated Him with a fury. What better way to hurt God than through the creation which He loved. So, he convinced Eve it wouldn't hurt to disobey God and eat that fruit. He told her she wouldn't die, but she would become like God.

'So, Eve ate the fruit, and then passed the lies on to Adam, who also ate the fruit. At once, a giant rift was torn between God and His creation. They suddenly knew shame and hid from God. Then they lied to God and tried to make excuses for their behaviour. But God is perfect, and He could not look upon their sin. They were cast out of the garden and had to toil and labour to survive.

'Now, as man increased in number on the earth, so did man's wicked behaviour. All the while God looked on, grieving over what His creation had become. His heart filled with pain and eventually He decided to wipe mankind from the face of the earth.

'But there was one man who loved God, and so God, who cannot resist responding to the love of His creation, saved him and his family. That man was Noah. God destroyed the earth with a flood, but saved Noah, his family, and the animals in the ark.

'Still, even after the flood, mankind did not learn to love God, continuing in wickedness and rejecting The Creator. God sent many messengers to speak on His behalf. He sent prophets with desperate pleas for His people to come back to Him, but they would not listen. Time and time again He was forced to punish His people, and still they did not return. The people killed the prophets and ignored the warnings. It seemed their hearts were set on worshipping idols made of wood and stone, and rejecting the living God who created and loved them.

'In a last, desperate act, God sent His only Son, whom He loved above all else to the earth as a baby. God could have intervened at any time with a display of awesome power and demanded His people love Him, but He wanted more than that. He wanted His people to love Him in return, freely, of their own choice. So, He sent Jesus who was born in a stable and His first bed was a feed trough.

'Jesus, although He was God made flesh, grew up as a man and experienced life as any one of us. At thirty years of age, He began to teach the truth about God. He taught that the kingdom of heaven was about giving, serving, and loving. T'was about being humble and merciful. He taught that it was more than keeping a bunch of rules; it was about an attitude of love in yer heart.

'Then He performed the most powerful act of all. He laid down His life to set His people free. Ye see, the only way the rift could be closed between God and man was through the death of a perfect lamb. The Israelites practised this ritual for centuries, but it had to be done daily to cleanse the people of sin. God could not watch His people remain trapped in such a harsh covenant. He sent Jesus, the perfect lamb who was without sin, to die for His people, once and for all.

'And Jesus made that sacrifice. He gave up His throne in heaven, and all His power to become a helpless human. Then He suffered unspeakable horrors as He was sentenced and then crucified on a Roman cross, naked, with soldiers mocking Him.

'All the sin of all the ages, including yours and mine, was placed on His shoulders as He hung there. He could have called ten thousand angels to cut Him loose, but He went to the cross without a fight. He knew it was the only way. Do ye know what He cried out from that cross? "Father, forgive them, for they know not what they do." Even amid such pain and suffering, He still loved his people and was willing to forgive.

'One of the things Jesus said to his disciples was this: "Greater love hath no man than this, that a man lay down his life for his friends." It was perfect, unconditional love for us that sent Jesus to His death, and that, my friend, transcends every other kind of love ye'll ever find. Our love fails, but God's love never fails. That is what yer lady friend cherishes above all.'

The captain paused to rise and pour himself a drink. Jack became solemn and thought over what he had just been told, but he had many questions.

'So, if Jesus died, where did God win? I mean, He lost his Son, and obviously there is still wickedness in the world.'

Tom gulped down some water and wiped his arm across his mouth. 'The story doesn't end there, Jack. That's where it really began. Three days after He died, God raised Jesus from the dead, defeating death, sin, and sickness. Jesus made the way clear for us to come to God freely. All we must do is believe what Jesus did and surrender our hearts to Him. All those who believe can live in that victory Christ won on the cross and are promised to live eternally in heaven.

'His grace and forgiveness are free, but ye must make Him the centre of yer life and live in fellowship and obedience to him. Ye see 'tis not about a set of rules, but about a relationship with our Creator who has loved us from the beginning and was not above sacrificing His life for us. Your lady is willing to forgo her happiness with you, because Jesus gave up His life for her.'

⤲⤳

The female inhabitants of Sainsbury Stud, barring the cook, were all seated in the sunny parlour. Mary and Kitty practised their embroidery under the scrutiny of their governess, while Gwen sat by crocheting a blanket.

In between the odd instruction from Meg, the girls chattered gaily. Mary had not yet run out of little anecdotes from the ball, which Kitty listened to with rapt attention, and giggled at intermittently.

'… then Uncle Jack stood up with Winnie, didn't he Winnie? And oh,' she sighed, 'it was just like a fairy tale.'

Meg stiffened, merely nodding her confirmation. How she wished Mary hadn't remembered.

'Which dance was it, Winnie?' Kitty asked, her eyes wide.

Meg opened her mouth to answer, but Mary cut in. 'They danced a waltz, didn't you Winnie?'

'Mm-hmm,' she acknowledged, focusing her attention on a stitch she tried to fix for Kitty.

'You should have seen her, Kitty,' Mary went on. 'She looked so beautiful they way Uncle Jack whirled her around the ballroom.'

Meg could stomach no more. 'That is nonsense, Mary,' she scoffed, very aware of Gwen's eyes on her.

'Well,' Mary argued, 'you looked much better on Uncle Jack's arm, than on that dull Mister Roderick's.'

'That's enough impertinence from you, young lady.' Gwen intervened. 'Go and put your sewing things away.'

Kitty looked at Meg as though she had just had a wondrous thought. 'Winnie,' she said with wide, innocent eyes, 'You should marry Uncle Jack. Then you would be our aunt and we could have you near us always.'

Meg felt the colour drain from her face.

'Kitty, hold your tongue.' Gwen remonstrated and directed her youngest to pack up also.

She looked apologetically at Meg. 'I don't know what has gotten into those girls,' she said with a grim smile. 'Are you all right, Meg?'

'Yes, of course,' Meg answered with a light cough.

'It's just you don't appear to be yourself and I wondered if ...'

'It is nothing,' Meg cut her off. 'I am just tired.'

At supper that night, Meg listened quietly to the familial conversation, and only spoke when one of them addressed her. She picked at her food, her emotions too churned up to be hungry. She frequently caught Gwen watching her, a worried look on her face, but thankfully she said nothing.

Philip had poured some cream onto his pudding when he remembered something that would be of interest to his wife. 'Fordham appears to have found another lady friend,' he told her.

Meg stared at her plate, her spoon frozen in motion. What now?

'He has?' Gwen asked.

'Yes,' he answered. 'I don't know her name, but there were a few rumours floating around at the ball that she is a commoner, a serving woman of sorts.'

Meg dropped her spoon, her hand suddenly weak, and then apologised for the noise.

'Although,' Philip continued, clearly oblivious, 'When I saw her, she did not look like a serving woman.'

Meg froze again. It was hard to breathe suddenly.

'You saw her?' Gwen asked.

'Yes, we passed them on our way back to the hotel the other night. They came out of a gaming house arm in arm and were about to get into that splendid coach of his. She was a dark-haired beauty, which is all I can tell you.'

Meg rose from her seat, her stomach swirling. 'Excuse me,' she whispered, 'I don't feel very well.'

She hurried out of the room but heard Gwen's next question. 'Are you sure it was Jack?'

'Of course,' he replied. 'I would recognise him anywhere.'

Chapter Thirty-three

Jack sat back and exhaled slowly. The captain's words stirred something deep within him, and if they were true then he could not ignore them. Hadn't he yearned for that kind of love? He could not have explained it if he tried, but as he listened to Tom, it was like he had discovered a treasure; one he had searched for all his life. He shook his head, trying to shake this strange sensation.

He leaned his head to one side. 'I never realised this is what religion is about,' he said. 'The only experience I have had at the hands of "Christians" is damnation.'

Tom grimaced. 'Unfortunately, some brethren are too quick to judge. The Scriptures indeed say if ye reject Christ, ye face a Godless eternity in hell, but Jesus taught that we should approach each other in love and grace. The Bible says, "For God did not send his Son into the world to condemn the world; but that the world through him might be saved."'

Jack pressed his lips together. 'I remember Meg saying something like that once. She is unlike any other Believer I have ever met. She is all those things you say a Christian should be.' He gave a half laugh. 'And to think I scorned her faith and thought her too fanatical.' Regret assailed him once again and he fell silent.

Eventually, Jack sighed and sat up straight. 'So, what happens now?'

Tom looked at him intently. 'Ye can be free of the shame that weighs heavily on ye,' he said. 'And that wound of betrayal can be healed.'

A shiver ran up Jack's spine. 'How? How do you know these things?' He had not told the captain anything about Antoinette, or his family's rejection.

The captain smiled warmly at him. 'God has his hand upon ye, my friend, I can see it clearly. He wants ye for heaven. Go, search yer heart, realise yer sinfulness and your need for Him, and surrender it all into His hands. He's waiting to meet with ye.' Tom handed Jack his Bible. 'Take this. Read the gospel of John. I'll be praying for ye.'

Jack opened the door of his cabin, his hands trembling as he turned the handle. Tom had said God waited to meet him, and Jack did not know what to expect. He peered around the room, but everything seemed to be in place. He relaxed a little, but he did not quite know what he should do. Was he supposed to pray? He didn't even know how. Would God just appear somehow? He could not imagine the Creator of the universe coming to visit Jack Fordham. He was not worthy of such an honour.

He looked at the Bible in his hands. The captain had told him to read the Gospel of John. With a light shrug, he sat down at his small table and, with a lantern nearby, began to read. He read about the life of Jesus.

It was all as the captain had told him. Deep respect and admiration for the Messiah who did not waver in his teaching and who did not flinch, even in the face of death, grew within him. When he read about Jesus' death and resurrection his heart was gripped in a vice. *He did that for you, Jack. He did that for you.*

It was late when Jack closed the Bible. He stared at the book. 'Why would you do that for me, when I have never even given you a thought?' He traced his finger over the lettering engraved in the leather. Holy Bible. You are holy,' he mumbled, 'and I am not worthy of anything you have to offer.'

Despite this, he yearned to know more about this man. He wished he could meet him personally and ask him questions. Christ alone would surely have the answers to anything he could ask. 'Are you really real?'

He remembered the words of the captain. *Go, search your heart, realise your sin and your need of Him.* All at once his life began to play before him. It seemed every incidence where he had lied to or hurt someone flashed before his mind's eye. The faces of many, many women appeared and disappeared before him; women who he had toyed with and then discarded, and he realised with shame he had been selfish, proud and without respect. Then other women came to his remembrance, the ones he had taken as mistresses. He saw not the selfishness they had displayed, but the selfish way he had treated them. He had dishonoured them, defiled them, and defiled himself.

The further he went on this journey into himself, the more he realised filth clung to him and a rotten stench filled his nostrils. He looked at himself and he could see his heart, not red and beating healthily, but putrid and dying. The garment he wore hung like filthy rags. He looked around him, but everything had gone dark. He felt around for his lantern but could not even feel the table he had leaned on.

'What is happening to me?' Jack cried out, nausea twisting his stomach.

This is what I see when I look at you.

Jack peered into the darkness. 'Who … who are you?' Fear gripped him.

I AM He that created you.

Jack dropped to his knees. The authority in that voice so overwhelmed him he could do naught but bow. 'God have mercy on me. What must I do to become clean?' His voice choked.

Take your evil deeds out of my sight!
Stop doing wrong, learn to do right!
Seek justice, encourage the oppressed.
Defend the cause of the fatherless,
plead the case of the widow.
Come now, let us reason together.
Though your sins are as scarlet,
they shall be as white as snow;
though they are as red as crimson,
they shall be like wool.

Jack shook with reverent fear. He had now bent forward with his face almost touching the floor. 'You have shown me my life, and it is black with sin. I am so ashamed. I do not deserve to live. Please, do with me what you will.'

Behold, the Lamb of God which takes away the sin of the world.

Silence surrounded him, but Jack began to feel a warm sensation, first touching his heart and then spreading out to his limbs. He opened his eyes and could see bright light enter the room. Deathly afraid, he slowly raised his head. The first thing he saw was the feet of a man. Though they radiated light, he could clearly see nail scars in them.

He lifted his gaze further and was dazzled by the blazing light that emanated from this being. And yet, he could not look away. He saw the man's arms outstretched toward him, palms up, and recognised the scars in his hands. Tears began to stream down Jack's face. The beauty of the sacrifice this man had made touched the depths of his being. 'Christ, my Lord.' he fell, face down before him.

Jonathon.

Jack did not move, even though he recognised his name.

Jonathon. Do not be afraid. Look up.

Amazingly, with those gentle, but commanding words, Jack's fear melted away and a sweet peace took its place. Slowly, again, he began to look up. He even found the courage to stand to his feet. The light that shone from him burned so bright Jack could not see his features clearly, but he sensed the man smiled at him, and his eyes were like fire.

See, your sins have been forgiven.

Jack looked down at himself. His robe was clean and pure white. It even glowed a little. And his heart beat strong and healthy in his chest. He also noticed the rotting stench had gone, and now a spicy aroma filled the air. Jack began to weep. It seemed too good to be true.

The next moment a wave of intense love surrounded, enveloped and saturated him. With pure joy he realised this is what he had longed for his whole life. He had come home at last. 'Thank you, Lord,' was all he could say, and he repeated it over and over.

Come. I want to show you something.

Still enveloped in Christ's arms of love, Jack felt himself gently guided back through time until he found himself face to face with Antoinette and his father. 'No, I don't want to go there,' Jack recoiled.

You must forgive.

'I don't know how.' Jack resisted.

Unexpectedly, he found himself reliving the moment when he had been told Antoinette had betrayed him and his father had condemned him. The pain stabbed at him all over again and he cried out in anguish. He wept bitter tears and grieved over his loss. Yet, all the while he knew those loving arms held him. He even sensed Jesus grieved with him, sharing his pain.

Let it go.

The words were not more than a whisper, but they echoed through his soul. At that moment he realised he no longer wanted to carry that resentment and everything that flowed from it anymore. It had only created a hard shell around his heart and distanced him from people who only wished to care. With a long sigh, Jack released his bitterness and anger, and forgave Antoinette, his father, and his sister as well.

The next thing Jack knew he was back in his cabin on the ship. His lantern had long since burnt out, and he remained seated at the table with the Bible in front of him. However, Jack knew his experience had been real. His throat was raw, and his cheeks were still damp from all the tears he had shed. But the clearest evidence was the lightness in his heart. He was clean. He was forgiven. He was made new. Unspeakable joy flooded him, and he began to laugh softly.

He rose from the chair and crept to the bed where he flopped himself down, still chuckling like a giddy child. 'I am a believer,' he said out loud, and then burst into another laugh. 'I am a Believer,' he told the ceiling, and hooted with delight.

'Thank you God for saving me,' he prayed as he began to settle down. 'My life is yours from this day on.'

Chapter Thirty-four

Meg had not left her room again that night. She couldn't face Mr or Mrs Sainsbury and the myriad questions she knew they'd have. She didn't know how she'd answer even one of them.

The following morning, soon after breakfast, Gwen sought Meg out, even though she did her best to stay out of sight. Obviously determined, Gwen came into the cook house, where Meg fiddled with a bowl of porridge, unable to raise an appetite. The older woman quickly glanced around the room to make sure they were alone.

'Meg, dear,' she began, 'may we talk?'

Meg knew instinctively what Gwen wanted to discuss with her and recoiled internally. 'I do not think it would serve any purpose.'

Gwen sat down next to her. 'You are obviously distressed. I just want to be able to help.'

Meg sighed. 'It concerns your brother, Missus Sainsbury,' she said bluntly. 'You will want to defend him. I need an unbiased listener.'

'But Meg,' Gwen insisted, 'you are like a sister to me. If he has hurt you, then …Will you not give me a chance?'

Meg, beginning to feel her emotions spin out of control again, got up quickly. 'I must take the boys to school.' She said and swept out of the kitchen.

Meg remained pensive all the way to the school. She had been deeply shocked by Philip's revelation the prior evening. When she realised Jack had gone from kissing her to another within hours it had been like a knife thrust in her heart. Waves of nausea assaulted her every time she thought about it. He had betrayed her. Her mind screamed at her that she should have known he would do this all along. After all, he had done it before. What made her any different?

Gwen did not bother Meg again until the children were in bed that evening. Of course, the minute the children were tucked in she went and shut herself in her bedroom, hoping she'd escaped Gwen's interrogation. But when a knock came on her door, she knew escape was out of the question.

'It's Gwen. May I come in?'

It was a few seconds before she forced an answer. 'If you wish.'

Gwen opened the door and peeked in. Meg lay on her bed, still fully clothed, staring at the ceiling. Gwen game in and closed the door softly behind her.

'Meg,' she said firmly, sitting down on the edge of the bed beside her, 'I want you to tell me what has happened.'

Meg did not respond.

'Listen,' she persisted. 'I care about you very much and I am worried about you. You have hardly eaten these past two days. You are pale and withdrawn. You are not yourself. What has Jack done to cause you such distress?'

Meg sighed. 'I really don't want to talk about it.' She rolled to her side, facing away from Gwen. 'There is nothing you can say to help.'

'Perhaps not, but I can listen.'

Once again Meg did not respond. How could she tell Gwen that Jack lived up to and went beyond every rumour said about him? Would she even be able to tell her about what happened at the ball?

'Are you in love with my brother?' Gwen asked her unexpectedly.

Unwelcome tears immediately welled in Meg's eyes and her lips began to tremble. 'A few days ago ... I thought I was,' she said in a broken voice and with reluctance, sat herself up. 'But now ...' she clenched her teeth. 'If I never see him again it will be too soon.' Angry tears spilled down her cheeks.

Gwen wrapped her in her arms. 'Oh, my poor darling. What did he do to you?'

Meg pulled her ragged emotions together once more, her anger giving her strength. 'Well, Missus Sainsbury,' Meg spoke candidly, pulling away from her. 'After we danced, he kissed me.'

Gwen looked horrified. 'How could he ...?'

'Then he offered to marry me ...'

'What?' Gwen's face changed from horror to surprise. 'He did?'

'He did, but I said no,' Meg quickly set her straight. 'And he then spent the rest of the evening with another woman.'

The pallor of Gwen's face now matched her own, no doubt.

'And what makes it worse,' Meg added, her voice shaking, 'he planned it all. He manipulated me to make me fall in love with him, and then he threw me aside like I was nothing. I cannot begin to tell you how sick with humiliation I feel.'

Meg slumped back onto her pillow and Gwen remained frozen in disbelief. 'If this is true,' she whispered as tears formed in her own eyes, 'then he has sunk lower than I thought possible.' She glanced at Meg. 'I mean, I knew he was a shocking flirt, but for all that he assured me most of his dalliances were harmless. Are you certain of all the details?'

Meg groaned. 'I knew you would defend him.'

'I am not defending him,' Gwen argued. 'I just want to know more information. You say he went to another woman after you.'

'You heard Mister Sainsbury. Do I have dark hair?'

'What is this plan you referred to?'

'It is what he does with every lady he pursues,' Meg answered. 'He manipulates her emotions and turns her head until she is blinded by love. Then, when he has had enough, he cries off. Jack told his best friend the game was over. I heard him retell it to his peers.'

Gwen got up stiffly. 'This is all my fault,' she said brokenly. 'I upset him terribly on Saturday. I should have made him stay.'

Meg shook her head in disbelief. 'How can you say this is your fault? Jack has a mind of his own.'

Tears slipped down Gwen's cheeks. 'But he was not in his right mind when he left here. Who knew what he would do in that state?'

Meg quietened, her tirade over.

'You know,' Gwen's voice was shaky. 'For a while, I have suspected Jack to be in love with you. I think that is why he took you to his orphanage, and the reason he proposed to you at the ball. But Jack has built a protective wall around his heart, and not even he knows what goes on inside it most of the time. I only know of one other time when he offered marriage, and that was a very long time ago. He would only have done so if he was sure about you.'

'No, Missus Sainsbury. He told me himself he only proposed out of a sense of duty.'

Gwen shook her head. 'That would just be a defence. Jack has not been himself lately. Trust me; he is in love with you.

Meg thought about her words. Was it possible? Jack loved her? It couldn't be. 'But, what about this other woman Mister Sainsbury saw?'

Gwen frowned, clearly upset. 'If it is true, then it is inexcusable,' she answered ruefully. 'That is what troubles me most. The Jack I know is not so completely void of moral principles. In fact, I *know* he is an honourable man. But perhaps my family has pushed him too far.'

'You must not blame yourself. I do not know what has happened between you, but Jack makes his own choices. He did this to me, not you.'

Gwen fell silent and sat down beside Meg again. They clasped each other's hands, and wordless comfort and understanding passed between them. After a time, Gwen looked up at her governess. 'I forgot to ask you if you gave Mister Roderick a dressing down?'

Meg didn't answer immediately, a new wave of regret washing over her. 'He, ah, saw Jack and I … together … in the garden.'

'Oh,' Gwen winced.

'Apparently, he became so upset he just left. I cannot be angry with him for that.'

'No,' Gwen agreed. 'Of course not.'

Meg gasped. 'That reminds me, Brian wanted to call him out the other night. I must write to him before he does anything so desperate. Excuse me Missus Sainsbury.'

'Yes, of course,' Gwen replied, rising from the bed. The two women embraced, and Gwen left Meg alone to compose her letter.

Meg sat at her bureau and penned a quick note to her brother to drop the offence with Mr Roderick, explaining her reasons. She would never forgive herself if Brian and Mr Roderick came to blows because of her own foolishness.

Chapter Thirty-five

When Jack emerged on deck the next morning, the lightness inside him from the night before remained. Excitement brewed within him, and he could not keep a broad grin from his face.

The captain took one look at him and seemed to recognise the change. 'So, it is well with yer soul now, eh?'

'Yes.' Jack nodded but could not find any words to elaborate.

Tom chuckled, his joy evident in that laugh. 'Welcome to the family,' he told Jack happily and embraced him tightly. 'What happened last night?'

'It was … He … I was …' Jack choked on his emotions and could not get the words out.

Once again Tom laughed. 'Never mind. Tell me whenever ye're ready.'

Jack spent another day standing solitarily at the bow of the ship. This time however, he did not dwell on problems in his life, but thanked God for his new-found faith. He gazed into the horizon and saw the perfect beauty of creation in a new light. He drank in the fresh sea air and thanked God for every little detail he could see from a cloud in the sky to a fish darting beneath the waves. He felt so light and clean it made him giddy.

After he had eaten dinner, he brought the captain's bible up on deck and spent time between reading parts of it and staring into the ocean's depths, musing over what he had just read. The more he began to learn, the hungrier he became. Like a thirst in him that had never been satisfied, now he could not stop drinking, re-hydrating his dry spirit.

The sun had begun its descent when Jack came upon a scripture that excited him to such an extent that he ran to search for the captain, finally discovering him below decks checking the cargo.

'Tom. Tom,' he called as he approached the sea man, the bible still open in his hands.

The captain poked his head out from behind a huge bale of wool. 'What is it, lad?'

'You must read this text,' Jack told him in a fever.

Tom took the bible and squinted at the pages. It was too dim in the hold to read, so he climbed back up on deck, Jack close behind him.

'Which verse did ye say?'

Jack pointed to Isaiah, chapter one, and verse sixteen. He read aloud. 'Take your evil deeds out of my sight...'

When he finished reading, he looked at Jack. 'What about it, lad?'

'God spoke to me last night,' his words rushed out. 'And that is what he said.'

Tom's mouth dropped open. 'He spoke to ye?'

Jack nodded.

'And ye've never read this before?'

'Never. Well,' Jack rethought his response. 'Perhaps when I attended services, not that I paid attention.'

The captain nodded and gave a low whistle. 'You are truly blessed. Tell me more.'

⁂

On Saturday, Meg awoke anxious. Mr Roderick was due to call on her and she had no idea what she would say to him. Should she give him a chance? Would she ever love him? She had fallen head over heels for Jack but had never experienced more than admiration for Mr Roderick. Was what she felt for Jack real? Was it something that would stand the test of time with the right person? If so, then she would only be deceiving Roderick if she promised him anything. On the other hand, if she had confused her attraction to Jack with love when it was only a passing fancy, then she and Mr Roderick had a real possibility of a happy future together.

The problem was though Jack had hurt her dreadfully, she still found herself pining for him. Her anger and pain had receded to a dull ache and heaviness within her, but disillusionment and confusion haunted her. Would it be right to make promises to another man when she knew she had not let go of Jack? Then again, good men like Roderick did not come by very often. Could he be her last opportunity to find a husband? He was attentive and courteous, and he shared her faith. He had declared how much he cared for her. Would she, in time, learn to love him?

When Mr Roderick arrived, Meg was no closer to an answer than when she had arisen that morning. She sighed with relief when he went straight to Mr Sainsbury to transact his business first. Looking out of the window she could see them talking in the distance. They shook hands and Roderick led two horses to his carriage and tied them to the back. He turned and walked towards the house.

Meg's nerves jumped and she hurried to the parlour. She would await him there while she tried to gather her senses. She had to decide.

'Good-afternoon, Miss Wingrove,' he greeted her not too many minutes later.

Meg stopped pacing in front of the hearth and looked at him. 'And you, Mister Roderick,' she gave a short curtsey.

He moved to her side and kissed her hand warmly.

Meg pulled away, awkward. 'May I pour you some tea?' She forgot his dislike of the beverage.

He looked at her strangely. 'No, thank you, Miss Wingrove. Shall we sit?'

'Yes, of course,' Meg nodded, uncomfortable. She sat on the edge of a chair and Mr Roderick sat opposite her.

'I trust you are improved from your distress of last week?'

'A little,' she replied with a shrug. 'It is considerate of you to ask.'

An awkward silence followed until Roderick cleared his throat.

241

'Well, you know why I am here,' he eventually said, 'So I shall not dilly-dally with small talk.'

'Yes, I …' Meg fumbled with her words.

'I am deeply fond of you, Miss Wingrove. Indeed, it wasn't until I saw you with Fordham I realised how much.' Mr Roderick came to kneel before her. He took her hand in his and gazed sincerely into her face. 'I hope you feel the same way. Will you promise me your hand in marriage?'

Meg only knew dismay. She knew she could not give this man the answer he wished for, but she hated to break his heart. She took a deep breath, trying to gather her courage. She looked sadly at him. 'Mister Roderick, I am afraid I cannot promise you anything. I am not sure if I care for you in that way, nor if I ever will. You are a very thoughtful man, and I appreciate your kindness, but I do not believe it will ever be any more than that.'

Mr Roderick hung his head for a moment, and when he looked up it was obvious, he felt deep regret. For a moment Meg thought she saw something dangerous, even sinister, flicker in his eyes, but then it disappeared, and she silently scolded herself for imagining such things.

'I am sorry to hear that, Miss Wingrove, more than you know. I had high hopes for us.' He stood to his feet. 'There is no use in prolonging this visit then,' he added. 'Good day.'

Once again Meg watched him leave, knowing nothing she could do or say would make the situation any easier. It would not be fair or honest to marry Mr Roderick when Jack Fordham remained a stumbling block in her heart. She stood there wondering why her life had suddenly been turned upside down. The only thing that made sense was that God held all in his hands and remained by her side, holding her up.

⇜⇝

The *Madeline* arrived safely in the port of Melbourne and Jack had been busy overseeing the transfer of his cargo to the ship that would take it to England. Once again, he kept a barrel aside to market to the local taverns. It was good to be on dry land again and in a thriving city.

Jack did not have to be back on the ship again until Tuesday. It was loaded with a new shipment of cargo to be taken back to Sydney, which kept Captain Connelly fully occupied as well. Jack used the time to visit the owners of the taverns in Melbourne, offering them a taste of his wine. Most of them were impressed with its delicate palette and ordered some on the spot. He sold all the wine he had kept aside and received many requests for future deliveries.

Pleased with his success he went aboard the ship on departure day, more than ready to go home again. He had so many things he wanted to share with his family … and with Meg. Thinking of Meg made him feel inexplicably nervous. He wasn't sure how she would receive him after what had taken place between them. All he knew was he had a deepened respect for her. She had always acted in accordance with her faith in God and the way He had called her to live.

Jack decided no matter how drawn to Meg he felt, he would no longer pursue a future with her. He had treated her shamefully and he did not deserve her. She had rejected him with good reason. She was far too pure to be united with one such as he. It would be better if he released her. He only wanted the chance to apologise to her; he owed her at least that. And then, if she would deign to listen, he wanted to share with her his experience on the ship and how God had changed his life.

❦

Jack was restless. The voyage home had been rough. Unstable weather seemed to track them all the way. Many times, he had succumbed to sea-sickness and had lain in his bed groaning. As they neared Sydney his disquiet over seeing Meg increased.

He tossed and turned in his cot, finding it difficult to sleep. The swaying of the ship from side to side combined with thoughts of Meg kept him awake until, exhausted, he finally drifted off. Images twisted and rolled before his agitated mind, seemingly in unison with the waves that tossed the *Madeline* to and fro.

He twirled Meg around the dance floor, giddy with delight as she smiled at him. The dance floor disappeared, and he saw he knelt before her, proposing. But, when he looked at Meg, she had been replaced by a stranger. 'Do you deserve a woman like that?' the image asked. 'Are you … pure?'

The ghostly figure vanished, and he found himself alone momentarily. Five women approached him, all scantily clad, with looks of disgust on their faces. One slapped him in the face, and another spat on the ground. 'You'll only ever be good enough for us,' they snarled.

Meg's innocent face reappeared before him and the harlots faded away. But her sweet smile turned into a defiant stare. 'I cannot, will not, ever, become involved with you.' Then even she disappeared and only the echo of her words remained. He heard his own voice telling him over and over, *You are not worthy.*

Jack woke in the early hours, despondent. It was true. He was a worthless scoundrel, and he didn't even deserve Meg's forgiveness.

Jack dragged himself into the galley, exhausted from the difficult night he had just passed.

The captain eyed him for a moment. 'Come, let's take our porridge up on deck.'

Wordlessly, Jack followed the large man, glad to move away from the extra passengers in the galley. Tom neared the helm and sat, leaning against a mast. He pointed with his spoon. 'Ye see there,' he pointed to the coastline. They were running northwards, along the coast which was visible in the not-too-distant west. The weather had eased off a little, and though it was overcast, the wind had softened.

Jack followed the captain's gaze.

'That's Botany Bay. Governor Arthur Phillip was commissioned to establish the colony there, but they found 'twas no' suitable. So, they changed the site to Port Jackson, which is only about three leagues north of here.'

'And that means …?'

Tom chuckled. 'That means we'll be in Sydney Cove before nightfall.'

'I see,' Jack perched his bowl on his knees.

They ate their oats in silence for a while, but eventually the captain spoke again.

'Ye look a mite worse for wear this morning.'

'Mm,' Jack mumbled. 'I did not sleep well.'

'What's ailing ye?' Tom asked candidly.

Jack shrugged. 'I had a dream.'

Tom watched Jack. 'Well, and are ye going to share it with me?'

Jack shrugged again and spooned some porridge into his mouth. He swallowed it down. 'It was about Miss Wingrove.'

'Aye ...'

'I asked for her hand and then all these people accused me and told me I was unworthy of her.' Jack told him flatly. 'They were right, too. I mean, she is completely innocent, and I ... well, I ... have been heartless ... with women. They call me a rake.'

Tom placed his empty bowl beside him and drew his knees up. Resting his forearms on them, he looked at Jack. 'Perhaps ye were a rake, once. But now ye're a new creature in Christ. Ye must remember He has forgiven ye and ye now have a clean slate. Ye need to learn to forgive yerself, too.'

Jack appreciated the captain for explaining these things. Forgiving himself though, that would be difficult. Apart from God, only he knew how cold his heart had been.

'Even so,' Jack said. 'I'll never deserve Miss Wingrove's affection.'

'Maybe,' the captain smiled. 'Maybe not. I think ye should let her be the judge of that.'

Just as Captain Connelly had promised, the vessel arrived in Sydney Cove before sundown. Once Jack's belongings were brought ashore, he hailed a handsome cab and had them strapped to the roof. He ordered the driver to wait and went to search for the captain.

'I wanted to say goodbye,' he said, shaking Tom's hand warmly. 'I cannot begin to thank you for showing me the way to salvation.'

The captain shook his head humbly. 'I was just an instrument. If ye'd not been open to it, well, ye'd still be lost.'

'Well, you shall always be welcome at my table.' He handed the captain a card he had written on earlier. 'Here is my address. Feel free to visit any time you wish, even if I am not there. My staff will be informed to receive you.'

Tom looked at the card and back at Jack. 'Thank ye, Jack,' he grinned broadly. 'I'll remember that.'

Jack smiled warmly at him and then slapped him affectionately on the back. 'Bon voyage, Captain,' he nodded and strode away.

Chapter Thirty-six

Meg had struggled through another week, still heavy with grief, although a little more comforted. The church brethren had surrounded her and prayed with her. Despite all her uncertainty, she knew peace, and she knew God upheld her. She tried not to think about Jack. Dwelling on his actions only fed her anger and made her bitter. She knew the Scriptures taught she must forgive, but she had not yet come to a place where she even wanted to.

The worst part about it all was despite all her hurt and anger, she knew she still loved Jack. How that was possible, she could not fathom. But the yearning remained, magnifying her grief.

As the week wore on, she became uneasy. She heard Philip and Gwen mention Jack was due back soon and they would undoubtedly see him out at the farm within a few days. Meg wished in vain Jack would stay away for good. It would be easier that way.

Those thoughts led her to another idea. Perhaps the time had come to sever her ties with the Sainsburys and find another posting. There would no doubt be employment available in Sydney where she could be closer to her brother and Katherine. That way she wouldn't have to see Jack at all and would be able to avoid having her wounds re-opened at every meeting. She would write to Brian and ask him to find out if there were any positions advertised.

∽∾

Travel weary, but more peaceful than he had been in years, Jack climbed into the cab and ordered the driver to move on. He leaned back in the seat and closed his eyes, thanking God once again for His great mercy.

When he arrived at the town house, Jack did not expect Miller to be ready for him. However, his valet had made enquiries at the wharf and found out approximately when Jack would return. He had, therefore, made sure fires were lit in the study and Jack's bed chamber for the last day or two. He had even put hot bricks in his master's bed in case he returned.

So, when Jack arrived that night, Miller had everything prepared. 'How did you fare, sir?' he asked as he took Jack's coat.

'I must say, Miller, it was the best journey I have ever taken.'

'Glad to hear it, sir,' his valet grinned. 'If you are hungry sir, there is a cold repast to satisfy you.'

'Yes,' Jack replied. 'Some food and a good night's sleep are what I need right now.'

'Very good, sir,' Miller nodded and headed to the kitchen.

Jack's head had barely touched the pillow before he fell soundly asleep and did not wake until bright rays of sunlight peeped through the drapes the next morning.

Miller found him a little later, sitting up in his bed, reading the bible Tom had given him. Miller's eyes bulged at the sight, not surprising since Jack had railed against religion numerous times. Jack grinned at him. 'You should read this, Miller,' he said. 'It really is worthwhile.'

'Yes, sir.'

Miller probably wondered if Jack was quite himself. He placed a tray with a hot cup of coffee on it next to Jack on the sprawling bed and waited for instructions.

Jack leaned back against the pillows. He had so many things on his mind he wanted to do. He wanted to try and straighten things out with Meg and tell his sister about his new faith. He wanted to organise for the boys in the orphanage to receive some religious instruction. He wanted to tell everybody he saw about the Truth. The list went on.

Then Jack remembered it was Sunday and thought he should probably find a church to attend, although he did not know where to go. 'I am going out,' he informed Miller at long last. The valet looked at him blankly and Jack laughed.

'To church, my dear chap,' he explained. 'I am going to church.'

'Church, sir?' Miller's voice sounded strangled.

Jack leapt out of bed and stood face to face with his valet. 'I have come to faith in Christ. It is the only way to true happiness.' He hoped Miller could see his zeal. 'Read the gospels and you shall see.' He thrust the bible into Miller's chest.

The valet smiled a small, uncertain smile and turned to lay out Jack's clothes for the day. Jack busied himself shaving and washing his face, smoothing his hair, and planning out his day.

As he dressed, he instructed his valet to lay out his riding clothes so he could change as soon as he returned. 'I am going to the country when I return. Have the cook pack me some cold meat and bread to eat on the way.'

❧❧

Outside the little church in Parramatta, Meg reflected on Reverend Kilpatrick's provoking message as she walked to her horse. He had spoken of God's forgiveness. It was hard to comprehend he could forgive and forget so much wickedness, when Meg knew she found it harder to remember the good. Her conscience pricked her when she remembered Jack's treachery.

As she walked thoughtfully to the horse that waited for her, she noticed a familiar carriage nearby.

'Miss Wingrove!' Mr Roderick called in what could only be described as an urgent tone.

'Mister Roderick,' Meg frowned in concern. 'What is it?'

'One of the Sainsbury children has been injured and they need you at the farm without delay.' His face was filled with alarm.

Meg hurried toward her horse.

249

'No,' Roderick cried. 'Come with me. It will be faster. We can fetch the other horse later.'

Without another thought, Meg ran to his carriage, and they were off at break-neck speed. Although tossed around by the roughness of the road, her only thoughts were on the children. Which child had been hurt? How serious was it? 'Dear God, let them be all right.'

❧

Jack found a church without too much trouble and enjoyed the service immensely. Unfortunately, though, there were several brethren attending that recognised him immediately. He could feel their eyes upon him the whole time and could sense their judgemental scrutiny. Clearly, they wondered what untoward circumstance caused Jack Fordham, notorious man of the world, to attend their assembly.

Uncomfortable, he escaped from the building as soon as possible after the service, stopping only to exchange pleasantries with the minister. He did not want to waste any more time in Sydney. He hurried home to change and was in the saddle and on the way to Parramatta before an hour had passed.

Jack spent much of the ride to the Sainsbury's wondering what he should say. Should he start by apologising for his heartless behaviour, or should he just blurt out about his new faith? If only he could know beforehand how Meg would respond. Whatever he chose to do, he knew he had to be completely honest with her. No more manipulation and no more deceit.

❧

It seemed to take forever to reach the stud farm. Meg was sure they should have been there by now. Perhaps, she thought, in her distress time appeared to pass much more slowly. She studied the view from the window but could not recognise any landmarks. Something was not right. Wherever they were going, Roderick was certainly not taking her home.

Concerned, she banged on the roof, but Roderick did not stop. She fiddled with the window until she managed to open it and shouted out at him, but he either did not hear her or he deliberately ignored her. Roderick had lied to her, she realised with alarm. The Sainsbury children were probably hale and whole.

Suddenly frightened, Meg wondered whether she should open the door and jump out. But there were two problems with that. They were still travelling at an alarming speed, and she would likely break her neck, and she had no idea where they were, nor how she would find her way home. The only thing she could think of to do was pray.

She tried to keep her mind positive and endeavoured to trust in God to protect her. She had no idea why Roderick should abduct her like this. Could it be because she spurned him? Was he that obsessed with her? She shuddered and wondered where he would take her. And even more terrifying, what did he intend to do with her when they stopped. 'Please God, don't let him hurt me,' she whimpered, and tears of fright spilled down her cheeks.

❦

Jack arrived at the Sainsbury's in the middle of the afternoon. He tethered his horse near the stable and strode towards the house, his nerves quickening his pulse. The children had not accosted him at the door this time, and he wondered where they were playing. Casually, he entered the house and headed for the parlour.

Before he got that far, however, he came across Philip in the hallway. The older man started and then put out his hand in greeting. 'Oh, Fordham,' he said. 'You are back.'

Jack studied him. Something was wrong. 'Yes, I returned last night.'

'Did you find success in Melbourne?' Philip sounded courteous but was clearly distracted.

'Very much so,' Jack answered slowly. He eyed his brother-in-law suspiciously. 'Phil, you are being overly polite. Is something amiss?

Philip sighed. 'I must say, Jack, you are not entirely welcome here at present.'

This took Jack by surprise. He had not expected a cold greeting. 'Why not?'

Just then Gwen appeared from the parlour, having heard voices in the hallway. 'Oh, it's you.' Her eyes glazed over with emotion.

Jack glanced back at Philip who gave him an "I told you so" look. Perplexed, Jack turned his gaze back to his sister, questioning. Perhaps it had something to do with the way he'd left before he'd gone to Melbourne. Was she angry at him?

'I think it is time we all had a talk.' Philip said when his wife did not speak further and then he herded them into the parlour and closed the door.

❧⟋

The carriage finally pulled to a sudden stop and moments later Roderick yanked open the door. Roughly he pulled Meg out and she yelped in pain. They were in an isolated place with only a small lean-to hut and a haphazardly built shed. Roderick shoved her towards the shed, but she turned and faced him angrily. 'What do you mean by this? Take me home at once.'

Roderick laughed, but there was no mirth, only scorn. 'I don't think so, Miss Wingrove.' Meg reeled from the venom in his tone.

He pushed her forwards. 'Now, move on. And don't bother yelling. There's no-one around here for miles. You won't be heard.'

Meg wanted to scream at Roderick, but the change in him alarmed her. The polite gentleman had vanished, and before her stood a calculating villain. Reluctantly she allowed him to lead her to the little shed where he tied her to one of the supporting posts, her hands behind her back.

Meg froze in fear. 'What do you want from me?'

Roderick stared at her with cold eyes that frightened her. 'I want your inheritance. And you're going to tell me where it is.'

Chapter Thirty-seven

Philip and Gwen looked expectantly at Jack. They had just demanded an explanation for his disgraceful behaviour towards Meg, and he found himself tongue-tied, his heart once again twisting with remorse.

'She told me about your little tête-à-tête in the gardens,' Gwen added. 'She believes it was all part of one of your cruel games.'

Jack's conscience was stricken but he could not find any words.

'Then there is the matter of the, er, woman I saw you with after the ball,' Philip looked uncomfortable.

Jack sucked in his breath, dismayed. 'Meg knows about that?'

Gwen nodded and her voice began to shake. 'Do you have any idea what you have done to that poor girl?' The accusation in her face could not be denied. 'She did not eat for two days, and she has not been the same since.'

Jack pressed his fist to his mouth. The aftermath of his actions had spread further than he knew.

'I am so disappointed in you, Jack.' Gwen's voice was husky, brimming with emotion. 'I never dreamed you would sink this low. I blame myself, of course. I suppose I drove you to it.'

Jack hung his head and looked at the floor. 'It's not your fault Gwen.'

'What?' Cynicism laced Philip's voice. 'No flippant remarks? No trivial excuses?'

Gwen stared at him. 'Do you have anything to say in your defence?'

Jack sighed heavily. 'No.'

'No?'

Jack stood up, agitated. 'No,' he repeated. 'I admit I have behaved treacherously. I have been so wrong in so many ways, and for far too long.'

Gwen watched him with a frown creasing her brow.

'Please hear me out,' he implored. 'I have finally seen the error of my ways and I have returned from Melbourne a changed man. I have found faith in Christ, and I yearn to tell you more, but right now I just want to talk with Meg to try and straighten out this mess.'

'You...you've become religious?' Gwen asked in obvious disbelief.

Jack pressed his lips together and nodded. 'All I can say is God has changed me. But please, can you tell me where Meg is?'

Still seeming stunned, Gwen shook her head. 'No, sorry,' she stammered. 'She hasn't returned from church yet. I assume she has gone to visit one of her friends.'

⤜∞⤛

Meg glared at Roderick as though he were insane. 'I believe I have told you I do not possess an inheritance.' She tugged at the cords that bound her. 'You are mad. Let me go. My brother will have you arrested for this.'

Roderick sneered at her, appearing to enjoy her struggles. 'Ah, but you do,' he told her. 'You have a very large fortune.'

Meg stopped wriggling and looked at him, exasperated. 'That is absurd. How would you know such a thing?'

'I worked as a clerk to your father's solicitor a long time ago.' Roderick's smile was nothing short of smug.

Meg stared at him in mixed surprise and dismay. What could this mean? What did he know that she didn't?

Roderick saw he had caught her interest and grinned. 'When we worked on your father's estate after he passed, I came across a document my employer hadn't discovered yet. It contained information about some family jewels that were passed down through the female line. I quickly realised that no other mention of these jewels existed in the whole of the Wingrove estate, so I simply made the document disappear.'

Roderick's gloating sickened Meg, but this information was new. Jewels? She pulled at the cords again.

'I planned to wait until the estate was sold and all the debts were settled, but unfortunately, I got myself caught for theft and locked away. When I was in the Old Bailey, I found out through my contacts that you and your brother emigrated. Lucky for me, I was sent to Van Diemen's Land for seven years on the penal colony.'

Meg wasn't sure whether he really meant he was lucky or if he was just being sarcastic. He had just happily admitted criminal activities. 'I am sure you deserved it.'

'Well, now,' he continued. 'It wasn't pretty, I can tell you that. If I hadn't known about the fortune waiting for me, I don't know if I would have survived.'

Meg shuddered. Where was this all leading?

'After a few years I was sent to work for the settlers on their farms, shearing and the like. It got easier then and I started to make plans. Once I had the farmers eating out of my hand, I ran away. I made it to the mainland before they barely knew I had left.'

Meg felt the colour drain from her face. He was an escaped convict. How long had he stalked her? She experienced a sinking sensation in her stomach as she realised that just like Jack, this man had fooled her into believing he was something he was not. Anger twisted her gut as she remembered Roderick had even pretended to be a Believer. Meg bit her lip. She was so gullible and pathetic.

⌘

'Uncle Jack!' The children had finally discovered he was in the house and had cheerfully burst into the solemn atmosphere of the parlour.

Jack embraced them all warmly but could not bring himself to sound playful.

'Are you all right, Uncle Jack?' the ever-sensitive Kitty asked, her face turned innocently up to his.

'I am, Kitty,' he kissed her on the forehead. 'I just have some important things to discuss with your Mama.'

'May we have a game later?'

'Yes, of course,' he gave her an affectionate squeeze.

Mary took Kitty's hand and the four of them filed out of the room.

When the door firmly closed behind them, Gwen faced Jack. 'I hope this religion thing is not another one of your machinations to win Meg's attention.' Her voice was grave and full of warning.

'No Gwen, it is real,' he assured her. He began to tell the couple all about his experience on board the *Madeline*. They listened to him but appeared to be sceptical.

Philip frowned. 'Forgive me Fordham, but this sounds a little far-fetched. If what you say is true; if you are indeed changed, then we shall let time be the judge.'

It frustrated Jack that they could not see the truth. He wanted to argue with them, but realised they had a point. He had never shown commitment to anything except the orphanage. Why should they believe him? He prayed a quick prayer in his heart that they would see the change in him.

Jack looked at the clock on the mantle. The afternoon had faded into early evening. 'I wonder where Meg is?'

Gwen also looked at the clock with a frown. 'She is not usually this late.

Jack sat up straight. 'Has Nellie returned? And what about Roderick?'

'Nellie arrived shortly before you did,' Philip informed him.

'But Roderick is another story,' Gwen added. 'We won't be expecting him around here anymore, except to pay for his horses.'

Jack frowned, not understanding.

'He claimed he lacked the funds but expects to receive some within a week or two,' Philip explained.

'That is not what I referred to,' Gwen said, her eyes narrowing at Jack. 'You know, he saw you and Meg in the garden at the ball.'

Jack closed his eyes, remorse flooding him again. More complications. Could this get any worse?

'It enraged him so much that he left the ball, and apparently, if what I hear is correct, he went to a tavern and filled himself with whiskey.'

'That was rather shabby of him,' Jack scowled.

'Shabby but understandable,' his sister debated. 'As though you can be the judge.'

Jack held up his hands in an attitude of surrender. 'I know, I know. I am the worst scoundrel here.'

'Philip had already left, and you were gone. Fortunately for Meg, her brother was still there to take her home. And you know, Mister Roderick wanted to marry her, but she couldn't because of you.'

Jack could do naught but shake his head in dismay.

'I had no idea you saw me outside that gaming house.'

'And I had no idea you had proposed to Meg earlier in the evening, else I would have kept my mouth shut. Indeed, you had just assured me you had no interest in Meg.'

Jack dropped his head into his hands. His sister and her husband were clearly not ready to forgive him. He sighed and got up from his chair. 'I am going to see Nellie.' He strode out of the room.

Nellie was easily found in the kitchen, stirring a pot over the fire. Jack entered the cosy room and sat down at the table. 'How are you, Nellie?' The cook jumped in fright.

'Well, good day to y', Mister Fordham,' she greeted him with a shy curtsey. Smiling and wiping her hands on her apron, she approached him. 'May I help y'?'

Jack smiled warmly at her. 'Firstly, I must tell you, because I could use a friend right now, I have come to Christ recently.'

Nellie's mouth open and closed and opened again. 'Well ... that is — I mean — that is, wonderful,' she grinned. 'Meg will be so pleased.' Her face fell, unsure. 'I think so, anyway.'

'Precisely,' Jack sighed. 'I understand she is justifiably upset with me at present, but do you know where I can find her?'

Nellie shrugged. 'She is usually home by now. I went to visit a friend after church, so I didn't — no, wait. I saw her get into Mister Roderick's carriage.'

Jack studied her. 'I was under the impression things haven't quite worked out between them. Did she decide to give him another chance?'

'Oh, no.' the cook waved that suggestion aside. 'I don't think so at any rate. I heard him calling to her urgent-like and then they drove off awfully fast. I think they were in a hurry to go somewhere.'

Jack sucked in his breath. Something was very wrong. 'Thank you for your help, Nellie. I must go and speak with Mister Sainsbury.'

Chapter Thirty-eight

Roderick looked as though he took great delight in telling Meg his story. He seemed to be extremely proud of his efforts in tracking her down. It appeared he had spent the last few years trying to find her whereabouts. That she lived in Australia and worked as a governess were the only pieces of information he had.

'You can imagine how relieved I was to finally locate you.'

Meg grimaced. As if she would be sympathetic to his cause. She didn't want to imagine anything about him.

'Ah,' he sighed, 'but then I saw you at the Sainsbury's and it was love at first sight. I said to myself, I said. "Roderick, you could marry the pretty wench and earn those jewels honestly." So, I bought some new clothes and came to call on you. If it wasn't for that cursed Fordham, I would have won your hand, too.' The villain shook off his melancholy and chuckled at his own resourcefulness. 'I even went to church, praise be to God.' His voice mocked everything she believed in. 'Some of those old Sabbath School lessons came in handy, I tell you.'

'You make me sick,' Meg gritted. 'You shall not be so arrogant when you stand before Him.'

Roderick laughed outright, and then he became serious.

Alas,' he sighed, I failed to win your affections.' His eyes became hard. 'I lack Fordham's talent for that, unfortunately. I don't know why you should prefer him. He is as much a rogue as I.'

'That must be the only thing we agree on,' Meg said bitterly, still wriggling with the ropes from time to time.

Roderick came close to her until their faces were only inches apart. ''Tis a pity you will not have me. I could have made you very happy, you know.' He paused and dragged his gaze down her body and panic rose in Meg.

'So, now I am forced to take what I want from you and leave you behind.'

Meg gasped and recoiled from him in fear, her eyes wide in terror.

Roderick reached one hand inside his coat and pulled out a dirty and creased envelope. He held it towards her. 'Read it and tell me what it means.'

Meg could barely find her voice, she was so afraid. 'B-b-but, y-you have tied m-m-my hands.'

Roderick growled, opened the envelope, and removed its contents. He spread the letter and placed it on Meg's lap, and then noticed the sunlight had faded too much to read. He lit a lantern and put it near her. Near enough to read by its light, but not near enough for her to reach it.

'Generous man that I am,' he bowed derisively, 'I'll give you time to think. When I come back, I want an answer, or I'll be forced to take more desperate measures. I'd hate to have to leave a scar on that perfect face of yours.'

❧

Jack went back to the parlour, where Philip and Gwen still sat talking. They had obviously been discussing him because they ceased as soon as he walked in. Jack reclaimed his chair and looked at the couple solemnly, ignoring their awkward glances at each other.

'When did either of you last see Roderick?' he asked.

'Saturday last,' Philip answered with a small frown. 'Why?'

'Tell me what happened during his visit.'

The puzzled man looked at his wife and back at Jack. 'As I mentioned earlier, he came to pick up his horses. We discussed payment, shook hands and he came into the house to see Meg.' He shrugged, not seeing any significance in this information.

Jack looked at Gwen. 'What happened inside?'

His sister seemed mystified, too. 'Why do you ask these questions?'

Jack sighed. 'Nellie saw Meg leave the church with Roderick,' he said matter-of-factly. 'Now will you tell me what happened?'

'I did not sit with them,' Gwen said, 'but I believe he offered for her, and she said "no". He left shortly after.'

'Did you see him when he left? Did he seem very upset or angry?' Jack pressed.

Gwen spread her hands in bewilderment. 'Any man would be upset if he was rejected. But I don't remember seeing anything unusual.'

Jack stood up and rubbed his chin thoughtfully. 'Would Meg have any reason to change her mind, do you think?'

'I don't know, Jack. She has been very confused of late. What are you getting at?'

'Well,' Jack looked at them both gravely. 'My guess is they have either eloped, or …'

Just then there came a knock on the door and Nellie poked her head in. 'Mister Wingrove is here, sir,' she addressed Philip.

'Wingrove?' Philip wondered aloud. 'Show him in.'

Moments later Nellie ushered the red-haired young man into the parlour where he nodded his greetings to Philip and Gwen. Continuing to look around the room he noticed Jack and stiffened.

'Fordham.' A cold greeting if Jack ever heard one. 'What are you doing here?'

'This is my sister's home,' Jack warned, defensive. 'If you have issue with my presence here, I suggest you take it up with her and her husband.'

Brian's gaze swerved to Philip and Gwen as he realised his mistake. 'I beg pardon,' he said. 'I have come to warn my sister about Mister Roderick.'

Before either of the Sainsburys could speak, Jack pounced on his words. 'Warn her about what?'

Brian met Jack's gaze with a challenge. 'I don't see it is any of your business, Fordham.'

In two strides Jack stood face to face with him and grasped him roughly by the shirt front. 'Tell me now.'

Brian's face grew red, although his voice remained low. 'Unhand me, sir. You and I have an account to settle. Shall we go outside and take care of it now?'

Jack remembered his betrayal and let go of the man. 'You may have your way with me; run me through or shoot me in the heart, whatever you wish. But let us see Meg is safe first.'

'Safe?' Brian's eyes became troubled and turned to the Sainsburys. 'She is not here?'

Gwen shook her head in answer. 'It appears she is with Mister Roderick as we speak.'

❦

Roderick had left Meg alone in the little shed. As the night began to close in the air became colder and her fear intensified. She trembled so much she found it difficult to read. Terrified tears also stung her eyes as she tried to make out the words on the discoloured paper. She blinked and squinted, and slowly began to read.

> *My darling daughter, Margaret,*
>
> *If you ever have cause to read this letter, then it is assumed I have passed on to glory and I pray God will be your comfort through this time.*

Meg had to stop reading, a rush of poignant emotions flooding her. This was her precious mother's handwriting. She tried to see the date on the letter, but it had been blotted by a smudge of dirt. It saddened Meg that this treasure had been in the hands of a criminal for the past decade.

> *Firstly, I want you to know how much I love you. You have been the joy of my heart as I have watched you grow, and I*

know you will be a strong young woman. I do not know what the future holds for you, but I have placed you in the Father's wise and gentle hands.

The purpose of this letter is to tell you a story about your great, great grandmother, Lady Eliza Greyford. A woman of great wealth, she believed the fate of a woman was too insecure at the hands of man, who is not immortal nor is he infallible.

If a lady's husband were to die or lose his fortune, who would provide for her? So, with that in mind she acquired some rare jewels, worth a great deal of money. These jewels, she said, were to be passed down through the female line. So, if ever one of her daughters, or granddaughters or so on, were to find themselves destitute, the jewels could be sold, and the girl would be able to provide for herself.

Thus, it is with pleasure I can pass these jewels on to you. In the event neither I nor your father can care for you, they will be enough to happily sustain you for the rest of your life. If you have no need of them, you are to pass them on to your first daughter when she becomes of age.

The jewels are well hidden in a secret place in Wingrove Hall. You will know how to find them when the time comes.

In closing, I wish to recall one of the fondest memories I have. It was one of the most precious times we shared together. Remember your eighth birthday? I will never forget that special time and I hope you also treasure that memory.

God bless you, my darling. With all my love, your mother.

Meg was moved deeply. For a moment she forgot where she was and drank in every word of the letter as though the words themselves were the jewels. It seemed she could almost hear her mother's voice as she read, and the pain of her loss came to life once more. Meg wept for a short time, wishing she could roll back time and prevent her parents' death.

As her mother's face faded back into the past, Meg remembered the predicament she faced. Were these jewels real? Did they really exist somewhere? The letter said she would know where to find them when the time came. Well, the time was imminent and yet, Meg had no idea.

She feared what Roderick would do to her when she told him she couldn't help. There must be an answer.

⮞⋅⮜

'Good grief,' Brian exclaimed and sank into a chair.

'What did you need to warn Meg for?' Jack asked again.

Brian shrugged. 'I have always had reservations about Roderick, but I could not fathom why. Then, yesterday I came across some papers in my office that put everything in place. He absconded from a farm where he was assigned to serve out his sentence over five years ago and he is wanted in Van Diemen's Land and Victoria for robbery. The troopers are going out to arrest him tomorrow.'

The muscles in Jack's jaw began to work. 'Tomorrow may be too late. I would to God you had remembered earlier,' he said, gathering his jacket.

'Too late? What … why?'

'I have reason to believe he has carried her off.' Jack shrugged into his coat.

Gwen gasped in horror and Philip exclaimed in disbelief, while Brian paled.

Jack continued, thinking out loud. 'He must have lured her into his carriage.'

'Something you would know all about,' Brian accused.

Jack looked at him sharply. 'Save it, Wingrove. You can unleash your venom on me another time. For now, we must co-operate. Do you know his whereabouts?'

'Yes,' Brian jumped up and moved into action, donning his own coat.

264

'Phil,' Jack turned to his brother-in-law. 'Bring me your fastest horse.'

Philip went to the door.

'And fetch me a pistol, too,' Jack called after him.

Ramming his hat on his head, he looked at Brian. 'Pray for her protection, Wingrove. And pray for Roderick's soul. For if he has hurt her, only God can help him now.'

Brian's face reddened again. 'Fordham! This is not the …'

Jack closed his eyes and prayed, cutting Brian off. 'Sovereign Lord, you alone know where Meg is right now, and you alone can keep her safe until we find her. Please, surround her and give her peace. In your name we pray, Amen.'

Brian stared at him open mouthed. When he finally realised Jack had finished his prayer, he shook himself free of his trance and weakly agreed. 'Amen.' He exchanged an amazed glance with Gwen. Jack rolled his eyes and strode out the door, Brian close on his heels.

Outside, Philip arrived with a powerful looking stallion in tow. The horse pawed at the ground restlessly.

'He looks as though he's ready to fly,' Brian commented.

'He's still very flighty, Jack. I haven't quite finished training him.'

Jack swung into the saddle as if he hadn't even heard. Philip handed him the pistol and Jack strapped it to his waist while trying to keep the horse still. He stared impatiently at Brian. 'Are you coming? Where is your mount?'

Brian handed him a piece of paper. 'Here's the direction. Don't wait for me. I shan't be far behind you. God's speed, Fordham.'

❧

Meg was too frightened to concentrate. Although she racked her brain for answers, all she could think of were the threats Roderick had spoken to her. She now knew why he had been so intent on knowing everything about her ancestral home. Desperately she fought with the cords that held her tight, crying in frustration.

Strangely, her panic began to fade away and she looked fear in the face. Scriptures began to repeat in her mind. *O death, where is thy sting? O grave, where is thy victory?* She was a child of God, and if it was time for her to leave this world, what had she to fear? She would go to her eternal glory with Christ, knowing she had been true to him on earth.

Fear thou not; for I am with thee: be not dismayed; for I am thy God: I will strengthen thee; yea, I will help thee; yea, I will uphold thee with the right hand of my righteousness.

Peace flooded Meg's being, and all her terror melted away. Her mind cleared and she knew everything would be all right. She read the letter again, praying for God to reveal the answers to this riddle to her. When she got to the last paragraph, she began to reminisce about her eighth birthday. That was the time her mother had given her the locket. Meg gasped. The *locket*. That had to be the solution. What had her mother said about it? *No matter what happens in the future, remember you are always loved and always cared for. This locket will help.* Yes, the locket had to be the key. Then she remembered something else her mother had told her. Something about the tiny portraits inside. *They are more than just pictures, darling,* she had said.

If only she could get the necklet off and have a closer look. But her hands were still securely fastened behind her back. And to think her mother had already hidden the jewels even then. She must have suspected that Father's gambling would lead to their ruin.

Meg was astonished to realise she could possibly be a wealthy woman. Her provision had been planned generations ago. Unfortunately, it now seemed she would lose that provision before she had even possessed it. Meg sighed and rested in the peace that strengthened her. God knew best, and His will would prevail.

Chapter Thirty-nine

The road disappeared beneath the stallion's feet at lightning speed. Jack's heart pounded at the same rate as the thundering hooves. He feared for Meg's safety. He feared for her innocence. But, above all, he feared losing her. No matter how fast the horse ran, it did not seem fast enough. All he could do was pray. 'Lord God, please don't let anything happen to her. I couldn't bear to see her suffer any more than she already has. Oh, God. I love her so much. Please protect her.'

The revelation hit Jack hard as he pleaded with God. He truly loved Meg. She was more than precious to him. He could not imagine a life without her in it. Somehow it would seem empty. No, he did not deserve her, but she did not deserve to come to her end like this.

'I must find her.' He willed the horse to gallop even faster.

❦

Meg waited, without qualm for Roderick to return. He had been gone a long while. She considered whether she would tell him about the locket. She did not know how desperate he was, or what he could be capable of.

In the end, she decided no amount of money was worth dying for. She figured Roderick could take her fortune if he wanted it; she had something greater. She had her faith, and God would provide her needs.

At long last, she heard his uneven footsteps returning. When he entered, she noticed he carried a half-empty bottle of rum, and his eyes were glazed.

'So, Miss Wingrove,' he slurred. 'Will you be nice and co-operative and tell me where those jewels are, or will you force me to do something distasteful.'

Meg looked at him calmly. He had obviously fortified himself with the rum. She decided to test his resolve. 'Well, now,' she said. 'I don't know. I think perhaps I might like to keep them for myself.'

Roderick roared and threw the bottle against the wall, where it smashed into tiny pieces. Meg flinched. He came close to her, so close she could smell the fumes on his breath. 'I have waited more than ten years for this,' he growled. 'Don't play games with me.'

Meg met his glare with a challenge. 'Who said anything about games?'

'Tell me where those jewels are.' His voice rose in volume.

'I don't actually know.'

'Liar!' He swung his arm to back hand her, stopping at the last moment.

Meg cringed but did not scream.

'Please, don't be difficult?' Roderick suddenly begged her. 'I don't want to hurt you, but I will if I have to.'

Meg studied him and realised he was intent on getting those jewels.

'How do you expect to get away with this?'

Roderick grinned at her. 'There is a vessel departing for England tomorrow, and I shall be on it. That is why I chose today to bring you here. I shall be long gone before anyone finds you.'

Meg stared fearlessly into his eyes. 'Can you be sure of that? Even now I am certain people are searching for me.'

Roderick looked at her with sinister determination. 'That is why you're going to tell me what I want to know right now.'

Meg knew it was time to let him have what he wanted. 'Very well,' she sighed. 'The locket around my neck holds the secret.'

'The locket. Of course! I should have known.' He reached out and yanked the necklet away from her throat and she cried out in pain.

Roderick rocked back onto his heels and fumbled with the locket, trying to open it.

'You have a strange way of showing a lady your affection,' a smooth voice drawled from behind him.

Startled, Roderick spun around to see Jack leaning in the doorway. 'Fordham,' he spat. Then he noticed the pistol aimed at his heart. 'Curse you.'

'Do not try to do anything foolish,' Jack warned. 'Or I might accidentally pull this trigger. In fact, I do not know why I haven't done so already.'

Roderick poised, undecided.

Jack was alert, ready for anything.

Suddenly, Roderick made his move. In a flash he had grabbed a cast-iron bar and swung it towards Jack. In the same instant Jack fired the gun deliberately into the ground to scare Roderick. Meg screamed. Somehow the iron and the gun collided, and the pistol flew from Jack's hand. Roderick, seeing he had the upper hand, swung the bar again, but Jack had a sharp eye and managed to dodge the blow. The force of Roderick's swing threw him off balance and the iron bar fell to the ground. Jack stepped in quickly with a powerful right hook, and landed a blow to Roderick's jaw which sent him flying backwards, unconscious, to the ground.

Jack quickly regained possession of the pistol in case the villain came around too soon. He checked Roderick over and bound his hands behind his back in case he should wake.

Finally, once he knew the bonds were secure, he turned to Meg. He had not allowed himself to look at her since he arrived. He knew if he glanced at her even once, he would have lost his reason and made a fatal error. He heard Brian arrive as he went to untie Meg. Wordlessly he gazed at her, not knowing what to say. Every fibre in his body wanted to take her in his arms and comfort her, but the look in her eyes held him back. They were large pools of confused emotion. 'You ...?'

Jack swallowed. 'Did he ... hurt you?' His voice was hoarse.

'No.' Meg shook her head, although he could see her trembling.

Brian came in then and rushed to her side. He gathered her up in his arms and held her tenderly. 'Are you all right?'

'I think so.' Meg's lips quivered.

'Let's take you home,' Brian soothed and scooped her up.

'Wait,' Meg said. 'The letter. And my locket. He took it from me.'

'I shall find them,' Jack assured her, and Brian continued to take her outside.

'What will you do with him,' the red head paused to ask.

Jack looked at the unconscious Roderick. 'A lot less than he deserves. I think I shall leave him tied up and let the troopers find him in the morning.'

'More than fair,' Brian nodded and went out the lopsided door.

Jack checked that Roderick remained firmly bound, tying more ropes around his ankles, found the letter and the locket where they had been discarded during the brief scuffle, and followed the Wingroves outside.

Brian had gently placed Meg in Roderick's carriage when Jack strode up.

'Will you drive?' Brian asked.

'Of course,' Jack replied. He fetched the stallion and Brian's horse and tethered them to the back of the carriage, then climbed into the driver's seat. He flicked the reins and the two-horse team eased into a trot.

The drive home was unhurried and much more peaceful. Relief flooded Jack. Meg was unharmed. He stared into the clear, star-lit sky and thanked God repeatedly for His protection.

Jack pulled the delicate, silver locket out of his pocket and examined it in the moonlight. What had Roderick wanted with it? He shrugged and put it back in his coat pocket. No doubt Meg would explain in her own time.

◈

Inside the carriage, the shock of what Meg had just been through hit her and she began to tremble violently. Brian cradled her in his arms, and her tears began to flow. 'I was so scared,' she sobbed into his coat. 'I thought he was going to kill me.'

Brian held her tighter. 'It's all right now. You are safe.'

He rocked her and stroked her hair. He prayed for her all the way home and gradually she calmed, until she rested peacefully in his arms. Silence reigned in the carriage for a long time, and when she finally spoke, it was muffled against his jacket. 'Why did Jack come?'

Brian sighed. 'I don't know, Meg. That is something you shall have to ask him.'

❧

The evening was well advanced by the time they arrived back at the farm. Brian gingerly carried his sister into the house amidst relieved welcomes. Gwen fussed over Meg, tending to her sore wrists, and sending for a doctor. Philip quizzed her gently about what had happened, although Meg was loath to talk about it yet. The children flocked about her, pouring out their affection. Even Nellie joined in the to-do, trying to persuade Meg to take some soup. And all the while, Brian stood stoically beside the sofa she lay on, as if he guarded her.

Jack remained in the background, observing how much every one of these people cared about Meg. He wished he had something to offer, but he had done his part. And Meg did not look at him, not even briefly. She obviously had all the support she needed, and he would just be in the way if he tried to assist in any way.

The doctor came and went, declaring that aside from a little shock and some minor bruising, Meg was in good health. Thus, having his mind put to rest, Jack removed himself to the dining room for a short while to eat the meal Nellie offered him. When he went back to the parlour, he found it deserted. He stepped back into the hallway and, judging from the noises coming from Meg's bedroom, figured she'd been ordered to bed.

Feeling redundant, Jack poured himself a mug of coffee and wandered outside. He strolled over to the yards where the horses were often trained and leaned on the fence, gazing into the starry sky. He reflected again on how beautiful God's creation was and drank in the jewel studded heavens.

After a few moments he became aware of the soft snort of the stallion he had ridden earlier. He straightened and walked over to the muscular animal and noticed that amidst the commotion, the poor horses had been neglected. They had not been given a rub-down or a feed. Jack affectionately stroked the stallion's nose. 'You did a wonderful job this evening, boy. You helped save a lady's life.' The stallion lifted his head and snorted again as though he understood.

Jack untethered him from the carriage and took him to the stables. He carefully groomed the stallion and covered him with a blanket. He gave him an apple, a nourishing feed of oats, and filled his trough with water. Then he began all over again with Brian's horse.

For some reason Jack felt much better now he had done something worthwhile and returned to the fence where he had left his mug. The coffee had long since gone cold and Jack tipped it out. He turned to go back to the house.

'Didn't get the recognition or glory you expected, eh Fordham?' Brian approached.

Jack smiled grimly. 'Ah, Wingrove. I wondered how long it would be before you renewed your antagonism towards me. So, what is it to be? Swords? Pistols? Or do you prefer the more modern form of pugilism?'

It was Brian's turn to smile. 'Actually, I wanted to thank you for what you did.'

Jack turned back to lean on the fence, staring into his empty mug. 'I am just glad she is all right.'

Brian joined him at the fence and peered into the darkness. They remained like that in silence for a while.

'You are not as heartless as people say you are,' he said eventually.

Jack gave a half laugh and kicked at the fence. 'No, indeed,' he answered without looking up.

'Meg always says there is more to you than meets the eye, and I begin to see why.'

Another awkward laugh. Jack was still uncomfortable with regret. 'I was very good at pretending. I tried to protect myself from pain, but it has cost me dearly.'

Brian glanced sideways at him 'You say "was"?'

Jack turned to face him. 'You may not believe this,' he began. 'In fact, nobody has really believed it so far, but I have been arrested by the love of Christ, and I am a new man.'

Brian's eyebrows rose and his mouth opened and closed a few times, but he said nothing.

'I know I have treated Meg disgracefully and I don't think I will ever be able to forgive myself for the pain I have caused her — but, I ... love her.'

Brian stiffened then. 'Love?'

'I do not presume to be able to continue a relationship with your sister,' Jack quickly assured him. 'I know I am not worthy of such virtue. All I want is the chance to set things straight between us and beg for her forgiveness. After that, I will not bother her with my presence again.'

After several more silent moments, Brian shrugged his shoulders. 'You seem to be genuine. I will take your word at face value and suggest to my sister she listens to what you have to say. That is all I can do, I am afraid.'

'And it is more than I had hoped for. Thank you. It means a lot to me.'

They both leaned on the fence and gazed into the velvety night.

'So, you are a brother in Christ, now,' Brian said finally, standing straight. He thrust out his hand and shook with Jack. 'Welcome to the family.'

Jack grinned at him, thankful he had been accepted, even if only warily. 'Still want to run me through?'

'Not nearly as much,' Brian answered with the hint of a smile. 'Besides, you seem to be doing a good job of punishing yourself already.'

'Friends, then?' Jack suggested hopefully.

Brian nodded. 'Friends.'

Chapter Forty

Meg sat in the parlour the next morning, by a small fire with a blanket over her knees. She had woken late, and though she felt quite well apart from her bruises, Mrs Sainsbury had insisted she rest for the day. Meg didn't bother arguing with her, she had too many things to think over.

The most obvious of these was her traumatic experience at the hands of Roderick. She reflected over what she had learnt from the villain. She remembered the letter, almost every word of it, and treasured the love her mother had put into it.

Thinking about the letter again made her remember her locket. Somehow that small trinket held the answers to where the hidden inheritance was. She reached for the necklet, but finding her throat bare, recalled that Jack had it. She had forgotten to reclaim it from him. However, seeing as she wanted to avoid Jack, she let her curiosity wait. Perhaps Mrs Sainsbury or Brian could get it from him and bring it to her.

She had asked Mrs Sainsbury earlier if Jack remained in the house. It troubled Meg to learn he did. 'Perhaps I should stay in my room.'

'Why should you?' Mrs Sainsbury had asked, draping the blanket on Meg's knees.

Meg had lowered her eyes to her lap. 'I do not wish to see Jack.'

Mrs Sainsbury stopped fiddling with the blanket and sat down next to her. She took Meg's hands and looked her earnestly in the eyes. 'I can understand you feel that way and I will tell him to keep away from you if you wish it, but I think you should give him a chance to talk. At the very least you need to thank him for flying to your rescue. After all, it was he who brought attention to your absence and figured out what had become of you.'

Meg bit her lip. It was true. She had not shown him any gratitude for the risk he took. Yet, the humiliation she had suffered at his hand was still raw and she was not ready to face him.

Brian came in then, stirring her from her thoughts. She brightened when she saw him.

'Brian, I am so glad you are here,' she welcomed him. 'Did you sleep well?'

'Knowing you were safe, yes. Do you feel better this morning?'

'A little stiff and tired, but other than that, quite all right. But Missus Sainsbury insisted I sit and rest here all day.'

'And so, she should have.'

'Oh, Brian, I have something wonderful to tell you,' Meg changed the subject. 'Well, it was horrid to begin with, but now I am home it is naught but good news.' She told her brother about the old, worn letter and began to explain what Roderick had wanted from her, finishing with the news that she believed the locket held the secret.

Brian was amazed such a mystery had even existed. He frowned and groaned at Roderick's treatment of her, but when her tale was told, he laughed out loud in astonishment. 'Show me the letter and that locket again.'

Meg screwed up her face. 'Jack still has them.'

'Oh,' Brian looked crestfallen for a moment. 'Well, we shall have to get them back then.' He turned to go and act upon his words, but then swivelled around and returned to his seat. 'I just remembered. Fordham has gone out for a ride.'

'Oh.' Meg was disappointed to have to wait even longer.

'I shall have to see it another time I'm afraid. I need to go and make sure Roderick is securely behind bars.'

Meg's face fell even further. 'Can't Jack do that?'

Brian cupped Meg's face in his hand. 'No, my sweet. He needs to be here.'

'I don't see why,' Meg grumbled.

'He wishes to speak with you.'

Meg's eyes widened. 'Brian, I can't ...'

'I think you should,' he persisted. 'You need to hear what he has to say.'

Meg looked at him in suspicion. It was uncommon for her brother to give Jack any latitude. Why, he was ready to come to cuffs with him after the ball. 'Has he spoken to you?'

Brian stared at her as if deciding how much he should reveal. 'Yes,' he admitted. 'And I think he deserves a fair hearing.' He rose and bent down to kiss her on the forehead. 'Now, I must go. Enjoy your rest, my dear. I shall see you again soon.'

Jack needed to clear his head. His nerves churned about speaking to Meg, even though he wasn't guaranteed she would even give him an audience. He needed to get out in the open air and pray for courage. He knew he must go and bare his soul to her, accepting whatever judgement she decided to confer on him.

Riding out in the fresh, crisp air did much to soothe him and he returned to the house ready to face whatever may come. As he approached the house, he met Brian on his way out.

'Going somewhere?' Jack asked as the red head looked up and noticed him.

'Back to Roderick's,' Brian answered. 'I have to make sure he is put away.'

'Good idea,' Jack nodded. 'I would rest easier being certain of the fact too.'

'I shall inform you of his fate.'

'Thank you, Wingrove.'

Brian shook his hand and made to depart, then paused and turned back. Oh, Fordham,' he said. 'I have put in a word for you with Meg. I am not sure, but I think she will listen to you now.'

Jack merely nodded his thanks, his nerves leaping into action again. Brian went on his way and Jack continued to the house.

Mary kept Meg company, sitting by her on the sofa, busying herself with needlework. They were chatting amiably when Gwen poked her head in the door. 'Mary,' she called softly. 'I need you to come and look through some fabrics I have purchased, so we can have Miss Montgomery make you a new gown.'

'Oh,' Mary squealed, jumped up and followed her mother without another thought.

Meg watched her with an amused smile and then saw Gwen wink at her before disappearing down the hallway. Meg stiffened, realising at once Jack stood outside waiting to come in.

Sure enough, seconds later, Jack quietly stepped in and closed the door behind him. For a moment, neither spoke. They glanced at each other, both awkward and conscious an enormous gulf had come between them. A few short weeks ago they had been the best of friends, but that friendship had been shattered.

❧

Jack hoped the distance between them would not be insurmountable as he stood there, his heart in his throat. He went to the window, unable to bear the hurt in her eyes. 'How are you this morning?' He stared out at the garden.

'Well enough.'

'It is a beautiful day outside,' he commented lightly. 'I think summer is just around the bend.'

'Jack,' Meg said with evident pain in her voice. 'If you have something to say ...'

'I'm sorry,' he turned from the window and sat down opposite her. 'I know this is hard for you, but I need to make sure you know the truth.'

'The truth?'

Jack took a deep breath. 'I have not come here to try another ruse on you,' he tried to reassure her. Meg dropped her eyes to her hands which were folded in her lap.

'So, you admit it was all a deceitful game.' Disappointment laced every word.

Jack's heart beat hard. This was more difficult than he thought. Admitting his folly to his sister had been a struggle, but confessing the truth to Meg was infinitely more painful. He ran a hand through his hair in agitation. 'Not all of it ...'

Meg's eyes flew to his face, full of question.

'Some of it was real,' Jack told her. 'I believe our friendship was real, and all the grand times we spent together with the children.' He watched for her response, but her eyes focused on her lap again.

'The time at the orphanage was real. I was so anxious about taking you there.' He laughed self-consciously. 'I knew the only way to get your attention would be to share with you my deep interest in helping the unfortunate.'

'So, although it was "real", you still used it to manipulate me. Correct?' Meg kept her head lowered.

'Ashamedly, yes.'

'And what about church?

Jack closed his eyes and swallowed, forcing himself to speak the truth. 'A thoughtless pretence to make you believe I was interested.'

Meg chewed on a fingernail, visibly trembling with her own nervous anxiety.

Jack pressed on. 'But what happened at the ball ...'

'Please do not speak about that,' Meg cut him off. She jumped up, wincing in pain at the sudden movement, and cast the blanket aside. She stood with her back to him at the fireplace. Jack groaned inwardly. Clearly, she was embarrassed about the incident.

'We need to talk about it.'

Meg did not respond.

'It was all real,' Jack told her, his voice full of meaning. 'All of it.'

Meg spun around, her anger apparent. 'How can you say that? You told your friend — I don't know his name — you finished playing your game.' She glared at him. 'And do not try to deny it, I heard him re-telling it with my own ears.'

Jack sighed. 'I shall not deny it. I did say that to him. But as with so many other things, I told him that to divert him, and even myself, from the truth.'

Meg frowned. 'The truth?'

Jack ran a nervous hand through his hair again and he swallowed hard. 'I cannot explain it very well. I am still figuring this all out, and I am not used to examining my own emotions.' His voice shook. 'Remember outside your brother's house, you guessed that I had been hurt by a woman. Well, her name was Antoinette, and I loved her many, many years ago. She deceived me and tore my heart in two. After that, I suppose I learnt to bury my feelings, even to the point of denying their existence.'

Jack gave Meg a searching look to see if she understood. But she watched and listened with an expressionless face.

'Months ago, before the ball, I decided you would make a suitable wife. It was a logical conclusion I came to because you had qualities which I admired. As I grew to know you, I found it more and more difficult to suppress my deepening regard for you. I was afraid ... and I was confused. Part of me wanted to push you away and the other part couldn't get enough of you.'

Jack paused, searching for the right words. His gut twisted with tension. Exposing his heart like this terrified him, but he knew he had to see it through. He stood up and paced for a few moments, while Meg continued to watch him with a stony face.

'The night of the ball I got to the point where I ... I just wanted to be done with all the turmoil. I wanted to cut you out of my life. But then I saw the look in your eyes ... it felt like a dam burst inside me. I guess what I am trying to say is my offer of marriage was genuine, the kiss we shared was very real, and I was — am ... truly ... in love with you.'

Meg's eyes filled with pain, her face contorting with anguish. 'Don't! Don't say that Jack,' she pleaded. 'Mister Sainsbury saw you get into your carriage with another woman that same night.'

Jack closed his eyes as a wave of remorse swept over him. He moved closer to Meg, and she turned her back on him again. 'Please, Meg, hear me out,' his voice cracked.

Meg didn't move.

'Nothing happened with her. I admit I thought about taking her home with me. We kissed briefly, but I couldn't continue. You were all I could think about, and I went home, alone.'

Meg whirled around, her eyes flashing with anger and grief. 'Is that supposed to make me feel better? Do you expect me to fall into your arms and forget all about it? The fact that you even thought about it ...' Meg's voice trailed off.

The last of Jack's composure crumbled, and he became choked with emotion. 'I don't expect anything from you, Meg. There is no excuse for the way I have treated you. You were wise to refuse me from the start. I disregarded your values and manipulated you for my own selfishness. I would to God I could undo the pain I have caused. Instead, all I can do is beg for your forgiveness and leave you in peace.'

Meg saw tears glisten in Jack's eyes and knew his words were genuine. It didn't lessen the intense pain though, and she let her gaze drop to the floor.

'Please don't ask me, Jack,' she whispered. She wanted to stay angry with him forever.

'Meg, look at me.'

She shook her head.

'Meg, please,' he begged.

Meg slowly raised her eyes to his, defiant tears streaming down her face.

Jack looked earnestly into her eyes, his own eyes brimming over. 'I am so desperately sorry for hurting you. I need your forgiveness. Please?'

'No ...' Something snapped within Meg and she crumbled to her knees, sobbing uncontrollably.

Jack took a few deep breaths, trying to rein in his own emotions. He raised his face to the ceiling and tried to blink back the tears. He wished he could take Meg in his arms and reassure her, but there was too much hurt between them. At a loss, he went to the door and called for his sister.

Gwen must have heard the emotion in his voice because she appeared very quickly. Jack was blowing his nose into a handkerchief when she entered. Gwen glanced at Meg and then back at her teary brother, her eyes full of question.

'She needs you,' he whispered.

Gwen hurried to Meg and gathered her in her arms. She began rocking the governess with motherly tenderness. Seeing Jack still standing there, she mouthed the word *go* and waved him off. Jack nodded and headed outside, where he took a long walk in the fields.

Chapter Forty-one

Meg had long since stopped crying, and now stared absently at the rug on the floor. She had let go of all her anger and bitterness in those tears and chosen to release Jack in forgiveness. Part of her was relieved to have finished with it, and another part of her was still wounded. Forgiveness did not immediately cure the pain.

She thought back over all Jack had told her and she was stirred by his openness. In all the time she had known him, she had never heard him be so honest. She realised it must have been extremely difficult for him and even admired him for his courage.

On the other hand, hearing he loved her only added to her grief. It was such a waste. His actions had driven a wedge between them so that she doubted they could even be friends again. Meg sighed. He had promised to keep his distance after this. That was the only solution for them.

Meg knew their conversation remained unfinished. She had told Mrs Sainsbury to send Jack back in whenever he appeared, and now waited for him to come.

When at last he did arrive, uncertainty clouded his face. 'Gwen said you wanted to see me?'

'Yes,' Meg nodded.

'Meg, I didn't mean …'

Meg held up her hand. 'Please, let me speak. I have a few things I need to say.'

Jack complied and sat down opposite her.

She took a deep, shaky breath. 'You asked me to forgive you. As hard as it is, I don't want to carry this for the rest of my life. So…you have my forgiveness. But, Jack,' she added. 'I need time to heal.'

Jack's eyes started swimming again. 'Thank you, Meg,' he whispered. 'You have no idea what that means to me. And I will give you as much time as you need.'

Meg nodded.

'I also wanted to say thank you for last night. You took a great risk to save me.'

Jack shrugged. 'Anyone would have done the same. You are more than worth the risk.'

'Jack please don't.' Meg shook her head, the ache in her heart still very raw. 'I'm sorry.'

He brightened slightly and put his hand in his pocket. 'By the way, I still have your things.' He handed the two items to her.

Meg grasped them eagerly and placing the letter in her lap, began to open the silver locket.

'What did Roderick want with it anyway, if you do not mind my asking?'

She didn't answer immediately while she fiddled with the heart-shaped locket. A moment later she held up a tiny piece of folded paper. 'This.'

Meg discarded the locket and unravelled the paper. It revealed a small map of her ancestral home with a red X marking where the jewels were hidden.

'I don't understand,' Jack frowned.

At long last a smile lit Meg's face. 'It turns out I may be quite wealthy. Apparently, my mother hid my inheritance at Wingrove Hall. Up until now, Roderick is the only person who knew about it. But thanks to you, he could not make his escape with this map.'

Jack grinned his congratulations. 'That is wonderful news. So, Roderick was after your fortune all along. It is a relief to know your future is secure.' He rolled his eyes. 'And to think, if I had known, I could have run off with it.'

Meg gave him a brief half-smile.

'Too soon?'

Meg lowered her eyes. 'You are already insanely rich, Jack. What would you want with this?' she attempted a comeback, their relationship still too fragile.

Jack smiled at this token of reconciliation. 'Perhaps, one day, we can be friends again?'

'Perhaps,' Meg agreed, 'In time.'

❧

They sat in a semi-comfortable silence for a time, while Meg examined her little map in detail. Jack watched her, trying to get used to the tenuous peace between them.

'There is something I want to tell you, Meg,' he ventured, hesitant.

'Mmm,' Meg turned the paper on another angle, squinting at it.

'I also have some good news, and I hope you will be able to share in my happiness.' He wondered if she would be open to hear about his salvation.

Meg looked up at him, stiffening. 'At least one of us is happy.'

Jack shook his head. 'You misunderstand,' he tried to reassure her. 'Will you listen to my story?'

Meg eyed him doubtfully and then sighed. 'If you wish.'

Jack cleared his throat. 'When I was on board the *Madeline* on the way to Melbourne, I felt miserable about what I had done, and I had a lot of time to examine myself. I …'

A commotion out in the hallway interrupted him, and the next moment a stranger burst into the parlour followed closely by the Sainsburys who protested loudly. Jack and Meg jumped up, startled by this intrusion.

'Mister Jonathon Fordham?' the man bellowed.

Jack stepped forward warily. The man appeared to be in a rage and was dishevelled. Clearly, he had travelled for many hours. 'I am he,' Jack replied. 'What is the meaning of this?'

The man glared at him. 'You have ruined my daughter!' The man pointed at him. 'I demand justice.'

The muscles in Jack's jaw tightened as he saw Meg pale. She didn't need this.

'How dare you disturb my sister's home and lay false accusations at my feet.' Jack's voice was low and tense. 'I have ruined no-one.'

The strange man's face went a deeper shade of red and he growled. 'She is with child, and she claims you are the father.'

Meg and Gwen both gasped in shock. Mr Sainsbury hung his head, dismayed, and heat flooded to Jack's neck.

'You have not yet told me your name, sir,' Jack stiffened, barely containing his fury at this piece of impertinence.

'Ambrose,' the man announced. 'Richard Ambrose.'

It was as though someone had just punched him in the gut. It could not be possible. 'Ambrose?' he repeated. 'I have not seen Sylvia in over six months.'

'And her confinement is due in less than three,' Ambrose countered.

'No.' Jack desperately searched his mind. This could not be happening. He paced up and down. He looked sharply at Mr Ambrose. 'How can you be sure I am the father?'

At this, Ambrose became enraged. 'Why you depraved villain,' he shouted. 'How dare you insinuate …? You dare to dishonour my Sylvia's name?' In one stride he accosted Jack and wrapped his hands firmly around his throat.

❧∽❦

Meg screamed. Her overwrought nerves had been assaulted one too many times. The room span before her eyes and then blackness engulfed her, shrouding her in painless, dreamless nothingness. The last thing she saw was the floor swiftly rising to meet her as she collapsed.

Minutes later, as she came around, Mrs Sainsbury and Jack's concerned faces swam before her, and Mrs Sainsbury waved a small bottle under her nose. They appeared to speak to her, although she could not respond. She was aware of a searing pain in her mouth and the taste of blood. Her head throbbed and she could vaguely hear arguing in the distance.

'Is it true?' she tried to ask, tears stinging her eyes, but her lips were swollen, making it difficult to speak.

Jack scooped her up and took her to her room, laying her on her bed. Mrs Sainsbury followed behind. Jack gazed at her momentarily, his face etched with grief. 'I am so sorry Meg,' she heard him say before he returned to the parlour.

Mrs Sainsbury dabbed at her mouth with a cold cloth and whispered soothingly, but Meg's grip on reality slipped and she drifted once more into the black void of unconsciousness.

It was some time later when she awoke. She blinked at the sunlight and tried to lift her head. A sharp pain stabbed at her, and she let her head fall back again. Silence had settled in the house now, except for some whispering nearby.

Meg focused her eyes and scanned the room. There, near the door, Mrs Sainsbury spoke in low tones with the doctor who had seen her the night before. The lady of the house looked worried, but the doctor appeared to be reassuring her.

A few moments later the doctor left, and Mrs Sainsbury came to sit beside her. Meg turned her head slightly to look at her friend and employer.

'Oh, you're awake,' Mrs Sainsbury said, relieved.

'Mmm,' Meg answered feebly. 'What happened?'

Mrs Sainsbury scanned the governess' face with a frown. 'You don't remember?'

Meg closed her eyes and thought for a moment. It didn't take long before the scene with Mr Ambrose flashed into her mind. 'Jack.'

Mrs Sainsbury nodded.

'Is he all right?'

Mrs Sainsbury smiled. 'You mean did Mister Ambrose strangle him?' She paused. 'No.'

Meg tried to lift her head again and groaned. 'My head hurts.'

The lady of the house frowned again. 'When you fainted, you hit your head rather heavily on the floor. You have a nasty cut on your lip and the doctor says you are a little concussed. You should feel better tomorrow.'

Meg groaned again.

'Can I get you anything, dear?'

Meg swallowed. 'Water?'

Mrs Sainsbury turned and poured a glass of water from a jug that sat on her bureau. She helped Meg sip at the drink and then sat down again.

'Is...is it true?' Meg ventured to ask, although she feared the answer.

Mrs Sainsbury looked at her sadly. 'I am afraid it is,' she sighed. 'It seems Miss Ambrose has hidden her pregnancy for quite a while, and it has only just been discovered by her father.'

'He was very angry.'

Mrs Sainsbury sighed again. 'Justifiably, I would say.'

'Poor man,' Meg sympathised with Richard Ambrose. She thought it must be very painful for a man to find out his precious daughter had behaved promiscuously.

'Strangely enough though,' Mrs Sainsbury added. 'When they left, Mister Ambrose appeared to be almost happy.'

'They left?'

'Perhaps it should wait until tomorrow when you are a little stronger,' Gwen avoided Meg's eyes. 'You need to rest now.'

Meg put her hand out and grasped her forearm. 'Tell me now please Missus Sainsbury,' she begged. 'Obviously you think it will upset me. I would rather be hurt now than wait for it until tomorrow.'

Mrs Sainsbury bent her head while she considered. When she looked up, she cleared her throat uncomfortably. 'I thought Jack would deny it all, or fight Mister Ambrose for the insult on his character. He looked so angry and desperate I feared he would do violence to the man. But he didn't. It appears he swallowed his pride and took responsibility for his actions. He agreed to marry Miss Ambrose to save her reputation and give the child his name. There will be a scandal of course, but it will fade in time.

'Jack and Mister Ambrose left a short while ago. Mister Ambrose wished to accompany Jack to make sure he followed through with his promise. As I said before, Mister Ambrose seemed quite pleased after that. I suppose it is because Jack is so rich — he knows his daughter will be well provided for, and a Viscountess one day.'

Meg sat in silence for a while, trying to let this information sink into her throbbing head. So, Jack was going to be a father. Jack would soon be wed. Jack, who had just confessed to her his love, was obliged to marry another.

'How was Jack?' she asked eventually.

Mrs Sainsbury shrugged. 'I think he is still in shock. He looked pale. I know he does not love Miss Ambrose, but he is doing the right thing.' She looked at Meg with understanding. 'I know you must feel confused and heartbroken. I know how much you cared for each other. I had hoped …' she swallowed. 'We told Jack so many times to stop living that way. We told him he would one day regret it. He never listened. And now it is too late, it can be no other way.'

Meg blinked back her own tears. 'It doesn't matter, Missus Sainsbury,' her lips trembled. 'Jack and I were never meant for each other.'

Mrs Sainsbury let her head sink to Meg's shoulder, and she put her arms around Gwen. They wept together, grieving over the fate of the man they both cared about more than anything.

Chapter Forty-two

Brian returned to the Sainsbury's that evening to inform Meg that Roderick was securely behind bars and faced an immediate return to the penal colonies. He was worried to find his sister confined to her bed with a cut and swollen lip and Meg had to explain all that had happened in his absence.

'I must say,' Brian said, one eyebrow raised. 'I never thought he had it in him.'

'What?' Meg did not follow.

'I never thought Fordham would take responsibility for his mistakes.' He told her, and she noticed that admiration filled his voice.

'You think this is a good thing.'

Brian shook his head. 'No,' he assured her. 'It is not a good thing. But it is the right thing.'

They settled into a much-needed heart-to-heart. Meg at last had a chance to show Brian the little map that had been inside her locket. Just like everyone else, Brian was astonished such a secret had remained hidden for so long. Meg gave the map into his keeping so he could organise for the jewels to be recovered and returned to her.

He looked at her seriously, scanning her face. 'Are you sure you're all right about Fordham?'

'Yes, I will be fine.' Meg let her gaze drop.

'You know, part of me cannot help feeling sorry for the poor chap.'

Meg looked up at him sharply.

'I mean,' Brian continued, 'I know he hurt you and his life has not exactly been admirable, but it seems a shame that just when he has turned his life around, he has to deal with this mess.'

Meg did not comprehend. 'Turned his life around? What …?'

Brian shot her a double take. 'He didn't tell you?'

'Tell me what?'

Brian sat back. 'He has found faith.'

Meg looked at her brother, dumbfounded. Her mouth moved but no words came out.

'I am sure he intended to tell you about it.'

'How do you know?' Meg searched Brian's face.

He shrugged. 'He told me about it the night he rode to your rescue. From what he said, I gather he had a dramatic conversion. But only time will tell, I suppose.'

Meg sat there staring at Brian. She didn't know what to say or think or feel. If true, this was wonderful news, but at the same time it renewed her pain. If only he had come to God earlier in his life, they might have had a chance. Meg chided herself for thinking so selfishly. If Jack had indeed given his life to Christ, then she should celebrate with the angels.

❦

Ten days later Meg still struggled with conflicting feelings about Jack's conversion. She caught herself several times distracted from her work. Meg had been occupied sweeping the dining room floor when Mrs Sainsbury bustled in, her eyes bright with excitement.

'A letter has come from Jack.' She waved the envelope in the air.

'Oh?' Meg did not pause in her work.

'I received one too,' Gwen added, lifting her other hand which also contained an envelope.

Meg stopped still. 'You mean that one is for me?'

'Yes,' Mrs Sainsbury handed the envelope over. She sat down at the dining table and opened her letter.

Meg followed suit, although hesitantly. What did Jack have to write her about? She carefully broke the seal and unfolded numerous pages. It appeared he had a lot to say. She sat back in the chair and began to read.

Dear Meg,

I know things between us were tenuous at best when I left, and yet I still had so much more to tell you. I dare say you have heard by now that I, too, am a believer in Christ, although I wish it were I who told you. In fact, I was on the verge of sharing my experience with you when Mister Ambrose interrupted us.

Meg stopped reading. Of course. Jack had been about to tell her something very important. She had forgotten all about that moment, and it pleased her to know Jack had not intended to neglect her in sharing his news.

I wanted, more than anything, for you to know about my salvation. His love has transformed me in ways I cannot begin to describe. I have been washed clean by the blood He shed, and for the first time in my life I feel truly alive. I am so thankful for the true witness of His nature you are, even though I did make light of it in the past.

There are other things I wish to share with you. I do not know how you will receive them, but you are the only person I know who will understand what I have to say.

I am to be married in two weeks time. It is not something I am happy about, but I am at peace with my decision. Yesterday it seemed completely unfair to me that I should have to suffer this

fate, but since then the Lord has revealed to me the just order of
things. I realise that although I am redeemed and forgiven, the
consequences of my past actions still take effect. As the Scriptures
say; they that sow to the wind will reap the whirlwind.

'Jack tells me he is to be married,' Mrs Sainsbury interrupted Meg's reading.

She looked up. 'Yes, in two weeks' time,' Meg replied, then noticed tears welling in Mrs Sainsbury's eyes.

'He says it will be a private ceremony, and due to the circumstances, we are not able to attend.'

Meg looked at her with empathy and clasped her hand across the table to comfort her. She sighed. The repercussions of sin spread wider than one would ever comprehend. The whirlwind indeed. What should have been a celebration would now unfortunately cause shame and grief.

'What does he have to say to you?' Mrs Sainsbury dabbed at her tears.

'It is all about his new faith.'

'Oh,' Mrs Sainsbury nodded. 'I shall leave you to it, then.'

The older woman rose with a heavy sigh and went off to check on her children, while Meg returned to her letter.

Yet, despite that, I can feel His hand upon me. I know He
will bless and uphold me. It occurred to me I could go on
spending the rest of my life wishing 'if only.' Or I could accept
my responsibilities with grace and do the best I can within
the situation I find myself.

I have chosen the latter, and I cannot tell you what peace it
gave me. So, I ask, from one Believer to another, please pray
for me. The woman I am about to wed does not share our
faith and is difficult at best. Please pray with me that she
will, in time, also find faith in Christ.

In turn, I pray you may find the happiness you deserve.
Once again, I am truly sorry for all the pain and confusion I
brought you. Thank you for showing me grace and forgiveness.
I will always remember your kindness.

With fond memories,

Jack Fordham.

Meg remained seated at the table for a long while, thinking over Jack's letter. She could not but admire and respect his courage. He behaved with wisdom and maturity, while she had indulged herself in self pity and despair. He had found peace in God's purpose, while she still struggled with her inner turmoil. Meg gave a half-laugh out loud. It was almost amusing. Jack, the devout agnostic, now conducted himself in a godlier way than she.

She scanned the missive again. Something in his words held an air of finality. It appeared he wanted to sever his ties with the past and focus on the future. He had let go of all his previous hopes and surrendered his will to the Father. Meg sighed. She needed to do the same.

Chapter Forty-three

The following Sunday was filled with tearful farewells. Meg ached to leave her beloved brothers and sisters in the Parramatta congregation and the family she had lived with for the past ten years. But it was time to move on.

She attended the small Parramatta church for the last time and embraced many of the brethren tightly. Nellie could not be consoled. She looked up to Meg as her mentor and doubted her strength without the governess there to support her. Meg reassured her with encouraging words, showing her how she could be the light of salvation to others in the Sainsbury household.

Back at the stud farm, the children were heartbroken. They sadly watched her pack her belongings all afternoon, and early in the morning they watched as her trunks were loaded onto the dray.

When the time came for goodbyes, Willy sat in a corner with fists rolled into balls pressed into his tear-filled eyes. PJ stood, solemn and quiet. Kitty buried her face in Meg's skirt and sobbed her little heart out. And Mary, though she tried to put on a brave face, had tears escaping down her cheeks. Mrs Sainsbury held her close for a long time, and Meg felt her shudder with silent tears. She whispered a blessing over the whole family.

Finally, when there were no tears left, and each person had said their farewells, Mr Sainsbury drove Meg to Parramatta where she could catch the mail coach to Sydney. As Meg's belongings were strapped to the coach, Mr Sainsbury turned to her. 'Goodbye, Meg,' he sighed. 'We could not have hoped for a better governess for our children. I don't know what we will do without you.'

Meg noticed his eyes misting over and she smiled affectionately at him. 'Thank you, Mister Sainsbury, but you have made my life here very easy.' She gave his hand a warm squeeze. 'Goodbye.' She boarded the coach.

Meg looked out of the window and waved once more to Mr Sainsbury. Then she leaned back into her seat with a deep sigh and closed her eyes. What would the future hold now? In one way it was a daunting unknown, and in another it would be an exciting adventure. With God, even the unfamiliar seemed safe, and she knew she could look forward without anxiety.

❧

Meg had informed Brian by wire she had quit the Sainsbury's and to expect her arrival. It would be comfortable to stay with her brother for a while. Mr Sainsbury had given her a brilliant reference and she knew she would have little trouble finding a new post.

Although Meg did not want to talk about what had happened with Jack, she thought about it a lot. There were things she still needed to work through in her mind and heart. Whenever anyone said they felt sorry for Jack having to marry Miss Ambrose, something within Meg reacted. She did not feel any sympathy for Jack at all and could not understand why anyone else would either. He deserved the fate he now suffered. He made the choice to live immorally. Jack himself admitted he had received his just desserts, so why should she pity him?

Sitting in Brian's church one day, Meg found herself being challenged by the sermon. The minister spoke about what happens when people surrender their lives to Christ. '*Therefore, if any man be in Christ, he is a new creature: old things are passed away; behold all things are become new,*' he read from the Scriptures.

The minister explained how the blood of Christ washes away all our sin, and that sin is not just forgiven, but forgotten, forever. 'When we accept Jesus' death for us, our old nature is crucified with him. It is no more. Our past stops with the cross and nothing can be seen beyond that. God now looks upon us through His Son and sees us as perfect,' the Reverend preached.

As she listened, Meg began to realise she still held Jack in judgement. She had condemned him for actions that he had been forgiven for. Meg immediately repented, asking her Father in heaven to cleanse her of her sin. 'From now on,' she prayed, 'I shall endeavour to look at Jack through Your eyes, blameless in Your sight. Help me to forgive and forget as You do.'

⊱⊰

Meg had resided at her brother's house for two weeks and had been mostly inactive during that time. While it had been nice to rest, she knew she could not expect Brian to keep supporting her when he would soon have to provide for his new wife. Shortly after breakfast on Monday morning, she prepared to go out and enquire about available work.

She had only just locked the front door of the house when a carriage pulled up at the foot of the steps that descended to the road. A man jumped down from the driver's seat and approached her.

'Miller.' Meg recognised Jack's valet at once but could not fathom what he would want with her. 'What are you doing here?'

The valet bowed deeply to her. 'I come at the request of Mister Fordham.'

Meg frowned and shook her head slightly. 'I do not understand,' she said. 'Is he not in Newcastle?'

'He is,' Miller bowed again. 'I beg your indulgence, Miss Wingrove.' He handed her a small, sealed envelope.

Still frowning, Meg took it and broke it open.

Meg,

Please go with Miller. He is quite trustworthy.

Jack.

It was Jack's handwriting. She recognised it from his previous letters to her. However, she remained at a loss to know his purpose. More out of curiosity than anything, Meg allowed Miller to hand her into the carriage.

Thankfully the journey was not a long one and they soon reined in. Miller opened the door, ready to help her out onto the busy, city street. Meg glanced around her in all directions. She saw many town houses and a few stores, but nothing that gave her any clue to Jack's purpose. The building they were in front of appeared to be a large, empty townhouse. The windows were boarded up and the small garden was quite overgrown.

Meg was surprised to find Miller leading her to the door of this house. She followed, a small frown creasing her brow again. The valet opened the door and motioned for her to enter. 'In here please, Miss Wingrove.'

Meg halted in the doorway, glancing into the empty house. She turned to look suspiciously at Miller. 'What is this about?'

The valet handed her the keys he had just used.

'In the back,' he said simply. 'I shall wait for you with the carriage.'

Meg watched him return to the horses, and then turned uncertainly into the house. Inside was dim and a little dusty, but her eyes gradually grew accustomed to the low light. The entryway she found herself in made the house seem bigger than it had looked from outside. There were a few doors leading off the hall and a narrow staircase rose straight up to the top floor.

She looked around carefully but could not see anyone. 'Hello?' she called. 'Is anyone there?'

No reply came, except for her voice reverberating off the bare walls.

Hesitantly, Meg moved towards a door that hung open towards the back of the entryway. As she neared it, she could see a faint light through the small gap where the door had been left ajar. Nervously, she pushed the door open and peered in, half expecting someone to leap out at her.

A small table and a solitary lantern were all that met her eyes. On the table, apparently waiting for her, she saw another sealed letter. Meg moved to the table, her fears now replaced with curiosity. She dropped the key on the stand and picked up the yellow envelope. Her name was written on the front, once again in Jack's hand. She brushed her fingers over its surface, hesitant to open it and read.

But her curiosity grew, and she broke the seal and unfolded the pages. Facing them towards the light, she began to read.

> *Dear Meg,*
>
> *Gwen informed me you have left the farm and are looking for a new post. However, I cannot bear the thought of you having to begin afresh in a stranger's home. Not when I am the cause of your resignation.*
>
> *You once told me you had a concern for unfortunate children. Well, I am happy to inform you, you now have the means to begin your own orphanage. This house is yours and I have opened a bank account in your name with enough funds to furnish it and provide for the children you take in. If you ever need any more, just contact Miller and he will notify me.*
>
> *If you think to yourself, you cannot accept this, then I beg you to reconsider. I was already in the process of purchasing this house for that purpose, and I cannot think of anyone more suited to take over. You can either keep it as a gift or choose to repay me when your inheritance is finalised. The choice is yours. But I hope in this way I can perhaps atone for my mistakes, even if only a little.*
>
> *You need not feel obligated to me in any way. I will be happy just knowing you follow your heart and give orphaned girls some hope for a future. May God bless you in your service.*
>
> *Jack Fordham.*

Meg looked behind the note and saw she held the title deed for the house.

The documents fell from Meg's hands as a wave of emotion overwhelmed her. Conflicting thoughts tumbled. Her pride made her want to refuse the help Jack had offered, but his letter made sense. As she looked around the house, ideas grew in her mind. A possibility had become a certainty. She had the means of her own to do this, but Jack had made a future hope, present day reality.

Meg took a deep, shaky breath to steady her emotions and began to explore her home. It was perfect of course. Jack knew exactly what would be needed for a girls' home and it was all here. Meg cried with joy as she went from room to room. She thanked God for this blessing and prayed she would be successful in all her efforts.

Chapter Forty-four

After weeks of decorating, furnishing, and fitting out the house, Meg employed the necessary staff and advertised the Wingrove Home for Girls as open. Within ten days, Meg had five children living under her roof and by Christmas that number had doubled. The weather became hot with the onset of summer, and one had to keep all the windows and doors wide open to keep the temperature indoors to a tolerable level. Fans and light cotton frocks were the order of the day. Despite the heat, the ten girls were happy in their new home.

Meg spent Christmas Day divided between Brian and all her other adopted families. In the morning she went to the church service where they celebrated the birth of Christ together with carols and a short sermon by the minister. Following that she accompanied Brian to the Montgomery's for Christmas dinner. They had an enjoyable meal filled with laughter and love and they exchanged small gifts with each other.

It was mid-afternoon by the time Meg headed back to the orphanage. The cook had baked a special supper for them all to share together. Meg told the children the story of Jesus' birth and all the wonders that surrounded it, while the girls listened on in awe. She prayed a blessing over them all and gave each one a gift to show how special they were to her.

On New Year's Day, Meg received a visit from the Sainsburys. She was elated to see them and embraced them all warmly. The children ran off to play with the orphaned girls, and Meg took Mr and Mrs Sainsbury for a tour of the home.

'I cannot believe you have your own girls' home,' Mrs Sainsbury said, astonished. She fanned herself furiously while grinning at Meg. 'What a wonderful thing to have done.'

'It really is a credit to you, Meg,' Mr Sainsbury agreed. 'I know these girls will benefit greatly from your guidance.'

'Thank you, Mister Sainsbury.'

'And are you all right?' Mrs Sainsbury asked with a meaningful look.

'Yes, I am,' Meg assured her. 'I am very happy.'

She looked relieved. 'I am glad to hear it.'

Meg led them into a private room she kept aside for special visitors and asked the cook to bring in some tea.

'Did you hire a new governess?' Meg asked.

'Yes,' Mrs Sainsbury replied. 'She is very good.'

Meg smiled in delight. 'I am glad you found a suitable replacement.'

'Although to be quite candid,' Mr Sainsbury added, 'the children believe no-one can replace you.'

The tea was brought in shortly and as they drank, they talked more of Sainsbury Stud and the Orphanage. Meg told them about her brother's upcoming nuptials and of the small church she attended.

One by one, the children drifted in and joined in the conversation. Meg asked them if their new governess was indeed a good replacement.

'She is very nice,' Willy answered. 'But I still miss you, Winnie.'

Meg melted and gave the young boy a hug. 'I miss you, too.'

Kitty evidently felt left out and added her own piece of news. 'We have a cousin now, Winnie,' she said with importance.

Meg hesitated, glancing from her to Mrs Sainsbury and back again.

'Hush Kitty,' Mrs Sainsbury scolded and then looked apologetically at Meg. 'Jack has a son. We received a letter from him two days ago with the news. I am sorry if it disturbs you to hear.' She gave her youngest daughter another scathing look.

Meg was quiet, but calm. 'It is all right, Missus Sainsbury.' She looked fondly down at Kitty who appeared both ashamed and confused.

'So, you have a baby cousin, do you? I'll wager you cannot wait to meet him.'

Kitty nodded, her braids bouncing.

'Does he have a name?'

'Jonathon,' Kitty replied, the smile returning to her face.

Meg took the child's hands in hers. 'You will have to look after him like a big sister.'

Kitty nodded again, looking very earnest.

Later, when the family was leaving, Meg drew Mrs Sainsbury aside.

'Please do not punish Kitty on my account,' she urged. 'I already knew it was going to happen.'

Mrs Sainsbury seemed to accept this and smiled briefly.

'How is Jack?' Meg asked. 'Did he seem pleased in his letter?'

Mrs Sainsbury's eyes shone. 'Oh, yes,' she replied. 'The whole letter was "Jonathon this" and "Jonathon that".'

'How is his wife? Did he mention her?'

Mrs Sainsbury frowned. 'I don't think he did,' she replied then shrugged. 'I suppose he was too excited about his son.'

Meg gave a short sigh. 'Well, I am glad he is happy.'

Mrs Sainsbury searched her face. 'And I am glad you are content.'

They embraced briefly and said their goodbyes. Meg waved until their coach was out of sight.

❧⚜☙

Summer rolled into autumn and Meg had settled into a comfortable way of life at the orphanage. The home for girls was now full and kept her busier than she had ever been. With twenty young girls in the house, every day was filled with noisy outbursts. Meg had wondered whether she would be able to care for so many children but found she had more than enough love for each one.

One day in April, Meg escaped from the orphanage to enjoy some space and freedom. She wandered through the markets, buying little nothings and drinking in the smells of horseflesh, leather, industrial furnaces, and freshly baked bread and produce.

As she strolled down the street, cane basket in her arms, she saw a man and woman exiting a general store not ten paces in front of her. The man cradled a small bundle in his arms and smiled at it affectionately. Meg had forgotten just how good-looking Jack was, and her breath caught. She shifted her gaze to the woman with him. Meg had expected Mrs Sylvia Fordham to be a stunning beauty, but the woman she looked upon was quite plain.

Meg knew she should walk away, but she found herself unaccountably frozen to the spot. The picture of Jack holding his son arrested her. As if he knew she stood there, Jack lifted his head and looked straight at her. A surprised smile lit his face and he turned towards her.

Meg briefly wondered whether she should run away, but she could not get her feet to co-operate.

'Hello, Meg,' Jack greeted her hesitantly.

Meg swallowed. 'Jack.'

'How are you?'

'Well, thank you.'

'Would you like to meet my son, Jonathon?' he offered a little awkwardly, holding the little boy so she could see him clearly. He glanced at Meg who remained unable to move. 'Unless it makes you uncomfortable.'

Meg looked past him, to where Mrs Fordham waited by the carriage, and then turned her gaze to the bundle in Jack's arms. Anxious, but more curious, she smiled. 'I would be delighted to meet him.'

Jack seemed relieved. 'He is a strapping lad, don't you think?'

A little shy, Meg leaned in and peeked at the baby's face. She could see at once this precious child resembled his father. 'He is beautiful.'

Jack beamed at her. He seemed pleased by her approval.

Meg leaned in and cooed softly to him, admiring his tiny features. Jonathon gurgled up at her and suddenly his face broke into a heart-melting smile. Meg giggled with delight.

'I think he likes you.' Jack grinned from ear to ear.

Meg beamed back at him.

'How is your brother?' Jack asked her as he headed for the carriage.

'He is well,' she answered, following. 'He is on his wedding tour in fact.'

Jack paused and looked at her. 'Ah,' he said. 'Give him my felicitations when you see him.'

'Thank you, I shall.' She wanted to tell him about the orphanage, but they had already reached the coach.

Jack handed Jonathon to his wife who waited in the carriage. Meg thought it strange he did not introduce her, but then perhaps he didn't want to make things more uncomfortable. Jack put one foot on the step of the coach. 'I am glad we happened upon you, Meg. It's good to see you again.'

'And you too, Jack,' she replied. 'Goodbye.'

Jack smiled at her and stepped into the carriage. Meg turned her back to them and continued her stroll down the street.

Chapter Forty-five

Inside the carriage, Jack glanced out of the window to see Meg walking away from them and something in his heart snapped. All of his inner being reached out to call her back, even as the coach lurched forward. Jack immediately knocked on the roof and the driver stopped.

He turned to the woman next to him. 'Will you take Jonathon home for me? There is something I must do. I will return in an hour or so.'

She nodded and Jack leaped out of the carriage, instructing the driver to continue without him. He watched only long enough to see the coach move forward and then turned to catch up to Meg.

Meg stopped dead in her tracks when he jogged up beside her. 'May I walk with you?'

Meg glanced around her at the folk everywhere. 'People will talk,' she said in a low voice.

Jack shrugged. 'Let them.'

Meg stared at him in disbelief. 'What about Missus Fordham?' She looked back towards where the carriage had been.

Jack smiled. 'Ah,' he said, understanding. 'That was not Missus Fordham.'

Meg frowned. 'Then who …?'

'That was Lucinda. The nursemaid.' He explained.

'Oh,' Meg finally understood, but seconds later frowned again. 'But what about *Missus Fordham*?'

Jack rolled his eyes. 'Never mind about Missus Fordham. I only wish to talk.

I have much I want to tell you, and I want to hear all about your girls' home.'

⤫

Meg scanned Jack's face and, perceiving no dishonesty there, turned and walked casually along the roadside. 'Very well,' she agreed. 'I wanted to thank you for helping me to get the orphanage started anyway.'

'There you go,' he grinned, falling into step beside her. He took her shopping basket from her hands in a chivalrous gesture. 'So, tell me about it.'

Meg told him all the details about the orphanage and the girls she now had there. Jack listened attentively to every word, asking questions at intervals, and showing his approval of what she had done.

'You should come and see it some time,' she suggested, then realised it was probably a bad idea. 'I'm sorry, I shouldn't have —'

'I would like that,' he interrupted.

Meg became so engrossed in the conversation she paid little heed to where they walked. It was wonderful to talk to Jack about the orphanage. He understood more about it than anyone and related to her deep affection for the girls. Meg was delighted their friendship could still flourish so easily after all they had been through. It amazed her how quickly the awkwardness between them melted away and she realised the time they had been apart had given them both a chance to heal.

Jack stopped walking and put the basket down beside a bench and invited her to sit. Meg realised with surprise that they had strolled so far, they were now in Hyde Park, away from the markets and bustling people.

'Jack, I …' Meg hesitated.

'What?'

'I do not think this is appropriate.'

'We are only talking, Meg,' Jack assured her. 'Or do you not trust me?'

'I trust you, Jack,' she replied. 'I am just wary of the scandalous rumours people can spread. You have had enough scandal in your life already.'

Jack sighed. 'I appreciate your concern, but will you let me worry about that? Please sit with me.'

Meg sat uncomfortably, making sure she kept a proper distance between them.

'I never had the chance to tell you about my conversion,' Jack told her. 'It is something I have longed to share with you, and I shall not let you go until you have heard it.'

Meg had to laugh at his determination. 'I must admit. I have been curious about that. I promise I will not leave until you are finished.'

Jack stretched his legs out, folded his arms and began his tale. He told her about the *Madeline* and about Captain Connelly. He told her every detail of his experience, recounting how dramatically God had met with him and changed his life.

His story mesmerised Meg. It was such a powerful testimony, and she could see the memory of it burning fervently in Jack's eyes as he spoke.

'… But, after experiencing the love of Christ like that, there is no way could I remain the same. Every day now, I wake up with new joy and I thank God for intervening before it was too late for me.'

He paused and looked at Meg who nodded, her eyes glazed with emotion.

'I'm sorry,' Jack seemed sheepish. 'I could talk about this all day.'

Meg laughed. 'Of course you could,' she said. 'You have no idea how happy I am you are now a fellow Christian.'

They lapsed into silence.

Meg wanted to ask him about his wife but was not sure how to approach it. She didn't know if he was sensitive about his marriage or not. But she had kept him in prayer, and she wanted to know how things were between them.

'You have a lovely little boy,' she ventured.

Jack sighed. 'I do indeed. He is the best thing that has ever happened to me, next to Christ, that is.'

'I know you will be a wonderful father.'

'I hope it is enough,' he replied, and Meg sensed a deeper implication behind his words.

'How are you and Sylvia faring?' she finally found the courage to ask.

Jack's lips twitched. 'I hope she is happy.'

'You do not know?'

'I have not spoken to her in a while.'

'Are things that bad?' Meg gaped in shock.

Jack grinned. 'No,' he said. 'It is merely that she is still in Newcastle.'

'Newcastle?'

'With her family … and her fiancé.'

Meg stared at him with her mouth open. 'Her fiancé?'

Chapter Forty-six

Jack began to laugh, and Meg looked at him as if he had run mad.

'I am sorry,' he composed himself. 'I should have told you earlier, but I didn't know how to enlighten you without telling you the whole distasteful story. I thought I would leave it till last.'

Meg shook her head but eyed him curiously. 'What happened? You were the one engaged to Miss Ambrose last I heard.'

Jack became serious. 'About two days before we were due to wed, I was lying awake in her father's house when I heard a noise outside my window. I peered out and saw a figure passing through the shadows. I was curious so I quickly dressed and crept outside. I followed the figure through the garden to the back corner of the property. I could hear voices so I huddled in the shadows until I could see who was there.

'Well, I was shocked by what I saw. Sylvia had a clandestine rendezvous with — er — another man. I only stayed long enough to hear his name and went back to the house. I could not sleep after that. I had resigned myself to enduring Sylvia's selfish nature and her childish tantrums, but I knew I could not abide her unfaithfulness.

'I prayed all night, but I could not find any answers. The next day I confronted her with her treachery. She flew into a rage, blaming me for all her problems and defending her wish to be with her true love. She ranted about how she hated me and the baby. She said things I could never repeat.

'Her tirade sickened me. I could not believe someone could be so full of hatred. But strangely I did not become angry with her. I saw another path I could take, a path that would possibly provide a better future for us.'

Jack's voice shook as he continued. 'I waited for her to calm down and then I asked her if indeed she had no interest in our child or marriage. She told me no. She swore I was the last person on earth she would marry. So, I suggested if she were willing to relinquish the baby to me, I would approach her father and see if he would release me from my obligation. If I succeeded, she would be free to live however she wished.

'It broke my heart to see the way her eyes lit with hope. Our son meant nothing to her. In part I felt horrid for taking him away from his mother, but then, I couldn't bear to see him grow up in a loveless home. Mr Ambrose agreed readily, but not until I promised to compensate him with an outrageous sum of money.

'I thank God for his grace which released me from a disastrous situation. I have a perfect son who I shall care for with all my heart. I have given him my name and he will be my heir. I plan to raise him in the knowledge of Christ so he may not make the mistakes I have. Then, hopefully some good will have come out of all this suffering.'

Meg could not respond for a while. It horrified her that a woman could reject her own child so completely. It was beyond comprehension. Miss Ambrose was nowhere near good enough for a man of Jack's generous nature.

She looked at him. 'I don't know what to say, but I feel you have done a very courageous thing.'

Jack reached out and squeezed her hand. 'You have no idea how much that means to me,' he said. 'Nobody really knows the full story. There are plenty of rumours around, and though I try not to take notice, I have had my doubts about it all. But your encouragement gives me strength.'

Meg smiled at him. 'I am glad.' She knew how it felt to doubt the choices one made, even when they seemed perfectly right.

Jack nodded gratefully.

'Jack, we have been talking for hours,' Meg said, standing. 'I have enjoyed every minute, but I really must get back home.'

'Then I shan't keep you,' he replied, although he seemed a little disappointed.

'It has been wonderful to hear all of your news,' Meg told him, not really wanting to leave.

'And yours,' he agreed.

'Well ... goodbye Jack,' she laughed self-consciously, having trouble getting her legs to move forward.

'Goodbye Meg.'

❧

Jack watched her walk away from him and a wave of intense longing came over him again. Was it possible to begin again? Would she even be interested? *You are free!* A whisper echoed through his soul. He noticed her basket still sitting by the bench and quickly picked it up. He jogged after Meg, his heart beating quickly.

'Meg!' he called. 'Your shopping.'

She stopped and turned around, waiting for him to catch up. He handed her the basket and she smiled up at him sweetly. 'Thank you, Jack.' She turned to continue her way.

'Meg,' he reached out and touched her arm and she turned back again.

Doubt assailed him, but his desire would not be smothered.

'What is it, Jack?'

Jack clenched his jaw. 'I have caused you so much grief.' His voice shook. 'I know I promised to keep my distance, but I cannot let you go. I wish to God I had lived a pure life.'

Meg reached out and put a hand on his forearm. She looked deeply into his eyes.

'What hideous sin have you committed? I look at you and I see a man swept clean, nothing else. If Christ has seen fit to forgive and wash you clean, who am I to judge you, and who are you to judge yourself?'

Jack could not speak. Meg's words touched him profoundly and he felt release from all the guilt he still carried. The Lord had forgiven him, and Meg had clearly forgiven him. Why should he still hold on to his guilt? *You are free!* He heard the whisper again. At that moment he thought he could fly.

'Thank you, Meg.'

Their eyes locked in an intense gaze.

'May I visit you?' Jack suddenly blurted. 'Regularly?'

Meg's eyes widened with delight. 'Yes, Jack,' she replied. 'Please do.'

Encouraged, Jack ventured further. 'If I brought you ... gifts ..., would you accept them?'

Meg smiled broadly and nodded with a giggle.

And if I were to tell you how exquisitely beautiful you are ...?'

Meg raised one eyebrow at him. 'I would tell you to get some spectacles.'

Jack laughed softly and stepped a little closer to her. He searched her eyes.

'But what if I were to say you are the noblest, most pure and upright woman I have ever met?'

Meg's eyes swam. 'It is a compliment beyond what I deserve, but I am honoured you feel that way.'

'Meg, you know I love you with all my heart, do you not?' He reached out and touched her cheek tenderly.

'And I have tried *not* to love you since the first day I saw you,' she replied, as a tear rolled down her cheek. 'Alas, I have failed miserably. I love you so much I hardly know myself.'

Jack took a deep breath and edged closer. 'So, if one day I asked you to give me the very great honour of becoming my wife, what would you say?'

Meg smiled at him, and her eyes were filled with longing. 'I would say please do not take too long, Jack.'

Jack's heart soared. She was his. He slipped his arms around her waist. 'Are you sure?' His lips twitched. 'Because you realise, I am known to be a desperate rogue.'

Meg seemed to ponder this. But then she dropped her basket and coiled her arms around his neck. 'It depends,' she replied with a dangerous twinkle in her eyes. 'Do you think you can endure a wife who is known to be an incorrigible mischief?'

Jack looked lovingly into her eyes. 'It sounds like an adventure, my lovely, lovely minx,' he murmured and slowly leaned in to kiss her.

The End

Acknowledgements

I would like to thank my husband, Morry, my children, Jessica, Jacinta-Rose and Caleb, and every one of my family and friends who have supported and encouraged me on this journey to pursue my dreams. I love you all.

Thanks also to Meredith Resce whose encouragement gave me the confidence to step out, and to the Omega Writers community who always provide inspiration, support and encouragement.

Of course, the biggest thanks go to the One who brings dreams to fruition. Thank you Jesus.

Other Titles By

Amanda Deed

The Jacksons Creek Trilogy

Ellenvale Gold

It is the time of Australia's harsh rogue-filled goldrush of the 1850's when Miss Penelope Worthington suddenly finds herself orphaned, isolated and alone. With a large sheep station to run single-handedly, she has little option but to enlist the aid of a mysterious, but sinister stranger.

But who is the more treacherous? Gus—the scruffy, trespassing, ex-convict who co-incidentally shows up looking for work just when she desperately needs a farmhand or Rupert—the handsome, wealthy neighbour who would willingly marry her at the drop of a hat and solve her apparent dilemma?

Repeatedly, her faith is tested as she faces the unforgiving elements, deceit, lies and uncertainty. But where and how will it all end? But…is it the end? Will vengeance return or will Penny's faith prevail?

Black Forest Redemption

A man resigned to a life without fulfilment or purpose. A woman desperate for adventure.

Set against the tumultuous times of the Eureka uprising in Ballaarat, 1854, the two find themselves victims of an abduction. To escape could mean death. To hope for rescue is not an option.

Together they must find a way to survive in an untamed land where bushrangers, dense forest and wild animals are only some of the dangers they must face. Can he find the courage to succeed? Can she realise her dreams of freedom? Will the ordeal forge a bond of love between them, or drive them apart? And above all, will they find their way home?

Henry's Run

Rupert Foxworth has made too many wrong decisions. He may be able to cast the blame on others, but ultimately he must face the consequences of his actions. With murder hanging over his head, can he make some drastic changes to his life before it's too late? Will he be able to find the lasting love he has yearned for in his pretty cousin who has come to visit?

Emily Harrison has some secrets of her own. Can she lay aside her past and learn to love a man who seems bent on destruction? She will discover that things are not always as they seem.

Available now at WOMBATRHIZA.COM.AU

FRACTURED FAIRY TALES

Unnoticed

Plain Jane O'Reilly is good at being unnoticed. Detested by her stepmother and teased by her stepsisters, Jane has learned the art of avoiding attention. That is until Price Moreland, an American with big dreams, arrives in her small town.

Does she dare to hope someone might notice her?

However, Price Moreland may not be the prince that the whole town thinks him to be. Was his desire to be a missionary a God-given call, or just a good excuse to run from his past?

Complete with an evil stepmother, a missing shoe and a grand ball, *Unnoticed* takes the time-old Cinderella fairy tale and gives it an Australian twist.

Unhinged

Serena Bellingham is faced with an impossible choice. Either leave her struggling family to serve the eccentric genius, Edward King, or stay, only to see the same man imprison her father.

Her decision leads her to Aleron House, a home shrouded in secrecy, strange attitudes and even stranger happenings. Is Edward King all that she has heard, or is the truth something entirely different? Is it possible

that the handsome architect might need her even more than her beloved family does?

Unhinged is an Australian retelling of Beauty and the Beast, complete with a mysterious curse and a precious rose.

Available now at WOMBATRHIZA.COM.AU

www.ingramcontent.com/pod-product-compliance
Lightning Source LLC
Chambersburg PA
CBHW070535120726
47909CB00007B/2138